In Defense of the Righteous

A journey through justice,

from the righteous

to the damned

by Charles Patton

IN DEFENSE OF THE RIGHTEOUS:

ISBN: 978-1-963809-43-5 (Paperback)
Published by Short Mystery Press
Orlando, Florida, USA
First edition

Cover design: chatGPT
Editing: Author/chatGPT
Printed in United States
10 9 8 7 6 5 4 3 2 1

Table of Contents

Character Key

Surface World
    Detective Dani Francis – Chicago cop, haunted past
    Jake Tinsley – Vietnam vet, steady and scarred
    Rally Gillum – Sixteen, restless, sharp-tongued
    Sheriff Dorman – Local lawman
    Grant Beaumont – Experienced caver
    Cam Lockett – Missing teen, rescued early
    Taye Reed – Missing teen
    Junie Bell – Missing teen
    Mason Cooper – Missing teen
    Nia Alvarez – Youngest (12), resilient
    Nia's Mother – Distraught parent

The City
    The Archivist – Ledger-keeper of deeds
    The Defender – Wry, theatrical counsel
    The Keeper (of Bray) – Stern, demands testimony
    Marla – Guide, exacts payment in pages
    The Deceiver – Shadow judge in Central Court
    The Enforcers – Faceless executors of law
    The Choir – Voices of Unless
    Counter-Witnesses – Opposing accusers

Inspired by Dante Alighieri's Inferno,
a path where justice is tested and redemption sought.

Chapter One: The Call

The ringing phone split the quiet like a gunshot.

Detective Dani Francis sat in the Sheriff's office with her shoulders hunched over a case file she wasn't reading. The Florida Panhandle heat pressed against the glass, and the ceiling fan's tired blades only shifted the warmth from one corner of the room to another. A fly ticked at the window, desperate to escape. On the folder's cover, a photograph of a boy was stapled crooked, the corner bent where her finger kept worrying it.

Nine years old. Wrong place, wrong time.

Her finger traced the photo's edge. In the picture he was mid-laugh at some long-ago joke, a tooth gone on the right, eyes bright. In her head, his eyes were always wide and empty.

Chicago. Self-defense, they'd called it. A clean shoot. Imminent threat. Clear and present danger. Every training manual would have written it the same way. But the manuals didn't include the sound a child's body makes when it hits the floor behind the man you were aiming at, or the part where that sound stays after the uniforms and statements and sympathetic nods are gone.

The phone rang again, sharp, insistent.

Dani blinked and closed the folder. She let her hand rest on it for a beat, like pressing a palm to a grave. Then she picked up the receiver. "Sheriff's Office, Francis."

The dispatcher's voice was tight with fear. "Detective, we've got kids missing. Six of them. Gillum boy and five others. Last seen heading into the caves out by Levy Ridge."

Dani straightened. "How long?"

"Four hours, maybe more. Locals say they mess around down there, but this time..." The voice cracked. "This time they didn't come back."

Dani's stomach went hard. Florida caves weren't in tourist brochures. They were limestone mazes, sumps and shafts and holes where a wrong step erased you. "Names?"

"Rally Gillum, sixteen. Taye Reed, Junie Bell, Mason Cooper, Cam Lockett, and a little one, Nia Alvarez, twelve." A breath hissed at the other end. "Nia's mother is here. She can't stop shaking."

"Where exactly?" Dani asked, already reaching for her jacket.

"Levy Ridge sink entrance off County 14. Sheriff's staging at the old sawmill lot."

"I'm on my way."

She set the receiver down and pressed her thumb and forefinger to her eyes until she saw pinprick stars. Then she stood, grabbed the folder out of reflex, and tucked it into her bottom drawer. The dead boy could wait. The living couldn't.

Jake Tinsley leaned against his old Bronco outside the office, a sun-faded beast with a cracked dash and a hood that wore the paint like old scars. He looked like he belonged to the truck, weathered skin, gray hair pulled into a no-nonsense tail, eyes that had seen enough to stop flinching. Vietnam had been forty years ago, but some places don't get the memo.

"You heard?" Dani asked, pulling her hair into a knot as she walked up.

"Kids in a cave," he said. His voice was gravel with a nicotine edge. "Sheriff wants a quick sweep." He spit into the dust. "Hell of a way to spend an afternoon."

"Afternoon's over," she said. "You in?"

He gave a half-smile that never made it to his eyes. "You know I am. Besides, caves and bad decisions? Be a shame to miss the set."

She almost smiled back. Almost. "We'll need rope. Helmets. Three lights per person. Radios won't carry down there."

Jake popped the Bronco's tailgate and gestured to a lumpy duffel and two hard cases. "Brought toys. Figure the county's still using flashlights you bait fish with."

"Depends on who's on budget committee," Dani said. "And what they're afraid of this fiscal year."

He studied her face as he set a coil of static rope aside. "You good?"

"I'm upright."

"Good enough." He tossed her a helmet lamp, then a pair of knee pads. "Those'll keep your prayers short."

The drive to Levy Ridge cut through scrubland and pine, the Florida most tourists never see, the flat kind, where horizon and road argue about which one is going to blink first. Heat shimmered above the blacktop. Cicadas sawed at the air. Dani rode shotgun, boots braced against the Bronco's floorboard, counting mile markers like the rosary she didn't carry anymore.

"You ever go down in these?" Jake asked, one hand on the wheel and the other tapping a rhythm on the dash with a coin.

"Once," Dani said. "Training. I didn't like it. Nothing like those I've been in up north and out west"

"Caves don't care if you like 'em." Jake flicked his eyes toward her. "You claustrophobic?"

"No." She paused. "Sometimes."

"Good. Means you'll listen to your lungs."

She watched pine blur past the window. "You ever stop hearing it?"

"Hearing what?"

"The one that sticks," she said. "The one you didn't mean."

He didn't answer for a while. A hawk lifted from a fence post and hung in the hot air like a thought. "No," he said at last. "But it changes pitch."

They turned off onto a dirt road that rolled them toward Levy Ridge, a hump of old limestone pushed up from a million years of sea. The Bronco bounced through ruts. Someone had left a white cross and a beer can at the first turn. Someone always had.

"City's got stories about a city under the ridge," Jake said. "Kids talk. Old men talk more."

"Cities under cities," Dani said. "Seems on brand."

"You think they're alive?" Jake asked it like a man asking the weather if it means to rain.

"They're kids," Dani said. "They do dumb things and come out bragging. Most times."

"And the other times?"

She stared ahead. "We don't leave families with empty holes where answers should be."

The sawmill lot lay in a clearing gouged out of the longleaf pines. Sheriff Dorman stood beside his SUV with a folding table snapped open and a map pinned under a water bottle and a box of flares. He was barrel-chested, mustache gone white in stripes, the kind of lawman who could talk down a drunken cousin at a barbecue before he put him in cuffs.

9

"Francis," he said as they approached. "Tinsley."

"Sheriff," Dani said, scanning the lot. A handful of deputies, two volunteer firefighters, a paramedic crew with a cooler. A small crowd of locals pressed at the tape beyond, curious and worried. A woman with streaked mascara, had to be Nia's mother, clutched a wadded tissue in both hands like she was trying to wring water from it.

Dorman tapped the map. "We've got three known mouths on the ridge. Two are flooded. They always are. The third's the sink here off County 14. Kids were seen going into this one at about one o'clock. Taye Reed's cousin says they were 'looking for the stairs.' Whatever the hell that means."

"Stairs?" Jake snorted. "In a hole?"

"Locals tell stories," Dorman said. "City under the ridge and all that. Rally Gillum's been sniffing around down there for a month. He's the one dragged the little ones into it." The sheriff's jaw shifted. "Kid's smart but mean as a cracked whip."

"We have cavers?" Dani asked. "Anybody who knows the system?"

A man in a faded Cave Conservancy shirt raised a hand from the shade of a pine. He had a neatly cropped beard and calves cabled with muscle above filthy boots. "Grant Beaumont," he said. "I've mapped a third of Levy, the part a sane person can map. Today's entrance heads to a Y after a hundred feet. Right goes dry passage to breakdown chambers and a dead end. Left goes slope to a sump, sometimes dry, sometimes not. There's a crawl through the Banjo to a second chamber if you know where to put your shoulders."

He eyed Dani and Jake the way sober men eye drunks with car keys. "This ain't a place for tourists."

"We're not tourists," Dani said.

Beaumont looked at the sheriff. "You want a team, you call one. Rope. Air monitors. Redundant lights. It'll take me forty minutes to drag in two more bodies with brains enough to follow hand signals. Or you can let these two play hero and I'll mark where to plant the plaques."

The mother behind the tape heard that and jolted at the word plaques. "Please," she called, voice cracking. "Please go now."

Dorman exhaled through his nose. He looked at Dani. "Your call."

"Time matters," Dani whispered. "Four hours is the difference between a bad story and a funeral." She nodded to Beaumont. "You come with us. We follow your line."

Beaumont hesitated, then rolled his eyes toward the pines like he was asking them for patience. "Fine," he said. "But we do it smart. Helmets. Knee pads. Gloves. Three lights. Tie in. If I say turn around, you turn around."

"If any of us say turn around, we turn around," Dani said.

"I can live with that," Jake said.

"You better," Beaumont muttered.

Dorman put a hand on Dani's arm as she turned away. "You don't have to prove anything, Francis."

Dani met his eyes. "I'm not trying to."

He squeezed once and let go. "Bring 'em home."

They kitted up at the Bronco's tailgate. Dani tightened her harness and ran her fingers down the rope for nicks. Jake checked his lamp, then stripped a yard of duct tape from a flat roll and wrapped it around his water bottle in neat bands.

"Insurance," he said. "For the thing I didn't think of."

"Which is?"

"It'll tell me when it shows up."

Dani clipped a small first-aid pouch to her belt and slid a spare light into the thigh pocket of her cargo pants. Her service pistol sat heavy at her hip. It was the only weight she hesitated over, the one she'd been trained to trust and the one that had betrayed her most completely. She adjusted the cant and closed the snap.

"Hey," Jake said softly. "You're here. That's the whole job."

"I know." She blew out a breath. "Let's go."

Beaumont met them at the taped-off trailhead with a coil of fluorescent surveyor's line around his neck and a Pelican case thumping against his leg. "You ever frog your way through a squeeze?" he asked Dani without preamble.

"I prefer doors that open," she said.

"Doors don't care what you prefer." He started into the trees. "Stay on my heel. Don't step where I didn't."

The crowd went quiet as they approached the tape. The mother pressed both hands to her mouth; her eyes shone with a fear that had bloomed past tears into the dry, watchful kind. A man in a fishing shirt folded his arms and squared himself like a barricade. "That Gillum boy is trouble," he said to no one in particular. "Been trouble since he was ten."

Dani stepped under the tape. "Mrs. Alvarez?" she asked, voice gentle.

The woman nodded jerkily. "She had a headlamp," she said, words tumbling. "Rally said there were stairs. He said he knew where they were. Nia, she wanted to see."

"Has she been down here before?"

The woman shook her head. "No. I told her no. But Rally..." Her throat worked. "He looks at kids and they forget they had mothers."

Dani wanted to tell her something like truth that didn't hurt. She had none. "We're going now," she said instead. "We'll bring them back."

"Bring her back," the woman whispered. "Bring her back and I'll forgive God anything."

The trail to the sink opening was a short tunnel of palmetto and slash pine, the ground a duet of sand and leaf litter. Through the trees the land dipped, the pines shouldering apart to reveal a dark oval eaten into the ridge, ringed by ferns and the bones of old deadfall. The air at the sink's lip was cooler, damp, the breath of something that lives in dark places.

Beaumont clipped a carabiner to a tree at the rim and threaded the line. He tested it, then tested it again, jerking down with impatient confidence. "Muddy slope," he warned. "It'll steal your knees if you gift 'em."

Dani nodded. To the deputies, she said, "Keep this entrance clear. If we call up, don't talk, listen. Sound carries weird." To no one, she said, "We'll be fast."

Jake touched the brim of an imaginary hat at her and Dani snorted despite everything. Then they followed Beaumont down.

The light narrowed behind them until it was a doorway, then a handprint, then a coin. The slope slid them down as if gravity had been waiting all along to hand them over to the dark. Mud sucked at their boots. Limestone sweated under their palms. The smell changed: pine gone to mineral, heat gone to cold breath and rot. Water dripped from somewhere not visible and hit somewhere else not visible and the sound made their spines itch.

Beaumont's lamp painted the rock a moving disc of white. He moved with the efficiency of a man who has learned his body's map. "Watch that shelf," he murmured. "You'll think it's rock. It's patience with a hard crust."

They reached the bottom of the slope and the passage leveled. Beaumont knelt and swung his beam low, sweeping the silt. "Footprints," he said. "Six. Fresh." His finger tapped a smear. "They ran."

Dani crouched beside him. The prints were chaotic, heel slides, a toe scuff where someone had lost balance. A crushed soda can lay on its side with mud pasted to the label. The aluminum had been stepped on, then stepped on again. A pale hair tie sat like a small broken halo in the grit. Dani felt something cold move under her sternum.

"Nia," she said quietly.

"Left or right?" Jake asked.

Beaumont's beam found the Y. Right was a shoulder-width corridor with puckered walls that looked like the throat of some old beast. Left sloped down into a broader passage, the floor scalloped with ripples frozen in stone from a river that had sulked away a thousand years ago.

The footprints went left.

Beaumont unwound line and tied off to a bulge of rock. "We mark every turn," he said. "We do not get clever."

"Clever's for kitchens," Jake said. "I make a mean omelet."

"Good," Beaumont grunted. "If we're stuck eighty feet down on a ledge, you can make us breakfast."

They moved. The roof came down. Dani ducked, then crouched, then found herself on hands and knees. Her helmet scraped stone and sang a small note. She closed her eyes, breathed in to find space around the breath, breathed out to make more. The passage narrowed until she could only turn her head half an inch before the rock said that was quite enough. Her heart went fast and hard.

"Hey," Jake's voice drifted back, calm. "You got room. You got air."

"I know," she said, and for a precious second wasn't sure. Then the rock opened an inch, then two, enough to make a laughable difference. They wriggled and slid and emerged into a low room where the ceiling gave them the breath back. Dani sat in the mud and let her pulse climb down the ladder in her throat one rung at a time.

Beaumont pointed to the wall. There, chalk ghosts, arrows thick as a child's finger, pointing deeper. "Stairs?" Jake asked softly.

"Kids leave breadcrumbs," Beaumont said. "We follow for now."

A few yards beyond, the cave floor tilted. The rock underfoot slicked to a treacherous shine. Water pooled in a shallow dish brimming with a film that smelled like old silver.

Dani's boot slid; she caught her balance with a palm slap against the wall. Her glove came away smelling of sulfur and something else, like the inside of a long-closed trunk.

"Watch the lip," Beaumont said. He hunkered and shone his light over the edge. "Drop, maybe eight feet. We can downclimb with a handline." He glanced up. "Hear that?"

They stilled. From somewhere below came the steady hush of flowing water. Not loud. Persistent. A pulse you only notice after your body has already matched it.

Dani listened past it for voices. Nothing. "Rally!" she called, and her voice pinballed through stone and came back as if someone else had said her name.

Beaumont set a line and went first. Jake followed, then he braced while Dani stepped down and found the notches Beaumont's boots had cut. The drop put them into a passage taller than any they'd seen yet, a long barrel with a spine of rock down the center like a dragon's back. On one side of the spine the floor was dry. On the other, black water lay flat as glass, not reflecting, only swallowing.

Jake's light found something across the water on a shelf: a smartphone with a cracked screen face down in mud. He stretched with a caver's care and hooked it toward him with two fingers. The case was cheap plastic printed with a crown and the word RALLY in block letters. The phone was dead. The case was warm from their hands, then cold from the cave.

"Found his," Jake said.

Dani felt the air thin. "Kids don't drop their phones unless they don't get a vote."

Beaumont's jaw shifted under his beard. "Or unless they think they'll be back in five minutes," he said. "It all feels like five minutes when you're dumb and sixteen."

They moved along the dry side, boots silent now by instinct. The water brushed the rock in small licks. At the far end the passage kinked and then opened into a chamber that made Dani's mouth drop. The ceiling arched high, ribbed with mineral like the inside of some ancient cathedral. Stalactites hung in patient rows. Stalagmites reached up like congregants with their hands raised. In the center lay a cairn of stones built up shoulder-high and topped with a skull of some small animal, bleached blind.

"Locals play pilgrim," Beaumont said softly. "Leave offerings to the hole so the hole doesn't eat 'em."

"Does it work?" Jake asked.

"About as well as anything."

Dani's light stroked the ground and found a scatter of candy wrappers near the far wall, a half-eaten protein bar, and a length of red paracord tied off to a jut of rock. Her lamp followed the cord across the chamber to a crack in the wall just wide enough for a teenager to think it might lead somewhere.

"Through there," she said.

Beaumont stooped at the crack and pushed his light in. "The Banjo," he murmured. "Opens into a slope on the far side." He eyed Dani's shoulders, then Jake's. "You'll fit. It'll make you swear first."

"I can swear quiet," Dani said.

"We'll see." Beaumont nodded to the paracord. "Smart kid. Left himself a way home."

Jake grunted. "Or breadcrumbs for a mythical wolf."

They took turns in the Banjo, each pause a prayer and a curse. The rock close-packed around Dani, pressed its cold teeth into her ribs and decided how many cubic inches she could afford to call hers. She exhaled, wriggled, exhaled more, found where bone learned patience, and dragged herself through with a grunt that made Beaumont chuckle in front of her.

"Beats church," he said.

"Your church and mine are different," she replied between her teeth.

On the far side the slope spilled them like loose change into a new passage. Here the air moved. Dani felt it on the wet hairline at her neck: a draft, cold and old, threaded with a smell like iron left out in rain. Her light slid over the floor and caught scuffs, a sneaker tread in sharp detail, the crescent scrape of someone's toenail through wet grit. The paracord ended at a fraying knot on a rock, cut clean.

"Cut?" Jake said, kneeling. "Or snapped?"

Beaumont touched it. "Knife," he said. "Either they wanted it on this side, or something needed it worse on the other."

"Rally!" Dani called again, louder. "Nia! Sheriff's Office!"

Silence answered. Then, faint and far, something else, not a voice. A low exhale that might have been wind. Or something that lived in the earth and made its own weather.

Beaumont lifted a finger for quiet. They listened until their ears rang with listening. The sound did not repeat. Or it did, and their hearts learned it before their heads.

Jake's lamp haloed his hair like tarnished silver. "We keep going," he said. It wasn't a question.

Dani stared into the dark and felt a shape move in her mind, the shape of Chicago like a door that never stops

18

opening. She tightened the strap on her helmet until it bit. "We keep going," she said.

They moved as a line, their line, into the throat of the ridge.

The cave breathed. The world above narrowed to a memory. They felt the cave close over them, as if the idea of daylight itself had been sealed away.

And the dark, patient and old as law, closed around them and listened.

Topside, the sawmill lot had swelled. A news van had knifed its way down County 14, satellite dish like a silver weed, and a woman with too-white teeth was rehearsing a somber look in the reflection of her phone. Sheriff Dorman hated cameras the way fishermen hate waves, everything gets sloshed, nothing stays where you set it.

"Turn that back," he told a deputy who'd lifted the tape for the crew. "This isn't a backdrop."

"We're just here to help get the word out," the reporter said, angling toward him. "Is it true you have six minors trapped? Are you resourced for a technical rescue? And is it true an unpermitted religious group has been using these caves?"

Dorman's mustache twitched. "Ma'am, we have children underground. That's the only truth I care about. Step back."

From the crowd, a man in a pearl-snap shirt called, "They're down there lookin' for the stairs. Preacher Hale told 'em."

"Preacher Hale told nobody that," said another voice, older, stern. Pastor Ernest Hale himself stepped forward,

Bible in one hand like a badge. "Stories keep folks out of holes. That's why they're stories."

"Then why is your pamphlet all over town?" the man shot back. He held up a crumpled handout, rain-spotted and sun-faded: a black serif title across the top, In Defense of the Righteous, and below it a woodcut of a gate in stone.

Dorman snatched it, jaw working. "Not today," he said, more to the paper than to the man. He folded it and slid it into his pocket like something you don't throw away in front of someone's mother.

He looked at the trees, at the dark oval of the sink that swallowed good sense and daylight alike, and wished his team down there a very old wish: May the ground be kind.

Underground, the ground was not kind.

The passage tightened again, not quite a squeeze, more like the cave putting its hand against their chests to test their hearts. The draft had teeth now, cooler, the metallic smell sharper, as if a tool had been put away wet and forgotten here for a century.

Beaumont raised his hand. "Hold," he whispered. He knelt, light low, and traced an edge in the silt with a gloved finger. "Boot tread. Adult. Not one of the kids."

Dani leaned in. The imprint was clear: a Vibram pattern with a chip missing on the right heel. The weight distribution told a story, a cautious step, a measured pivot.

"How old?" she asked.

Beaumont tilted his head. "Hours."

"Caver?" Jake asked.

"Could be," Beaumont said. "Could also be a hunter with no sense." He swept the beam. "Or a man who knows exactly where he's going."

They pushed on. The ceiling rose unexpectedly, and they found themselves in a tall slot where their voices didn't bounce back so quick. Their lamps threw long spears up the walls, catching pale draperies of calcite, thin as fingernails, and places where the stone was blackened as if someone had burned a lamp too close too often.

"Someone's been staging," Beaumont said, touching a soot smear. "Not kids."

A hundred feet ahead the slot widened into a balcony over a black pool. The water was perfectly still, a mirror that refused to show your face. At its far edge, the rock sloped down into it like a drowned stair. The draft came from somewhere above, an unseen gap, making the surface quiver with the smallest of tremors.

"Sump," Beaumont said. "Usually shallow. Today, hard to say." He pointed to a narrow shelf three feet above the waterline. "There's a traverse if you've got respect for your ankles." He anchored a line and tested it until the carabiner sang against the bolt.

Halfway across, Jake paused. "Hear that?"

They froze. From deep in the rock came a sound like a far-off hammer, two slow knocks, then silence. Dani felt the hairs rise along her arms.

"Echo," Beaumont said, too fast. "Water drip."

"Too regular," Jake murmured.

Dani swallowed. "Rally!" she called, careful to shape the name so the cave didn't eat it. "Nia! It's Dani!"

A second silence answered. Then, faint and thin as thread, a whistle, one, two, three chirps, from somewhere ahead and below.

Beaumont's eyes cut to hers. He didn't say don't hope. He also didn't say hope smart.

They finished the traverse, and the passage funneled them into a room so narrow it forced them single file. Here the air was colder still. On the wall, someone had drawn arrows again, but not in chalk, these were charred, draggy marks made with the burnt end of a stick. Between the arrows, a single word in blocky letters: STAIRS.

Beaumont exhaled through his teeth. "Kids think a legend needs a sign."

"Sometimes legends plant one," Jake said.

At the floor's edge lay a blue plastic inhaler, muddied, the name written in Sharpie on the side half-scrubbed but visible: NIA A.

Dani's throat closed for a painful beat. She forced it open. "They're ahead," she said. "Move."

Above, the crowd had curdled into factions. Some prayed. Some filmed. Some muttered about lawsuits and county budgets. Pastor Hale had placed a gentle hand on Mrs. Alvarez's shoulder and was murmuring something soft; she didn't hear him. She was listening to the dark like a woman at a door.

A county commissioner's SUV rolled in hot, door still opening as he barked, "Dorman. Media's calling this a crisis. What's our liability if that cave collapses with county personnel inside?"

Dorman looked at him the way men look at wasps. "My liability is six kids and their mother."

"Stand down until State Search & Rescue arrives," the commissioner said. "We can't risk..."

"State's two hours out," Dorman snapped. "Caves don't hold their breath because you scheduled it." He turned away, ending the conversation by not having it.

The reporter caught that, satisfied that she had both a conflict and a villain, and started talking faster to her phone.

The room beyond the inhaler broke left into a corkscrew chute so slick it demanded three points of contact and a fourth of prayer. They took it slow, Beaumont first, then Dani, then Jake. At the bottom the chute spat them into a chamber, unlike the others, flat-floored, the walls strangely regular in places, as if hands had once smoothed them. Fossil shells stippled the stone like constellations.

In the corner stood a cairn not like the others: this one was topped by a small metal object gone to rust. Dani angled her light. A square of grating? No, an old iron step, the kind you cast in a foundry and bolt into bedrock.

"Tell me that's natural," Jake said.

"It's iron," Beaumont said. "Nature makes a lot of things. Not that."

Dani brushed mud from the metal with her glove. Letters revealed themselves in bumps and pits: L.C.C., and beneath them, a date mostly eaten by rust. 19, something.

"Lafayette Citrus Company," Jake said slowly. "They ran phosphate out of this county before my old man learned to shave. Mined caves, ran rails into holes."

Beaumont's mouth went tight. "Means voids. Means places that aren't mapped."

Dani pictured six kids walking toward a story and finding a century-old one waiting. "Rally brought them to a gate," she said, and didn't know why she used that word until she saw it: beyond the step, at knee height, a slit in the wall and, inside, the ghost of something straight, the line of a corroded hinge plate set into rock.

Cam Lockett's backpack lay half-tucked in a pocket of the wall. Dani pulled it free, unzipped with careful fingers. Inside: a cracked headlamp, a tin of mints, a half-eaten sandwich in plastic, a Polaroid of four kids on bikes in front of a gas station, and a folded pamphlet, same black serif title as the one topside: In Defense of the Righteous. On its inside a page had been marked with grease pencil, a circle around an old map engraving of "Under-Ridge Works" and an X drawn at a dark square labeled Access.

"Where'd a sixteen-year-old get this?" Dani asked.

"Someone gave it to him," Jake said. "Someone who knew there was more than legend under here."

Beaumont turned his light away as if the paper burned. "If there's old industrial, there's pockets, bad air, false floors, metal you can't trust. We back out, call a mine team…"

A sound stopped him: the whistle again, closer now, then a thin, ragged voice, not a kid's bravado but a child's prayer cutting upward through stone: "Help."

Dani was already moving. "Point it," she said.

Beaumont swore, then pointed to a rift no wider than his shoulders. Cold air poured from it like breath. "That splits into a keyhole. I can fit. You two'll swear you can't and then you will."

"Story of my week," Jake said.

They filed in. The keyhole pinched at the hips, then opened at the chest, then pinched again. The trick was to trust the rock to give back what it took. The floor dropped without warning; Dani caught herself on elbows and slid into darkness on her forearms, lamp swinging, heart a drumline in her throat.

The slide ended on a ledge. The room below was a vault of cold blue air where her breath smoked. On the far side a narrow slope descended to a black ribbon of water. At the water's edge, huddled in a wedge of shadow, a boy in a camo hoodie hugged his knees. He had dirt on his face in comet sweeps and blood dried at his hairline.

"Cam," Dani said, voice tight. "Hey. I'm Dani."

The boy flinched at the light, then looked up, hope and terror tangled. "Nia's not with me," he said immediately, as if that was the only sentence he'd practiced. "Rally said there were stairs. We found 'em. But then they moved." His breath hitched. "He said go left. The man said go left."

Jake's voice was a blanket. "What man?"

Cam shut his eyes like the name itself hurt. "The one with the whistle."

Beaumont had already rigged the handline. "We haul him up," he said. "We do not dally."

As Jake clipped Cam in, Dani scanned the floor. Next to the boy's shoe prints were others, larger, the same Vibram with a chip in the heel. And another set: smooth-soled, like dress shoes, absurd here, the print of a man who didn't spend time in dirt. Her light followed those tracks to the water. They disappeared into the ribbon like someone had stepped onto a hidden shelf.

"Platform," she whispered. "Or a boat anchored in black."

Beaumont heard her tone and didn't argue with things he couldn't see. He hauled. Cam rose up the line trembling and silent until he reached Dani's ledge, then clamped to her like a small drowning thing remembers land.

"It's okay," she lied, because sometimes lies were tourniquets. "You did exactly right, Cam."

From below, water ticked against stone. A whisper of air changed direction, brushing their cheeks as if the cave had turned its head to listen.

"Dani," Jake said. "Hear that?"

She did. Under the water's tick and the cable's faint creak, a steady machine hum no cave should make. It was faint but unmistakable: a fan somewhere, or a generator, running behind rock.

The cave breathed in. Lights seemed to dim, though they did not. Somewhere far away, or too close to measure, two slow knocks, then silence.

Dani reached for the rock and found the iron again, the edge of a second cast step buried in flowstone. Not a memory. A path.

"Beaumont," she said, her voice not loud but carrying. "There's infrastructure in here. We're not just in karst. We're in somebody's footprint."

"Then we leave," Beaumont said. "We get the kids out and we let a team with gas and meters risk their pensions."

Cam tugged her sleeve. "The man said we were brave," he whispered. "He said some people have to do hard things to keep the bad out. He had a pin on his hat. An R in a circle."

Jake met Dani's eyes. "Righteous."

The pamphlet in her pocket might as well have weighed a pound. She heard the reporter's neat questions. She heard Mrs. Alvarez's dry prayer. She heard Chicago, always.

"We're taking Cam up," she said. "Then you and Jake bring a stave party down with air and steel. And I go to the gate."

"No," Beaumont said flatly. "You go nowhere alone."

Dani smiled without showing teeth. "Then keep up."

Topside, the first ambulance lights ghosted the pines red and blue. Dorman felt his phone buzz and buzz again, ignored it, and met the ambulance halfway with his hand up for quiet. He listened. The forest had a sound it made when a storm was walking in, and it wasn't making that sound. It was making a different one, remote and regular, a mechanical heartbeat. He looked at the sink and knew it was not the earth he was hearing.

Mrs. Alvarez's lips moved without sound. Pastor Hale had stopped talking. The crowd, restless as cattle, stood very still.

The reporter, sensing the shift without knowing why, dropped her script voice and whispered into the camera, "Something's happening."

They moved. Cam upward, clipped between Jake and Beaumont like a bead on a string, hands shaking, but he moved. At the traverse, he froze and made a small animal noise; Jake murmured an old song under his breath, something from a war the cave didn't care about, and the boy moved again. When they reached the chute, Beaumont went to ground and made his back into a step; Cam climbed as if the man had always been a staircase.

At the slot before the light grew, Cam turned his face into Dani's jacket and sobbed once, soundless. She pressed her palm to the back of his head and felt the fragile roundness of his skull. "You saved yourself," she said. "That's the bravest, stupidest thing any of us ever do."

"I left them," he said, guilt scalding.

"You're going to help us find them," she said. "That's what comes next."

They reached the slope and its glimmer of daylight. The crowd's noise leaked down in threads. When Cam's head appeared at the lip, a sound rose from the clearing like a flock of birds taking off, relief and fear finding each other in the same breath. Mrs. Alvarez pushed through hands and tape and rules, and the medics knew better than to be the first touch. She took Cam's face in both hands. "Where is she?" she asked gently and with knives.

Cam cried in a way that had words and didn't. Dorman's hand found Dani's shoulder. "One," he said. "Get him warm. Get me the rest."

Dani nodded once. "We're going back in," she said to Beaumont and Jake. "Short resupply at the tailgate. Then the gate."

Beaumont scrubbed a hand over his face. "I'm logging a protest on record that this is rash, stupid, and personal."

"Logged," Dani said.

"Also," he added, meeting her eyes, "I'm with you."

Jake grinned like a man who'd found his lighter. "Let's go knock on somebody's door."

28

They moved faster the second time down, but not sloppy. Fresh batteries. Spare lines. A small gas meter Jake insisted on, "Stole it from a contractor who owed me a favor," he said, like that was a confession and a boast.

Back through the familiar: the slope, the Y, the Banjo's hungry throat, the dragon's back, the cathedral of stalactites that didn't care. Past the cairn with the skull that did. In the chamber of the iron step, Dani knelt again at the slit. She put her light inside and the beam struck metal: a grating three feet in, bricks beyond, and the shadow of a corridor laid in lines human hands intend.

Beaumont set a small expansion bolt in sound rock and rigged a body belay. "I don't like this," he said conversationally. "I like a lot of things. This isn't one."

Breathe," Dani said to him and to herself. She slid sideways into the slit, shoulders grating, with a sound like steel scraping concrete. The hole opened into a pocket barely big enough to crouch. The air was colder, the machine hum clearer. She pushed her hand through a veil of calcite and touched iron. It was rough with damp rust, but under that roughness was the blunt certainty of a thing made to last.

The grating had been cut. Not recently, edges were flaked with old corrosion but cut. Beyond, a narrow corridor ran left-right, brick arched, the mortar soft from weeping stone. To the left, the hum grew louder. To the right, in the dust, the clear print of a small shoe and the smooth ellipse of a dress shoe beside it.

She looked back, met Jake's lamp through the slit. "I've got man-made," she said. "And fresh sign."

"Air?"

She glanced at the meter clipped to her vest. "Good enough to think you're lucky."

Beaumont's line went tight on her harness. "We do this like we mean to come back," he said.

"Copy."

She ducked and slipped through the cut grating. The corridor took her like a throat. On the wall, painted a lifetime ago and decayed now into the color of old teeth, flaked letters read: L.C.C. SERVICE TUNNEL, NO UNAUTHORIZED ENTRY.

Dani smiled grimly. "Too late," she said to the wall.

Behind her, Jake's shoulders filled the slit, then Beaumont's. The three of them stood in the long narrow pulse of a machine that was not dead.

From ahead came a sound like a door engaging. And then another sound, the smallest, simplest, most human of sounds in a place designed to erase them: a child coughing, trying to be quiet and failing because lungs are honest.

Dani raised a hand. Jake killed his lamp; Beaumont dimmed to a halo. The tunnel held its breath with them.

"Rally," Dani whispered, no louder than a story told in a church. "Nia." She waited. The cough came again, from the left this time, behind a door that hadn't been opened in a hundred years until someone oiled its hinges last week.

Dani put her palm to the cold iron. She knocked once. Twice.

From the other side, two knocks answered, not echo. Not water. Someone there, counting the seconds, counting the knocks, deciding whether to answer a world that hadn't been kind.

The lock turned.

.

Chapter Two: Shadows of Justification

The darkness pressed down like a hand that squeezes the breath from your chest.

Dani's headlamp threw a narrow beam of light that wobbled with her breath. It skated over limestone the color of old teeth, catching seams of quartz that winked like watchful eyes. Water dripped from somewhere she couldn't see to somewhere else she couldn't see, each plink echoing with maddening patience, as if the cave were a clock no human had wound. The echoes measured the room into a geometry her body didn't understand, angles that bent the mind sideways.

"Left or right?" Jake's voice was soft, but the cave took softness and mocked it, doubling it, tripling it, sending it back from impossible corners. His words became a chorus of Jakes, all of them waiting for her answer.

Dani squatted, lamp angled low and swept her beam across the floor. Mud told the story better than words: six sets of prints, small and erratic, overlapping into chaos. A heel slide gouged deep, as if someone had skidded in panic. A skid where somebody had lost footing and caught themselves with a hand, she saw the palm print pressed into the silt like the ghost of a child trying not to fall. A crushed soda can bore the bruise of a boot tread, its aluminum belly split, still reeking faintly of sugar and rust.

"Left," she said. "They went for slope, not throat."

Jake grunted behind her, the sound carrying through rope and rock. "Kids always pick gravity."

They moved single file, tethered by rope like beads on a rosary. Dani's rope clipped to Jake's harness, Jake's to Beaumont's. The caver moved with the patience of a priest who knew the ritual and had no interest in shortcuts. At each junction he chalked arrows, bright white smudges against the stone, temporary as breath. He touched the cave like it was alive and owed him nothing.

"You keep wanting to look up," he said over his shoulder. His voice held no judgment, only fact. "That's how you scalp yourself. Rock doesn't care about foreheads."

"Put it on the list," Jake replied dryly, ducking as his own helmet nearly found a low tooth of stone.

The tunnel narrowed to a letterbox. Dani went to her knees, elbows digging into cold grit, and pushed her pack ahead like an unwilling mule. Her helmet scraped stone with a shriek that made her teeth ache. The air smelled like wet mold and rotting leaves, metallic and organic, a combination that turned the stomach. Her chest tried to take a full breath, but the rock denied it. She made her breath smaller, like folding paper until it fit a pocket.

"You okay?" Jake's voice floated from behind, muffled by the stone.

"I've been worse," she said. She meant it and didn't mean it. Chicago worse. Nightmares worse. But claustrophobia had a way of rewriting definitions. She dragged forward another foot, then six inches, then an inch, bargaining with stone, promising herself there was a future in which she wasn't doing this.

Beaumont's voice carried from ahead, steady as rope. "Think of it like a hug from the earth."

"I'll send a thank-you note," Dani muttered.

The stone relented, lifting into a shallow room no bigger than a cheap motel bathroom. She sat back on her heels, drew her helmet to her knees, and let her pulse climb down a rung at a time. A bat fluttered past her head, wings whispering like leather rubbed together. She flinched, then cursed herself for flinching.

Jake slid in behind her, mud smeared to his thighs, lamp catching his cheekbones in sharp planes. "You ever hear the one about the boy in Hue?" he asked, voice casual in the way men make confessions sound like jokes.

"No," Dani said, though her gut told her she didn't want to.

"Seventeen," Jake said. "Shot through the leg. Enemy. He begged me to kill him. No medic. No chance. So I did." His tone was even, stripped of color. "Mercy."

Dani stared at the rock between her boots. "You call that mercy."

"I call it not listening to screaming until dawn." Jake's smile was a line without temperature. "The paperwork didn't cover that scenario."

"Paperwork never does," Dani said. She pressed her palm to the wall, cool and damp. "Sometimes I think we invented forms because we couldn't invent absolution."

Beaumont clipped the line to a nub of rock, efficient, uninterested in their ghosts. "Save theology for the bivy," he said. "We'll make a ledge in the next chamber."

The passage widened like a throat swallowing them into a cathedral stolen from under the earth. Dani's lamp strained to hold it, but the chamber mocked her beam. Stalactites hung like teeth grown since the law was young; stalagmites reached up like hands tired of waiting. The ceiling breathed. She told herself it was temperature differentials, nothing more, but she could not shake the feeling of lungs.

They picked a flat patch near a rock that looked too much like an altar and called it camp. Beaumont unpacked a small lantern, its orange glow softer than the stark lamps, feathering shadows into strange shapes. Jake unrolled a foil blanket and coiled rope beside him, pressing his back to the stone like he could keep it from moving.

Dani inventoried her pack, spare lamps, blister packs, a scarf that still smelled of her washing machine, the ghost of her apartment. Not the Chicago file. She hadn't brought it. But it had come anyway, a weightless thing that pressed harder than stone.

"Eat," Beaumont said. "Hydrate. Your body won't remember until your head's halfway to stupid."

Jerky that fought their teeth. Trail mix gone stale. Chewing sounded obscene in the vast silence, human noise intruding on something older.

"Why stairs?" Dani asked when the food sat heavy. "Kid said he wanted to find stairs."

Beaumont shrugged. "Every county's got its ghost works. WPA projects, Prohibition storage, conquistador graves. Kids like the idea that somebody put these places here for a reason. Makes the dark feel less like an accident."

Jake crumpled an empty peanut bag between his fingers. "I saw stairs once," he said. "In Laos. Led to a hole with snakes."

"Everything in Laos leads to snakes," Beaumont said.

"Everything leads to something," Jake countered. His tone chilled the back of Dani's neck.

The cave took their silence and filed it away.

Sleep didn't come so much as bargain. Dani lay on her side, knees tucked, helmet off but headlamp within reach, foil blanket crinkling when she moved. The lantern sputtered to a dull ember. Darkness reasserted itself, heavy and complete. It wasn't the kind of dark that made you close your eyes. It was the kind that kept them open, convinced there was always something to see if you stared hard enough.

Every sound stood up and introduced itself: the cooling tick of stone, the drip that refused to keep rhythm, the shallow whisper of Jake's breath behind her, Beaumont's heavier exhalations to her left. Her own pulse made the rock under her cheek feel alive.

"You awake?" Jake asked quietly.

"Yeah."

"Me too." She could hear the smile in his voice even without seeing his face. "Hell of a first date."

A laugh caught in her throat, half-humor, half-exhaustion. "This isn't a date."

"Tell that to the brochure." Jake whispered as he shifted. His shoulder found hers, warm through the thin barrier of her jacket. It was the most human thing in the cave, and it was dangerous for that very reason.

"Don't mistake me for a confessional," Dani whispered.

"Not looking for absolution." His hand brushed hers. Rough, calloused, alive. "Just proof we're still here."

Her forehead rested against his for a breath longer than it should have. Their mouths found each other in the only direction left to go. Clumsy, gear in the way, fear between them. It promised nothing beyond the moment, which was the only promise worth making this deep.

When they parted, the cave hadn't changed. But her pulse had a new shape.

They lay side by side, silence stretching until it felt like a truce.

That's when the moan came.

Low and long, it filled the chamber like something shifting in its sleep. It was not wind. Dani sat up fast, headlamp snapping on, beam quivering. The hairs along her arms stood up as if a hand had run across them.

"You hear that?" she whispered.

"Yeah," Jake said. His voice was flatter now. "Not the kind of song you hum on the way home."

Beaumont propped on an elbow, lamp in hand, face hard. "Could be air squeezing through a pinch." He didn't sound convinced. "Could be…"

The sound came again, closer, different. Almost words. The cave chewed syllables until only bones of them remained.

"…no justification here…"

The words brushed Dani's skin like cold breath.

She was on her feet without remembering the decision. The lantern went up. Headlamps snapped on, shrinking the dark just enough to move.

They followed the sound to the far wall. Up close, what looked like solid stone revealed a seam. A slot no wider than a shoulder turned sideways. From it the moan leaked like air through a throat too narrow.

Beaumont angled his lamp inside. A shaft dropped away, light falling, falling, until it caught on nothing. From below came a glow. Not bright. Just persistent. Red, not the color but the idea of red. It pulsed like something alive, swelling with the moan, ebbing when the sound died.

"Gas?" Jake asked. "Or fungus?" He knew it wasn't fungus. He needed it to be fungus.

"No stink," Beaumont said. His nose wrinkled. "No heat. Not gas. And not bio-lum I know. I'd have seen it on a map."

Dani tied off to a stalagmite. "We go down."

"Hold." Beaumont's voice snapped, sharp as rope under tension. "We haven't marked our exits. We don't know if it bells out or narrows. We don't know if there's a re-belay. You can't…"

"Six kids," Dani said. Her hands moved as if argument wasted more time than climbing. "We don't make the perfect plan. We make the possible one."

Beaumont stared at her, lips tight, then gave the smallest, most practical nod. "Fine. Possible and alive. Tinsley anchors. Francis first on rope. If it bells, you lock and wait. Two tugs, you come up. Three, we cut line."

"Cut?" Jake growled.

"If the shaft narrows and jams her, we don't add bodies to the jam," Beaumont said. "I like her, but not enough to decorate limestone."

Dani smiled without heat. "Flattered."

They worked in silence, hands moving by muscle memory. Anchors checked and rechecked. Carabiners set. Jake's knots were precise, military neat. Beaumont tested the rig with his full weight until the carabiner sang against the bolt.

Dani clipped in, swung her legs into the slot, and felt the shaft take her.

The glow licked her boots.

"On rope," she called.

"On belay," Jake answered, steady as scripture.

She eased off the lip. Rock closed around her like a coffin. The shaft was straight, an elevator no one designed for people. Her lamp painted three feet ahead, three feet back. The glow seeped up her like blush.

"Talk to me," Jake's voice floated down. "Give the hole your voice."

"I'm fine. I'm not stuck. I'm going down."

"You still own your feet?"

"For now."

The shaft narrowed. Her shoulder scraped. She adjusted, body twisting in ways it hadn't been asked to since academy training. Rope hummed in her descender. Her breath fogged her visor.

Then it widened. Her boots found a ledge slick with not-water. She crouched, balancing on stone that wept. The glow wasn't below anymore. It seeped from the walls, bleeding from seams like light underwater.

And the words came again.

No justification here.

Not sound. Not echo. Recognition. A key fitting a lock she hadn't wanted to admit she carried.

Her stomach turned cold.

"I'm at a ledge," she called. Her voice sounded like it belonged to someone else. "There's a chamber."

"Do not unclip," Beaumont ordered. "Wait for my light."

Two more beams joined hers, braiding light until the chamber ahead revealed itself.

It wasn't a room. It was an artery.

The walls curved, smooth and worn by more than water. Symbols smeared in blood-dark paint ringed the stone: scales, blades, raised hands, bound hands. The glow bled between the marks, slow as breath.

And the moan wasn't a moan anymore.

It was voices.

Layered like a choir that couldn't agree on the hymn.

"…had no choice…"

"…orders are orders…"

"…mercy…"

"…necessary…"

Excuses stacked on excuses, bones of rationalizations left to rot.

Dani's light swept the chamber and froze. A figure stood in the artery. Too tall. Too thin. Coat hanging like it remembered another century. A face, pale and stretched, eyes like ink spilled in water.

It raised one hand. Not greeting. Not threat. Just acknowledgment.

Dani blinked. It was gone.

Her mouth went dry. "We're not alone," she whispered. "Move."

The artery funneled them downward, rope humming, lamps tracing walls alive with excuses written in old paint. Dani landed first, boots splashing shallow water pooled in a hollow. Jake followed, then Beaumont, eyes scanning like a man reading a language he didn't admit to knowing.

The floor angled. Footprints pressed into the silt, small, panicked, overlapping. Sneakers, not boots. Scuffs where someone had stumbled, toe marks gouging hard.

"They're close," Dani said.

"Or they were," Beaumont muttered.

They moved as a line. The air changed again, cooler, threaded with the smell of iron, as if something metallic was sweating nearby.

At the far end, a slope spilled into a vault with a black ribbon of water cutting it in half. On the near side, huddled against the wall, a boy in a camo hoodie hugged his knees. His lamp lay dead beside him, cracked and useless.

Jake clipped the boy in with careful hands. Dani kept her lamp sweeping the edges of the vault. Prints beside the boy's were wrong: heavier boots, Vibram soles with a chip missing on the heel. And another, smooth-soled, narrow, absurdly like dress shoes. They led to the water and ended there, as if the wearer had stepped onto a hidden shelf.

"Platform," Dani whispered. "Or a boat."

The water's surface quivered with the faintest tremor, though no stone had fallen.

"Move," Beaumont snapped. He braced the rope, muscles corded. Jake lifted the boy, guiding him like freight more precious than anything he'd carried in war. Cam rose up the line, trembling but silent now, survival overriding terror. Dani scrambled beside him, hand on his shoulder until he reached her ledge.

"It's okay," she lied, crouching to his level. "You did exactly right, Cam."

"I left them," he choked.

"You saved yourself," she said firmly. "That's the bravest, stupidest thing any of us ever do. And you're going to help us find the rest."

They started the climb back, Cam clipped between Jake and Beaumont like a bead on string. He froze at the traverse above the black pool, whimpering. Jake murmured an old tune under his breath, something from a war Dani didn't know, words slurred with memory. The boy moved again.

At the chute, Beaumont made himself a step, letting Cam climb his back like he was stone. When Cam's head broke into the light of the slope, the clearing above erupted.

The sound of a crowd seeing proof of survival is unlike any other: relief and grief crashing together, sharp as glass.

"You don't have to prove anything, Francis," Dorman said.

"I'm not proving," she answered. "I'm preventing funerals."

The crowd surged again, voices fracturing: some thanking God, some cursing Rally Gillum, some accusing the Sheriff of negligence, some whispering about the pamphlets.

The news crew's lights seared the clearing, catching the tears on Mrs. Alvarez's cheeks like diamonds mined too cruelly.

The commissioner raised his voice. "Stand down until State SAR arrives! We can't risk county employees without…"

Dorman turned, jaw set like a man resisting the urge to throw a punch. "Kids are breathing underground right now. I don't wait two hours while you write liability memos."

The commissioner looked ready to argue, but the reporter had already seized the conflict, whispering urgently into her camera: "Rescue operation split between Sheriff and county leadership. Questions swirl about who authorized the descent."

Dani ignored them all. At the Bronco's tailgate, she rechecked gear with shaking hands she forced steady. Batteries. Spare rope. Gas meter Jake had smuggled from a contractor.

"We're logging a protest," Beaumont said as he strapped on fresh knee pads. His beard dripped sweat and cave water. "This is rash, stupid, and personal."

"Logged," Dani said without looking up.

Beaumont's mouth twisted, then steadied. "Also, I'm with you."

Jake grinned with the thin humor of men already committed. "Let's go knock on somebody's door."

,

The return into the ridge was faster, but not careless. Past the slope, the Y, the Banjo squeeze that scraped Dani's ribs until they burned. Past the dragon's back and the cathedral of stalactites that had watched civilizations rise and fall without interest.

At the chamber where Cam had been found, the water still whispered against stone. Dani's lamp followed the adult tracks again, tracing their end at the edge. Her gut clenched. Whoever had been with the children had gone somewhere the cave didn't advertise.

Beaumont set bolts into clean rock, rigging lines. His movements were efficient, but his jaw was tight. "I don't like this," he said. "Caves don't change this fast without help."

Dani crouched at a slit in the wall, half-concealed by flowstone. Her lamp touched iron. Rusted, rough, but unmistakably wrought. She pushed and the calcite veil flaked away, revealing grating.

It had been cut, not collapsed.

Behind it lay brick.

She squeezed through, shoulder scraping, and landed in a corridor. The arch overhead was man-made, mortar dripping like tears from decades of seepage. On the wall, in flaked paint the color of old teeth, the words still clung:

L.C.C. SERVICE TUNNEL, NO UNAUTHORIZED ENTRY

Jake ducked in behind her, lamp sweeping the dust. "Lafayette Citrus Company," he said slowly. "They ran phosphate out of this county before my old man could shave. Rails into holes. Mines under farmland."

46

Beaumont crouched, fingertips brushing mortar. "Industrial voids," he muttered. "Gas pockets. Collapses. I don't want to be here."

"Kids went down here," Dani said. "So do we."

Her lamp caught prints in the dust: sneakers, small and recent. Next to them, dress shoes. The absurdity of it chilled her more than the cave air.

The hum grew louder now, mechanical, steady, a generator somewhere close.

Jake raised his head. "You hear it?"

Dani nodded, throat dry. "Somebody's home."

At the end of the corridor, a door waited. Iron hinges slick with oil that hadn't been there a month ago. From the other side came the faint, unarguable sound of a child coughing.

Dani laid her palm against the metal. It was cold, but not dead.

She knocked once. Twice.

Two knocks answered.

The lock turned.

The lock turned with a metallic click that echoed through Dani's bones. She pushed, and the door swung inward with a sigh, as if it had been waiting for this moment.

The corridor beyond was narrow, brick-walled, and wrong. The walls wept with condensation, mortar streaked like tears. Rust stains bled from corroded bolts sunk into the brick a century ago. The air was colder, tinged with the faint smell of ozone, as if wires somewhere out of sight were sparking against stone.

Jake's lamp cut long shadows ahead of them. Beaumont closed the door behind, testing it, and grimaced when it latched easily. "Somebody's maintaining this," he muttered. "Doors don't stay smooth a hundred years without hands."

The passage turned left, then right, then pitched downward. Each turn carried new graffiti, some old, charcoaled symbols that matched those in the artery; some newer, etched by knife, phrases scrawled jagged: FOR MY FAMILY. NO CHOICE. ORDERS. MERCY.

Excuses layered until the walls themselves seemed to murmur.

"City of Justifications," Dani whispered without knowing why. The words fit the place like a key.

At the bottom of the slope the tunnel widened into a chamber, square, brick-arched, too regular to be natural. In its center stood a table of rough stone, piled with objects: a child's backpack, cracked plastic headlamps, cheap watches, papers curled with damp. Atop it all lay a Bible, warped, its pages swollen, a red circle drawn on its cover in marker, a capital R inside.

Cam's voice came back to her: The man said we were brave. He had a pin. An R in a circle.

Dani touched the book with a gloved hand. The cover was warm.

"Sheriff's Office," she called into the chamber, her voice hard. "Kids, answer me."

For a moment there was only the drip of water and the whisper of their own breath. Then from the far wall, behind another iron door, a cry: thin, hoarse, unmistakably a child.

Nia.

48

Dani surged forward, but Beaumont caught her arm. "Wait. Traps. Air. This isn't a playground."

"Neither is a coffin," she snapped, tearing free.

They approached the door. Its hinges were slick with fresh oil, its frame lined with riveted steel plates. Someone had reinforced it recently. The crying rose, ragged, then broke into coughs.

Jake set his shoulder against the door. "One push," he said. "Together."

They shoved. The door screamed and gave.

Inside was another corridor, shorter, lined with barred cells hacked into the limestone. Old mining supports jutted like ribs. In the nearest cell, huddled against the wall, was Nia Alvarez. Her hair was plastered to her face, her lamp broken beside her. When she saw Dani, she tried to stand but collapsed to her knees, sobbing.

"Nia!" Dani dropped, reaching through the bars. "It's okay. We're here."

The girl clutched Dani's hand with both of hers, fingers cold as stone.

Keys hung from a hook beside the cell, absurd in their convenience. Beaumont grabbed them, fumbling only once before the lock gave with a click. The gate swung open, and Nia threw herself into Dani's arms, clinging with desperate strength.

"We're taking you out," Dani murmured into her hair. "You're safe."

But even as she said it, the cave argued.

From deeper in the corridor came footsteps. Slow. Measured. Two sets.

One heavy, heel chipped.

The other smooth, absurd, dress shoes whispering against stone.

Jake's lamp swung toward the sound. The beam caught only emptiness, but the steps continued, echoing like they owned the place.

"Back out," Beaumont hissed. "Now."

The crying had woken others. From the farther cells came voices, faint, pleading, not all of them children. A man's voice whispered, "Orders are orders." A woman sobbed, "I had no choice." Their words tangled with the painted phrases on the walls until it felt like the cave itself was speaking.

The generator hum deepened. Somewhere behind the brick a machine shifted, gears engaging.

Then the lights died.

Total dark.

Only their headlamps remained, fragile cones in an ocean.

And within that cone, at the end of the corridor, the figure stood.

Tall. Thin. Coat hanging from narrow shoulders. Face pale, eyes black. It lifted one hand again, not threat, not greeting. Acknowledgment.

This time it did not vanish when Dani blinked.

Behind it, another shape emerged. Shorter, broader, features hidden, but a whistle hung from a cord around its neck. The man raised it slowly to his lips.

The first note pierced the corridor, shrill and endless.

Nia screamed.

Dani yanked her close, lamp beam fixed on the figures.

Her other hand went to her holster out of instinct, though every fiber of her training screamed that a bullet wouldn't matter here.

One moment Nia was at her side; the next, the City reached in and claimed her, as if judgment itself had chosen.

Jake stepped up beside her, rope taut at his hip, eyes narrowed. "Looks like we found the stairs," he muttered.

Beaumont's voice was a rasp. "No. Looks like the stairs found us."

The whistle note cut off. The dark inhaled.

And the door behind them slammed shut.

Chapter Three: Crossing Thresholds

The rope hummed against Dani's hip as she dropped the last twelve feet and felt the floor take her weight. Cold surged up through her boots like the earth exhaled frost. Her knees flexed, body absorbing the impact, but her breath still hitched at the air itself.

This wasn't cave air. It was curated, chosen, like the thermostat in a courtroom where judgment never wanted to sweat.

She swung her lamp in a slow arc.

The chamber wasn't a chamber. It was a vein, widened and smoothed, its walls polished into curves. Not water. Not erosion. Something had designed this for bodies to flow the way rivers carry silt.

Jake landed behind her, boots thudding, rope whispering back into stillness. His shoulders rolled like a man shaking off old armor. He scanned, squinting into the glow that leaked lazily from the seams in the wall.

Beaumont came last. Rope neat in his hand even here, his motions precise, methodical, as though tidiness could fend off the wrongness pressing in.

Symbols lined the stone.

Not graffiti, not art. Symbols laid in ranks: scales, blades, hands lifted, hands bound. They glowed faintly under Dani's lamp, as though fire had once kissed them and the memory still lingered.

A pulse throbbed through the seams, slow and indifferent, like a heartbeat that had never known hurry.

"Welcome to where explanations come to die," Dani said, repeating the whisper she'd already heard. Her own voice sounded brittle in her helmet, but speaking it aloud was the only way to prove she wasn't imagining it.

Beaumont's throat worked. "This isn't cave," he said softly. "It's... infrastructure."

Jake's jaw flexed. "Built by who?"

Beaumont shook his head. "Wrong question. Built for what."

The answer slid out of the dark, dry as parchment dragged across stone.

"For judgment."

They spun. Lamps converged.

A figure stepped from the wall as though stone had given him up. Tall, gaunt. His coat might once have been formal but was now colorless with age. His face was long, austere, human until you met the eyes: two drops of ink spreading endlessly in water.

In his left hand he carried a ledger, thick and worn, corners rounded by time, its edges blotched from years of fingers. He balanced it like a craftsman balances his favorite tool.

"I am the Archivist," he said. His voice was mild, not loud, but stone carried it to every corner. "You have been brought to the threshold."

Jake's palm hovered above his holster but didn't settle. "Brought by who?"

The Archivist turned a page with a rasp. "By your acts. They have asked for accounting. You came because you have been doing the accounting badly."

The words slid under Dani's ribs and clicked into place like a key finding its lock. Her chest ached. "We're looking for children."

The Archivist's gaze fell to her badge, then her pistol, then her face. "Yes," he said. "You are always looking for children."

Beaumont raised his lamp, trying to cut through wrongness with wattage alone. "Listen, whatever this is, we're not here for riddles. Six kids are missing…"

"Five," the Archivist corrected gently. "One has already crossed. He will be your guide."

The glow swelled. From the far curve, a figure detached and shuffled forward as though waking through syrup.

Rally Gillum.

Alive. Altered.

Relief shot through Dani like a flare, followed immediately by dread that smothered it. "Rally," she breathed. "We're taking you home."

His lips parted. The voice that spilled out used his breath but not his ownership. "Justifications crumble here."

Jake cursed under his breath. "Hell no."

Beaumont took a half step toward the boy, instincts pulling him forward. The stone answered with a dry scrape.

Shapes slid from the seams: tall, ash-gray, balanced wrong. Their skin stretched thin, their faces smooth where faces should have been. They did not rush. They did not threaten. They moved with the patience of ushers closing theater doors.

"They're herding us," Jake said evenly.

"They will not touch you unless you insist on being a problem," the Archivist said. "Please don't be a problem."

Beaumont's lamp trembled. "We go back," he muttered to Dani. "Up the rope. Call in a real team. This isn't for us."

Her eyes stayed locked on Rally. His pupils swam, his face flickering between boy and stranger. She saw not just him but every kid she'd ever cuffed, every one who'd cried in the chair, every one she couldn't save. "We can't leave him."

Rally blinked. "Leave who?" His voice was guileless and monstrous at once.

"Enough," the Archivist said. He gestured with his ledger. "You are at a door. You may enter and continue. Or you may refuse and be escorted out."

Beaumont seized it. "Out," he said. "We're leaving."

The Archivist's mouth softened, almost regretful. "Only those summoned may pass back alone. Those who come for them must go as far as they go."

Jake jerked his chin toward Beaumont. "You can climb, Grant."

Beaumont swore, the word worn smooth with use. His gaze found Dani's. "I can clean the anchor, bring the sheriff more line. Two hours. If you're not back, I come with men and we make everyone mad."

Dani's chest cinched tight. She wanted him with them. She wanted him gone. Both truths screamed. "Go," she said. "Hold the door open."

He nodded once, touched the wall with a pilgrim's reverence, and backed to the rope. "Two hours." His lamp rose, shrinking until it winked out.

The ushers closed the space he left, indifferent, shaping geometry around absence.

The Archivist turned, ledger steady. "This way," he said. "You're late."

The artery narrowed, funnelling them like livestock toward slaughter. The glow from the seams pulsed slower here, each beat dragging against Dani's pulse until she felt herself syncing to it, whether she wanted to or not.

Her lamp played over symbols repeating in endless ranks. Some were chipped and ancient, but others looked refreshed, as though a caretaker still touched them up, repainting guilt in fresh blood tones.

She couldn't help it. "Who draws these?"

The Archivist didn't look back. "Those who have something to defend."

"And the ushers?" Jake asked. "What are they supposed to be?"

"Geometry," the Archivist said simply, as though that explained everything.

They walked in silence until the artery pinched into a landing. Set into the wall loomed a door that wasn't rust and wasn't iron. Sigils covered its surface, glowing with a slow, patient red. The marks moved if Dani stared too long, shifting like diagrams she almost understood.

Her chest tightened. She remembered reading Miranda rights to a boy in Chicago whose voice cracked when he swore he hadn't pulled the trigger. The way he'd looked at her, demanding she believe him, and the forms she had filled anyway. The sigils seemed to etch those same words across the metal: He said it wasn't him. She wrote it was.

Jake leaned close, eyes narrowing. "Those aren't symbols. That's instructions."

The Archivist put his palm flat against the door. The sigils flared brighter. Dani's teeth ached. The seam split with a groan, and cold air exhaled from the gap, tinged with ash.

"Wait." Jake's hand shot out. "What's behind it?"

"A city," the Archivist said.

"What kind of city?" Dani asked.

"The kind that grows wherever human mouths learn to say, I had no choice."

The door yawned open.

Dani dragged Rally through. The boy's skin was clammy, his breath uneven. Jake followed, pistol loose in his hand. The Archivist came last, ledger hugged like scripture.

The corridor beyond was paved in black stone worn to gloss. Red torches bracketed the walls, flames steady, light flat and without heat.

The air whispered. A thousand voices bleeding through cracks in the stone: excuses, pleas, defenses. Dani heard fragments like radio static: Orders are orders. Collateral damage. For my people.

Rally twitched, mouthing words not his own. She tightened her grip on him until her knuckles whitened.

Then the corridor forked.

The Archivist paused, as if calculating. "Stay with me," he said.

But one usher moved left, blocking the direct path. Another peeled away, gliding right, its faceless head tilting toward Jake.

The Archivist turned, frowning faintly. "This is not scheduled."

The usher lifted its arm and pointed, not at Jake, but at his chest. At something inside him.

The stone to their right quivered, seams splitting open. A passage yawned where no passage had been. Cold air rolled out.

Jake stiffened. His jaw locked, eyes narrowing. "Nope."

The usher tilted its head again, patient. Geometry insisting.

"Jacob Tinsley," the Archivist murmured. "The record asks for clarification."

Jake spat on the stone. "Clarify this."

But the passage widened, waiting.

Dani's lamp skated across the opening. Beyond lay a small chamber, its floor flat, its walls painted with crude murals. Soldiers etched in charcoal. A jungle sketched in red strokes. Fire. A boy with a rifle.

Jake's breath hitched.

"Jake?" Dani asked carefully.

He didn't answer. His boots carried him forward, body rigid.

The usher followed, silent, sealing them in. Dani cursed, shoved Rally toward the Archivist, and pushed in after Jake.

The chamber snapped shut behind them.

Her lamp illuminated three figures that hadn't been there a moment ago. Young men, lean, dressed in rags that resembled uniforms. Their faces were half-erased, features smudged into anonymity, but their eyes burned like embers.

Jake froze. "No." His voice broke. "Not them."

The first figure staggered, clutching a leg wound that bled endlessly. His voice came soft but clear. "Seventeen. Enemy. Shot through the leg. You left me screaming."

The second lifted his chin. "Orders, Jake. You followed orders. But who gave them?"

The third stepped closer, a rifle in his thin hands. He was no older than sixteen. His eyes hollowed into pits. "You killed me at dawn. Called it mercy. Was it mercy, or convenience?"

Dani swallowed. The chamber tilted around them. "Jake, they're not real."

"They're real enough," Jake rasped. Sweat gleamed on his forehead. His pistol shook in his hand, barrel wavering between phantoms.

The usher stood silent, faceless, geometry watching.

Jake dropped the pistol. It clattered against stone. His voice cracked. "You begged me. I couldn't, couldn't..." He dropped to his knees, palms pressed to his skull.

The first figure stepped closer. Blood dripped on the stone but left no stain. "You called it mercy."

The second whispered, "You called it orders."

The third lifted his rifle, the barrel black and endless. "What do you call it now?"

Jake's body shook.

Dani lunged, catching his shoulders. "Jake! Look at me."

His eyes lifted, wild.

"Say it," she snapped. "Say what happened and stop talking."

His throat worked. "I killed him." The words tore out raw, unadorned. "He was seventeen. I killed him."

The chamber froze. The phantoms held still, then slowly dissolved into smoke. The usher lowered its faceless head, satisfied.

The passage behind them opened again. The Archivist waited in the main corridor, expression unreadable.

"You handled it," he said.

Jake staggered, breath harsh, face pale. "That wasn't handling. That was reliving."

The Archivist made a small mark in his ledger. "It is recorded now."

Dani helped Jake up, her own chest aching. Rally clung to her arm, eyes wide, whispering fragments: "Orders are orders. Mercy. Necessary."

She squeezed him tight. "Not you," she murmured. "Not yet."

They rejoined the path. The corridor tilted downward. The murmur grew louder. The glow deepened.

And then the world opened onto the balcony.

The corridor breathed them out onto a balcony.

Dani stopped dead, one hand on the rail, her chest forgetting how to move.

Below stretched a city that should not exist.

It was vast, sprawling across the cavern floor and climbing the walls in defiance of geometry. Towers of black stone tilted at angles that mocked physics, leaning so far they should have toppled but never did. Bridges stitched them together in spans that arced too thin, too long, but still held. Streets curved like arteries, doubling back on themselves, intersecting in impossible loops.

Her lamp tried to measure the distance but failed. Every time her eyes settled on a line, it bent. Every time she thought she understood the scale, it shifted. The city seemed alive in its design, an organism of stone and excuse.

Windows blinked open and closed like eyes. Red light seeped from seams in the ground, glowing up through cracks and fissures as though the earth itself bled ember.

The sound came last.

Not the moans from the shaft. Not the whisper of air. Voices. Thousands. Tens of thousands. Layered so thick they formed a constant pressure. Not loud, but everywhere.

They weren't chanting. They weren't praying. They were justifying.

Dani caught fragments as if they were broadcast on frequencies tuned to her shame.

It was him or me.

For my people.

Collateral damage.

I warned him.

I had no choice.

Not my fault.

Each phrase multiplied, echoed, repeated until the meaning bled out but the rhythm stayed, a chorus of self-defense muttered forever.

Rally leaned forward, his weight dragging toward the rail as though a hook had been set in his chest. Dani yanked him back. His skin was icy.

Jake stared out, his face carved blank, the way soldiers get when they're back in a place no one else can see. His voice was a dry rasp. "I've had worse shore leaves."

Dani shook her head, trying to anchor herself in sarcasm, but the city's enormity crushed humor flat. "What is this?" she whispered, though she already knew the answer.

"The City of Justifications," the Archivist said, his ledger open against the rail as though checking the city off inventory. His voice held no triumph, no pity. Just clerical satisfaction. "Built from every excuse ever spoken. Every defense rehearsed. Every reason offered to balance guilt. Walk carefully. The streets shift under the weight of words."

Dani's skin prickled. "Why the kids? Why Rally? Why any of them?"

The Archivist gazed over the railing, ink-black eyes reflecting the red glow. "Because the city is hungry. And the young carry the freshest food. Your reasons are old. Hardened by repetition. Theirs are warm."

Rally trembled in her grip. His lips parted. "I didn't mean…"

The city answered him in a thousand overlapping voices: didn't mean, didn't mean, didn't mean.

Rally's knees buckled. Dani caught him, pulling him tight against her side.

Jake leaned on the rail, eyes tracking movement below. In the city's central square, clerks in ash-gray robes weighed stones against gleaming discs. A great iron scale swayed, its chains creaking. The toll of a bell rose, cold as steel against bone.

"Looks like a courthouse bazaar," Jake muttered.

The Archivist marked something in his ledger. "The Market of Balances," he said. "Where words are measured against weight."

Movement across the gulf made Dani's breath stop.

On a balcony like theirs, five figures stood. Children. Mud-streaked, wide-eyed, still as mannequins.

Taye Reed slouched against the rail, his hoodie torn, his gaze hollow.

Junie Bell fiddled with her braids, whispering to herself, lips moving in silence.

Mason Cooper clenched his fists rhythmically, jaw tight, shoulders twitching.

Cam Lockett stood rigid, scanning like a soldier, chin raised as if facing a drill sergeant.

And Nia Alvarez, twelve, fragile, stood at the edge, her hand resting on the rail with reverence, as though she were touching sacred water.

"Nia!" Dani shouted before she could think. Her voice tore from her throat, rang across the cavern, then shredded in the air, chewed to tatters by the city. The words never reached.

Nia's head tilted, curious, like a bird hearing something faint. But her eyes were blank, reflective, as though she were listening to the city instead of Dani.

Dani's chest cracked. She almost climbed the rail, almost launched herself across the gulf, but Jake's hand caught her arm. "Don't," he said. "Not yet."

Rally struggled in her grip, reaching out. His mouth moved, muttering fragments: She begged me. I warned him. Collateral damage. Words he should never have known.

The Archivist didn't look. "You will not reach them from here," he said. "You will reach them where your reasons and theirs are sold by the pound."

"The Market," Jake said, eyes narrowing. "That bell."

The Archivist nodded. "Keep descending."

The stair wound down along the cliff, cut narrow, dangerous. At times it was broad enough for three abreast; at others, it was no wider than a plank with a chain hammered into the wall as a handhold.

Dani's lamp swept the abyss below. Shadows shifted, moving like crowds in streets. Sometimes they resembled faces. Sometimes they blinked. She forced her eyes back to the chain, to Rally, to the next step.

Half a turn down, the stair bent onto a knife-thin landing. Rally stopped, his body tightening.

"Rally," Dani warned.

"There." His voice was his own this time, sharp, insistent.

She followed his gaze. Across a gap, on that distant balcony, the five kids pressed closer to their rail.

Nia raised one small hand, palm outward, solemn.

Her lips moved. Dani strained, desperate to read them, but the city shredded even silence. No words carried. Only the impression of sound stolen.

Dani's throat burned. "Nia," she whispered, uselessly.

The Archivist's tone was calm, almost bored. "You cannot reach them from here."

Jake's eyes tracked the central square again. He pointed. "Market."

The bell tolled. The sound rolled up the cliffs, a verdict disguised as sound.

The stair continued.

The stair spat them into a corridor paved with black tiles slick as pond water at midnight. Reliefs carved along the walls showed scenes Dani forced herself not to linger on: hands tied, mouths open in pleas, blades held hilt-first against backgrounds of fire. The air smelled faintly of scorched paper and iron.

Rally lagged, sometimes dragging behind, sometimes surging ahead as if listening to instructions whispered only for him. Twice his shoulder brushed the wall and he flinched, jerking away from invisible touches. Dani kept her hand clamped around his wrist until her knuckles whitened.

"Hey," Jake said quietly, sliding in beside the boy. "You with us, kid?"

Rally's lips moved. "Where else would I be?" His tone was guileless, but Dani caught the shadow of something else riding it, an echo not his own.

The Archivist paused at an archway. Red sigils flared brighter in the stone, pulsing in rhythm with Dani's racing heart. He lifted his ledger like a priest raising scripture. "You will be tempted to argue," he said without turning. "You will be tempted to dress your actions in words. That is not the story here."

Jake's voice came flat. "Then what story does it want?"

"The one where you say what happened," the Archivist said, "and then stop talking."

He stepped through.

Dani tightened her grip on Rally and followed. Jake came last, his jaw hard.

The square opened before them.

It stretched wide, ringed by stalls like a marketplace. Clerks manned them, ashen-skinned, their bright eyes sharp and unreadable. Ledgers lay open, pens scratched without pause. Scales gleamed on counters, their chains polished from constant use.

But the goods here were not spices or fabric. They were words.

At one stall, a ragged man clutched a thin metal disc stamped with I had no choice. He begged, tears streaming, as the clerk placed it on the left pan. On the right, the clerk dropped a river stone. The stone hit with a sound like a heart stopping. The scale tilted hard. The disc gleamed weightless. The man wailed, and then dissolved, his body unraveling into smoke, leaving only the disc behind. The clerk stacked it neatly on a growing pile.

At another stall, a woman whispered, "For my family," as though prayer might add weight. The clerk ignored her plea, placed the disc, balanced it with a stone. The result was the same. The stone outweighed. The woman vanished, her disc gleaming, her words empty.

Dani's stomach turned. "Jesus."

Jake's face stayed hard, but his hands curled into fists. "This place would make prosecutors rich."

The bell tolled. The sound struck deep, echoing in her sternum.

The crowd parted.

Two ushers herded forward a boy, seventeen, maybe. His body flickered, as though memory had dragged him here half-complete. A clerk pressed a disc into his hand: I followed orders. His lips trembled. He set it on the pan. The scale tipped instantly. The disc gleamed weightless.

The Archivist marked a line in his ledger. The boy dissolved.

Rally whimpered. Dani pulled him close, but he muttered, voice broken: "Orders are orders. Not my fault."

Her chest locked. "Not you," she whispered, fierce. "Not you."

Another bell. Another soul. A soldier this time, shoulders squared as though still at attention. His disc read Collateral damage. He placed it with shaking hands. The stone dropped. Verdict made. He dissolved without a cry.

The market went on, relentless. Justifications weighed, found wanting, discarded.

Then Dani froze. She knew that voice.

Across the square, a clerk led forward a man in a suit that flickered between forms, uniform, robe, tie, like memory couldn't settle on what role he'd played. His eyes burned with

68

authority. He slammed his disc onto the pan: For the greater good.

The clerk dropped two stones. The pan crushed downward. The man screamed, the sound like metal tearing. Then he vanished, disc gleaming, excuse discarded.

Dani's skin crawled. For the greater good. She'd heard those words in briefings, in strategy meetings, in every room where one life was traded for many. The city had recorded them all.

Rally pressed closer to her side, trembling. His lips moved again, parroting: "Collateral damage. Greater good. Necessary."

She wanted to shake him, to scream the words out of him. Instead she held him tighter.

The Archivist turned a page. His ink-black eyes rose to her. "Danielle Francis."

Her heart stopped.

"No," she whispered.

"Yes," he said gently, like a clerk confirming an appointment. "Detective. Shooter. Carrier of the boy."

Her throat burned. Chicago crashed over her: the folder, the photo stapled crooked, the boy's toothless grin frozen forever. The sound of his body hitting tile. The words she'd written: self-defense, justified.

The ushers stirred, geometry shifting. They began to herd her forward.

Jake stepped between. "You want her, you go through me." His hand hovered near his pistol.

The Archivist didn't blink. "This does not begin with you, Jacob Tinsley. You have been recorded."

Jake snarled. "Recorded this." He reached for his gun,

and froze mid-motion, as though the air itself had hardened around him. His face twisted, fighting it, but the geometry didn't care.

Dani's chest heaved. The ushers loomed closer, patient, inevitable.

Rally's hand slipped into hers. His skin was ice. His whisper bled against her knuckles. "Don't leave me."

The bell tolled. Louder this time, shaking the stones of the square.

The great central scale swung, empty pans yawning like hungry mouths.

The city fell silent. Thousands of voices stilled, justifications paused, waiting.

All eyes turned to her.

"Step forward," the Archivist said. His ledger lay open, her line waiting.

The ushers closed in. They didn't touch her, didn't need to. Their mere presence bent the space, nudging her forward as surely as gravity.

Dani dug in her heels, but Rally tugged her hand. His eyes were wide, frightened, yet something else glimmered in them too: recognition. Like the city's chorus had been whispering to him long before tonight.

Jake strained against invisible weight, his face twisted with fury. "Francis, don't you do this alone."

Her throat locked. Alone was how Chicago had ended. Alone was how she carried that boy in her chest, all these years.

She took one step forward. Then another.

The Market hushed. Clerks leaned back from their ledgers, watching. Scales stilled. Even the constant murmur of justifications dimmed, as though the entire city had leaned in.

The central scale loomed. Iron beams, chains thick as her wrist, pans polished from endless verdicts. It swayed gently, hungry.

The Archivist opened his ledger. His ink-black eyes glimmered like ink dropped in water. "Danielle Francis. Detective. Shooter. Self-defense, justified. Child collateral. A contradiction."

Her breath came shallow. She felt the weight of her service pistol at her hip, the file drawer back in Chicago, the bent photo corner where her finger had traced the boy's grin.

Her voice was barely air. "I tried to save him."

The Archivist's head tilted. "That is not what is recorded."

"I didn't mean…"

The city answered. Didn't mean, didn't mean, didn't mean.

The words battered her until her knees trembled. Rally whimpered, clutching her hand tighter.

The Archivist gestured to the pan. "Place your disc."

She looked down. A thin metal disc lay in her palm, cold and gleaming. She hadn't felt it appear, but it was there, stamped with words that twisted her stomach: Imminent threat.

Her hand shook. That was what the report had said. The language she had used. The shield she had hidden behind.

"I can't," she whispered.

"You must," the Archivist said softly. "Every entry must be weighed."

She lifted her hand.

Jake roared, breaking free of whatever held him, lunging forward. He grabbed her wrist, stopping the disc from leaving her fingers. His eyes burned. "Francis. Look at me."

She looked.

"Don't give them your report," he said. "Give them what happened."

Her chest heaved. The boy's face filled her vision. The grin, the missing tooth. The sound of his body falling.

Her voice cracked. "I shot the man. And the bullet went through. And it killed him."

The disc in her hand changed. The letters warped. Imminent threat burned away, replaced with three words: I killed him.

The crowd murmured. The sound spread through the Market like wind through leaves.

The Archivist's ink-black eyes shone. "Now weigh it."

Dani's fingers trembled. She set the disc onto the pan. It rang like struck glass.

A clerk dropped a stone onto the opposite pan. The thump echoed like a heartbeat.

The scale wobbled. The stone dragged it down, heavy. The disc gleamed, weightless.

The Archivist marked his ledger. "Recorded."

Dani swayed. Her legs buckled. Jake caught her elbow, steadying her.

She gasped. "So that's it? Always the stone? Always guilty?"

The Archivist's gaze did not waver. "This is not a place of verdicts. It is a place of records. Words are weighed. Stones remember. The rest belongs to the city."

Around them, the Market's murmurs swelled again. More excuses weighed, more discs discarded, more stones stacking into invisible mountains.

But Dani heard something different. A thread of voice rising above the others. A girl's voice.

Nia.

She turned, searching the balcony above. For a moment, she swore she saw Nia's lips moving, her small hand pressed against her chest.

Then the bell tolled again.

The sound slammed through the square, louder than before, making the iron chains groan. Clerks stilled. Ushers lifted their heads in unison.

The Archivist closed his ledger with a snap. "It is not finished."

The great scale swung, pans yawning wider.

"Next," he said, and his ink-black eyes fell on Jake.

Jake's jaw clenched. "Come on, then."

The ushers shifted, geometry bending, space funneling toward the scale.

Rally whimpered, pulling against Dani's grip. His whisper slithered into her ear, wrong and terrible: "No justification here."

Dani's skin crawled. She tightened her hold, but his body jerked as though strings pulled him.

The crowd leaned forward. The Market waited.

And in the stillness before the bell struck again, Dani knew, this wasn't just about her. It wasn't just about Jake. The city wanted them all.

The bell had just tolled, the ushers bending space toward Jake, when Rally jerked violently in Dani's grasp.

His hand slipped from hers like water. His eyes went wide and glassy. "No justification here," he whispered, and then he bolted.

"Rally!" Dani lunged, fingers brushing his jacket, but he was gone, darting through the crowd, weaving between clerks and scales. The city opened for him, a narrow lane yawning where a wall had stood.

Jake swore, shoving past an usher that bent away like rubber geometry. "Move!"

Dani followed, shoving through murmuring bodies that didn't touch her but pressed like water in a tide. She caught flashes of Rally, his headlamp swinging, his small frame swallowed by red-lit alleyways.

The lane bent into darkness. The Market's clamor dulled behind them, replaced by whispers tighter, meaner. Excuses hissed from cracks in the walls. She begged me. He was armed. It wasn't my fault.

Rally stumbled ahead, his breath ragged. Dani saw him slam a hand to his ear like he was hearing orders through an invisible radio. "I'll do it," he muttered. "I'll say it right."

"Kid!" Jake's voice snapped like a whip. "Stop!"

Rally didn't.

The alley spat them into a chamber.

It was wider than the Market square, but not orderly. This was chaos, dozens of figures crammed shoulder to shoulder, clerks dragging them forward in clumps, ushers forming walls of faceless geometry.

A massive scale loomed in the center, its pans broad enough to hold several at once. The clerks shoved people forward, pressing discs into trembling hands: For the greater good. It was an accident. I was just following.

They piled onto the pans, excuses clinking like coins. Stones rained onto the opposite side, one after another, each drop thunderous. The scales sank, jerked, tilted.

The voices rose, screaming, pleading. "It wasn't me!" "I had no choice!" "I saved more than I hurt!"

One by one, they dissolved, dozens vanishing into smoke, their discs stacking on the clerks' growing heaps.

Rally froze at the edge, transfixed. His lips moved, repeating the words he heard. Dani grabbed him, pulling him back. His small body fought, weak but desperate. "Let me try!" he shouted. "I can balance it!"

"No!" Dani's voice cracked. "There's nothing to balance!"

But the clerks had seen him. One extended a disc with delicate fingers, the stamp glimmering red: I didn't mean it.

The usher nearest bent geometry, space folding to funnel Rally toward the scale.

Jake shoved forward, slamming his shoulder into the usher. The thing bent but did not fall, faceless head tilting as if noting the interference.

"Francis!" Jake barked. "Get him out!"

Dani hauled Rally against her chest, wrapping both arms around him. His body writhed, but she held fast. His breath hitched against her shoulder, a child caught between terror and indoctrination.

She spun, looking for escape. The alley behind them had sealed, stone where entrance had been.

The only way out was through.

The mass trial thundered on. The great scale tilted violently, its chains screeching. Another wave of souls dissolved, their excuses left behind.

The Archivist stepped into the chamber then, ledger open, eyes calm. He did not hurry, did not press. He simply appeared, as though the city had unfolded him here.

"This is overflow," he said mildly. "The record grows faster than the Market can tally. So it spills."

Dani glared. "He's a kid! He doesn't belong here!"

"All belong," the Archivist said, not unkindly. "The question is only when."

Jake's face twisted. "Then we're leaving. Now."

The Archivist marked a line in his book. "Then leave. If you can find the door you closed behind you."

The crowd surged. More souls pressed forward, discs in shaking hands. The ushers funneled them, their faceless geometry sealing exits.

Rally shrieked, clawing at Dani's arms. His voice cracked. "I didn't mean it! I didn't mean it!"

The clerks turned toward him, sensing fresh words.

"No!" Dani screamed. Her voice cut raw, but it didn't carry far in the cacophony.

Jake drew his pistol. He leveled it at the nearest usher. His hand shook, not from fear, but fury. "Move."

The usher didn't.

Jake's finger tightened.

"Don't," Dani snapped. "They don't bleed."

But the usher bent aside suddenly, space opening where there had been none. A lane yawned, a way back, lit by faint red glow.

The Archivist's voice floated over the crowd. "You are recorded. You may return to the Market."

Dani didn't question. She hauled Rally into the lane. Jake backed after her, pistol steady, eyes never leaving the chaos.

The alley sealed behind them with a soft sigh.

They stumbled back into the Market's square, the bell tolling once more. The crowd barely noticed their return; another soul was already stepping to the great scale.

Dani sagged against the rail, clutching Rally. The boy's body trembled. His lips moved silently, still mouthing excuses, but weaker now, as if repetition had dulled the fire.

Jake exhaled, shoulders rolling like he'd just finished a battle. "Hell of a detour."

The Archivist emerged beside them, ledger steady. "The city is generous," he said. "It shows you more than your own weight, so you may understand scale."

Jake spat on the stone. "Generous isn't the word I'd use."

The Archivist looked at Dani. "The Market is not done. Your friend will step forward. The bell waits."

The great scale swayed, its chains groaning.

Jake's jaw set. He holstered his pistol slowly, his eyes on the ushers closing space again. "Then let's get this over with."

Chapter Four: The Weight of Choices

The stair spat them into a square crowded with red light and the sound of counting.

Stalls choked the flagstones, tables of black wood, brass counters, trestles sagging under ledgers bound in leather as thick as belts. Everywhere Dani looked she saw scales: hanging from beams, bolted into pillars, sunk into the floor on stone pedestals. Their pans flashed and clinked. Tokens passed like currency from hand to hand, stamped with tiny phrases that made her jaw tighten.

I WARNED HIM. NO TIME. FOR THE GREATER GOOD. ORDERS.

The air smelled of sulfur and the ghost of smoke. A woman with ash-pale skin and eyes bright as ball bearings stood at the nearest table, weighing a squat cube engraved with a single word: CHILD. Opposite it, a desperate man stacked his tokens, He was armed; He would have killed others; I didn't see, thin as coins, gleaming as if they were worth something. The scale refused to move.

The woman made a neat notation in her ledger and slid three small embers across the counter. "Documented gratitude," she said.

The man snatched them like winnings. They went gray in his palm and dusted the floor.

Jake's breath slid out through his teeth. "Roadside court from hell."

"Market," said the Archivist, appearing at Dani's shoulder as if he'd always been there. "Justice by arithmetic. Intent is scrap. Outcome is coin. Welcome to the Market of Balances."

Rally stared, face slack in the red glow. The hum under his skin seemed to answer the square's murmur. Words brushed his ears the way moths brush a porch light. He swayed.

Dani's hand found the back of his jacket and squeezed. "Stay with me."

They moved through the crowd. At one stall a merchant arranged tiny vials in velvet-lined trays, mist coiling under wax stoppers, whispering through glass. Handwritten labels read Proportional Response, Chain of Command, Collateral Damage, Self-Defense. Buyers selected a vial, inhaled, and sighed, shoulders settling as if the words had fitted a brace around their spines. Minutes later a Weigher guided them to a scale, where the new phrases flashed and weighed nothing at all.

"Language dealers," Jake muttered. "I've bought worse. I've paid more."

At the next table a boy no older than Nia clung to his father's sleeve while the man argued, voice hoarse. "He threw first because they came into our block with guns. He defended our name. You weigh that."

The Weigher's stylus flicked. She dropped a pebble stamped BREATH onto the opposing pan. The beam slammed down so fast the boy flinched. She made another neat mark. "His breath weighs more than your name," she said without heat.

The father sagged against the counter, rage folding into itself until it looked like grief.

Rally's fingers twitched at his sides. Dani felt the tremble run through him. "I didn't..." he started.

"Save it," Jake said quietly. "This place eats speeches."

A bell tolled, bright and precise. The crowd surged toward the square's center.

A dais rose in the middle of the plaza, a massive beam scale mounted along its length. The pans were wide enough to hold a person. On the left knelt a woman with her hands bound behind her back, face calm in the red light. On the right, polished stones sat stacked in a pyramid. TEN SAVED was etched on each in tidy capitals.

A Tallymaster in a hooded robe stood between the pans with a ledger the size of a family Bible. "Emergency apportionment," he announced, voice carrying cleanly without echo. "Petitioners claim ten lives spared by the defendant's act. Opponents claim one life taken unlawfully. Weighing commences."

The murmur around the dais crisped to silence. The Tallymaster lifted a TEN SAVED stone with both hands and set it on its pan. The beam quivered, then steadied, unmoved.

He added a second. Quiver, settle. A third. A fourth.

A fine sweat broke across the Tallymaster's lip. He reached under the dais and hauled up a dark block shot through with condensation. No word cut into it, just a shallow groove like a fingerprint worn into the surface by someone who had held it too long.

He set it on the woman's pan.

The beam slammed down. The TEN SAVED stones hopped and clinked and came to rest high in the air.

"Cost," the Archivist said softly at Dani's side. "The part arithmetic never carries."

The Tallymaster drew a single short line in the ledger. The woman exhaled once. Her shoulders lifted and fell, then didn't lift again.

A thin man in the crowd hissed, "Rigged," and threw a TEN SAVED stone at the dais. It glanced off the beam with the weight of chalk. A Weigher caught his elbow without looking up from her figures. He folded like a broken hinge and was led away, muttering at his shoes.

Dani felt something settle in her chest, anger or recognition or both. She'd stood in rooms where a single breath outweighed a stack of good outcomes and lived with how little the math could hold it.

"Keep moving," Jake said. "We'll drown if we stand still."

They didn't get far. A Broker stepped into their path, coat shiny with age, fingers jeweled to the knuckles. His smile was undertaker-warm.

"Detective Francis," he purred, as if he were greeting a regular. "Mr. Tinsley. And young Rally Gillum." He rolled the name on his tongue like a lozenge. "How fortunate. I can ease your passage."

"We're leaving," Dani said. "With him."

"An ambitious direction," the Broker said. He flicked a latch on his counter and a small elegant scale rose like a conjurer's trick. On one pan sat a sliver of mirror, thumbnail-sized, its surface catching her face and breaking it into a dozen tiny versions. On the other pan he set a thin iron tag stamped RALLY GILLUM. The beam tipped decisively toward the name. "Purchase is possible," he said. "Place a pledge."

"What kind of pledge?" Jake asked, already annoyed.

"A future life," the Broker said pleasantly. "Not yours. Name one. Someone you are willing to stand aside for when deserved. Fate will collect. You will not have to be present."

"You want us to pick a stranger to die," Jake said.

"Such an ugly phrasing." The Broker's smile didn't move. "You merely agree not to interfere when the balance requires it."

Rally swayed. Dani tightened her grip on his sleeve. "No," she said. "Not happening."

"Refusal accrues interest," the Broker warned.

"Bill me," she said, and pulled Rally past him.

The Broker watched them go with a genial patience that felt wrong. "You will be back," he said conversationally. "Everyone comes back to price the things they pretended were priceless."

The crowd thinned toward the square's far edge where a narrow bridge arced over a trench of softly glowing slag. A sign hung above the arch in serif letters: PASSAGE BY DECLARATION ONLY. The bridge's railing was a chain of tiny linked scales. Each pan was no bigger than a teacup and they shivered in the air like chimes.

Two Appraisers stood at the entrance, abacuses hanging from their necks like necklaces. A guard beyond them, no armor, no weapon, eyes the temperature of morgue steel, gestured to a lectern in the bridge's mouth. Inlaid in the wood was another sliver of mirror, larger than the Broker's, big enough to show a face whole.

Jake slowed. "I hate tests I didn't study for."

The Archivist stood off to one side as if the whole thing bored him. "To leave the Market you must declare an accounting," he said. "Not a defense. A statement without argument. Clarity is the toll."

Dani stepped to the lectern before she could talk herself out of it. Her badge flashed in the mirror, then the alley in Chicago, then the man with the pistol, then the boy behind him, falling in a loop that never wore out. Her throat tightened.

"I fired to stop a lethal threat," she said, voice coming from far away. "I didn't see... "

"Stop," the guard said without raising her tone. "You are arguing."

Dani swallowed until she could feel the act like a hinge. She looked at the mirror and saw her mouth the night it happened. "I killed a man who was trying to kill me," she said. "A boy died because I didn't know he was there."

84

The tiny scales along the railing chimed, a scatter of silver pings. A narrow span of planks slid forward with an almost cheerful click.

"Proceed," the guard said.

Jake exhaled like he'd been underwater. He stepped up and stared at his own face. The jungle rose in the mirror, rain coming down like thrown nails, a boy on the ground with eyes like wet stones. Two versions of the memory stood shoulder to shoulder in the glass: mercy and execution; plea and threat. His hands shook and he stilled them.

"I shot a boy to end his pain," he said. "Maybe to end mine."

The pans along the chain trembled as if a gust had passed. Another span of planks slid into place.

The guard turned to Rally. "Declaration."

Rally stared at the mirror like it might bite. It showed him in a school hallway, laughing with his crew, a gun, heavy and important, in his waistband. It showed his mother in a kitchen with the light off, hands in her hair. It showed Jamal's face, open and hurt, and the way it had looked later, empty and gone. Rally's chest hitched.

"I wanted to be somebody," he said. "I hurt people to feel like I mattered."

The chain sighed. Pans tilted toward him in a slow tide and then steadied. A third set of planks slid into place.

The guard stepped aside. "Cross."

They went single-file, Dani first, Rally clinging to the chain, Jake behind watching the crowd. The tiny scales brushed their sleeves like cold jewelry. Below, the slag pulsed. Midway, a man on the return side tried to rush the bridge, eyes wild, declaration unsaid. The bridge rejected him with a clean mechanical clack. He stumbled back into the arms of a Weigher who guided him away with terrible gentleness.

On the far side the Broker stood at a respectful distance, hands tucked into his coat. "See?" he said. "No need for me."

"You never are," Jake said.

"Oh," the Broker replied, smile mild. "But I always am."

The Market thinned behind them like a fever breaking. The street ahead straightened into an avenue flanked by slabs of white stone carved deep with tidy commandments: DO NOT LIE. DO NOT STEAL. DO NOT KILL. The words repeated down the blocks until they lost their edges and became the suggestion of words.

"The Temple quarter," the Archivist said. His voice had gone almost reverent. "Where context kneels."

Rally shivered. "Do we have to?"

"Yes," Dani said. "We do."

They passed a narrow alley where a Public Defender sat on a crate stamping papers with quick, nervous hands. He glanced up at them, eyes hungry, and lifted a small rubber stamp shaped like a question mark. "Marginalia?" he offered hopefully. "Confuses footnotes."

"Careful," Jake said under his breath. "Men who sell question marks are either saints or liars."

The Defender deflated and returned to his stack. Dani kept moving. The market's noise had fallen away entirely. Even their boots seemed to make less sound.

At the end of the avenue, a building rose with the clean lines of geometry, all right angles and measured columns. The steps were worn in arcs that looked like knees had carved them. The doors were tall and plain, their hinges set deeper than they should have been into the stone.

"Temple of Absolutes," the Archivist said. "Where law speaks without throat and listens without ears."

"I'm overjoyed," Jake said. He wasn't.

Rally hesitated at the bottom step, gaze caught on the plaques along the approach, brass plates stamped with single verbs: KILLED. LIED. STOLE. Each had a tiny groove worn where someone's finger had traced it a thousand times. Dani touched KILLED without meaning to. The metal was cold.

The doors swung inward without being touched. The air that breathed out from the temple was colder than the stone itself.

The figure in the threshold wore robes the color of old bone. Its face had the suggestion of features, as if someone had sculpted eyes and mouth and then blurred them with a thumb. It lifted a single hand and the huge doors opened wider.

"Enter," it said. Its voice was neither male nor female, but resonated like the word of a rule read out loud. "Leave your explanations outside."

The Archivist stopped at the threshold, ledger tucked under his arm. "I do not cross," he said, and for the first time sounded smaller than the place. "The record is not welcome where law denies context."

"Fine," Dani said. "We'll bring you the minutes."

Jake glanced at the ink-black eyes, then at the bone-white face, then at the boy trembling at his elbow. He rolled his shoulders as if bracing for rain. "After you, Detective."

Dani took the step.

The doors sighed shut behind them, sealing the Market out with a thunderclap that didn't echo.

The Temple's light was flat as paper. The walls were lined with stone tablets carved with the same three commands in a dozen languages. A beam rose at the far end like a horizon frozen into architecture. Human figures stood in alcoves along the hall, mouths open, words caught and petrified on their lips.

Rally whispered, "They look like they were still explaining when it stopped mattering."

"That's exactly what they look like," Dani said.

From the dais the bone-robed Judge lifted its faceless head. "State your act," it said. "Intent is discarded. Only act remains."

The Market had demanded clarity. The Temple was about to demand something colder.

Dani squared herself under the carved words, DO NOT KILL, and opened her mouth.

And the City of Justifications held its breath.

Chapter Five: Judgments Rendered

The doors shut like a verdict.

Cold light flattened the Temple so that shadow had nowhere to hide. Columns held up a ceiling engraved in tight lines of text, scripts Dani recognized and many she did not. Walls wore tablets from floor to height of a man's reach, DO NOT KILL, DO NOT LIE, DO NOT STEAL, repeated until the words lost the comfort of semantics and became teeth.

Rally stood between Dani and Jake, his breath visible in the air. "I don't like it here," he whispered.

"You're not supposed to," Jake said. "That's how you know you found the right room."

At the far end, a dais rose like an altar. The figure upon it was robed in bone-white, features smoothed as if the sculptor had run a thumb across wet clay and then let it harden. When it raised a hand, the air changed pressure, the way a courthouse hush has weight.

"State your act," the Judge said. The voice was human only in the way thunder is a sound. "Intent is discarded. Only act remains."

Dani drew a breath and felt it stall at the top of her lungs. The Market had demanded a statement. This demanded more: surrender. She stepped forward until she could feel the floor tilt ever so slightly toward the dais.

"I killed," she said.

The light shifted. The space above the dais shivered into image as if the ceiling was water. The Chicago alley appeared: the yellow streetlamp hum, the stain of the brick, the man's gun, the muzzle flash, the boy behind him falling without a sound. The picture stripped away everything but motion. No sound. No smell. No pleading. Only act.

"Act: killing," the Judge intoned.

Rally jerked as if struck. "That's not fair," he blurted. "She… "

The Judge turned that blank suggestion of a face toward him. "Fairness is a human compromise," it said. "Law is not compromised."

Jake's jaw flexed. "Alright. Me next." He stepped to stand beside Dani, defiant because defiance was how he kept from shaking. "I killed."

The air rippled again. Rain hammered leaves. Mud sucked at boots. A boy stared up from a jungle floor, eyes fever-bright; Jake's younger hands lifted a pistol. Another version of the same instant split beside it like a cell dividing: the boy's hand curled around a hidden rifle. Two images, two narratives; one act.

"Act: killing," said the Judge. "No exception."

Jake huffed a single mirthless laugh. "Thought so."

Rally's turn came without being summoned. The mirror-space showed him in the school hallway, flashing a grin he'd learned from older boys, a gun heavy in his belt, Jamal's face open with trust; then the alley, the heat and stupid joy of firing, the shock afterward when there was blood where there had only been a story before.

"Act: violence," the Judge said. "Act: theft. Act: threat. Act: killing."

Rally's legs went soft. Dani caught his elbow before he sat down hard. "Don't fold," she murmured. "It likes the sound."

Statues stood in alcoves along the hall, men and women caught mid-sentence, eyes wide, mouths shaped around syllables that would never be finished. As Dani watched, one of the figures' lips quivered without moving, as if a rehearsed defense still wanted a last breath. The tablets flickered. The statue stilled.

Jake tilted his head. "They come here to talk their way out."

"They come here because they believe talking has magic," the Judge answered. "Talk is a veil. In this hall there are no veils."

"Then what do you want from us?" Dani asked. "We said the act. Now what?"

"Recognition," the Judge said. "Adherence." One bone-pale hand swept to the tablets. "There are three commands. Your world has made a thousand footnotes to avoid them. Here there are no footnotes."

Rally swallowed. "So that's it? We're just... guilty. Forever."

"Guilt is the residue of act against rule," the Judge said dispassionately. "Residue endures."

Jake's hands opened and closed at his sides. He inspected the urge to put his fist through sanctified stone and found it pointless. "You know, I used to think priests scared me," he muttered. "Turns out it was the math."

A door opened in the dais as if the wall itself had taken pity on a tired argument. Beyond, a corridor sloped down into colder light.

"Proceed," said the Judge. "You have shed words. You may descend."

Dani stared. "So the toll here was to agree we did it."

"The toll here was to stop performing a defense," the Judge said. "We are finished with you."

Jake exhaled through his nose. "We get that a lot."

They moved toward the opening. As they passed under the tablets, Dani reached out without thinking and brushed the words. Cold surged up her fingers to her wrist. A fine web of frost stitched across her glove and vanished. When she looked back, the imprint of her hand had paled the carved letters for a moment, as if the stone had tasted her and found something to file away.

The corridor beyond the dais was narrower than the hall. Niches opened along one side, each holding an instrument displayed with museum care: a blade; a length of rope; a small bottle with a stopper; a pistol; a rubber stamp shaped like a question mark. Under each was a brass placard with a single word: MEANS.

Rally lingered at the pistol. "Looks like yours," he said to Dani.

"They all look like mine," Dani said.

At the corridor's midpoint, a smaller chamber opened like a burrow into the wall. Inside, ten tablets ringed a stone pedestal. Each tablet bore a single name. Only one was legible: NIA ALVAREZ.

Dani's heart slammed once, hard enough to make the room sway. "She's here," she said. "She's... "

The pedestal's surface shivered. For a second the image of a small hand appeared, fingers spread. Then the stone went blank again.

"Not judgment," the Judge's voice said from everywhere and nowhere. "Index."

"Index of what?" Jake asked.

"Those presently measured," it said.

Dani fought the urge to smash the pedestal to shards and pocket the pieces as if that might alter facts. "Where?" she asked. "Where is she?"

Silence. The Temple does not answer location with mercy.

Rally closed his eyes and pressed his forehead to the tablet with NIA on it. He whispered something small, maybe a prayer, maybe the beginning of an apology. When he opened his eyes again, the name had darkened as if absorbing what he'd given it.

"We move," Dani said. "Now."

The corridor ended at a shallow pit bridged by a single plank thick as a man's wrist. Above it, a line of text carved into the lintel read: LAW DOES NOT BEND.

"Great," Jake said. "We found the motivational poster."

A figure waited on the far side of the plank. Not the Judge. Smaller. Human. A woman in a plain gray dress, hair tied back. She held a ledger identical to the Archivist's but unmarked, pages blank.

"Cross," she said. "Say only the act and cross."

Dani stepped to the edge. The pit did not look deep, but the bottom didn't quite come into focus.

"Killed," she said, and put her weight on the plank.

It held.

Rally choked on his word. He looked at Dani, at Jake, at the pit. "If I say it," he whispered, "does it make it more true?"

"It makes it plain," Dani said. "Plain is the toll."

He closed his eyes. "Killed." He crossed, knees shaking, hands out for balance.

Jake followed, voice rough. "Killed." The plank gave under his boots and then stiffened again, as if reconsidering an objection.

On the far side the gray-dressed woman dipped a pen into a well and wrote nothing on a blank page. The pen scratched audibly. "Proceed," she said, and stepped aside.

"Who are you?" Dani asked, surprised by the need to know a name in a place that didn't seem to have them.

"Function," the woman said without inflection. "Not person."

"Same," Jake said dryly. "Some days."

They left the plank and the function behind.

The passage narrowed again and bent in a series of exact angles that felt like moving through a diagram. The air

94

sharpened until breathing carried an edge. When the corridor opened out, the light had gone chalk-white. Flat. As antiseptic as a hospital corridor at two in the morning.

Here the Temple put them through a small cruelty.

Ten doors lined the walls, five on each side. Each bore a single verb in raised letters: LIE, STEAL, KILL, ABANDON, BETRAY. Five more repeated the same five verbs. The handles were simple brass rings.

"Choose," the Judge's voice said, as if offering a menu. "Then speak only the act. Do not add. Do not subtract."

Dani stared at KILL and felt herself get both smaller and heavier. "He's going to make us walk into our own word," she said.

"Feels tidy," Jake said. "We're walking into worse places to get this kid out."

Rally stood rooted. His eyes skittered over ABANDON and BETRAY and fled to LIE like a lesser sentence.

"LIE," he said. "I lied. I told Jamal we were just going to scare him. I told my mom I threw the gun away." He reached for the ring.

Dani caught his wrist. "Don't let it downgrade you," she said. "This room wants to file you where you fit smallest." She tipped her chin at KILL. "He'll make you walk through the right door eventually. Save time."

Rally stared at the letters a long second, as if he could bargain them into rearranging. Then he nodded once, hard, and took the KILL door.

It opened onto a short corridor and then a small square cell. No furniture. No sound. No image. Only the word KILL incised into the far wall, each letter deep enough to plant a seed.

Rally stood in the cell and looked at the wall as if it might strike him for looking back. "I killed," he said. His voice came out callused.

The word on the far wall glowed red for a heartbeat and then went dull.

The door opposite opened. Not back to the Temple, but forward to another corridor.

Jake and Dani took their own doors, KILL, because the Temple would not be satisfied with anything else. Each cell was identical. In each, they said the word. In each, the red flicker acknowledged them like a stamp. Across the hall, their doors opened to the same corridor that took Rally onward.

"Processing," Jake said as they rejoined. "Just in case sanctity needed a clerk."

Dani didn't answer. Something in her posture had become more precise, as if each sentence since the dais had been hammering her into a cleaner shape.

They emerged into a final chamber as spare as a bone: a long hall with a single beam mounted at shoulder height, a single bell suspended above it, and a single mallet resting on a pedestal.

The Judge stood at the far end. The archivist was not here. No ushers. No marketeers. Only the blank-eyed law.

"You sought certainty," it said. "You found it."

"We didn't seek it," Dani said. "We were dragged to it by a kid's bad decisions and a city that eats reasons."

"Your path is irrelevant," the Judge said. "Only act endures."

"Then ring your bell and let us out," Jake said. "We've got living children to retrieve."

The Judge inclined its head toward the mallet. "Strike."

"Why?" Dani asked.

"Because that is what you do," the Judge said. "You strike. You end. You divide. Strike now and depart. Or refuse and be weighed until you are quiet."

Rally looked at the mallet with dread. "If I hit it, does it... mean I'm worse?"

"No," Dani said. "It means we are not staying for a sermon." She lifted the mallet and found it heavier than wood should be, as if the head were stuffed with lead filings and old verdicts. She glanced at Jake.

He nodded once.

She struck the beam. The sound was clean and terrible, the kind of tone you recognize even if you have never heard it. It rolled down the hall and gathered itself and unrolled again. Somewhere deep in the Temple, doors opened. Somewhere else, they closed.

The Judge raised a hand. A seam parted in the rear wall, revealing a downward sloping passage where the light went from white to gray.

"Proceed."

They did.

Behind them, the bell's last harmonic faded into stone.

The passage bled the Temple from them in increments: the white drained to slate, the cold softened, the smell of iron gave way to mineral and damp. The words on the walls thinned and went away, replaced by blank faces of stone.

"What did we buy?" Jake asked after a while. "What did the bell cost?"

"It cost the comfort of believing we were exceptions," Dani said. "We paid in words we didn't say."

Rally walked in silence, mouth a tight line. After a long time, he said, "I thought if I said it out loud, it might rip me in half."

"How many pieces you in?" Jake asked gently.

Rally considered. "A lot," he said. "But they all still walk together."

They rounded a corner. The Last Tablet hung above the threshold: a slab without writing. Dani touched it. The stone did not chill her, or burn. It did nothing. Which, here, felt like grace.

Beyond the threshold, the corridor widened into a broad stair that sloped down and away. The light took on a greenish cast, and a sound reached them that was neither market nor bell: a murmur, like conversation behind a wall, full of opinion and confidence and contradiction.

"The Quarter of Shadows," Dani said, remembering the Archivist's map only in the body, not the mind. "Where nothing stands still."

"At least we'll feel at home," Jake said.

Rally stopped at the head of the stair. "What if the rules change again?"

"They will," Dani said. "That's why we're better than this place. We can tell when rules are being used to hurt people."

"And when we're using feelings to hurt them," Jake added. "Two-way street."

They started down.

The Temple did not watch them go. The Temple did not watch anything. It counted and was done. The door behind them closed with a sound like a page turning in an enormous book.

Ahead, the city breathed again, and the light took on the restless color of argument.

The Temple's certainty stayed behind them like a scar: healed, but tender if you press.

They did not press. They descended. And the City of Justifications waited with its next street, one that turned every act into a different story, and demanded they step carefully through their own shadows.

Chapter Six: Morality in Flux

The stair corkscrewed down until the white of the Temple wore to gray and then to a black that wasn't absence so much as saturation. The descent was longer than it had any right to be. Each step seemed to repeat itself, a loop that uncoiled beneath their feet but refused to bring them closer to level ground. Dani counted the turns by instinct, five, six, seven, and lost track when the sound changed.

It wasn't silence, not the kind they had known in the Temple where every word was devoured by tablets. This was a layered murmur, a crowd beyond a wall, a courtroom in recess, a stadium before the whistle. The sound of judgment deferred, always waiting. Not words she could parse, but weight she could feel pressing into the marrow.

She brushed her glove along the damp wall, half for balance, half to remind herself it was solid. Beneath her palm, the stone vibrated faintly, as if water carried whispers through rock. The hum nested in her jaw, made her teeth ache, and stayed even after she pulled her hand back.

Rally walked with his shoulders raised, like a boy waiting for a blow. The stair's curve pulled them tight together, his arm brushing hers every few steps. He hadn't spoken since the bell in the Temple. Dani let him be. Some silences belonged to survival.

When the stair spat them out, it did so without ceremony. One more step and the coil ended on a stone landing that opened into a square.

The square was wrong the way a dream is wrong: proportions subtly violated, lines leaning away from gravity. Buildings loomed too close, taller than their balance allowed, stitched together from centuries that should not have met. Pitted limestone pressed against worm-scarred timber. Corrugated steel jutted from plaster walls streaked with soot. A roof of tarpaper peeled like a scab, edges fluttering in air that never reached them. Balconies sagged under the weight of iron pots left to rust, the plants inside fossilized into dust.

Light came from cages that dangled over the square, lamps made of braided wire. Each cage held a flame that shifted color without pattern, gold, then green, then a washed-out red that bruised the world. The wires creaked as though moved by wind, but no hair lifted on their heads. When the lamps swayed, the square itself seemed to swivel, angles sliding against one another as if geometry were opinion.

Jake stopped at the edge, his eyes scanning up the facades with the same wary calculation he used for ridgelines and treelines. Sightlines, sniper nests, corners that could conceal rifles. He frowned as though the city's architecture mocked him by refusing to obey even the math of cover.

"Feels like combat," he muttered. "People talk about glory, but war's just sickness dressed up in brass and banners. I still smell it, oil, steel, rubber, and flesh burning together. You march through mud and maggots till you forget your own name, and the dread of going back is worse than the fight itself. War takes good boys and hollows them out. Fast friends, quick deaths, that's the trade. And what it leaves you with is silence, nightmares, and the nerve to call it peace."

His fingers tapped the butt of his pistol, not drawing it, only confirming it was still there.

"City built by liars," he said. "Or built to make liars."

The Archivist's voice came from a doorway that hadn't been there a second ago. The words had the texture of paper, pages turning. "The Quarter of Shadows. Perspective is the architect here. Every act wears whatever eyes put on it."

Rally hunched deeper. His sneakers squeaked once on the damp stone, too loud. "I don't need anybody else telling me who I am."

"Then you came to the wrong street," the Archivist said.

Dani felt her ribs tighten. She knew this kind of quarter, not a place but a trial. A street that would not let you leave until it had taken what you thought was yours and shown it to you in someone else's handwriting.

They moved along a wall that had once been a warehouse. Its bricks had sweated salt that dried into veins. Now it wore the skin of a mural, thirty feet wide, ten high, the paint still damp enough to glisten under their lamps. The smell of pigment hit her before the image did, sharp as turpentine.

Dani's throat locked when her beam fell across it.

A drive-by. A sedan rolling slow under midnight. A boy's arm jutting from the window, the muzzle flashes a white bloom. The faces on the sidewalk weren't faces, only masks of terror. The bullet's path was frozen mid-air, a line drawn like chalk across black sky.

"Stop," Dani said, though they already had.

The mural moved when she looked at it. The shooter's arm lengthened, muscles hardening with age. The victims shrank, features softening. The bullet's chalk line stretched until it intersected with the outline of a child.

"No," Dani whispered. "No, that's not..."

Rally didn't hear the same picture. His eyes glowed with the same fever she had seen when his crew walked a school hallway and other kids scattered aside like leaves before wind. The mural gave him what he brought. In his gaze, the shooters gleamed with coronation, bathed in the light of respect. The blurred sidewalk faces looked like enemies, shadowed threats. The gun was a crown.

"That's respect," he said.

"That's murder," Dani snapped. The word tore from her throat like something thrown.

The mural obeyed the word, changed for another witness.

To Jake, it shifted into a jungle track. The car stretched into a truck with sandbags stacked high. The shooter's arm transformed into the wiry limb of a boy holding a rifle where his childhood should have been. The victims became men, rifles braced against their shoulders where laughter might have been once.

Jake rubbed the bridge of his nose, weary. "It's not the wall changing," he said. "It's us."

"Keep moving," Dani ordered. Her voice was harder than she felt. She needed her body busy, or she would drown in pigment and memory.

They moved. The mural's smell followed them, sour as fresh paint trapped in closed lungs.

The Quarter unfolded itself block by block, each corner a new verdict.

A soldier with a torch marched across the wall of a shuttered tavern. In one glance, he was a monster setting fire to roofs of straw. In another, he was starving fighters out from their hiding places among children. In a third, he was desperate, burning food he couldn't carry because choices had narrowed to one.

Every truth demanded the others' death.

They passed a storefront window glazed with grime. Instead of reflection, it showed scenes behind their eyes.

Dani saw the Chicago alley, the lamp buzzing overhead, her breath a fog, the muzzle steady in her hands. Then the picture widened into a courtroom. The floor gleamed. The judge's haircut was neat enough to slice. He called her "Officer," the word a title and a blade.

Jake's pane was streaked with rain. The sound smothered thought. A boy knelt in mud, mouth forming pleas, hands open. Another pane flicked and the same boy rose, rifle cocked, eyes lit with something past mercy.

Rally's glass carried him into a school hallway where his crew laughed too loud. The pane shifted, and he stood at a funeral, Jamal in a suit too cheap and too final, his mother's hand gripping the pew so hard the wood groaned.

"Eyes front," Jake murmured. He wasn't looking at his window either.

On a stoop across the lane, a woman watched them. Or the outline of one. She wore a house dress, the fabric stiff with age, her chin lifted in the way of mothers who do not trust police but want to. When her gaze touched Dani, the mural behind them shivered again, mothers, verdicts, none binding enough to shift a bullet's course.

"Do not bargain with paintings," the Archivist warned. His voice followed them like a margin note. "They take offers and give back terms."

"Then why is this here?" Dani snapped, sharper than she meant.

"It teaches that your eyes are hungry," the Archivist said. "And hunger always eats."

Dani kept walking, fists tight.

The lane narrowed, paving stones uneven beneath their boots. A row of pennants fluttered overhead, red, then white, then red again, flapping in a wind no one felt.

Windows lined the walls. Every window held a face. Some were human. Some were sketches only half-drawn. All of them watched. None blinked.

The lane ended in a courtyard.

Statues ringed the space, twelve in total. All the same man. Each carved into a different verdict: Warrior. Criminal. Martyr. Traitor. Prophet. Fool.

The sculptor had been cruel in detail. Veins swelled in the wrists that clutched sword hilts. Creases etched mouths that might have been laughter or agony.

In the center stood a plinth. A brass plaque bore only two words:

HE ACTED.

The lamps swayed. The light bent green. The statues shimmered, insisting on their truth from every angle.

Dani saw fury in the warrior's eyes, calculation in the traitor's, cheap theater in the prophet's.

Jake saw tenderness stitched to ruthlessness, leadership soldered from contradiction.

Rally saw only the laurels. He wanted them. Hated wanting them. Hated himself for hating it.

"This is a trap," Dani said.

The statues cracked.

Lines split their stone bodies down the middle. From the fissures spilled shadow, not liquid, not smoke, but the memory of both. Shapes coalesced and dissolved, faces that became fathers, sons, cops, targets. A man clutching a child. A child holding a gun.

The whispers came next.

"You defended your block."

"You murdered my son."

"You honored your family."

"You disgraced your name."

"You saved a life."

"You took two."

Rally collapsed to his knees, palms clamped against his ears. "Make them stop."

Dani stepped between him and the closest shadow. The gesture was worthless against smoke, but it mattered to Rally. She drew and fired at the flagstones.

The crack leapt between the walls, echoed back raw. The bullet sparked stone. The shadow rippled, multiplied, stretched its whispers wider.

"He had a gun."

"He had a life."

Jake hauled Rally upright with a soldier's grip. "These only eat what you feed them."

"I'm not..." Rally sobbed.

"You are," Jake snapped. "We all are." He turned his back to the blur and raised his voice. "I killed a boy. Thought it was mercy. Maybe it was. Maybe not. He's still dead."

The shadows twitched as though startled. Some thinned, edges fraying. Others pushed closer, their mouths wide with accusations.

"You enjoyed it."

"You hesitated."

"You'll do it again."

Dani's throat tasted of copper. Behind her, the wall replayed the alley. The boy blinked, blinked, as if death could be undone by insistence.

"I killed," she said. "He's dead. I'm not."

The shadows recoiled as if shocked by current. Somewhere in the city, a bell tolled. The courtyard flinched.

Rally lowered his hands. His face was wet with tears he didn't remember shedding. "I wanted to be somebody. I hurt people to feel like I mattered."

The nearest shadows stepped back as if their own names had been spoken. Some burned out, collapsing like ash. Others slid back into their statues' cracks.

Jake muttered, "Facts. It hates those."

The Archivist's voice drifted from the archway: "Relativism dissolves. Simplicity cuts."

"Then cut us a door," Dani demanded.

"Through yourselves," the Archivist said. His tone had the weariness of ink that had been read too many times.

The courtyard drained into a crooked street lined with shutters. The shutters were warped, the paint bubbled and flaked. They looked like wood, but when Dani brushed a finger along one, it flexed like skin.

Each shutter cracked open as they passed, and voices leaked out like steam. Not voices of people standing behind them, these were fragments, statements broken from their speakers.

"Officer-involved," sighed one shutter, and the alley rearranged itself into a press conference backdrop. Microphones bristled like thorns. A police chief in a starched uniform adjusted his notes, his mouth shaping sorrow syllable by syllable. His eyes stayed dry.

"Best practices," hissed another, and Dani felt her training fold around her like origami armor. Hallway. Stance. Sight picture. All the boxes checked, each a justification.

"Mercy," breathed a third, and Jake's boots faltered a half-step. He looked down, jaw tight, as though mercy were a blade he had once carried and lost.

"Don't listen," Dani said, but her voice rang false because she was listening too.

Rally stayed between them, shoulders hunched, lips pressed so tight they went white. The shutters whispered his lies as well, and though Dani couldn't hear them, she saw the way his face twitched with every syllable.

They reached a corner where the street fractured into three directions at once. A signpost stood in the center, made of black slate. The arrows were painted by hand, each in a different script, each pointing somewhere no compass would recognize.

HEROES →

MONSTERS →

VICTIMS →

Jake eyed it and gave a humorless huff. "That's tidy. None of the above, thanks."

Rally frowned at the arrows, lips moving silently. Dani knew the math he was doing. Hero was what he'd wanted. Monster was what he feared. Victim was what he hated. The words pressed against him like labels on jars, ready to seal.

"If we don't pick," he asked, "does the city pick for us?"

"Yes," said the Archivist, his voice like ink soaking into paper. "It always does. That is how streets work."

Dani reached out and touched the peg that pinned the signs together. The wood warmed under her skin, then cooled. The arrows rearranged themselves.

LIARS →

COWARDS →

SURVIVORS →

She let go, lip curling. "Cute."

Jake stepped forward, ignoring all of them. He rapped his knuckles on the post and chose the narrowest way, the one with no sign at all. "We make our own street. Been doing that all day."

They followed him into the alley.

The alley pinched tight, then opened into a chamber that wasn't outside at all. A ceiling pressed low enough for Jake to touch with his palm. Mirrors hung on every wall, old glass warped by age, frames mismatched like salvaged furniture.

These were not the Mirrors from the Temple. These were cheaper cousins, but cousins all the same, glass that showed not what was, but what strangers swore they saw if only you would be reasonable.

Dani's reflection appeared first. The alley replayed itself. The man stood in front of her. His hand was empty, no gun. The boy behind him was only a boy. Dani fired anyway, said this glass. Fear pulled the trigger. Another mirror hissed the opposite: the man's gun massive, the boy a shield, Dani surgical, Dani righteous.

The mirrors argued like drunks, louder and louder, each scrambling to drown the other out. None listened.

Rally's mirrors were worse. One gave him a crown, gold catching light. Another offered a shiv disguised as a crown, its edges honed for betrayal. A third showed him in a cell with a clock that had no hands, time arrested. His mother appeared in three panes, once slapping him, once hugging him, once hanging a towel over the glass because she couldn't stand to see his face look back at her with prison in its eyes.

Jake's reflection was blunt. The boy in the mud. The pistol in his hands. The boy's mouth forming a plea. Another pane: the same boy, rifle hidden, ambush waiting. A third: Jake older, the lines on his face deeper, his weapon holstered, a man who carried silence heavier than steel.

"Enough," Dani said, voice sharp to keep her knees from buckling. She flicked her baton open and smashed the nearest mirror. The crack ran across the room like a sentence written in glass.

Jake followed, heel into one frame, elbow into another. Rally hesitated, then slammed his shoulder into the mirror that showed Jamal's mother crying. The impact left his breath ragged, but the guilt eased just enough to let him keep moving.

One by one the panes shattered, each fall of glass like an accusation losing its voice. When the last frame hit the ground, the chamber exhaled.

A door stood where a blank wall had been.

The door led them into a street paved with mosaics. Tiny tiles, their colors dulled by time, formed pictures that rearranged themselves with every step. Under Dani's boots, a king shifted into a tyrant, then a father holding a child. Jake's steps turned a thief into a provider, then into a patriot. Rally's path drew a police officer into a thug, then into a shield.

The stories climbed into their soles, crawled up calves, whispered at their ears. Dani shook her head as if to fling them off, but they stayed, tattooed in motion.

Ahead, a boy stood in the center of the street. Seventeen maybe. His hair was dark, his stance relaxed, his face deliberately familiar, familiar enough to catch their trust if they let it. He held his palms up, showing what he carried.

On the left, a knife. On the right, a folded scrap of paper.

He smiled without warmth. "Your call."

Jake kept his voice steady. "What's on the paper?"

"An apology you'll believe," the boy said.

"And the knife?" Dani asked.

"The truth," he said. "It cuts."

"Both are traps," the Archivist said from a balcony above, his ledger under one arm. "Some streets only have traps."

The boy's smile widened, turned toward Rally. "Pick. You know which you're good at."

Rally flinched. He had been good at both. Lies and blades, both came easy when you wanted belonging more than breath. His jaw worked, eyes flicking between the hands. "I don't want either," he said.

"Then say what is," Jake told him.

Rally folded his arms, holding himself together. "I wanted to belong. I hurt a friend. That's it. That's all of it. Nothing here makes it smaller."

The boy's face cracked like old paint, flaked into chips, then into dust. The knife tumbled, turned into a seed. The paper became a moth, wings beating once before it disintegrated. Both rolled into cracks in the mosaic and were gone.

"Onward," the Archivist said, as if stamping a page.

They walked until the street bent into a crossroad. Four directions, none agreeing on which way was up.

A lamplighter stood in the nexus, pole in hand, touching flames. Each flame shifted color when he breathed on it, blue to red, red to green, green to white.

Dani approached warily. "If we're looking for kids, which way?"

The lamplighter didn't lift his face. He lifted his attention. "Children go where stories make them tall," he said, "or where shadows make them vanish."

Dani's throat tightened. "We need the ones who can still come back."

"Then you do not go where they are tallest," the lamplighter said. "You go where they are smallest. And pull."

Jake nodded toward the bright street, where murals crowned children with crowns too heavy for their skulls. The other path narrowed into a slot where light drained to nothing. He chose the dark. "Small," he said.

Dani stopped him with a hand on his arm. She pulled paracord from her pack, tied a loop, hitched it to a rusted ring sunk into the stone. "We don't lose the way."

"The city will cut it," the Archivist warned.

"Then it can try," Dani said. She fed the cord through her fingers and stepped into the dark.

The slot twisted mean. It should have been twenty paces but stretched into a hundred, bending left where it promised right, rising where it looked ready to fall.

The air thinned, then thickened, then went neutral, as though deciding what to be. The smell of mildew turned into stone, then into nothing at all.

The crack opened into a playground.

Swings hung from beams that weren't beams. A seesaw rested on a fulcrum carved from an altar stone. A slide descended from a second-story window of a building that had no first floor.

The metal was cold, and where the red lamp-light touched it, the steel gleamed wet, though Dani's glove came away dry.

Sooty handprints streaked the slide. Six sets. The sizes didn't match. One set stopped halfway down, fingers cut off mid-glide.

"Nia," Dani whispered. Her voice came steady, but her pulse slammed once, hard.

A shadow crouched at the slide's end. For a second Dani thought it was an animal, but the shape corrected itself. It was the outline of a choice. A child's decision given body. It smiled at Rally with a mouth full of invitation and no teeth.

"Jump," it whispered. "I'll catch you. That's what kings get."

Rally's breath hitched. His foot shifted forward. He had jumped at worse promises. He had been caught by worse.

Jake hooked an arm across his chest and yanked him back so hard his heels skidded. "No," Jake said, voice flat. "You don't practice dying."

Rally's fists pounded Jake's grip once, twice, then went limp. His head dropped. "I don't know what I am," he said, not to them but to the shadow, to the soot-stained slide, to the phantom hands that had vanished.

Dani's voice cut, cruel only on the surface. "Pick the story where you stop hurting people. That's the one you get to keep."

The shadow flattened like paper underfoot. The swings swayed though no air moved. The seesaw tipped, then settled. The Quarter had tried to shrink a child small enough to keep. They refused to give it one.

They backed out. The paracord still held, threads intact. For now.

They backed out of the slot one careful step at a time, the paracord whispering over stone as Dani reeled it in. The cord felt wrong in her hand, stiffer than when she'd fed it out, as if the Quarter had tongued each fiber and left a film. When the last loop slid free of the rusted ring, the cut end showed a single half-sliced thread like a hair held in a knife.

Jake held the loop up to the lamplighter when they re-emerged at the crossroads. "You said it would try."

The lamplighter touched the nearest flame, breathing it from green to a flat white that made shadows honest. "Streets dislike leashes," he said. "You did not leash the city. You leashed yourselves to one another. That, it tolerates. For a time."

Rally stared back into the dark slot they'd left. The swings had stilled. The altar stone looked like a skull with its teeth ground down. "Those handprints," he said. "Why didn't they move?"

"They were moving," the lamplighter said, turning the next flame from white to red. "They moved you."

Dani anchored the cord back onto her pack, feeling the grit grind under her straps. "Which way to the ones who chose to be tallest?"

The lamplighter pointed with the pole toward a bright corridor heavy with banners and voices. "That way," he said. "But you will not find a child by chasing the height she borrows. There is another way."

"Which is?" Dani said.

He breathed on the last lamp until it guttered to a coal. "Listen for a voice that argues wrong about you with conviction. The children who can come home learn to hear that voice without obeying it."

Rally's jaw worked. "All the voices in here argue wrong."

"Not all," the lamplighter said, and went back to tending colors.

They chose a street that headed toward noise but ran at a slant to it, like a predator flanking a herd it didn't intend to stampede. The cobbles clicked under their boots. Signboards hung by two nails and one stubborn thread. Air warped where heat should have been, though the wind still never touched them.

The Quarter put on a fair it never intended to sell. Stalls lined the way, piled with objects that were only almost real: medals stamped with unfamiliar wars; uniforms a half shade off from departments that never existed; diplomas bearing seals from academies with Latin that meant something you wouldn't want to translate. A hawker held up a mirror no bigger than a hand, the glass black unless you tilted it just so. In the brief flash of visibility, Dani saw herself years younger and then not herself at all; the angle changed and the mirror showed only the hawker's palm lines, deep as riverbeds.

"Keep walking," she said. "No purchases."

Jake laughed once, a sound too dry to be mirth. "All sales are final anyway."

They passed a stall where sentences hung on hooks like fish. Plaques read I HAD NO CHOICE and WE WERE AT WAR and HE SHOULDN'T HAVE BEEN THERE and IF

I HADN'T DONE IT SOMEONE ELSE WOULD. The vendor wore a butcher's apron and a smile that never touched his eyes. Dani didn't slow. If she smelled the varnish on the words too long, they'd stick to her tongue.

Rally drifted toward a rack of jackets, leather, letterman, suit coats with other men's shoulders still in them. He stopped himself. Put both hands in his pockets like a kid around breakables.

"Want the one that fits," the vendor said lightly. "Or the one that makes them think you fit?"

Rally didn't look up. "I already tried that store," he said, and kept going.

The street spilled them into a plaza tiled in a checkerboard so neat it felt like a dare. Black squares slick as wet obsidian. White squares matte and chalky. Figures moved on both, criss-crossing in patterns that would have read as choreography if anyone had agreed on the same song. Some of the moving shapes wore faces; others wore suggestions. Each time Dani thought she recognized someone, Junie's cap, Taye's jacket, the swing of Mason's gait, the figure turned and was a stranger with the wrong mouth.

Dani stepped up onto a low stone bench for height and hated how the Quarter rewarded the instinct to get off the ground. "Nia!" she called, hands cupped. The name slid across the plaza and returned to her thinner, as if the air had eaten in transit. She tried again with the names that had weight in Rally's throat. "Junie! Mason! Taye!"

The tiles drank sound the way sand drinks water: without visible change and with complete efficiency.

A man with a cart drifted past, hat brim low enough to turn him into a moving horizon. On the cart lay little wooden placards like the ones at the signpost. He picked one up and held it toward Dani.

CHOOSE YOUR NARRATIVE, it read, letters carved sharp by a hand that liked straight lines. He flipped it over. ALL SALES FINAL.

Jake plucked the sign out of the man's grip, turned it, set it back down with care, as if putting a loaded tool back on a shelf. "We don't buy."

"You already did," the man said without malice, and wheeled on.

Rally tugged at his sleeve. "There," he whispered. Across the plaza, a doorway had appeared where blank wall had been. No lintel inscription, no sigil. The darkness beyond wasn't red like the Quarter's jealous light or green like envy wearing mercy's mask. It was the color inside a theater before a film starts — the kind of dark that expects you to look at yourself.

The Archivist stepped into their line of sight as if he'd always been standing there and they had simply earned the ability to see him. Ledger under his arm. Neutral expression with mass behind it.

"The Hall of Mirrors," he said. "Not the Quarter's cheap glass. The place where you stop arguing with strangers and argue with yourselves."

"Can we skip it?" Jake asked, knowing the answer.

"Not with children in your pockets," the Archivist said. "The city has a bureaucracy. It does not release minor souls without process." His mouth flattened almost into a smile at his own joke, then unflattened.

119

"Are the kids ahead?" Dani said. Her voice tried and failed to be procedural.

"Some," he said. "Some behind. Some beside." He tipped his ledger toward the dark. "One of you moves because stopping feels like confession. One stops because moving feels like guilt. The third hasn't yet chosen which pain to keep. If you wish to leave with anyone, choose your own."

Rally scrubbed a hand over his face. "I hate this place."

"So do I," Dani said. "That's why we're leaving."

Jake scanned the plaza one more time, the soldier in him refusing to trust a single entry point. "We go together."

"Not always how halls work," the Archivist said, not quite a warning.

"Try anyway," Dani said.

The threshold didn't feel like a step so much as a relevance shift. Noise behind them thinned and tightened, like a crowd deciding to listen. The air inside the Hall tasted clean in the way that hospitals sometimes taste clean: antiseptic on top, rot grafted beneath.

They stood in a nave long enough for echo. Mirrors rose from floor to ceiling on both sides, fifteen a side, the frames carved in a style that never existed and never stopped being copied. Some of the glass was dark; some held milky storms like snow globes impatient to be shaken.

A narrow balcony ran the length of the walls halfway up. It held nothing and no one. It was there so you knew where witnesses would sit if the Hall decided to have them.

Rally's breath came in two-measure counts. Jake's boots made a sound that felt too loud even though it wasn't. Dani walked exactly on the center seam of the floor the way she'd been taught to move down a hallway with doors on either side.

"Do we announce ourselves?" Jake asked.

"Too late," the Archivist said.

The mirrors cleared.

They did not show reflections. They showed frames. The shape of a person with the details stripped away, height, weight, a way of carrying shoulders recognized by muscle memory, not yet a face.

"Say only the act," a voice said, not the Judge's, not the Archivist's; the Hall itself. "Do not add. Do not subtract."

Rally swallowed. "Again?"

"Again until you stop trying to get interest on the payment," the Hall said. "Say only the act."

Dani stepped forward because movement had always been her lever against fear. "Killed."

The nearest three mirrors flared like struck steel, white and merciless. The empty bodies inside them filled with her. Not her face, not her uniform. Something older. Her stance when she believed rules harder than people. Her posture when she believed people harder than rules. Her hands, twice, one unflinching, one shaking, both steady enough to finish.

"Jake," she said, because going second is a kindness, and she had learned to spread kindness like sand on ice.

"Killed," he said. No qualifiers. He didn't look at her, refusal not to divide blame but to hold his own.

"Rally," Dani prompted, quiet.

He had to rock forward to find his voice. "Killed."

The word lifted hair on his arms as if something static had built and needed a lightning rod.

"Proceed," the Hall said. "You may carry nothing but the act."

They stepped deeper. The mirrors tracked them like rows of heads in a church following a pall.

The first bay arrived without a door. A circle in the floor demarcated the space the way chalk demarcates a body. Inside the circle: three pedestals. On each pedestal, a small object rested on velvet the color of clotting: a penny, a key, a ring.

The penny was steel, not copper, the kind the country minted when copper was needed for bullets. It was nicked on one edge, the kind of nick caused by a table leg that never quite stopped wobbling.

The key was heavy, warded, a courthouse key from the era when institutions wanted you to feel the weight of entry in your pocket.

The ring was a thin band, tungsten, the inscription inside worn so shallow you'd have to believe it to read it.

"Pick," the Hall said. "Penny for chance. Key for rule. Ring for bond."

Rally looked at Dani with the helpless fury of a boy who'd run out of right answers and still insisted there ought to be one. "What if I don't want to be any of those?"

"Then the city picks," the Archivist said from very far away and very near.

Jake stepped up to the pedestals and hovered his hand over each object without touching. "You already know," he said to no one. "You don't set a test if you don't know what you want to see."

The Hall was patient. Patience here felt like teeth closed over a pulse.

Dani's throat worked. "We take rule," she said, nodding at the key, "we're back in the Temple. We take chance," she jerked her chin at the penny, "we're in the Quarter. We take bond and we keep each other from drowning."

Rally stared down at the ring until his eyes burned and the shape blurred. He had broken bonds. He had traded them for applause that cut when it quit. He reached and took the ring.

The velvet dented, slow as a bruise. The ring weighed more than it should have, as if it had borrowed gravity from somewhere more honest.

"Act acknowledged," the Hall said without praise and without censure. A door-shaped emptiness opened in the wall ahead.

The second bay narrowed. The mirrors here were taller, closer, breath on glass close. They did not show figures now. They showed rooms.

Dani's mirror held a precinct's back hallway. A cot with a thin mattress. A locker with a lock that stuck when it rained. The sound of a coffee pot burning its own dregs because no one had turned it off. She watched herself walk down that hallway in a suit jacket that had learned her shoulders. She watched herself not stop at the cot even though her body wanted to lie down and delete.

Jake's mirror held a tent half-collapsed by storm, canvas popping and snapping like large animals. A map pinned to a board with knives that the map pretended were pushpins. He watched himself take the pistol apart and put it back together with the muscle memory of a psalm.

Rally's mirror held a school stairwell painted in colors that had been cheerful two coats ago. Jamal leaned against the railing at the landing, telling a story with hands and eyebrows. The story made the boys around him bigger. Rally watched himself walk up into the story with a grin he'd learned in a mirror and with a darkness behind that grin not even he had agreed to look at.

"Say only the act," the Hall repeated, more gently. "Not the reason."

"I killed," Rally said to the stairwell. Jamal still laughed. The sound blossomed and died and left the air occupied by its shape.

Jake's hands curled into the shape of a gun and then uncurled. "I killed," he said to the map. The knives didn't shift. The storm didn't notice.

Dani put her palm against her own glass and felt cold so clean it almost felt like heat. "I killed."

The mirror fogged in a circle where her skin met it, then cleared.

"Proceed," the Hall said.

The third bay had seats. Three benches on one side, three on the other, aisle in the middle, like a chapel or a courtroom or a waiting room that had ambitions beyond its budget. People sat on the benches. Not people, maskings. They wore the outlines of former colleagues, former neighbors, former classmates who'd called Dani brave until a week later when they called someone else that with the same certainty. They wore the outlines of Jake's chain of command, the ones who had given him the order and then the ones who had asked in careful voices whether the order had been interpreted too enthusiastically. They wore the outlines of Rally's crew in their best performative swagger and then in their worst quiet, heads down, hands on knees.

"Do not listen," the Archivist said reflexively.

"You listen," the Hall corrected. "You do not bargain."

The bench-people spoke.

To Dani: "You did what any officer would have done." "You aimed wrong." "You saved someone." "You killed a child." "You were scared." "You were brave." "You didn't mean…" "You did."

She stared at them and felt the old itch between shoulder blades where a bullet could have been. "I hear you," she said. "None of you get to decide what I do next."

To Jake: "Rules of engagement are clear." "Fog of war." "How many seconds did you have?" "You always were too quick." "You always were too slow." "You know which one is true."

He didn't flinch. "I know a boy is dead," he said. "I know I'm not. That's enough truth for this room."

To Rally: "They would have done it without you." "You didn't pull the trigger that killed Jamal." "You brought the gun." "You wanted what it did to your name." "You didn't know." "You knew enough."

Rally stared at the floor until the checkerboard bled from plaza to bench to brain. "I wanted to belong," he said, so soft Dani almost missed it. "I wanted to be tall." He raised his head. "I made myself small. I hurt my friend. I'm not asking you to forgive me. I'm saying it so the room quits pretending I didn't."

The bench-people fell quiet not in agreement, not in defeat, but in lack of purchase. The Hall's air shifted. Somewhere, a bolt unlatched.

They reached the fourth bay and the Hall changed grammar. No more benches. No more pedestals. An empty square, floor markings faint as rubbed chalk, mirrors all dark. A single pedestal in the center held an object wrapped in cloth the color of old bones.

Dani stepped into the square and the mirrors brightened like eyes opening.

Each one showed a child. Not all the same child. Not all alive and not all dead. The glass didn't distinguish with the indecency of fact. Faces flickered, Nia at eight with scabbed knees and a chipped tooth; a boy in a hoodie whose name Dani didn't know and knew anyway; a girl who had braided her own hair twice too tight because the world would tug; Jamal laughing; Jamal falling.

Rally made a sound that had been a word before the Hall stripped vocabulary to cords and breath. He reached for the cloth.

"Careful," Jake said. Warning by habit, not command.

Rally undid the knot. The cloth fell open around a small object so ordinary Dani almost laughed. A wooden ruler, the kind teachers once used for measures and for tapping knuckles. Twelve inches. One edge nicked.

"What is this," he asked, and knew.

The Hall finally sounded like a person, almost kind. "Scale."

Dani's vision doubled. She stood in three rooms at once, the alley, the school stairwell, a kitchen with a refrigerator plastered in magnets shaped like states a family had never visited. She saw the ruler used to measure spelling margins. She saw it used to teach the fact that hands could be instruments. She saw it snap in half, stress point white, and felt the relief of broken things no longer serving.

"Measure what?" she asked. "Us? Them? The act?"

"Yes," the Hall said.

Rally lifted the ruler. The wood was warm, not from the cloth but from a thousand palms. He set one end against his own knuckles and spanned across to his thumb. "I was small," he said. "I wanted to be tall. I used a gun as a ruler. I made the street measure me and I came up wrong."

Dani took the ruler from him. Her hands remembered length the way bodies remember fall distance. She aligned it against the ghost of the muzzle she carried in her muscles. "I used the wrong tool," she said. "I used the right tool wrong. I measured the wrong thing. I measured my fear instead of his body."

Jake laid his palm against the ruler, pressing until the wood creaked. "I measured time," he said. "A second and a half is enough for a life to change shape. I pretended that number made me clean."

The mirrors did not soften. The Hall did not absolve. The pedestal opened like a pupil dilating. The ruler slid back into the cloth without anyone moving it and the cloth tied itself in a knot so precise Dani could feel the hand that had practiced it.

"Proceed," the Hall said. "Last bay."

They walked. The Hall narrowed again until their shoulders almost brushed glass. The final space opened not with grandeur but with the exhaustion of a machine built to grind that had finally ground enough to reveal what had always been caught in its teeth.

A single bell hung from a cross-beam. Not the Temple's bell. This one was smaller, tarnished along its lip where hands had gripped it when they shouldn't have. A mallet rested on a pedestal below it.

"No," Rally said immediately, stepping backwards. "I'm not ringing anything here. I'm not standing under another bell and pretending it doesn't make me worse."

The Archivist's voice slid around the beam like a draft. "It doesn't make you worse."

"Then what does it do?" he demanded. "What does any of this do?"

"Ends this chapter," the Archivist said.

Dani almost laughed. The Hall made her too tired to find the breath for it. "We're not done," she said. "Not with the Quarter. Not with the kids."

"The Hall cares for process," the Archivist said, ledger resting against his ribs as if it had a heartbeat. "The Quarter cares for argument. Neither cares for rescue. That's on you."

Jake picked up the mallet. It was heavier than it looked, dense, gravity stuffed into wood. He met Dani's eyes.

"Together," she said.

He offered the handle to Rally first. The boy's hand hovered, shook, then wrapped around the wood. Dani slid her palm over both their knuckles, not to steady, to join. Jake layered his over theirs. The mallet felt like a burden they had agreed to share in public.

They swung. The bell's note wasn't pretty. It started flat, found a clear tone, then wavered at the edge like a truth spoken by a mouth that hadn't earned it and then decided to.

Sound hummed through the Hall, found the seams in glass, lit them, darkened them. Mirrors clouded, cleared, clouded again, like breath that could not decide whether to leave or stay.

When the tone died, the last mirror on the right did not clear. It shattered. Not explosively, quietly, as if giving up.

Behind it, an opening, too small for a grown body, exactly the right size for a child who'd tried to leave through the smallest door she could find.

"Nia," Dani said, and this time her voice wasn't an order. It was a permission.

A small face stared from the dark. Soot marked her forehead in lines that might have been finger streaks, might have been a city's attempt to keep what it believed belonged to it. Her eyes went to Rally first.

He broke. Not in a way that needed catching. In a way that rearranged him. He fell to his knees and pressed his forehead to the floor because there is a kind of apology you only know how to make that way. "I see you," he said. "I see you, I see you."

Nia lifted her chin. The motion had the exact tilt of a girl who had run from more than she should have and was ready to keep running if the world did not change its mouth. "Are you here to take me to where they stop telling me what I am?"

"Yes," Dani said, before the Hall could answer for her. "Yes, we are."

The child's gaze slid to Jake, measured him the way the ruler had measured hands. "You look like a man who can carry weight," she said. "Can you carry mine?"

Jake's throat worked. "I can try," he said. "And I can put it down when you ask me to."

Nia nodded once, as if that were the only answer that would fit the lock.

129

She wriggled through the opening. The glass edges did not cut her. Dani did not call that grace. She called it a rare day when the city forgot to sharpen its tools.

"Proceed," the Hall said, quieter than before. The bell's echo faded so slowly it felt like permission instead of sentence.

They stepped back into the plaza blinking, the Hall's dark returning them to the Quarter's bruised light. The checkerboard had shifted: more white than black now, or maybe that was how their eyes wanted to count.

The placard seller had vanished. The signpost stood at a tilt. The cart with slogans was gone, or had never been more than a suggestion the Quarter could afford to drop.

Dani crouched in front of Nia, so they were eye to eye. The girl smelled like playground metal and a little like smoke. Close up, the soot on her forehead looked like the print of a small hand, then like the absence of one, as if a grip had been removed after years.

"You hungry?" Jake asked, voice deliberately ordinary.

Nia considered. "Only for leaving," she said.

Rally wiped his face on his sleeve and failed to make himself presentable in any way that mattered. "We're going," he told her, like a promise, like a defense he didn't need to raise here.

The lamplighter's voice drifted in from a street they hadn't chosen. "Do not argue with the Quarter about what you are," he said without turning. "It will always have more words."

"We're done arguing," Dani said, rising. "We're walking."

"Good," the lamplighter said. "Walking makes fewer mistakes than speeches."

They set off across the plaza. The Quarter watched them without blinking. The lamps swayed in a breeze that, for the first time since they'd entered this part of the city, brushed their cheeks and almost felt like air.

At the far side, a street opened that hadn't been there when they arrived. It ran down and away into a greenish glow, not Temple white, not market gold. The stones of its threshold were worn the way thresholds get worn by feet that knew they were leaving and kept going anyway.

Dani glanced back once. The Hall of Mirrors looked smaller with distance, like all buildings do when you've taken what you came for and the rest is filing.

Nia slipped her hand into Rally's without looking at him. He flinched, surprised by being allowed. Then he made himself steady, not for show, for the weight of small fingers that had measured him and decided he could bear it for a while.

"Next street?" Jake asked.

"The city of Justifications," the Archivist said from somewhere that could have been his throat and could have been marble. "It prefers argument to mirrors. You may find that a relief. Briefly."

"We'll take brief," Dani said.

They crossed the threshold. The Quarter let them pass with the irritation of a bureaucracy someone had managed to satisfy with exactly the right form.

Behind them, the last lamp in the plaza breathed itself back to green and then to gold, as if color were a way streets congratulated themselves for being inevitable.

Ahead, the murmur changed again, from verdict to debate, from debate to negotiation. The city breathed with them, or despite them, and the light took on the color of argument.

Nia's hand tightened once on Rally's. He squeezed back, not too hard. That was the measure now. Not tall. Not small. Just enough.

They didn't look for more voices. They didn't correct any murals. They didn't purchase anything that pretended to be a reason. They moved, the four of them, and the Quarter, sulking, did not get another word in.

The street sloped downward, the stones underfoot damp with a sheen that looked like dew but smelled faintly of ink. The walls leaned inward, the kind of architecture that wanted you to know you were passing through something owned.

Nia's small hand stayed tucked in Rally's. The boy walked stiff at first, like he'd been cuffed, but the longer her fingers stayed in his, the more his body adjusted. He didn't strut, didn't slump. Just walked.

The Archivist walked parallel in a way that never looked like he walked at all. Ledger at his side, mouth at rest, voice absent unless required. That was its own judgment.

Ahead, a low arch marked the exit from the Quarter. The words carved across its lintel had been smoothed by so many eyes that Dani couldn't tell what alphabet had been there. She lifted her lamp. The light slid over grooves faint as veins. She didn't need to read the script to understand its appetite: YOU ARE ONLY WHAT WE SAY.

She kept her hand off the stone. Some temptations weren't worth confirming.

"Feels like leaving court," Jake muttered. His voice was sandpaper. "Everybody talks, but the verdict already had its coat on and was halfway out the door."

"Except this time," Dani said, "we don't stay to hear it."

They passed beneath the arch.

The change came gradual. The light shifted first, bleeding green into a muddier amber. The air warmed, touched with something sulfuric. Then the sound returned. Not the whispers of judgment but something more familiar and somehow worse: people talking over each other with the confidence of men who have never been wrong in their own stories.

The street straightened into a boulevard, wider, with stalls pressed shoulder to shoulder. Every stall had a speaker, every speaker had a crowd, and every crowd had already chosen sides.

"The Quarter of Justifications," the Archivist said, almost with boredom. "Where every act is explained until explanation becomes a crown."

Nia frowned up at him. "Doesn't explaining help?"

Dani squeezed her shoulder. "Sometimes. Usually it just makes the knife look clean."

They moved deeper.

On one side, a man shouted into a megaphone about necessity. "We had no choice. You understand? Our hands were forced." His crowd nodded, some chanting back the word necessity like it was oxygen.

Opposite, a woman held a Bible so worn its cover had furrowed. "The Lord knows intent. He knows the heart. The act is a test!" Her crowd murmured amen until the sound turned into a hive's buzz.

Rally slowed, his eyes drawn to the first man, then the second. Dani tightened her grip on his shoulder until his knees bent. "Don't shop here."

He blinked, shook himself like a dog coming out of rain, and nodded. "Right."

Jake kept his gaze high. "Streets like this," he said, "are why wars last decades longer than sense."

They passed stalls selling words. Not plaques this time, but slogans printed on parchment and nailed in rows.

IF NOT ME, THEN WHO?

CLEAN HANDS CAN'T BUILD.

THEY DESERVED IT.

THEY ASKED FOR IT.

MISTAKES WERE MADE.

Each parchment had a price tag: blood, bone, silence, sleep.

Rally stopped at one that read I DID IT FOR RESPECT. His hand lifted without permission. Nia's smaller fingers squeezed his until his knuckles ached. He let his arm fall.

"They all look like lies," she said flatly.

"They are," Dani said. "That's why they're easy to sell."

The vendor smiled with a mouth too wide. "Easier to carry than truth," he said.

"No," Rally said, surprising himself. "Just heavier later."

The vendor's smile cracked. The parchment curled on its own and blackened at the edges, shriveling until it was ash.

Jake gave Rally a single nod. "That's how you bankrupt a stall," he said.

A procession clattered past them: masked figures carrying banners stitched with reasons. Each banner told a story of why something had to be done. The masks were blank, but the voices behind them were fervent.

"We were defending ourselves!"

"We were following orders!"

"We had to send a message!"

"They would have done it first!"

The crowd parted for the procession as though reverence required space. Nia pressed closer to Dani, her small face set in something older than childhood.

"Why do they shout so loud?" she asked.

"So they don't have to hear what they did," Dani said.

The Archivist wrote something in his ledger with a quill that hadn't been there before. "Volume is the enemy of accuracy," he murmured.

"Then why record any of this?" Jake asked.

The Archivist's eyes flicked up, the faintest quirk at their corners. "Because you asked me to come."

Jake grunted. "Fair."

The street ended in a wide square. In the center rose a dais with three thrones, each carved from a different material: one from marble, one from iron, one from charred wood.

Figures sat on them, dressed not in robes but in ordinary clothes, suits, jeans, a jacket with a badge still pinned. Their faces blurred and shifted, too many features layered, like multiple photos overexposed.

A crowd gathered at the base, shouting up arguments like tribute.

"He didn't mean it!"

"She had no choice!"

"It was war!"

"It was justice!"

The three figures did not move. They didn't need to. Every justification was a coin tossed into their laps.

Dani stepped forward, hand near her weapon, though she knew nothing here could be shot. "What is this?"

"The Court of Excuses," the Archivist said. "Less binding than the Temple, more popular."

Jake's lip curled. "Looks like politics."

"Same architecture," the Archivist agreed.

Rally stared up, his mouth dry. He wanted to shout something, to see if the throne-faces would nod. Nia tugged his sleeve before he could.

"They don't care," she whispered. "They just eat."

He swallowed the words back down. For once, silence felt like victory.

The crowd surged, restless. Some turned toward Dani, Jake, and Rally, sensing new voices to recruit.

"What about you?" a man demanded, his eyes too bright. "Why did you do it? Say it here and it will be understood."

Dani shook her head. "Understanding isn't the same as forgiveness."

Jake added, "And neither bring the dead back."

The man recoiled as if splashed with cold water. His neighbors muttered, displeased at wasted bait.

Nia's hand tightened on Rally's. "Don't," she said.

He didn't. For once, he didn't.

They circled the dais and found, on the far side, a narrow stair that descended beneath it. No sign marked it. No guard blocked it. Just a path hidden in the shadow of excuses.

"This way," Dani said.

Rally hesitated. "What if it's worse?"

"It will be," Jake said. "But we'll walk it anyway."

They descended.

The stairway led to a cavern lit by a single brazier. Shadows clung to the ceiling, reluctant to leave. Around the brazier, objects lay scattered: broken weapons, torn clothing, pieces of toys, badges, half-burned letters.

Nia's breath hitched. She pointed at the letters. One had her name written on the outside in a child's scrawl.

Dani crouched, picked it up carefully. The paper was half gone, but the name was whole. "It's hers," she said softly.

The Archivist looked down into his ledger. "Here the city keeps what it cannot justify. The fragments that won't take polish. The residue of acts too sharp to swallow."

Jake's hand brushed the hilt of a broken knife. The metal was dull, the edge chewed. "Looks like the truth bin."

"Yes," the Archivist said.

Rally crouched beside the toys. A small car missing a wheel, a doll with one arm. He touched the car, lifted it, turned it once in his palm. "What happens if we take something?"

"It stays with you," the Archivist said. "The city is glad to be rid of it."

Rally set the car back down. "Then let it keep its garbage."

Nia took Dani's hand. "I want to leave."

"We are," Dani promised.

A passage opened beyond the brazier, the stone split by roots that had forced their way through. The air carried damp earth and a whisper of wind.

They followed it up. The slope eased, the walls widened. The sound of voices faded behind them.

At last, the passage broke open onto a hillside. The city stretched below, its quarters sprawled like organs in a body too large to survive. The Temple's pale white dome rose in the distance. The Market's lights flickered gold. The Quarter of Shadows smoldered green. And here, the Quarter of Justifications buzzed red, its arguments rising like smoke.

Dani breathed deep. The air tasted like rainfall.

Jake stood with his hands on his hips, eyes narrowing as he mapped their next path. "We've still got ground to cover."

Rally nodded, his free hand still holding Nia's. For the first time, his posture wasn't defiance or collapse. It was balance.

Nia looked at Dani. "Do we have to go back down?"

"Yes," Dani said. "But not here. Not in this quarter. We move forward."

The Archivist closed his ledger. "Then let us record it so: You walked through shadows, argued with mirrors, refused excuses. That is one chapter. Another waits."

Dani straightened her shoulders. "Then let's turn the page."

Together, they started down the hillside, leaving the Quarter behind.

Chapter Seven: Reflections of Self

The Hall of Mirrors swallowed them whole.

The arch sealed behind them with the sound of stone rubbing stone, a lid dragged over a box that didn't intend to be opened again. Pressure rippled indalong the corridor as if the masonry itself had taken one long breath and refused to let it go. Sound didn't vanish; it was refined. The hush was honed to an edge so sharp Dani felt it against her teeth. Even the scrape of a boot came back magnified, a coin dropped in a cathedral and made to sound like a bell.

Their lamps threw silver blades across the walls, but the light wasn't needed. Every surface already gleamed with its own steady pallor, not illumination so much as appetite. The glass did not reflect; it stared back.

Dani slowed, instincts bracing her skeleton. Training told her to keep moving, momentum was its own armor, but older sense cautioned her: you don't sprint through a room that wants your attention. The panes returned more than light. Each carried a waiting weight, like a mouth ready to speak with her face.

"Stay close," Jake said, voice obedient to the room and therefore low.

Rally tried to whisper and failed. "Feels like we're inside an eye."

The Archivist's voice came from everywhere and nowhere, like annotations scribbled in the margins of air. "No strangers here. No prosecutors. No juries. Only what you choose to admit to yourself."

The ledger tucked beneath his arm glimmered as if the mirrors were trying to read it, hungry for precedent.

The corridor split after thirty paces into three identical halls, each dressed in floor-to-ceiling glass so clean the seams were guesses. Left curved inward, right outward, middle straight, if geometry could be trusted. Here it came compromised.

"Middle," Dani said, because a choice made early denies a maze its first laugh. She stepped forward. Her boots counted five measured beats before her body noticed the wrongness: a second echo following her heels by half a heartbeat, as if a slightly late Dani came behind them, insisting on a place.

Her fingers brushed the baton at her thigh. Not to draw. To confirm weight.

The first mirror offered the simplest thing, her own image: pale under cave grime, jaw clenched, pistol holstered.

Then the frame widened without her permission. The Chicago alley unrolled like bad film: yellow sodium halo, wet bricks, the man's pistol rising, the muzzle bloom, his body twisting down. Behind him the boy folded in the quiet way some deaths prefer.

Smell came with it. Powder burn and rain, copper and rot. Memory does that: it doesn't ask the room's consent.

Her reflection lifted its chin, eyes cleaner than hers. "He had a weapon. I followed protocol. It was justified."

The boy lifted his head from the pane's floor. His lips formed words with no sound but no ambiguity: You didn't save me.

Dani's hand rose of its own accord. Her palm met glass so cold it ached her wrist. "I didn't see you," she whispered. "I didn't..."

A crack stitched down the mirror's center. Her face split into two precise halves. Both smiled back at her with a knowing that had never been kind.

Jake's grip landed on her shoulder and pulled. "Not here, Francis. Not like this."

She let him move her, boots skidding. The split reflection kept smiling until it slid behind them and out of range.

The next panel chose Jake.

Rain beat the jungle flat, drops so heavy they blunted leaves, made mud into suction. A boy sprawled in that mud, leg opened by shrapnel, skin the color of fever. His mouth worked in a plea every language knew. Please.

Jake's reflection crouched. Pistol steady. One shot to the chest. The boy stilled in a way that had nothing to do with peace.

The reflection raised its eyes. It borrowed Jake's voice. "Mercy," it said. "A gift."

The glass changed its mind. In the same pane, another reel: the boy alive, eyes hate-white, rifle in his hands, muzzle angling toward men who had not yet seen him. The pistol fired again. This time the word nobody spoke was execution.

Two Jakes remained in the rain. Savior. Butcher. Both turned to Jake with his own mouth.

Rally's voice arrived from somewhere behind his teeth. "Which is it?"

Jake didn't flinch from the pane. "Doesn't matter. I pulled the trigger either way."

Fog blossomed on the glass. Not theirs. The film itself breathed.

Dani wanted to drag him on the way he had pulled her, but his body told her not to. He stood until the weight finished using him as an anvil and moved on.

The hall tightened, stone shouldered closer, mirrors leaned in like spectators who had paid for the front row. The light brightened without changing and made shadows where there were none. Dani's pulse sat high in her throat and refused to be swallowed.

Rally's turn came with no ceremony. The glass changed.

First, him with his crew in the school hallway. Sneakers unscuffed. A gun heavy and comforting in his belt. Jamal beside him, grin too wide for the boy's own face, like the joy didn't fit and had to leak. Rally drew and fired at nothing the mirror thought worth showing. The crew laughed, their hands landing on his back like blessings. Respect. Survival. Belonging.

The next pane repented all that. A kitchen with a single bulb that flickered with the rhythm of a bad heart. Jamal's mother bent over a table, shoulders shaking. Sirens smeared color across the window. Disgrace, the glass said without subtitles.

Then the hallway got crowded. Rally crowned with a wreath cut from a license plate. Rally on the pavement, blood darkening chalk letters. Rally in a cell, time handless. Rally younger, a shirt pressed to a wound, eyes so wide the whites told their own story.

The mirrors spoke over one another in Rally's voice until argument turned to weather.

"You belong."

"You betrayed."

"You're a king."

"You're nothing."

"You killed."

"You lied."

Rally's hands clamped his ears. "I don't know which one I am!" It came out more break than speech.

Dani took his face between both palms and forced his eyes to hers. "Not the glass. You decide. Not them, you."

The mirrors hissed as if insulted by theft. Predators deprived of the stillness they required.

They pressed forward because motion, here, was a refusal to be furniture. The Labyrinth disliked that. Some panes stopped acting like walls and started acting like doors.

A version of Dani stepped half through her own surface. Her skin was liquid silver, hair falling in mercury ribbons, eyes lit from within by a light that did not want witnesses. The hand it reached toward Dani was colder than a morgue drawer. Dani recoiled, baton snapping open on muscle memory; the strike rang like a hymn gone wrong. Glass shrieked and fell in neat, razor squares.

Jake swore as his double pushed out with a pistol raised. He didn't give it time to aim. He drove a shoulder through the reflection and back into its panel; the thing cracked and fell, shards clinging to his shirt like scales. His breath sawed once, then steadied. Impact had been real enough to bruise.

Rally's double came last, smirk carbon-copied, gun tucked in waistband. It raised the barrel, not at him; at Dani.

Rally screamed. He didn't remember starting forward; he only remembered hitting. He and the reflection crashed into the pane. Glass went off like a slow explosion. A spear of it cut his forearm. Blood splashed the floor and the floor drank greedily.

Dani hooked him back by his collar, free hand clamping the wound until his breath returned to the shape of words. The chill in the stone bit deeper, the bleeding slowed, and the cut sealed as if the City wanted him moving. "Keep moving," she ordered. "These walls want you to freeze."

They obeyed and the mirrors leaned after them, disappointed predators.

The corridor forked again, this time without symmetry, like a choice made by a drunk cartographer. The left path carried a faint smell of rain on hot stone. The right smelled like old paper and courtroom coffee. The middle held no scent at all.

"Middle lies," Jake said. "Left's a memory, right's a verdict. Pick the monster you know."

Dani listened the way cops listen when the body isn't yet found but the room already knows where it is. She nodded left. "We've done verdict. If we drown, we drown on real water."

They turned. The air cooled, a mercy that had teeth. The mirrors on this stretch were narrower, portrait-height, hung like family photographs. They did not show geography. They showed acts.

Dani again: the alley, yes, but also a girl in a stairwell years ago, hand on a boy's shoulder, telling him to go home, now, voice harder than she believed she owned. The boy had gone. The glass titled this Stayed and made it sound like Preserved.

Jake: a doorway in a village, his palm up, weapon down, his mouth moving steady, the shape of it saying walk. The pane named this Escorted; Jake's eyes insisted Evacuated.

Rally: a school cafeteria, a tray, Jamal sitting across from him, both boys laughing at something stupid and alive. The mirror didn't title that one. It let the silence do the work.

Rally reached for the glass with two fingers, didn't quite touch. "I remember this lunch," he said. "He put too much hot sauce on. He was crying without crying." He swallowed sand. "I didn't deserve that day."

Dani's voice softened because soft had an edge too. "You don't have to deserve the good to admit it occurred."

The pane fogged where his breath reached it and then cleared itself like a cat unwilling to be petted. They moved on.

A figure waited at the next bend, a docent for a museum that had never had a map. She wore the Archivist's gray, but her ledger was blank. The pen in her hand scratched on empty paper and made a sound anyway.

147

"Say only the act," she intoned, without looking up. "Do not add. Do not subtract."

"We did this already," Rally muttered, exhausted around the eyes.

"In this hall," the woman said, "you pay in installments."

Dani almost laughed at the accuracy. She didn't. "Killed," she said, and kept walking.

Jake: "Killed." No ornaments.

Rally's mouth opened and nothing came. Dani didn't rescue him. He found it and laid the word down like a silver coin he'd been rubbing smooth for years. "Killed."

The pen scratched. The page stayed empty. The woman didn't move aside. She was never in front of them to begin with. She had been inside the step, not in the path. They moved through where she was as if passing through fog that preferred bureaucracy.

The Labyrinth tried one more trick before surrendering the section. A pane tall as a church door rose ahead. Not silver now, black, polished to an obsidian shine that returned no detail. It showed them as silhouettes only, three figures and a fourth that didn't commit to being a person.

It waited. The room waited with it.

Dani lifted her lamp. The beam slid off like oil on water.

Jake exhaled through his nose. "Doesn't want light. Wants confession."

Rally shook his head. "I'm empty."

"Good," Dani said. "Then it gets nothing."

She reached forward with the baton and tapped the glass once. The sound rang a single clean note. The pane answered not by cracking but by thickening, as if it had inhaled. Their silhouettes on the surface moved, not them, the them in the glass.

Dani's mirror-shape turned on Jake, gun drawn. Jake's turned on Rally. Rally's turned on Dani, mouth curled into a sneer he recognized and hated. The reflections shouted words the room supplied like captions: Murderer. Coward. Nothing.

Three shots in the glass. Thunder without air. Spiderweb fractures blew out from the center, racing the edges. The pane collapsed not as shards but as black dust so fine it hung in the air like consequence. Where it settled, an archway unstitched itself into being.

"Through," the Archivist's voice said, sounding tired of being correct.

Dani's grip adjusted on the baton. "We go."

Beyond the arch, the Labyrinth tightened its weave. Mirrors crowded so close their frames touched, a picket line of selves. Whispering rose, a textile of verdicts rubbed together until heat built.

Dani's glass: a review board, colleagues whispering words like accident and negligence because those were the syllables with pensions attached. She saw the way faces looked at the floor when they believed you and at the ceiling when they didn't.

Jake's: medals pinned in a ceremony under a tent, a speech about restraint, the dead boy's face ghosted behind every saluting hand.

Rally's: Jamal forgiving him, then damning him, then forgiving him again, the panes fighting over which one felt truer when both were impossible and necessary.

"Enough," Dani said, and her voice sounded like a hallway command. She smashed her mirror. Jake followed,

149

elbow, shoulder, iron will. Rally hurled a loose cobblestone into his own pane.

The hall screamed with the kind of sound glass makes when it is too committed to its story to break nicely. Then it quit. The floor drank the glitter to dull. The whispering died the way a crowded room dies when the power cuts: mid-word, resentful.

The corridor exhaled and widened its chest just enough to admit three human bodies still insisting on forward.

"Keep your feet," Jake said, because he had learned what floors do when you trust them in the wrong war.

"I am," Rally said. He meant: I'm trying.

Dani rolled her shoulders, tasting iron at the back of her tongue, and led them into the next turn where the Labyrinth promised to stop pretending to be impartial.

The Labyrinth rounded the bend and narrowed to a throat. Dani felt it the way a diver feels depth, pressure collecting in the hollows of bone. The mirrors here sat flush to the stone as if poured into it still warm. Their surfaces were so clean the lamps lost their edges. Shapes bled into shapes.

Rally sniffed and wiped his sleeve with the back of his wrist, leaving a thin, rust-dark crescent. "How long have we been in here?"

"Long enough to stop asking," Jake said. "Keep your spacing."

They moved single-file: Dani in front, Rally close, Jake watching rear. The whisper that had threaded earlier corridors returned, this time riding a low burr, machinery about to seize. Words tried and failed. Guilt written in a language a throat doesn't speak.

The corridor eased wider without getting taller. Three mirrors faced them, shoulder to shoulder, frames touching like knuckles.

The left pane held a living room: couch sunken by years, TV off, a crooked family photo. Dani stood there in uniform; a woman blocked the doorway with her arms; behind her a boy peered out, eyes wide. Caption: Enter. Then it flickered: Invade.

The center pane was Jake's: a dirt road, a convoy, a child running toward them with a plastic bag. Jake's reflection raised an open palm, stop. Caption: Engage, Non-Lethal. Flicker: Delay, Negligence.

The right pane offered Rally's stoop: cheap deadbolt, a sticker promising security, Jamal grinning with two sweating cups of orange soda. In Rally's pocket: a gun. Caption toggled Welcome / Recruit and then failed, blank.

Rally reached. Dani caught his wrist. "Don't give it a fingerprint."

Jake's mouth thinned. "Left is rules. Center is rules. Right is rules. Different uniforms."

"It wants agreement," Dani said. She lifted her baton. "We don't."

She struck the left pane. A crack leapt corner to corner. The woman didn't move; the boy's eyes did, met Dani's for a heartbeat, then the room emptied to blank glass.

Jake slammed the heel of his hand into the center pane. The convoy jittered; the child's bag turned into a paper bird and dropped. The caption scrambled and failed. He hit it once more; the glass sighed and cleared.

Rally spoke to his pane instead of breaking first. "You were my friend," he said. "I made you a crown and nails." He drove his elbow into the corner. The pane collapsed fast as if choosing it. The soda fell and disappeared.

The wall behind opened into a short corridor with no mirrors. They went anyway.

Stone on both sides was a relief, even for twenty paces. Then mirrors returned, narrow strips, slivers glued up in haste. Each reflected only a slice: an eye, a shoulder, a mouth. No whispers; a soft click instead, like teeth considering closure.

The passage spit them into a gallery. Plinths stood in measured lines under pale cones of light. On velvet sat small objects: a plastic whistle, a rusted dog tag, a key to nothing modern, a chipped white pawn turned coffee-stained.

Rally's fingers hovered over the pawn. The Archivist's voice descended, patient as rain. "Tools," he said. "Not for hands. For stories."

"What happens if we pick one?" Jake asked.

"You pay with certainty."

"I've bought that before," Rally muttered, and pulled back.

Dani felt the key tug her palm, entry, permission, order. She closed her hand empty. "We take nothing."

"Wise," the Archivist allowed. "Not required."

They threaded the plinths untouched. Each object gave a tiny sound as they passed, the whistle's breath, the clink of tags, the delicate knock of a pawn catching itself. Petty punishments. The far door opened of its own accord.

Honesty arrived next, which is a specialization of cruelty.

Ten mirrors, five a side, woke as they approached. Each held a single still.

Dani's first: a training screen, shoot/don't-shoot silhouette raising something she can't identify, breath wedged high beneath sternum. Caption: Hesitation. Second: a hallway, a man on his knees, a woman behind him with a knife, two children staring through a bedroom door that wouldn't close. Caption: Clear, a word that tasted like bleach.

Jake's: a map table, pieces moved like promises. Label: Plan then Justify then blank. Second: a cracked well, water black, his hands cupped, a child's hands cupped beneath. Share, both charity and ration.

Rally's: a doorway party, chin high, boys lined up along walls. Perform. Then a school bulletin board, tutoring, basketball, a grief group meeting Wednesdays. Caption wrote itself slow and ashamed: Ignore.

"I could have gone," Rally said. "Any day."

"You performed," Jake said. "Sometimes staying alive looks like that. Sometimes dying does."

"What do we do with these?" Dani asked.

"Note them," the Archivist said. "Then let them be notes. Scores are not songs."

"Say the act," Dani murmured. "We killed."

The mirrors shut their eyes.

The ceiling climbed. Pillars of mirrored stone rose like trees; beneath their feet a floor of glass set over shallow water. Reflections multiplied, on pillars, underfoot. Water made repetition look like depth.

Rally looked down and saw himself drowning. He jerked his gaze up.

"Up," Dani said. "The room will beg you to look down."

Halfway through the pillars, they found a platform. A bench. A man sat with his hands folded, posture blank, uniform hanging like clothes could be tired. He watched their reflections in the water, not them.

"Officer," he said. Not to Dani. To the surface.

She recognized the type before the face: apology in a pressed suit. "This is where you make the speech."

He nodded. The words came polished. "We regret the loss of life. Our thoughts are with the family. Our officers responded to a dynamic situation." He studied Dani's reflected jaw. "Do you believe any of it when you say it?"

"The speech belongs to a building," she said. "I belong to the people who live outside it."

A noise that wanted to be a laugh and failed. "That line plays." He stood; his reflection rose a half-second earlier. "It doesn't matter. The glass records. It doesn't vote." He stepped off the platform and vanished as if booked for a slot.

"Function," Jake said.

"Moving," Dani said.

A fork promised three easy outs. Above each path, letters written backward in silver leaf, readable only in the mirror opposite.

Left: CONFESS AND BE LOVED.

Right: DEFY AND BE CLEAN.

Center: STAND STILL AND BE UNDERSTOOD.

"If I pick, I get a story," Rally said. "I get to stop walking."

"That's the trap," Jake said. "Stopping feels like justice when you're tired."

Dani snapped a rescue hook around the center plaque and pulled. Silver leaf tore like old skin. Underneath, incised small and honest: KEEP GOING.

"That's our brand," Jake said, and stepped into the path that had pretended to be nowhere. It deepened and became a corridor after all.

A chapel waited, pews of mirrored glass facing a mirrored pulpit. On it, a blank book reflecting an infinite stack of blank books. No congregation. Air like melted snow.

"What's the sermon?" Rally asked.

"The one that says if you sit long enough, the glass will tell you who you are so you don't have to," the Archivist said, contempt a thin thread in his tone.

"I've been to that church," Rally said.

"So have I," Dani said, and closed the book. The discreet click unlocked a door behind the pulpit.

"Through," she said.

The corridor after the chapel narrowed to a knife slit. Thunder rolled ahead, impact in threes, repeating: a gavel, a rifle bolt, a door slamming.

With each drumbeat, the flanking mirrors flashed a single word so fast it branded: GUILTY. CLEARED. ALONE. Then again. Then again. The cadence of institutions.

"I hate this hallway," Rally said.

"You're supposed to," Jake answered.

The slit opened to a hexagonal vestibule. Every wall a mirror. In the center hung a bell the color of old copper. A mallet waited beneath, head wrapped in leather blackened by other hands.

155

"No," Dani said at the same time as Jake. "No more bells."

"What happens if we ring it?" Rally asked.

The Archivist hesitated. "In some halls the bell ends a chapter. In others it repeats one."

"We don't need a rerun," Dani said. She guided Rally around it. Three exits waited, unmarked. Jake sniffed air like weather and chose the one that smelled least like incense and most like outside.

They stepped through together.

The Labyrinth clenched. Mirrors pressed so close they bulged as the trio passed, reaching for fabric, skin. Dani drew elbows in. "Hands in. We give it nothing."

The bulges subsided when they found no purchase. Twenty paces later the pressure released as if the hall had sighed.

"Why does it care if we touch?" Rally asked.

"Signature," the Archivist said. "Agreement. A handshake you don't remember offering."

"Consent," Dani said. The word gave her heat. "No one takes it from us."

A final bend opened into a hall with a vaulted ceiling and a wall at the far end that was less mirror than horizon: one continuous pane from floor to arch, so perfectly polished it didn't reflect, it displayed. Color moved across it in slow tides.

Rally breathed, awed despite himself. "Is that… "

"The Atrium," the Archivist said, impressed despite himself. "Total Reflection."

Jake's hand fell toward his holster by reflex even though nothing here respected bullets. "What does it show?"

"Everything you already know and won't say," the Archivist answered. "And one thing you don't know yet."

Dani's jaw set. "Fine. Then we're almost done."

She stepped forward. The Atrium woke, colors sharpening into shape. Air dropped five degrees; gooseflesh rolled her arms. She glanced back at Jake and Rally.

"Whatever it shows," she said, "we hold the line. And we say the act."

They nodded. The pane brightened. The first scene resolved.

The glass rolled like a tide finding shore. At first it was abstract, lines of light sketching angles, and then the image clicked into focus so suddenly that all three flinched.

Chicago again, but not the alley. A precinct hallway late, the vending machine humming, tile fluorescents too bright. Dani stood with a paper cup of coffee gone cold, listening through a door. Inside, voices, the chief, a union rep, a city lawyer, low, practiced. Words slid under the door like oil: optics... liability... community.

The Atrium did what mirrors can't do: it overlaid what was being said with what those same mouths had said a year earlier in a different room about a different officer. The sentences matched, syllable for syllable. Only names changed. Only dates.

Dani's reflection on the glass looked at herself and looked older. She spoke into the hall without turning to Jake. "This is the part where the building decides what I mean."

"What did you decide?" he asked.

"That I could still knock on doors in my own city without a story eating the air before I said my name." She took a breath and let it sharpen her voice the way the Temple had. "Act: killed."

The Atrium shivered. The hallway vanished, replaced by rain. Jungle. The convoy again, but closer, not memory, feeling. Jake's camera-eye, the one he didn't have, panned the mud. The boy with the plastic bag ran. The bag wrinkled. The sound it made didn't belong here, grocery store noise in a war. Jake raised a hand in the image and in himself. The men at his back shouted something the Atrium didn't bother to translate. His finger didn't touch the trigger in the picture; it touched orders.

He said it before Dani could. "Killed." He didn't try to add mercy. He didn't subtract execution. The pane hummed once, a tuning fork finding pitch.

Rally braced. He didn't know which scene the Atrium would choose for him because there were too many that wanted the job. It chose none of the famous ones. It showed his mother's living room on a Tuesday: her feet up, slippers he had bought two Christmases ago, a TV tray with a plate of rice and beans cooling. On the screen: news that pretended to be bored by violence. His name wasn't in the crawl. Jamal's was. The camera cut to a street he knew and cops he didn't. His mother's face went still the way faces do when a breath is taken away and never returned.

Rally's mouth opened and closed. He had no words for taking a breath away from someone who had taught him to take one. Dani stood close enough for him to borrow hers if he needed them.

He found his own. "Killed." It was small and exact. It landed, and the Atrium absorbed it without ornament.

The pane darkened as if to say: That much we agree on. Then light flowed back in, a new picture gathering itself, details sketched and waiting.

"Next frame," Jake said.

"Hold the line," Dani said. Her voice steadied them both.

Rally wiped his nose on the inside of his wrist and didn't apologize. "I'm here."

The Atrium brightened, and shadows inside the glass moved like people taking their places on a stage they hadn't been invited to but would dominate anyway.

The Atrium lifted a scene from shadow as if the glass itself inhaled.

Not Chicago. Not jungle. A school stairwell in a cheap municipal building where the paint had learned to flake in long curls. The angle was slightly high, as if viewed from a camera tucked up under the ceiling tile. Students blurred through the frame: backpacks, sneakers, the wild choreography of teenagers who don't yet know they are choreography. Rally broke through the flow, walking too tall. Jamal leaned against the landing rail, telling a story so big he had to use both hands to hold the shape of it in the air. The image had no sound but made plenty: you could hear the joke's drop, the laughter's hit, the skid of a kid running late.

Rally in the picture hoisted his chin another notch and put his knuckles to Jamal's shoulder, playful and not. The glass didn't linger on the almost. It didn't need to. The scene pressed forward to a future the boys hadn't asked for, color grading subtly darker with every step.

The camera tilt changed, now an alley; later; heat; a gun that felt heavier for being introduced by a school staircase. Rally's jaw twitched, watching himself assemble a person he had not been born to be.

"It makes it look like it was inevitable," he said. He pressed thumb and forefinger hard into the ridge of his brow.

"Like there was a belt and I got buckled to it and didn't notice."

"It wasn't inevitable," Dani said. "It never is. That's just how shame narrates."

Jake's eyes stayed on the glass. "Shame and law tell tidy stories for different reasons."

The Atrium turned the stairwell back into a room Dani recognized: a conference space at the precinct that pretended to be neutral and only managed beige. She stood at the table on the glass, hands on the polished surface, elbows locked. Around her, men and women in suits, one in uniform, all with folders, all with thin smiles that threatened to become thin frowns at the slightest provocation. A PowerPoint glowed on a wall in a font that wanted to be decisive. There was a clicker in someone's hand. There is always a clicker in someone's hand when a city wants to believe in control.

The mouths moved. A bullet point changed. A graph slid up to show complaints as a line ascending like a diagnosis. The glass overlaid this meeting with another from three years prior, different faces, same slide, the line tilted the other way. Same words: this is about trust. Same words: the community is watching.

In the reflection, Dani did not speak. The building liked to hear itself. She let it. On the real side of the glass, she said softly, "This room is where they try to clean the knife by naming it something else."

Rally frowned. "What did you say in there? For real."

"I told them the building is not where trust lives," Dani said. "It lives where you knock. In the hallway. In a kitchen. On a stoop. And I told them I had killed and I would knock anyway."

160

The Atrium took that and turned it, as if calibrating the lens. It landed on Jake at a podium in a tent somewhere that tried not to be jungle by being aggressively temporary. His dress uniform looked borrowed from a better man. A general pinned a medal to his chest with a practiced tenderness that made the pinprick feel like theater. Applause rolled like surf seen through glass.

Behind the tent, the jungle waited. In the jungle, the boy Jake had shot waited. The picture split the way some days do: half ceremony, half mud. It laid them over each other until the medal's gleam lit the boy's still face and the tent's canvas flutter sounded like overrun water.

Jake did not flinch. "Act," he said. "Killed." The word landed and refused further grammar.

The glass shivered. It darkened. It brightened.

A living room: a couch, a TV, a woman with slippers off, heels pressed into carpet. Rally's mother, younger by months that felt like years. The news at the bottom of the screen turned its crawl into an accusation. The image clicked to a hollow-eyed anchor, then to a street, then to yellow tape, then to a reporter who performed urgency for a lens that did not love him. The name Jamal on the screen, white letters in a red box that tried to look like tragedy and looked like branding. The camera panned, dizzy; the footage cut; the camera held too long on a kid who hadn't learned what to do with his mouth when grief took his words.

Rally leaned so close his breath filmed the Atrium with fog. He wiped the glass with his sleeve and left a smear of oil and the ghost of blood. "I wasn't there," he said. As defense it failed. As truth it succeeded. A person can fail at defense and succeed at truth in the same sentence, and that's one of the reasons halls like this get built, to make sure you know the difference.

"Say it," Dani told him. Not a command. An access code.

"Killed," Rally said. He didn't apologize to the glass. He apologized to the air. "Killed."

The Atrium accepted the payment and went still. The colors receded like a tide. The pane returned to depthless silver.

"Is that it?" Jake asked.

"No," the Archivist said. His voice held the fatigue of a man who has already read the next page. "Atriums are polite. They walk you to the door before they lock you in."

The light in the glass changed in a way that had nothing to do with electricity. It was the difference between morning and noon, between overhead and oblique. A shape emerged across the width of the pane, a single block of glass blacker than obsidian, polished to the kind of shine you only get by burning something. It rose from floor to arch at the far end of the hall beyond the Atrium, a wall that was more verdict than architecture.

Dani felt the hair on her arms lift. "Another one," she said.

"Not another," the Archivist corrected. "The one behind the others. The glass the other mirrors pretend to be."

Rally swallowed. "What does it want?"

Jake's hand flexed. "For us to hate each other the way we hate ourselves."

"Then it's out of luck," Dani said, and hoped the Hall didn't hear the prayer inside her certainty.

They moved, the floor vibrating underfoot as if the Atrium's surface had gears. The great black pane, the

Obsidian Wall, absorbed them before they reached it. It showed them not as reflections but as cutouts, outlines with their edges serrated. Their silhouettes turned on one another without being asked.

In the wall, Dani raised her pistol toward Jake, her mouth shaping the word murderer. In the wall, Jake leveled his toward Rally, his mouth shaping coward. In the wall, Rally aimed at Dani, his mouth making nothing with a relish that made Dani's stomach fall.

"Don't," Rally said aloud, flinching as if he had watched himself spit.

"Hold the line," Dani said, and didn't reach for him because reaching looked like the motion the silhouettes would make if they meant to fire.

The wall fired anyway. Three muzzle flashes stuttered in black glass. Thunder jumped out and crawled down the bones of the hall. The pane split, a spiderweb racing its own edges, but it did not fall. It held its damage the way some people do, keeping fracture as identity.

"Again," the wall seemed to suggest, eager. The three silhouettes cycled through, smaller this time, faster. Gunshots repeated. The fractures multiplied but still the glass held.

Jake grinned like a man chewing on pain and using it for protein. "It wants us to feed it."

"Let's starve it," Dani said.

She holstered her weapon slowly, the motion theatrical on purpose. In the wall, her silhouette did not obey. It kept its gun up.

Rally dropped his arm. His silhouette raised the barrel higher.

"Not ours," Jake said. "Just the city's puppets."

"Then we stop dancing." Dani folded her baton and slid it into place.

The wall didn't like that. A pressure wave rolled out from the pane, shoving a wind through the hall that smelled like copper pennies left in a mouth. The fractures healed a fraction, then snapped apart wider.

"On my count," Jake said. He knew when to hit a structure and make it decide what kind of thing it really was. "One. Two. Three."

They hit it with words, not steel.

"Killed," Dani said.

"Killed," Jake said.

"Killed," Rally said, voice tearing.

The wall flinched. The spiderweb paused. The silhouettes went static, as if a stage manager had called hold.

"Again," Dani said. She could taste the Temple in her throat now, white cold, judge's blank face, bell tone bruising bone. "Killed."

"Killed," Jake said, louder, not because volume helps truth but because sometimes your chest needs to feel the sound.

"Killed," Rally said, and his voice broke in the place where a boy becomes a man because no one gives him another option.

The wall couldn't find its next frame. The fractures whitewashed. Then the blackness held itself together by stubbornness alone.

"Not enough," Jake said, sweating. "It wants the fight as offering."

"Then it wants something it can't have," Dani answered, and looked for somewhere old. There, the taste of a hallway where a plank had held because they said the act and crossed. The Quarter's lesson: plainness is the toll. "We don't feed it with hating. We feed it with only the act."

She stepped forward until the cold of the Obsidian Wall mummified the air before her mouth. "I killed," she said to her own serrated outline. "You can burn all the context to ash. I killed." She flattened her palm on the glass. It didn't accept the touch. It recoiled and pretended not to.

Jake did the same, broad hand to the pane, scar on knuckle catching faint light. "I killed," he said. "That's the spine. You don't get to chew any more meat off the bones."

Rally's fingers shook on the glass. He put them down anyway. "I killed." The confession had become less a surrender and more a brick he could stand on.

The wall made a noise like stone under pressure. The spiderweb fissures whitened to opacity, then turned to powder. The entire pane collapsed not as shards, not as dust, but as ash so fine it rose instead of fell, a column of black breath lifting and then going still in the air like a figure drawn in smoke.

Where the wall had been, a narrow arch revealed itself, cut keen into the far stone. The light beyond wasn't the Atrium's reflective glow. It was the pallor of a corridor that didn't care whether you had earned it.

"Through," the Archivist said, no triumph in it, only relief. "You finally stopped performing a defense."

Dani turned to Rally. "You in one piece?"

He glanced at his arm, the bandage she'd made from his own shirt dark through the weave. He flexed. Pain flared and faded. "Enough pieces for walking."

They went through the ash. It clung to hair, to lashes. It tried to remember them. Dani shook her head once, a motion she'd used to clear rain out of her eyes on nights the city wanted to drown itself. The ash drifted off and fell behind.

The corridor after the Obsidian Wall was pinched and smooth as a throat. Mirrors didn't line it. The absence should have been a relief and wasn't. The stone surface had learned enough from watching glass to reflect without help. Their shapes stretched along it, more shadow than image.

"Feels like the Labyrinth is over," Rally said, whispering because the stone suggested it. "But it's not."

"It never is," Jake said.

The passage uncoiled into a room that pretended to be simple: six walls, each a door, each door a mirror. No frames. No hinges. Just six panes of perfection that turned the chamber into a jewel box where you couldn't tell which facet cut.

In each door, a scene waited. Not rotating like the Atrium, not flickering like the corridors. Patient. Chosen.

Dani's door showed a boy, not the alley boy, not any boy she knew. Ten, maybe. There was a dog behind him with a muzzle half gray. They were on a stoop. The boy's chin lifted the way boys' chins do when they are trying on courage like a jacket they expect to grow into. "Are you the police?" his mouth asked the glass. The door titled itself Future in letters that did not belong to any language Dani had practiced.

Jake's door showed a river no map named, brown and fast, the far bank higher than this one, a rope strung across in a sag. Men moved along the rope, hunched and careful. On the near shore, the boy Jake had killed stood alive, anachronism, canted slightly, looking at Jake not with accusation now but with the tired curiosity of someone who has figured out that memory is just another theater. The title read Retained. Jake's throat worked.

Rally's door showed Jamal's mother again, but not crying. She was asleep in a chair, mouth slightly open, a quilt over her legs. Daylight veiled the room. On the TV a game show ran without sound and without anyone caring. A title burned faintly at the bottom of the pane: Ordinary.

"Pick," the Archivist said. "Not which door. Which title."

"What happens if we pick wrong?" Rally asked.

"There's no wrong here," the Archivist said, and made it sound like a threat.

Dani walked to her door and laid her palm flat to the glass. "Future," she said. "Means knocking still matters." She took her hand away before the glass could ask for more.

Jake touched his and chose "Retained," and in his mouth it meant I keep what I did, and I keep the parts of me that don't make a speech about it. The pane accepted it without flourish.

Rally walked up to "Ordinary" like a kid approaching a dog he wanted to trust. He placed his hand on the glass. "Ordinary," he said, and the syllables cracked like ice doing the brave thing in spring. "I want this. Not a crown. Not a sentence. Just... ordinary. Jamal should have had it. I'll carry it."

The six doors unlatched in the same second. You could hear it, a tiny click like bone setting. They didn't swing. They became corridors. Each poured perspective away from the room at a different angle.

"Together," Dani said. She chose the one with the least shadow.

The corridor didn't argue. It declined. The mirrors thinned to a suggestion. The air lost its gloss and settled into something weight-bearing. The floor pitched down, the way streets do when they intend to bring you to another part of town without asking your opinion.

"Almost out," Jake said. It had none of the careless hope of boys who say the same line in monster movies right before the wall cracks. He meant it like a report.

"Listen," Rally whispered.

They did. The sound ahead wasn't glass. It was metal: the scuff of greaves, the hiss of plates on plates, the echo the city's guardians make when they've been trained to think weight equals righteousness.

Dani's jaw tightened. She knew that cadence even if the uniform was different. "Enforcers," she said. The word had to be said as if its first letter were a threshold.

The corridor widened its mouth into an arch. Beyond, the light went steel. The echoes grew teeth.

"Hold the line," Jake said.

"Say only the act," Dani said.

"Don't shop for stories," Rally said, surprising both of them with the right lesson at the right time.

They crossed into the cold where mirrors ended and men began.

The arch gave them a last cold kiss across the shoulders and then they were out of the mirrors and into weather made of metal.

The corridor widened into a plaza of slate. Light here had been scrubbed of color; it fell in sheets the shade of gunmetal, and it did not waver. Buildings rose in planes: no filigree, no mural, no argument, only right angles like laws that never met an exception they couldn't starve. A fountain occupied the center, not water but beads of mercury pumping in a measured heart-beat from one bowl to the next. It ticked.

"Neutral District," the Archivist said, and the way he said Neutral had in it a small, contained disgust. "Where intent is archived in a locked drawer and effect is labeled and shelved."

Bootsteps arrived before the men. Choreographed. Four at first, then twelve, then a line that made the plaza look smaller than it had been a breath ago. They wore matte armor that drank light: breastplates with edges like paper knives, pauldrons quiet as a shut book. Helmets mirrored nothing; instead they presented a brushed surface that refused faces. Each Enforcer carried a baton as long as a forearm and a halberd with no ornamentation. Their tabards were gray enough to be an absence.

One stepped forward. If he had rank, it was in the stillness of his posture. He held a rod with marks burned down its length at uneven intervals. When he spoke, the plaza's angles listened.

"Border crossers," he said. "Identify your acts."

Jake exhaled like a man setting down a weight he knew he'd have to pick back up anyway. "Killed."

Dani: "Killed."

Rally's throat tightened, then opened. "Killed."

The leader's head tipped a fraction, as if the rod had vibrated at each word. "Confession is recorded. Measure follows."

He pointed with the rod. A rectangle opened in the plaza, floor plates sliding apart with the embarrassed sound stone makes when it admits its seams. Within rose three pedestals, shoulder high and wide as a man's back. Each bore a shallow dish of black glass. At the base of each pedestal lay a coil of, what? Rope? No. A chain made from interlocked characters: small letters forged into links. DO NOT KILL. DO NOT STEAL. DO NOT LIE. A thousand times, a thousand anodized segments, a catechism made into hardware.

Dani's fingers flexed. "We've done our measuring," she said.

"In the Temple," the Enforcer replied. "It weighed what law writes. Here we weigh what balance demands."

"I'm fresh out of faith for scales," Jake said.

"Balance isn't faith." The Enforcer turned the rod in his hand. "It is arithmetic."

Rally's eyes strayed to the chain that repeated DO NOT KILL until language became a fence. He could feel the weight of it in his lungs. "What do we put in the dishes?"

"Something of equal mass to what you did." The Enforcer's tone held no sarcasm. It was a man describing weather. "Or you stand there while we decide what that is."

Dani glanced at Jake. The air between them took a reading: how much blood left, how much fight afforded, how many kids still somewhere ahead in a city that liked to rename them inventory. "We don't carry trophies," she said. "You knew that when you built a scale."

The Enforcer stood very straight. "Words are acceptable. So are names."

Rally swayed. "No."

Jake's jaw moved, grinding a thought into decision. He stepped to his pedestal. The black glass smiled up at him and showed him nothing. He placed his palm on the dish. "I give up the story where this made me a hero," he said. "I paid it in years, so you're not getting interest. But you can have that story. It weighs a lot. I carried it too long."

The chain at the pedestal's base twitched as if a current had been passed through it. One link unlatched and fell with a sound like a coin returning to a jar.

The Enforcer looked down the line, gauging yield. There was no triumph in him. Only ledger. "Recorded."

Dani took her place. The glass bit cold through the skin. "I put down the sentence that says accident," she said carefully. "Not because it isn't sometimes true, but because it makes me smaller than the act. I don't get smaller than the act." She took her hand back, shaking once without letting the shake reach her fingers.

Two links fell from her chain. The sound they made was little and huge.

Rally stared at his dish until his own face stopped being readable and only the shape remained. "I don't have a story," he said. "Only mistakes." He lowered his voice. "But I have Jamal's name. You don't get it." He lifted his hand, tears subtracted from the equation by the District's apathy. "You don't get his name."

The Enforcer's head turned toward him with the dispassion of a compass finding north. "Then you must give weight," he said. "Weigh him with a promise."

Rally blinked. "A promise?"

"Acts accrue interest," the Enforcer said, almost gently. "Someone has to service the debt."

Rally swallowed. His mouth tasted like the alley: copper and asphalt and the way sirens make air taste electrical. "Fine. I promise ordinary," he said. "I promise small. I promise to carry groceries. To fix things without a badge. To apologize without a microphone. I promise to be a man you don't have to measure twice."

The chain jerked once and dropped three links, like a quiet approval from a machine that didn't understand mercy but recognized inputs.

The leader touched the rod to each dish in turn. It made a small, ugly tone, and the black glass dulled, sated for now.

"You may pass," he said.

Dani exhaled. She looked at the Enforcers arrayed behind him and saw no malice and no joy and something worse than either. "You don't care if we deserve it," she said.

"We care if the weight holds." He nodded at the fountain. The mercury pulse kept perfect time to his voice. "If the city tips too hard, people fall."

"That already happened," Jake said. "We're here to stop some of it."

"It is not our function to stop," the Enforcer said. "It is our function to keep line."

"Lines were used to shoot children," Dani said, and felt her temper try to light. She snuffed it with discipline and made it into a blade. "If your line helps that, it's not balance. It's camouflage."

The Enforcer did not react. But he did not argue, and that was the smallest of victories, no link dropped, but a notch made in a rod.

He gestured with the rod. "Transit gate," he said. "You earned it. You forfeit it if you break anything in this plaza on the way."

"Noted," Jake said dryly.

They moved. The Enforcers did not turn their backs and did not need to. Their attention was a web.

The transit gate stood like an uncolored door in a city that had opinions about pigment. It had no ornament but carried weight in the hinges: black iron, old as a principle and twice as stubborn. In its lintel had been cut three small slots shaped like breath. Above them, an inscription in a hand that did not apologize for liking symmetry: ADMIT ACT. ADMIT LOSS. ADMIT COST.

"Admissions office," Jake muttered.

"Cheaper than lies," Dani said, and put her palm over the first slot. "Act," she said clear. "Killed." The slot breathed out once, a faint rasp, as if a lung had agreed.

Jake palmed the second. "Loss," he said. His mouth worked. He didn't say the boy's name; the District did not deserve it. He said what might stand for the boy. "I lost the right to decorate that day with any ribbon." The slot breathed.

Rally took the third. He felt the Alphabet Chain's repetition in his bones and did not hate himself for it. "Cost," he said. "Jam…" The name stuck. He tried again and found another sentence that fit. "A mother eats alone." The slot took that breath like food.

The gate unlatched inward with a groan that lived in the hinges and in the city. It opened onto a corridor of iron lattice, a tunnel hung over emptiness. Beyond the lattice, the Neutral District extended in geometry. Other tunnels cut at other angles. People, or functions in the shape of people, moved like a diagram come to life. In the distance, a different quarter's color bled, saffron, electric, wrong for this place.

"Enforcers won't cross into the quarters that argue," the Archivist said. "Beyond the lattice, the rules loosen. They will not protect you while they do."

"We're not here for protection," Dani said. "We're here for kids."

They walked. The lattice vibrated under boot heels, humming with the frequency of constraints. Through the metal diamonds they saw a room four stories below where men in gray fed papers into a machine that turned them to ash and then pressed that ash into slabs labeled LAW. A forklift lifted a pallet of the stuff and drove away. Industry of justification. The smell of it reached even here.

"That's a joke," Rally said softly. "Right?"

"Nobody here tells jokes," the Archivist said. "Only cautionary tales."

"You're getting funny," Jake said. "I think it's bad for you."

"Unavoidable byproduct of proximity," the Archivist said, and almost smiled.

Halfway down the latticeway, two Enforcers stepped out from a hatch and blocked the tunnel. Not the leader, but the same blank posture. One had a net slung across his back, not rope but line made of glass? It glittered in a way that made teeth ache.

"Hold," said the first. "Additional measure."

Dani stopped. "Your leader measured. We paid."

"He measured confession," the second said. "We measure risk."

Jake's neck muscles corded. "We're all risk. So is air."

The Enforcer unfurled the net with an efficient flip. It opened like a parachute. The filaments rang the way crystal sings. "We have orders to detain repeat vectors," he said. "The boy is a repeat vector."

Rally swallowed. He felt the weight of every hallway behind him tilt. He felt the Labyrinth whisper from his shirt cuffs and from the bandage around his arm. He felt every mirror say king and nothing at once.

Dani stepped half a pace forward. Her baton remained holstered. "He confessed twice," she said. "He gave weight. You drop that net and you make your District a liar."

"We have a ledger," the Enforcer said. "It disagrees."

The Archivist sighed without using lungs. "Show me."

The Enforcer did not offer the book to any hand. He touched the cover. Symbols moved under his fingers. "Vectors increase when the subject remains undifferentiated."

Jake blinked. "English."

"He means the city thinks I'll go back to being the me that makes knives into crowns," Rally said. "It says I haven't turned into someone else yet."

"That takes a day," Dani snapped. "Or a decade. You can't forge a promise and then weigh it like a stone while it is still hot."

"Nevertheless," the Enforcer said, and cast the net.

Dani moved before the net finished its arc. She stepped into its fall instead of away from it, one hand up, grabbing glass line. It sliced her palm with a clean, neat loyalty to edges. Blood slicked the filament. She twisted, pulling the net off its path, throwing her weight sideways. Jake pivoted the other direction, hands on line, forearms cutting in a way that would look heroic in a worse story. The mesh hissed like a thousand little bells. Rally ducked, then lunged in, forearms raised to give the net something to catch that wasn't his throat. The three of them turned together, pivoting on grit and pain, and slammed the net into the lattice railing. The glass line snarled in the metal diamonds and tightened on itself.

The Enforcer tugged. The net held. Jake grinned around his breathing. "Arithmetic, my ass."

"Enough," the other Enforcer said. He drew his baton and stepped forward with professional boredom. He meant to crack kneecap, to end this with a dull sound and a drop.

Dani met him with her baton, drawn late and still faster. Wood (or whatever this city called wood) rang against alloy. The impact vibrated Dani's bones up to her teeth. She pivoted, let his momentum pass, and rapped the joint of his wrist. The baton clanged to lattice and skittered. Twenty feet below, a clerk in gray looked up with the irritation of a man whose machine had a hiccup.

Jake took a step and stopped because it wasn't a fight they could win by out-Enforcing Enforcers. He hated that, but he knew it. He opened his hands, palms out. "Act," he said. "We're not adding a new one. You want to make a ledger entry for assault an officer? Make it on your own line."

Something about the shape of that sentence fit the District's lock. The first Enforcer held very still. His net arm trembled with effort. He looked at the twisted mesh, at the blood on the filament seeping into the lattice's geometry, at the boy who'd already bled this room's measure into his sleeve.

"Release vector," the Archivist said quietly, as if narrating a procedural everyone already knew. "Or this district will record an imbalance you can't afford in your numbers."

The Enforcer considered. The fountain ticked. Somewhere in the complex, a bell that wasn't the Temple's bell chimed the quarter hour. The mercury pulse matched it perfectly.

"Stand down," he said at last. He did not sound convinced. He sounded obeyed. He clicked a stud on the rod; the net slackened, then melted, not heat, but permission rescinded. It fell away from the lattice and withdrew into itself like a bad dream being folded and put back in a drawer.

Rally's knees went uncertain and then true. He breathed. He kept breathing. Dani wrapped her palm quick with a strip torn from the inside hem of her jacket. The blood looked black in this light. Jake flexed his hands and decided to dislike that net for the rest of his life.

"Transit permitted," the Enforcer said. "Further acts measured at next quarter."

"Noted," Dani said again. She wanted to say more. She didn't. The District had already eaten more words than it deserved.

They reached the far end of the lattice and stepped into a vestibule where three corridors met. Here the light lost some of its iron. A current of air moved that did not smell like filings. Signs hung in the archways in two languages: one was words, the other was color.

Left: a wash of deep red where the letters read QUARTER OF PASSIONS.

Center: the saffron bleed from before: QUARTER OF STORIES.

Right: a thin, blue-white thread that felt like midnight on a screen: THE ENGINE.

"The children won't be in Passions," Dani said. "Too easy to lose them there and too easy for the city to approve."

"Stories, then," Jake said. "Where if you listen wrong, you disappear. Or the Engine, where they turn everything into power."

Rally inhaled like he meant to answer and then caught himself. "What do you hear?" he asked Dani. It still mattered to him that she answer. It would for a while.

Dani tilted her head as if the city spoke like distant traffic. It did, and she'd learned to hear it. From the Stories corridor came the murmur of plot, crowds rehearsing lines they'd forget were fiction. From the Engine came a hum, low and hungry, the sound a generator makes when it has no thought to spare for the hands that feed it.

"Stories first," she said. "It's where frightened kids go when they need to be told who they are before somebody else says it louder."

"And after?" Jake said.

Dani looked toward the blue-white thread and didn't flinch. "After, we go cut the power."

Rally scrubbed his face, left a streak of blood she pretended not to see. "I'm not a vector," he said to himself like a boy reciting something rescued from a test. "I'm ordinary. I'm going to be ordinary so hard the city has to update a page."

"Make it bored with your goodness," Jake said, and clapped him once, gentle.

The Archivist wrote nothing and everything. "You have learned their tricks," he said. "You may still be learning your own."

"Good," Dani said. "We'll use them."

Before they stepped into the saffron wash, she paused and looked back the way they'd come, toward slate and scales and the fountain that pretended to be a heart.

"Balance," she said under her breath, not to them and not to herself. "If you want to know how we carry weight, watch."

The plaza did not answer. Plazas rarely do. But a single link on one Alphabet Chain lifted and dropped of its own accord, as if a tool had remembered it was supposed to be a law once.

"Forward," Dani said.

They entered the Quarter of Stories, and the light warmed as if agreeing to pretend.

Behind them, the gate to Neutral folded shut with a click the bones of the city would remember.

Chapter Eight: Law Without Mercy

The corridor tilted down in a long, patient slope, as if the city had grown tired of staircases and decided to grind its pilgrims down instead. Stone gave way slowly, gray fading to slabs of black marble, then to iron plates worked flush with the floor. Their boots rang against it, a dull metallic clatter that sounded too loud in a place that wanted every noise filed and cross-referenced. The air grew sharp. Metallic. Each breath cut as if they were inhaling copper dust, the taste of old batteries gathering under the tongue.

Somewhere ahead, a rhythm throbbed: boots striking in unison, measured, endless. Not the ragged step of a patrol, not the heartbeat of soldiers marching with zeal, but something worse. This cadence was patient. This cadence was law, an intake of order through mechanical lungs.

Dani slowed, the hairs at her wrist lifting under the cuff of her sleeve. She glanced at Jake and Rally. Jake had heard it too; the lines around his mouth drew tight, that quiet pre-fight geography his face took on when options narrowed. Rally swallowed, an audible click, his eyes flicking to the ceiling as if sound might pour from there as well.

The Archivist appeared at their shoulder the way only he could, ledger tucked beneath his arm, voice calm, unhurried. "Do you hear it?"

"We'd have to be dead not to," Jake muttered.

The Archivist inclined his head. "It is not a march. It is an intake. Enforcement breathing."

The corridor opened into an arcade lined with arches that stared down upon a channel of water so black it drank light. Not a river. Not even a canal. An aqueduct cut with merciless geometry, edges so sharp they felt dangerous to look at too long. The water was too still, like glass forced to impersonate liquid.

Along the banks, offices stretched in endless sequence, their shutters closed, their brass plates polished to bright indifference. Dani's beam picked the words out one by one as they passed: Department of Outcomes. Registry of Breach. Office of Prohibitions. Each plate had been buffed by hands that never trembled; each hinge gleamed; each threshold had the unworn look of a place that preferred forms to footsteps.

Every door was locked. Every lock gleamed from never being touched. No traffic had worn the handles. No chairs waited for clients. It was not a workplace, it was the skeleton of one. Rooms where the air had been taught to remember rules and forget people.

Jake grunted. "Feels like the government district of hell."

"Not hell," the Archivist corrected, as though a cartographer drawing lines. "Neutral District. Here the law does not weigh or debate. It enforces."

Rally hunched his shoulders. "Neutral? Doesn't feel neutral."

"That," the Archivist said softly, "is because you are people."

From the vanishing point of the arcade, they came. The Enforcers.

They appeared as silhouettes first, tall and faceless, outlines cut from a template. As they drew closer, detail sharpened: helms polished blank, armor the color of unfinished stone, neither reflective nor dull, simply dismissive. Shields hung at their sides, mirrored plates turned outward, not inward, so they reflected others but never themselves. Batons rode their belts, long and narrow, their heads shaped like gavels. Even the scabbards looked procedural.

The floor shivered with every step, though no step was heavy. They did not stomp. They did not run. Their pace was steady and inevitable, a metronome built into muscle, if muscle had been replaced by statute.

Rally's voice rasped from his throat. "What are they?"

Dani answered, low. "The part of justice that forgot people."

The Enforcers halted six paces away, the line locking with a precision that made Dani's chest ache. One raised a hand. Metal plates flexed at the wrist. A circular glyph glowed in the palm, faint as a coal, brightening on each syllable of their synchronized breath.

The voice that came from the helmet was not voice but mechanism, pitched monotone, drawn from no human throat. "Declaration."

"We already declared," Dani said, hand grazing the butt of her weapon, a touch she made herself stop. "At the Temple. At the Quarter."

"Declarations expire," the helmet replied. "Re-verify. Breach will be punished."

The mirror of the nearest shield angled. Rally's reflection splashed across it, warped by the convex plate. He wasn't himself, he was hunched, feral, some small animal cornered and trembling. Another shield turned, catching him in another age, eight years old again, eyes wide, lip caught between teeth. The mirrors did not repeat the present; they annotated it.

A baton lifted in the Enforcer's hand. "Minor. Prior acts: assault. Theft. Risk: high. Custody: authorized."

Rally stumbled back, breath breaking. Dani stepped into the gap before him, feet finding the floor's faint seams. "He's with me."

"Interference recorded," the helmet droned. The glyph in its palm pulsed brighter, as if a seal warming to press.

The strike came as punctuation. A baton swung without flourish, aimed for Dani's ribs, no anger in the arc, only geometry. She dropped her weight, turning her hip into the blow and rolling off the line. The wind of the weapon grazed her jacket; pain bloomed where it clipped a seam. Another baton whistled toward Jake's head; he rocked back and it clipped the curve of his ear hard enough to make sound fracture in his skull. White seared his vision. He tasted copper.

The formation advanced without urgency. Every time one Enforcer moved, another adjusted, filling the gap. A lattice of motion, choreography built not for beauty but inevitability. No shouted orders. No visible glances. Just an engine of bodies where cogs had once been men.

"Run!" Dani barked. The word snapped free before the next baton fell. Her voice ricocheted under the arches, came back thinner, like an echo handcuffed.

They ran. Boots slammed against iron plates, echo bouncing like alarms down the arcade. Locked doors whipped past, Registry of Breach, Office of Prohibitions, each brass label a verdict. Behind them, the Enforcers followed, not quickening, not faltering. Just moving, steady, as if the chase itself were already measured and entered into the ledger.

Then a sound broke the air: a siren tone. Not rising, not falling. One note. Flat. A judge's gavel turned to sound. The note pressed against their spines, scolding them forward.

The arcade ended in a fork. Left: a narrow alley threaded with chains that rattled in a wind that did not blow. Right: a black iron bridge arched across the aqueduct. A sign overhead, letters bitten deep: BRIDGE OF PROHIBITIONS. The deck was webbed with wires, each strung taut, each tagged with placards etched in capitals: TRESPASS. FALSEHOOD. CONTEMPT. MALICE. The words were instruction and snare.

Jake hissed through his teeth. "Looks like a lawyer built a spiderweb."

Before they chose, a door in the alley cracked open. A gaunt man leaned out, eyes fever-bright, suit stained with ink and ash. He smelled like damp paper and cold coffee that never cooled. "Quick! This way. Court won't wait!"

Dani stopped short, keeping her body between him and Rally. "Who the hell are you?"

The man grinned, teeth sharp in shadow. "Public Defender. Excommunicated." He tipped an imaginary hat. "I sell delays. Come!"

Rally blinked. "You sell... what?"

"Time," the man said brightly. "Law doesn't forgive, but it pauses. Sometimes."

They stumbled inside before the Enforcers rounded the corner. The Defender's chamber was a throat of a room that had swallowed a century of petitions and never digested a single one. Mildew and ink slouched in the air. Stacks of yellowed pleadings rose like columns. Every wall was drawers, labels written in a hundred hands and none of them neat. He shoulder-checked one open, riffling through files marked MERE THREAT, TECHNICALITY, ACT OF GOD, and, alarmingly, MISFILED.

With a triumphant noise, he produced a heavy seal carved with an umbrella. "Stay of Motion," he announced proudly, like a conjurer revealing a rabbit. "Touch it to your chest, you freeze time. Two seconds, maybe three."

Jake eyed it. "To fight them?"

"To run," the Defender corrected. "Law never tires. It only pauses. If you fight, you're arguing with physics."

He rummaged again, hands leaving little ink constellations on the wood, and dredged up a smaller stamp carved with a question mark so barbed it looked illegal. He pressed it into Jake's palm, the metal cold as the District's humor. "Marginalia. Confuses the footnotes. Never underestimate a footnote. Whole cases collapse on a footnote. Judges do too, if pushed."

Dani shook her head, not in refusal but in disbelief. "You're insane."

"Sanity is inadmissible," the Defender said cheerfully, as if reciting a rule he'd written himself.

The door shuddered under a knock, polite, measured, inevitable. The helmet voice spoke through wood as if it were nothing but another statute. "Office inspection."

The Defender paled, sweat glossing his upper lip. "Ah. The random audit that is never random." He yanked open a hatch in the floor, revealing a culvert lined with rusted bolts.

Cold metallic air wafted up like the exhale of a vault. "Through the culvert. Now."

They crawled through the pipe above the aqueduct, bodies scraping iron, knees bruising against bolts. The air had the taste of nickels and quiet threats. The underbelly of the Bridge of Prohibitions loomed ahead, its struts weeping condensation. Above, the Enforcers had already begun to march across, their boots a thunder that traveled through the bridge's bones; the structure made the sound into law.

Jake led, Rally squeezed in the middle, Dani guarding the rear. The girder shivered with their weight. Overhead, wires twitched to the cadence of boots, each bearing placards etched like scripture: NEGLIGENCE. MALICE. FRAUD. The words faced downward, as if intended for those already beneath judgment.

One wire brushed Jake's sleeve. The chime rang clear, ding. The placard flared: NEGLIGENCE. The light kissed his skin like a reprimand.

The march above ceased in unison. Silence pressed down, thick and diagnostic. Then the helmets spoke together, a choir of machines: "Detection. Below."

Hooks snaked over the railing, blind iron fingers feeling their way through air, tapping, hunting. Each hook bore a tiny plate stamped with an offense, as if even the act of grabbing required a citation.

A hook caught Rally's shirt. He screamed as it yanked him upward, ribs grinding against iron. Dani didn't think. She slammed the Stay of Motion seal to her chest.

The world froze.

Water ceased mid-ripple; the pendulum-drip from a beam arrested in a glass bead. Dust hung like a little galaxy suspended on an injunction. The hook paused, teeth an inch from Rally's skin. Dani lunged in the silence, tearing cloth, dragging him free. Her muscles burned in that wordless instant; she could hear her own heart the way a judge might hear a lie. She shoved Rally flat against the girder, the seal's pressure hot against her sternum, her breath the only motion in a halted world.

Then time snapped. Sound returned with a slap. Hooks slashed the space where he had been, cutting only air and a thread of his terror.

"Go!" Jake roared, voice hoarse, already moving.

They scrambled for the abutment, girder rattling under their scramble, hands skidding on damp iron. The Enforcers regrouped above, no curses, no confusion, formation knitting itself without visible command. Dani hauled Rally the last three feet and dumped them both into a gutter on the far side, stone biting knees and elbows through cloth.

She looked down at her palm. The Stay of Motion seal lay there as powder, an umbrella collapsed to ash. Its power spent. Its promise over.

Behind them, the siren note resumed, flat, patient, unconcerned. The law had missed them by inches and did not take it personally.

They lay in the gutter, breathing metal. The gutter smelled of old judgments, dust, oil, rain that had learned not to fall here. Above them the flat siren note resumed, patient, unconcerned, as if the miss by inches had been penciled in as a rounding error.

The Defender closed the hatch behind them with his heel and blinked into the gloom. "You see?" he whispered,

189

delighted and terrified at once. "Pauses. Exquisite little pauses."

The Defender closed the hatch behind them with his heel and blinked into the gloom. "You see?" he whispered, delighted and terrified at once. "Pauses. Exquisite little pauses."

Dani wiped grit from her cheek with the back of her wrist. "We need distance."

"Distance is an argument," the Defender said. "I prefer misdirection." He pointed down the gutter, where a run of grates cut the floor into panels. Each grate was stenciled with a single word: INTENT. ENTRY. EXIT. PURPOSE.

"Step only on PURPOSE," he advised. "The others have opinions."

Rally coughed. "Grates have…"

"… opinions," the Defender finished. "Don't take it personally. Everything here does."

Jake tested a grate marked PURPOSE with his boot. It dipped half an inch and held. The grate marked EXIT creaked like a throat clearing to object. He ignored it and moved. Dani shoved Rally forward and fell in behind, counting the steps as if number could persuade the place not to notice them.

They passed beneath a run of drainage mouths shaped like masks. Each had a hole where the mouth should be, and from each hole a breath issued, soft, measured, like someone sleeping a room away. The sound made Rally try to move quietly. It punished him with louder echoes.

"Left," the Defender hissed, gesturing to a low arch. They ducked under it and into a narrow maintenance corridor that doglegged twice and dead-ended in a wall of riveted iron. The Defender slapped the wall twice, then smudged it with his thumb. A rectangle of darker iron floated up like a door reconsidering its life choices and slid aside.

On the other side was a stairwell. It descended in shallow flights with landings every twelve steps. Each landing held a stand with a brass box and a lever. The brass boxes were labeled with words that did not look like words until Jake tried to read them; then they resolved into something like meaning: DISCRETION. SYMPATHY. EQUITY. MERCY.

The Defender wrinkled his nose. "Decorative levers. Never touch. They bite."

Rally stared at the MERCY lever like a man staring at a warm window when it's snowing. "What do they do?"

"Nothing you want." The Defender patted his pocket as if checking for his own heart. "Think of them as decoys. The District hates mislabeling, so it indulges it."

They spiraled down into colder air until the stair opened onto a service tunnel running parallel to the aqueduct. The wall on their right was pierced by narrow observation slits; through them, the black channel glided, a mirror forced to pretend at water. On the left, recessed doors wore plaques etched with single nouns: WARRANT. SUMMONS. FINDING. All locked. All gleaming.

Jake kept moving and tried not to think about what it would feel like to be caught on the far side of one of those doors, standing at the wrong end of a noun.

They reached a junction where the tunnel split. Signs hung from the ceiling on thin chains. One pointed right: CUSTODY. One pointed left: PETITION. Straight ahead: HEARING.

Dani didn't slow. "Petition."

"Petition is crowded," the Defender murmured. "Hearing is punctual."

"Petition," Dani repeated, and turned left.

The corridor narrowed and the ceiling lowered until they had to duck to pass under a length of ducting that vibrated with distant boots. The air went from metallic to sour, a hint of old sweat and paper. Voices grew audible ahead, low, muttering, the sound of a hundred throats rehearsing arguments under their breath.

They came out into a vaulted chamber with benches arranged like chapel pews and counters that resembled altars. No priests. Only clerks in gray, each with a chain running from wrist to desk. The chains were slack but present, like jewelry that insisted on being law.

Above the counters, slate boards listed case titles in chalk handwriting too precise to be human: NEXT UP: IN RE: BREACHED CURFEW / IN RE: UNLICENSED ASSEMBLY / IN RE: MINOR FALSEHOOD.

A line of petitioners curled through roped lanes and curled again. Each carried an object as if it were a talisman, broken lock, torn notice, photograph with the faces rubbed away. The noise in the room wasn't pleading; it was preparation. People arranging their lives into bullet points.

Rally shrank automatically, instinct driving him to the wall. Dani touched his shoulder. "Eyes up," she said. "They read posture here."

The Defender didn't join the line. He weaved along the outer aisle toward a side counter labeled CORRECTION REQUESTS. A clerk with a chain wrist looked up without curiosity.

"Name," the clerk said. The voice was tired, like a shoe that had been polished too often.

"No," the Defender said politely. "We're here to file a procedural confusion."

"Those go to HEARING," the clerk replied, nodding with his chin toward the central counters.

The Defender smiled with two-thirds of his mouth. "Not when it's footnoted."

The clerk blinked. A long blink, like a cat annoyed into tolerance. "Show the footnote."

Jake produced the question-mark stamp the Defender had given him. The clerk didn't touch it. He stared at it the way one might stare at an insect. "Origin?"

"Temple," Jake said. He wasn't sure that was true. He said it anyway, and the word felt heavier than lying.

The clerk's chain hummed against the counter. "Footnote is admissible if attached to primary document."

The Defender leaned on the counter, hands flat. "Primary document is in motion," he said. "We would like to append."

The clerk tugged his chain once and extended an open palm. Jake placed the stamp in it. The clerk turned his hand over and the stamp didn't fall; it stayed on the palm as if gravity had been temporarily convinced of another argument. The clerk breathed on it. The metal beaded with condensation that spelled out words, faint and backward. The clerk read upside down and backward as easily as if reading his own notes.

He slid the stamp back. "Marginalia accepted for one traverse," he said. "Limit of three entries. Attach to steps, not statements."

Rally frowned. "What?"

"Attach to steps," the clerk repeated, as if telling a child not to run with scissors. "Not to statements. Attach to what you do, not what you say."

Dani took the stamp from Jake and weighed it, feeling the subtle lean of its cold. "We need route," she said. "Off the Bridge of Prohibitions. Something they won't expect."

The clerk's eyes flicked to her and away. "They expect everything," he said. "But there is a maintenance catwalk behind the Chamber of Sentences. It has no name."

The Defender's eyebrows went up. "No name? How did it survive?"

The clerk's eyelid twitched, which in this place felt like flirting with insubordination. "It is not on the boards. Its purpose is service. Service is not a proceeding."

"Where's the entry?" Jake asked.

The clerk nodded toward a blank wall to the right of a door labeled PRONOUNCEMENT. "Behind that." He pushed his chain toward them; the links clinked without slack. "You did not hear that here."

Boots thudded in the corridor they'd just used. Not running. Arriving. Dani tucked the stamp into the cuff of her sleeve. "Move."

They slid along the wall, keeping heads down without looking afraid. Dani pressed a palm to the blank stone where the clerk had nodded. It was colder than the surrounding wall by just enough. She pushed and the stone swung inward on silent pivots, revealing a slit of dark.

Jake pushed Rally through first; the Defender oozed after; Dani slipped in last and pulled the panel behind her. Darkness replaced the room so completely it made sound louder. Someone, Rally, breathed too fast. The Defender fumbled for a match; the scrape sounded like a dare. The little flame licked up and showed a catwalk welded to the wall like an afterthought. It ran behind a series of narrow windows, each a slit into a tall chamber where benches faced a dais.

194

"Sentences," the Defender whispered. "Lovely."

They edged along the catwalk. The windows offered a running series of vignettes in near-silence, a man standing alone with hands behind his back, a clerk reading words into a book that wrote itself, a woman removing a ring and setting it on a ledge as if depositing a coin.

On the far end, the catwalk widened to a platform clasping the back of a high arch. Beyond the arch, the aqueduct gaped again, the black water scrolling. A metal lattice spanned the void here, not a bridge but a grid like the inside of a throat. Across it, forty feet away, a door stood, a simple door, unmarked, the kind that existed for function. Between them and the door, the grid glinted with hair-thin wires, most of them barely visible until you focused. On some wires, tiny tags hung like chrysalises. The tags bore the same words they'd seen before: TRESPASS. FALSEHOOD. CONTEMPT. MALICE. Others were new: DELAY. PRETEXT. APPEARANCE.

Rally tried to exhale humor and got half a breath. "Spiderweb," he said. "Lawyer spider."

"Not a web." The Defender's voice had lost its cheer. "An index."

Dani crouched at the edge of the grid. "Teach me."

"Every step you take is an entry," the Defender said, crouching beside her. "Each wire is a cross-reference. Touch a wire and the reference attaches to your step. Too many cross-references and your step becomes a precedent. Precedents call Enforcers like bells."

Jake looked at the question-mark stamp in Dani's cuff. "And the footnote?"

195

"Attach it to a step," the Defender breathed. "You can misdirect one cross-reference per entry. Maybe two if you bribe the line-breaks with panic."

"You're not helping," Rally whispered.

"You asked," the Defender said. He gestured to a slender run of three squares in the lattice, a diagonal path with fewer wires hanging. "That route is sparse. It will still sting."

Dani slid the stamp into her palm and tested her weight on the first square. The grid hummed under her boot, a faint metallic vowel. A wire brushed her calf like a thought; a tag spun once. DELAY.

She lifted her heel and pressed the stamp into the square. The question mark bit the metal with a crisp click. The sound disappeared as if swallowed whole. The DELAY tag shivered, then drifted two inches to the left, attaching to a wire she would not touch if she kept her hips steady.

"Good," the Defender breathed. "You wrote 'see also' into the floor."

Dani breathed out and stepped to the second square. This time a wire grazed her sleeve. The tag: APPEARANCE. She froze, and the tag flared bright as if satisfied. "I'm wearing the wrong face," she said, aware of the absurdity of narrating it.

"Stamp," Jake said.

She stamped. The question mark left a tiny indent in the lattice, an irony vandalizing perfection. The tag dulled, then scooted sideways to attach itself to a wire above where her head would be only if she stood taller. She did not stand taller.

Rally swallowed. "I can't..."

196

"You can," Dani said, without turning her head. "Follow my exact steps." She placed her boot on the third square. A wire kissed the side of her ankle with a cold more insult than temperature. The tag on it read TRESPASS. It glowed, ready to lodge itself.

Dani pressed the stamp. The TRESPASS tag paused. It didn't drift. It quivered like a decision reconsidering. She pressed harder. The tag dimmed, but did not move.

"Sometimes they refuse," the Defender whispered. "Law hates being obvious."

Dani adjusted, rotating on the ball of her foot to change her angle. The wire slid away from her ankle by a quarter inch. The tag swung and missed. The glow faded, aggrieved.

"Your turn," she said to Rally. "Step where I stepped."

Rally set his foot. The lattice sang a note his bones didn't like. He closed his eyes and set the second foot. A wire grazed his knee. The tag read CONTEMPT. It pulsed.

Rally stopped breathing.

"Stamp," Jake murmured.

"I…" Rally's hands were shaking. Dani put the stamp into them without looking back and kept moving. Rally pressed it. The CONTEMPT tag hesitated, then slid down and attached to a wire that hung an inch below his shin. He lifted his foot. It missed. His laugh was explosive and dangerous so he strangled it into a cough.

They moved like that, Dani carving, Rally imitating, Jake walking the arithmetic Dani left behind, the Defender tiptoeing the margins as if he had been born to them. Twice an invisible wire sang without touching, as if bragging. Once a tag flashed with a word none of them recognized, a word that wasn't English or law, and the Defender hissed and made the sign of a librarian against it. It went out.

Halfway across, the air changed, the indefinable shift a room takes when someone else enters. The siren note under the district flattened another hair, which meant it was listening harder. Boots, distant. They were running out of pauses.

The last stretch was worse. The wires thickened into a thatch with fewer gaps. Dani tested a path and felt the lattice give a grudging nod. She touched the stamp to the square and nothing happened.

"The ink's gone," Rally whispered, as if the object had ever contained ink.

"No," the Defender said softly. "The footnote's bored."

Dani pressed harder. The stamp did not bite. She pulled her hand back and looked at the metal head. The question mark was the same. Her pulse thudded at the base of her throat in time with the patient note that meant they were being measured.

"Different tactic," Jake said, very calm. "Attach to a step, not a statement."

Dani looked at the space between her leading toe and the square she wanted. She raised her foot, then lowered it with an intention as particular as writing a single letter correctly after a page of almost. The lattice vibrated. Somewhere, a pencil decided to be dull. The stamp head clicked without pressure. The tag nearest her knee rotated away and attached to a wire two hands-widths to her right.

She smiled without showing teeth. "Okay," she said. "We write by walking."

They wrote by walking. The lattice complained, then tolerated. The tags made their little decisions and sometimes had them changed. Rally's breath stayed inside his teeth. Jake's eyes went flat and bright the way they did when he had too many variables and had decided to accept only three. The Defender whispered useless advice that sounded like prayer and worked like encouragement anyway.

They reached the far platform. The door waited, maddeningly ordinary. Dani put a hand on the latch and a tiny spark stung her palm. She looked down. A hairline wire touched the latch, almost invisible, tagless.

She leaned closer. The wire quivered, delighted to be found.

"What is that?" Rally whispered, as if whispering might keep it from hearing.

The Defender's face soured. "PRECEDENT," he said. "Sometimes they don't label it."

Dani didn't touch the latch. She put her shoulder to the door six inches away from it and pushed. The metal flexed, not much. The wire hummed the way a memory hums when you're about to make the same mistake. She stepped back.

Jake took the stamp. He crouched and pressed it to the floor in front of the door. The question mark clicked. The wire's hum wavered. Jake stood and put his palm to the door three inches closer to the latch than Dani had managed. The door flexed further.

Footsteps now, in the corridor they'd left. Not far. Measured. Synchronized.

"Again," Dani said.

Jake stamped, shifted, pushed. The wire buzzed like a gnat. The door shivered and then gave with a sigh that sounded like a court adjourning. They slipped through into a narrow service hall and pulled it closed behind them. The buzz damped to a cross little murmur.

The service hall ran fifty feet and ended at another door, this one with a simple bar. No wires, no tags, no pretense.

They lifted the bar and emerged into a low-lit corridor with exposed pipes and a floor painted with yellow lines. The lines branched and rejoined and ducked through doorways. Every ten feet a small stencil offered a directive: MAINTENANCE ONLY. NO PASSAGE. NO STANDING. The directives contradicted one another in an orderly way.

Dani touched the wall, orienting herself by the feel of vibration rather than sight. "Aqueduct to our right, hearings to our left. We head…?" She looked to the Defender.

"Forward," he said. "Always forward here. Going back is a motion you'll never win."

They moved. Twice they crossed under grates and heard the Enforcers overhead, the boots precise, the silence around them like a lid. In one side passage, a figure in gray swept with a broom that had no bristles. The figure didn't look up. The broom made no sound. The air smelled briefly of chalk.

They reached a junction where the yellow lines piled into a tangle, a knot of paint that had been repainted too many times. A sign on the wall tried to give directions and failed, pointing in seven directions and labeling all of them ACCESS. Dani turned in a slow circle, mouth a hard line.

"Which way?" Rally asked, voice thin, trying not to hear how thin.

"Up," the Defender said, and pointed to a steel ladder bolted to the wall. "Everything important goes up here, except the punishment."

They climbed. The ladder was cold enough to bite through gloves. After twenty rungs they reached a ledge, then another door, this one with a small glass pane wired against breakage. Through it, Dani could see a wide chamber with a raised platform, a dais, framed by iron scrollwork. Benches fanned out below it. The scrollwork read CHAMBER OF PROHIBITIONS.

"Of course," Jake said.

The door wasn't locked. That felt worse.

They slipped into a side aisle. No one sat in the benches. At the dais, a single lectern stood, and on it a book so large it looked like architecture. Its cover was a matte gray that swallowed light. No one minding it. No one guarding it. The silence in the room was expectant, like the moment before an oath that ruins a life.

Rally shivered. "What is this place?"

The Defender didn't step past the last row of benches. His hands stayed at his sides like a defendant who'd been told not to reach for anything. "Where prohibitions are affirmed," he said. "Where the words on the bridge get their teeth."

Dani took a step down the aisle toward the dais. The book's cover seemed to thicken with each step, the way distance sometimes behaves when you're walking into wind. She stopped.

A figure detached from the shadow beside the dais and walked into the low light. Not an Enforcer. A woman in a plain dark dress, hair pulled back so tightly it filed the idea of softness down to nothing. She wore no chain. She wore a small pin at the throat in the shape of a lock.

She regarded them the way a doctor regards a chart. "You should not be here."

"We keep hearing that," Jake said.

The woman's eyes touched the stamp in Dani's sleeve as if they could see through cloth. "Footnotes," she said. "How quaint."

Dani felt her fingers curl. "We're passing through."

"No one passes through," the woman said. "They pass into."

Dani did not ask into what. "We need the northern escalade."

The woman tilted her head the smallest possible amount. "You know the phrase," she said, not quite surprised. "Then you know it is sealed."

The Defender found his humor again like a coin in a couch cushion. "Perhaps we're here to unseal."

The woman's mouth almost smiled. "Perhaps you think the book is a lock and the right touch a key."

Rally murmured, "Isn't it?"

"No." The woman's eyes flicked to him. "The book is a mirror. It only closes on those who try to open it."

Boots now. Closer. The sound came down the long corridor behind them, a new rhythm joining the room's steady breath. The woman glanced past them at the door that had not been locked.

Dani set her weight the way she did when the choice was about to go against her. "We have to cross," she said.

"You have to decide what to carry," the woman replied. "Law doesn't care if you cross. It cares if you try to bring something that is not allowed."

"What isn't allowed?" Jake asked.

The woman's gaze slid from him to Dani to Rally and back. "Debts," she said. "Promises. Names."

The words struck like a cold hand. Dani felt the memory of the Defender's earlier rules ghost past and tried to catch it. Names bind. Promises drag. Debts call themselves in.

Jake's jaw worked once. "We're clean," he lied, and the lie tasted like a copper coin sucked too long. The woman didn't react. Maybe lies here were too small to notice unless they carried paperwork.

The door behind them opened. The Enforcers entered in a file of four and stopped at the aisle's mouth. The siren tone flattened the room until it felt paper-thin.

"Declaration," the helmets said together.

Dani didn't reach for anything. She didn't look at the book. She looked at the woman with the pin. "If we speak, do we bind?"

"If you speak, you enter," the woman said. "If you remain silent, you risk nothing, except what silence costs outside of here."

Rally's breath hitched. The Enforcers took one synchronized step forward. The woman didn't move. She put one palm on the corner of the great gray book and the page edges whispered.

"Choose," she said. "What you carry, what you drop."

Dani's eyes flicked to Rally. The boy had assault and theft clinging to him like burrs, history trying to make itself into future. Jake had a string of necessary lies tied to his spine like a line of charms that cut. Dani had a promise tucked behind her left lung that didn't belong to her anymore. The words in the room reacted like acid with each thought.

She took the stamp from her sleeve and set it on the nearest bench. "We drop the footnote," she said. "No more misdirection."

The Defender made a soft hurt sound. "But…"

"… we wrote enough," Dani said.

Jake's hand went to his pocket. He pulled out a thin strip of fabric, blue, faded, knotted twice. He had carried it through checkpoints, across borders, into rooms where men weighed power against price. He set it on the bench beside the stamp.

Rally looked down at his own hands. They were empty. He swallowed. "What if I don't have anything to drop?"

"You do," Dani said, and touched his forearm. She felt the old fear snap at her fingertips and didn't snatch them back. "You drop the story that you can't be other than the worst thing you did."

"That's not an object," Rally whispered.

"Here it is," the woman with the lock pin said. "Here, stories weigh."

Rally closed his eyes. When he opened them, something had left his face. It didn't make him clean. It made him possible. He nodded once.

The Enforcers took another step. The air tasted like a coming storm taught to be polite.

The woman moved her hand half an inch on the book. The gray surface didn't open. It reflected. Dani saw, for a second, not their faces but their outlines the way the District preferred: less than people, more than entries. She hated it and held still.

"Traverse," the woman said softly, as if granting an extension neither deserved nor expected. "North escalade will admit you. It will not forgive."

"We won't ask it to," Dani said.

"Next time," the woman said, and that almost-smile appeared again, "bring nothing."

The Enforcers raised their batons together. The room bowed under the math of it.

"Go," the Defender said, pointing to a narrow passage under the dais, a maintenance door disguised as ornament. "Go now."

They did. The passage was so tight Jake had to turn his shoulders sideways. It smelled like metal and a trace of paper that had been allowed to burn only to ash. The corridor bent, bent again, and opened on a narrow escalade that ran up along the inner skin of the District's northern wall, an iron stair masquerading as a service duct. The first step looked ordinary. It had been polished by none of the thousands who had never been allowed to use it.

Dani put her foot on the step and felt it move, not down, not up, but forward, as if the stair itself were an argument advancing. Somewhere behind them, batons struck and struck again, sound making law out of contact. The argument of the stair continued, steady, almost kind.

They climbed. The air thinned until breath turned into bookkeeping, intake, output, balance. Lights passed at intervals, each numbered, each a small sun that refused to do more than light its own circle. At the twentieth light they stopped to breathe without saying they'd stopped. At the thirty-second, Rally started to laugh and turned it into a cough. At the forty-fifth, the stair opened into a landing with a grate that looked out over a chamber full of lockers.

Each locker wore a brass plate. Each plate bore a single word: NAME.

The Defender's face went paler. "Don't," he said. "Whatever you're about to do, don't."

Dani had not moved toward them. "Noted."

They pushed on. The stair turned one final time and ended under a hatch. The hatch was painted the color of old restriction signs. Dani pressed her palm to it. It was not wired. It was not tagged. It was just heavy. Jake put his shoulder to it. Rally set his hands and pushed with them both.

The hatch rose. Cold air washed over them, honest cold that had not learned anyone's habits. Beyond lay a gallery under the skin of the District's roof, a place of vents and beams and, in the far distance, a rectangle of light that looked too clean to be a trick.

"North escalade," the Defender murmured. He sounded both proud and afraid. "Admitting."

Behind them, far below, the siren note altered again, a fraction, a re-keying you wouldn't hear unless you already believed in differences that small. Dani looked at the light rectangle and then at the miles of pipe between here and there.

"Go," she said.

They went, their bodies low, their steps negotiated with the beams. The light did not recede. The District didn't chase them here. That worried her more than pursuit. She touched the place on her wrist where the stamp's cold had been and found nothing, no mark, no weight. The bench below held their dropped things like a tidy moral.

"Do we get them back?" Rally asked, not stopping, not really expecting an answer.

"No," Dani said.

"Yes," the Defender said, at the same time.

Jake smiled without humor. "That tracks."

The light resolved into a hatch like the one they'd come through, only this one breathed. It exhaled damp air that smelled of rain that had fallen somewhere else. Dani set her palm to it and the hatch released with a complaint pitched like paperwork.

They emerged into a narrow lane between two rows of offices with windows too clean to be honest. The brass plates here had different words: COMMUTATION. CLEMENCY.

PARDON. Every door was unlocked. Every office was empty except for a single chair and a single pen.

Rally's voice was a whisper that couldn't decide whether it was hope or mockery. "Mercy row?"

"No," Dani said. "Display."

"Also a trap," the Defender added, cheerful again as if exhaustion and fear were spices he preferred. "But a pretty one."

At the end of the lane, a door stood open. Beyond it the world changed color, warmer, the metallic tang giving way to the smell of stone when sun thinks about it. The open door looked out onto a staircase that ran down into a square of daylight.

Dani turned once, looked back along the lane, and then forward again. "No names," she said, mostly to remind herself, and started down.

Halfway to the square, the light flickered. A shadow crossed the opening like a bird no one had seen in years. The hair lifted again at the base of Dani's wrist. She stopped.

Jake stopped beside her. "What?"

"Listen," she said.

They listened. No boots. No siren. A new sound, soft, irregular, as if someone were shuffling cards slowly on a cloth table.

The Defender frowned. "That's not District."

At the base of the stair, just before the square, a man sat on the step with his back to them. He wore a coat that had once been expensive and now was simply the kind of expensive that had given up. His hair was neat. His hands were not. He held a deck of paper cards and turned one over, then another, laying them face down in a row at his feet.

Dani descended the last steps with care. "You're in our way," she said.

He didn't turn. He placed one more card and patted it like a pet. "Everyone thinks that," he said. His voice was mild and threaded with something that wasn't local law at all. "But I'm where the way is."

Jake's hand hung close to the place where his weapon wasn't useful. "Who are you?"

The man looked back over his shoulder. His eyes were the kind you only got after years of telling people what they didn't want to hear for money. He nodded at the cards. "Appeals," he said. "Filed, misfiled, and will be filed."

Rally sputtered. "We're not appealing. We're leaving."

The man smiled sadly at the square. "You can leave," he said. "Or you can decide what follows you out." He tapped two of the face-down cards. "There are always two. You only get to take one and you can't look."

Dani stared at the cards. The square beyond them was honest light and honest air and somewhere out there the Neutral District ended or turned into another thing that had the decency not to call itself neutral. Behind them the law hummed its patient breath and counted. In front of them, two dumb rectangles of paper waited to change everything.

She looked at Jake. He was watching her and not the cards. Rally was watching the light like a person who has never learned if light is a promise or a threat.

The Defender cleared his throat. "If it helps," he said, "I have always chosen the wrong one."

"It doesn't help," Dani said.

"No," the Defender agreed. "But it is true."

The man with the cards patted his knee. "Choose," he said softly. "And mind you don't promise what you can't pay. Out there, promises have teeth too."

Dani reached down. She did not close her hand. Not yet. The square breathed, and for once the breath did not belong to the District.

The two cards lay face down on the step, edges frayed, backs stamped with a pattern that meant nothing until you tried to ignore it. The man waited without speaking, one hand resting on the cards, the other on his knee, patient as old stone. The District's silence wasn't empty, it pressed, the way a courthouse does when you're waiting for the verdict and the jury has left the room.

Dani crouched, her shadow spilling over the paper rectangles. The air around them felt heavier, as if the District itself leaned in, curious how they'd play. Jake shifted his weight, one hand hovering close to where his weapon would have been useful anywhere else. His eyes stayed fixed on Dani, letting her carry the burden. Rally's breath stuttered, too quick, too loud in the silence, like a man guilty of every crime he'd never committed.

She reached. Her fingers hovered. The man tilted his head, not guiding, not warning, only noting how choices bent the spine of a person. Dani pressed her fingertips to the left card. Warm. Too warm. She lifted it.

A single word filled the card's face: WITNESS.

The man smiled faintly. "So be it." He turned the other card over for himself. DEFENDANT. He slid it into his coat pocket as if filing it away for later. "You'll walk out as a witness. That's lighter. Sometimes."

He rose, dusting imaginary ash from his coat. The daylight square stretched behind him, broad and open, the kind of space that felt like freedom only because the corridor had been so narrow. "Go," he said. "The District has no more claim on you. For now."

They stepped past him one by one. Rally lingered, his eyes darting to the card still on the ground, now blank, the word gone. He wanted to ask what it had been, but Dani's hand on his back moved him forward. He let the question dissolve in his throat.

The square opened before them, wide and paved with stone that looked heartbreakingly ordinary. A courtyard, if you squinted. Stalls lined its edges, but each was empty, awnings flapping gently without wind. Wooden signs swung on hinges with words that shifted when you read them: SUPPLY. RELIEF. RESTITUTION. Each sign beckoned, but no goods stocked the stalls. Promises without follow-through.

Jake scanned the exits. Four gates, iron-barred, each with inscriptions overhead: EASTERN INDICTMENT. WESTERN PRECEDENT. SOUTHERN DOCKET. NORTHERN ESCAPE. The inscriptions glowed faintly, their capitals precise as verdicts.

"Which?" he asked, his voice flat.

The Defender chuckled and wagged a finger. "Not Northern. Never Northern. The District names exits the way gamblers name dice."

Dani's eyes lingered on the Western gate. "Precedent?"

"Dangerous," the Defender said, "but survivable if you're clever."

"Indictment?" Jake asked.

"You'll come out altered. The kind of altered that feels permanent."

"And Docket?" Rally's voice cracked.

The Defender's grin faltered. "That one eats people in order."

Dani made the decision before anyone else could. "Precedent." She led toward the western gate.

The corridor beyond was lined with statues. Each figure was life-sized, carved from black marble polished until reflections bled across their surfaces. Men, women, children, all frozen mid-gesture, hand raised, fist clenched, mouth open mid-shout. Pedestals bore inscriptions in neat capitals: OBJECTION. APPEAL. MOTION DENIED. Every statue looked ready to continue its movement, but the District had filed it into stone.

Rally slowed near a boy not older than ten, captured with one hand outstretched, eyes wide. The pedestal read: DISSENT. The boy's marble lips were parted as if to speak again, caught forever before the second word.

Rally's throat clicked. "They're... real?"

The Defender shook his head too quickly. "Not anymore."

But Dani noticed the fingerprints still smudged on the boy's arm, preserved in stone as though the District had decided even panic should be indexed. She touched Rally's shoulder, urged him forward.

At the corridor's end, a vast hall opened. Shelves climbed to heights ladders couldn't reach, crammed with tomes of leather, wood, even bone. A library or a mausoleum, it was hard to tell. Pages yellowed, bindings cracked, but the weight of them pressed the air into obedience.

"Welcome to Precedent," the Defender whispered, reverent and afraid. "Every step forward here is judged by what came before."

Jake's voice was quiet, flat as iron. "And if what came before was wrong?"

"Then it's more binding," the Defender said.

They passed between the shelves. Whispers slithered from the books, scraps of sentences too faint to catch, but heavy enough to crawl under their skin. The air smelled of dust, of ink older than speech. Dani felt her legs drag harder with each step, as if every verdict ever written here was cross-referencing her existence.

At the far end, a staircase spiraled upward, its railing slick with oil. Above, faint daylight filtered through a square grid. An exit, if exits in the District could be trusted.

They climbed. Rally went first, Jake after him, Dani, then the Defender trailing. Halfway up, the shelves groaned. Books tore themselves free, pages fluttering as they launched into the stairwell. Words spilled from them like smoke.

"Minor: prior acts, assault, theft," a voice intoned, repeating Rally's past. "Custody authorized."

Rally froze. Jake yanked him upward, jaw tight. "Ignore it."

The books shrieked shut, but more opened higher, circling them like vultures. "Defendant," another voice droned, this time Jake's lies. "Contradiction noted. Reprimand pending."

The Defender hissed. "Precedent's awake. Run!"

They surged upward, boots slipping. The grid widened overhead. One final book cracked open in their path, pages bursting to block the stair. On them, scrawled in black strokes that bled through: BREACH.

Dani didn't hesitate. She shouldered through, the paper slicing her skin like razors. Blood streaked her sleeve, but she burst into daylight. Jake shoved Rally through after, the

Defender tumbling last, palms smudged with ink that clung like burns.

They collapsed on the stones outside. The air was sweet, unfiltered, too clean, almost painful. Behind them, the grid slammed shut, locking the library away. The siren-note cut off. For the first time in hours, maybe days, they were out.

Or at least outside one boundary.

The square stretched wide. A skyline jagged in the distance. Bells tolled, neither celebratory nor mournful, only procedural. At the square's edge, the Archivist waited, ledger tucked beneath one arm.

"You traversed," he said, no surprise in his tone.

Dani wiped blood from her cheek. "Barely."

"That," the Archivist replied, "is the only way anyone does."

They didn't celebrate. They didn't speak. The District loomed behind them, faceless but present. Ahead, the city sprawled, alive but fragile. Dani pressed her hand against the cut on her arm, the word BREACH burning beneath the blood, and wondered what it meant to leave the Neutral District alive but not untouched.

Chapter Nine: Deceiver's Debate

The boulevard narrowed into silence. Not the silence of peace but the silence of a courtroom after the verdict has been read. Every sound they carried with them seemed muffled and devoured, as if the black stone had a hunger for echoes.

Overhead, chains rattled without being touched. Bells dangled from them, their iron mouths cracked, tongues broken. They swayed in a rhythm not tied to any wind. Each dull swing made the chains groan, the sound burrowing into ribs like an uninvited memory.

The walls gleamed with a sheen like old blood, dark red caught beneath the polish of centuries. No liquid stained them, but the stone still looked wet. The surface reflected nothing back, only warped shadows.

The hum they had felt since entering the labyrinth grew louder here. It was not a sound so much as a force, a steady compression in the chest. Every breath resisted it. Jake caught himself tightening his jaw, as though clenching could keep his lungs from giving in. Rally clutched his own ribs without realizing it, his shoulders twitching every time the hum deepened. Dani swallowed against the pressure, telling herself it was only air, only sound, not the District itself trying to inhale them.

Her boots clicked against the flagstones. She glanced down and froze. Names had been carved into the stones, letter after letter etched so deeply her beam could not soften them.

At first, she thought they were just lines. Then the words resolved: rows upon rows of names, stretching endlessly down the boulevard. Soldiers. Judges. Farmers. Children. Some names carried titles, Sergeant, Bishop, Advocate. Some were simply UNKNOWN.

She crouched, touched one. The grooves were fresh as if cut that morning, not centuries ago. Her fingertip came back red as though she had pressed into a scab. She rubbed it against her thigh, and the stain vanished like it had never been.

"They're graves," Rally whispered. His voice cracked at the edges. "Ain't they?"

"Not graves," Jake said, though his eyes stayed on the stones. "Records."

Rally scanned the bells above, their shadows swinging across the names. His throat bobbed hard. "All of them tried to defend themselves?"

Jake didn't look at him. "Looks like they lost." His tone was flat, not unfeeling but practical, the way he used to list supplies before a mission, checking boxes even when the list meant death.

The hum shifted again, pressing like a tide. The chains clattered in answer, their weight jerking as though something tugged from above.

They pressed forward, every step deliberate. To stop was worse than to move.

The boulevard widened. It emptied into a cavern vast as a cathedral. Pillars of black stone rose in perfect lines, climbing into a ceiling so high it seemed infinite. Torches lined the pillars, their flames motionless, locked in a glow that gave heat but never flickered.

Benches curved around the walls, tier upon tier, rising higher than the torchlight reached. And on those benches sat figures. They were not entirely flesh. They were not entirely shade. Faces flickered and shifted with each heartbeat. Widow. Soldier. Child. Executioner. Teacher. Prisoner. The faces replaced themselves too quickly to hold.

Their voices filled the cavern. Not a single voice, not even a chorus, but an avalanche of speech: every face muttering, whispering, confessing. The words overlapped until they were impossible to separate, yet every one landed sharp in the ear.

"Collateral damage..."

"Proportionality..."

"Orders followed..."

"Honor restored..."

"Necessary evil..."

The sound wasn't a roar. It was something worse. A storm of excuses, every syllable self-justifying, every phrase designed to soothe guilt while making it eternal. The words stacked and braided themselves until they formed ropes that pulled on the mind. Rally gritted his teeth. Dani blinked hard. Jake pressed the base of his tongue against his molars until the sting steadied him.

The Central Court had already begun.

The realization moved through them like a draft under a sealed door; this was not a hearing they could interrupt but a weather system they had already stepped into.

The moment they stepped into the cavern, the Court noticed. Heads snapped toward them in unison. Faces froze mid-shift. The muttering collapsed into a hiss that filled the silence with a sharper pressure than noise ever could.

At the far end, high above the lowest benches, loomed a throne of twisted iron. It was not crafted but tortured into shape, bars bent and locked together as though the throne itself had once been a cage.

Upon it lounged a man. Or what looked like one.

His features were symmetrical to the point of parody, as if beauty had been drawn with a ruler. Skin unlined, balanced, flawless, but vacant in a way perfection always was. His robe shimmered like woven embers, bleeding from crimson to black with each slow breath. His smile was warm and wide, but his eyes were mirrors. Looking into them was like staring into water with nothing beneath it.

"Welcome," he said, voice rich enough to drape over the walls. The sound carried no echo. It existed everywhere at once, filling lungs, vibrating in bones. "At last, petitioners with weight."

Jake's mouth twisted. He hated warmth that pretended to be mercy. "And you are?"

The figure spread his hands. Palms empty. A host at his feast. "I am what you make me. Judge. Advocate. Accuser. Call me host, if you must name me at all."

The benches laughed. Not a thousand voices together, one voice split into a thousand throats, bouncing in waves from the stone. The cavern shivered with approval.

They walked the aisle. Each step echoed too loud, stamped and recorded. Shadows leaned down from the benches, faces shifting closer until they were less than an inch from skin. The whispers came, soft but inescapable.

To Dani: "You saved yourself. Would you rather be dead? The boy was an accident. His life bought ten more. Isn't that fair?"

To Jake: "Mercy is mercy. He begged. Ending pain is a gift. You spared him the humiliation of bleeding out. You were strong when others faltered."

To Rally: "Respect is survival. Without it you are nothing. You gave your block a name. They feared you. Fear is power. Power is life."

Each voice slid beneath thought, not appealing to reason but to ache. They sounded like friends who had once forgiven, like mothers soothing children, like commanders praising soldiers.

Dani clenched her jaw. For a split second, she wanted to believe. She wanted release more than she wanted justice. Rally's steps wavered, his shoulder brushing hers, as if one more whisper might tilt him over. Jake's teeth bared in something between a grin and a snarl. He had heard lies before, but not lies shaped to his marrow.

They reached the throne.

The Deceiver leaned forward, robe flowing like liquid flame. "You seek an exit," he said. His smile was gentle, almost sympathetic. "There is one. Accept what you already know: you were right. Your actions were justified. You owe no one guilt."

The benches thundered, a storm of applause. Stone trembled. Dust trickled from the ceiling. The cavern itself seemed to nod in agreement.

Jake muttered, "Sounds too easy."

"Justice is easy," the Deceiver replied softly. His mirrored eyes warmed like glass in a fire. "As long as you call it yours."

His tone turned coaxing, like a lullaby sung too close to a crib, gentle until you noticed the hands on the rails.

Mist seeped up from the flagstones, curling around their legs, climbing into the air. It thickened into mirrors, floating clouds of reflection that pulsed with borrowed light.

Dani's mirror shaped into her in uniform, badge polished, her shoulders straight. Children crowded behind her, smiling, safe. Headlines unfurled above: HERO COP SAVES LIVES. The boy erased from history, his name scrubbed away like chalk in rain. She looked proud. She looked clean.

Jake's mirror formed a soldier kneeling before him, weapon lowered in gratitude. His record clean. His hands unbloodied. The boy's broken body never existed. Instead, Jake's name whispered in barracks as the man who chose mercy. His weight lifted. His shoulders unburdened.

Rally's mirror crowned him king of his block. His crew knelt in adoration. Jamal alive at his side, his smile wide, unbroken. Respect eternal. Fear bowed into loyalty. Rally the survivor, Rally the name no one could erase.

The illusions burned brighter, bleaching the chamber in false radiance. Even the benches leaned forward, their whispers synchronized, urging them to step in.

Heat gathered along their cheekbones the way shame does before a lie, you feel it first as warmth, then understand it as warning.

Dani's hand trembled. The headline's praise called to her like cool water after a day in desert heat. She could step forward, dissolve the stain in her chest, and walk out pure.

The Deceiver extended his hand, robes pulsing crimson and black. His smile widened, promising absolution. "Take what is yours."

Dani stared at the vision in the mist. Her badge gleamed as if it had been freshly pinned to her chest, polished and bright, untouched by dirt or blood. The children behind her beamed, their small hands waving as though she had saved them all, every one of them spared because of her. The boy, *that boy*, was gone. Not erased, not forgotten, simply never written.

Her throat tightened. For one unbearable instant she wanted to step in, to fold herself into the picture, to accept that headline as truth. She would sleep without waking to the sound of a single shot replaying in her skull. She would wake each morning clean.

Jake's reflection glowed beside hers. The kneeling soldier thanked him, gratitude pouring from his face. Jake's hands looked steady, unbloodied, the tremor gone. His reflection's lips formed the word *mercy*. For a moment, Jake's chest lifted with the relief of being honored, not haunted. His shoulder loosened. The ache that had lived under his collarbone like a stone shifted as if at last it might fall away.

Rally's crown shone brightest of all, a crown of fire and gold. His crew bent the knee, his block chanting his name like a hymn. Jamal stood beside him, alive, eyes full of pride. It was everything Rally had ever wanted, respect without question, loyalty without fear. He was no longer a corner kid with a pistol. He was king.

The Deceiver's voice poured over them, honey over ash. "Take it," he said, palms open. "What you deserve. What you've *earned.*"

Dani's boots scraped against the stone. Her hand trembled at her side. For a heartbeat, she took a half step forward.

Jake's hand shot out, fingers hooking her sleeve, pulling her back. His jaw clenched so tight the muscle in his temple jumped. He spoke first, voice cracking like a rifle shot in the chamber: "No."

The illusions flickered, edges wobbling as if someone had breathed on a mirror.

Jake's chest heaved. He raised his voice, louder, steadier with each word. "I killed that boy. Not mercy. Not necessity. Just fear. That's the truth."

The benches hissed. The sound of a thousand throats drawing sharp breath at once filled the chamber. Faces blurred, flickering faster, growing grotesque. The hum beneath the floor quaked with disapproval.

Dani's head whipped toward him. The words ripped open her own reflection, and she saw the crack in her illusion. Her badge split beneath a hairline seam. The children behind her blurred at the edges as if smudged by a tired hand.

Her turn. Her throat closed. She forced the words out, raw. "That's not what happened. I killed him. And I killed the boy behind him. No headline erases that. If I call it justified just to sleep..." She swallowed hard, forcing the last inch of truth past her teeth. "...I'm not a cop. I'm a liar."

Her mirror shattered. The badge split down the middle, shards tumbling into mist. The smiling children shrieked once, thin, metallic, then dissolved like chalk under rain.

Rally was left alone with his crown, Jamal's smile lit bright, his crew cheering. He dropped to his knees, eyes locked on the vision. His lips moved soundlessly, caught between want and confession. Then the words broke free, cracked. "I just didn't want to be nothing. Maybe that's all I was. Nothing with a gun."

The crown tipped. Jamal's smile wavered, then turned to smoke. The crew bowed their heads, not in respect but in vanishing. The vision collapsed in a hiss, leaving Rally kneeling on bare stone, palms empty.

The illusions died. Cold slid through the chamber like a knife laid flat.

The Deceiver's perfect smile faltered. The mask of his face twitched, an imperfection spider-webbing across his flawless skin. His eyes darkened from polished glass to coal.

"Very well," he said, voice no longer velvet but iron dragged across stone. "You resist. Admirable."

The benches shrieked. Thousands of faces screamed together. The cavern quaked. Pillars split, hairline cracks brightening with heat from below.

The Deceiver rose from his throne. His body stretched taller, robe unraveling into wings of shadow. His mouth widened, no longer a smile but a dark aperture where warmth went to die.

"Then you shall not leave unchanged," he roared, voice layered with a hundred courts. "You denied justification. Face judgment *naked*."

The amphitheater came apart at the seams. Shades tumbled from benches into widening fissures. Some clawed at their faces. Others reached for Dani, Jake, Rally, begging to be believed. Their voices merged into a storm of pleas and accusations:

Cracks spidered with bureaucratic neatness, as if even catastrophe obeyed filing rules here.

"I had no choice…"

"They forced me…"

"I did it for love…"

"For country…"

"For God…"

Stone buckled. Lava flared beneath. Fire roared up the chasm, devouring whole rows. The smell of scorched parchment and burned hair filled the air.

A slab the size of a door sheared from a pillar and slammed into the aisle behind them, showering them in chips that stung like bees. Heat hit their faces hard enough to peel tears from their eyes.

"Move!" Dani shouted. She shoved Rally ahead, her palm between his shoulder blades. Jake took the rear, eyes up, searching the collapsing geometry for a line.

The nearest bench tore free and slid toward them on a stream of embers. Dozens of shades still clung to it, mouths open in permanent argument. Jake grabbed Dani's belt and dragged her aside as the bench ground past, sparks skittering over their boots.

A figure in a judge's wig grabbed Dani's sleeve as it slid by. Its hand was soft, sticky with melted wax. Eyes burned into empty bowls. "Say I was right," it begged in a voice like boiling water. "Say it and I'll let go."

Dani tore free, skin and fabric ripping, and ran.

The Deceiver's laughter boomed, layered and inhuman, echo without walls. His shadow wings unfurled across the ceiling like storm fronts. "You chose guilt," he thundered. "Then drown in it!"

Ahead, the far arch glimmered faintly, pale light seeping like a promise. Between them and it, the aisle had split into islands of stone floating in a river of flame.

Rally balked. "We can't..."

"We can," Dani said, catching his wrist. "Step where I step."

She leapt to the first island. Heat clawed up through her soles. Jake tossed her the half-melted remains of a banister as a pole. She planted it, gauged the distance to the next stone, and vaulted. Rally followed, landing crooked, arms pinwheeling. Jake took the jump flat-footed, absorbing the shock in his knees and rolling the last inch to keep momentum.

A gout of flame speared between islands and the stone under Rally's boot cracked. He pitched forward with a shout. Jake lunged, fingers catching Rally's forearm. The crack widened with a sound like paper tearing.

"Kick off!" Jake barked.

Rally kicked. For one suspended breath the boy hung above the seam, then slammed into Jake's chest and both crashed to the next island in a tangle. Dani's pole clanged against rock as she hauled them upright.

The Deceiver's voice followed, lower now, intimate, a whisper under the roar. "It is not too late," he crooned. "Confess justification and the floor will still. Say only that you *meant well.*"

Dani spat, the moisture hissing on hot stone. "We meant what we did," she shouted back. "And we live with it."

The shadows above convulsed, affront rippling through wings. The heat redoubled.

They moved. Leap. Plant. Pull. The arch loomed closer, its pale light cold against the furnace's glare. A final gap yawned, twice as wide as the others.

Jake measured it in a glance he hadn't used since Kabul. "Too far."

Dani backed up, judging the run. "Not for three," she said. "Rally, middle. You go light."

He nodded, jaw working, fear replaced by the simple math of obeying. They ran together. At the edge, Dani and Jake heaved. Rally flew, a ragdoll fired from the guilt-cannon of two adults who refused to fail him. He hit the far lip, slid, scrabbling for purchase.

"Catch!" Dani flung the pole. Rally grabbed the hot iron and yelped but held. Jake and Dani jumped together. The stone they pushed from sheared away into the lava. For a dizzy second they were over nothing. They hit the lip neck and neck with Rally and slammed shoulders into the arch's jamb. The three of them jammed for a heartbeat, then spilled through in a heap.

Stone thundered closed behind them, the arch sealing with a noise like a judge's gavel big enough to break a city.

They landed on black soil. The impact ripped the breath from their lungs. They rolled, choking on ash that tasted like old paper and pennies.

The sky was a ceiling of smoke. Rivers of fire cut the horizon into glowing arteries. The ground was not ground at all but cinders fused into crust. With each step, the surface crackled like thin glass. The heat licked their faces, but the air itself was cold, as if heat and cold had agreed to divide the world between them.

Rally gagged, coughing grit. "We said no," he croaked. "We told him no. But where are we?"

Dani pushed to her knees, palm leaving a print that filled with fine gray dust. She wiped soot from her face, eyes stinging. "Not out," she said. "Not yet."

Jake got to his feet more slowly. He turned back toward the sealed arch, a freestanding slice of stone set into nothing, and listened. Laughter still echoed faintly, filtered through yards of rock and yards more of hatred. His mouth thinned. He looked out over the ash plain without comment.

"Deeper," he said.

The word did not echo. It simply sank into ash.

They stood together, orienting. There was no wind, yet ash drifted in coils, sliding across the surface like snakes drawing cursive no one could read. Far off, structures rose from the plain, black silhouettes like gallows or the skeletons of towers. Between them ran the fire-rivers, their banks glassed and cruel.

Rally wrapped his arms around himself. "What is this?"

"After," Jake said, eyes narrowing. "Where excuses go when they burn."

Dani scanned left. A line of poles jutted from the ash, each topped with a small iron cage. Inside one, a bird of ash and wire beat its wings in slow hopeless circles. In another, a pile of papers tried to lift itself into a shape with hands. The cages were stamped with single words: ALIBI. CIRCUMSTANCE. INTENT.

Rally looked away. "I can't…"

"You can," Dani said, not looking at him. "Eyes up."

They moved off the scab of solid ground into ash that sank a little underfoot. Every step wrote itself, a dark footprint briefly visible before the slow drift erased it. The erasure was not random. It began at the edges and worked inward, leaving the center last, as if the plain liked to save the heart of a step for dessert.

The nearest fire-river hissed as they approached, the sound like a crowd shushing itself. Heat washed across their faces and sucked the moisture from their eyes. The river was not lava, too quick, too clean. It looked like liquid glass with light trapped in it and trying to get out.

"Bridge?" Rally asked, hope and dread braided into one syllable.

"No bridge," Jake said. "But there." He pointed to a series of flat, dark shapes rising just above the flow. They were plaques. Each had a word cast into it. Some words were common, FEAR, DUTY. Some were snakes, ENVY, PRIDE. One read NECESSITY in letters slick with grease.

Dani stepped onto FEAR. The plaque held, just, dipping with a wheeze. Heat licked her shin. She stepped to DUTY and felt the metal try to seize her boot like gum. She tore free, heart thumping fast enough to feel in her throat.

"Read before you step," Jake warned.

Rally hopped to PRIDE and nearly went in to the knee. Jake grabbed his collar and hauled him back. PRIDE slurped and spat, offended.

They picked a path. FEAR to DUTY to DUTY to LOSS. At REGRET, the metal tried to keep them. Dani yanked her foot free with a flash of panic that left her dizzy. Jake chose WEIGHT and nearly sank but muscled through by brute refusal. Rally picked SHAME, wobbling, then steadied, face pale but eyes clearer.

On the far bank, the ash resumed, cooler by a degree. A low skittering sound approached from their right. They turned, hearts closing the distance faster than their bodies.

Along the ash came things like crabs made of filings and wire, their pincers little guillotines snipping at nothing. They moved in a line, cruise-speed, purposeful. Their carapaces bore stamped words: WITNESS. DEFENDANT. APPEAL. Some were blank, waiting for labels.

Rally took a step back. One crab tracked the movement and swerved toward him.

"Don't run," Jake said. "They chase motion."

"What do they want?" Rally asked, not taking his eyes off the closest pincer.

"Attachment," Dani said. "To clip themselves to you. To make you carry the word they are."

The nearest crab reached Dani. It raised its pincer, angle querying. She held still. The pincer lowered, tapped her boot, moved on, unsatisfied. WITNESS skittered past Jake, hesitated, then chose a direction that wasn't them.

A blank one homed in on Rally. It climbed his shin like a toy seeking a charging port. He swore, fear spiking his voice.

Dani dropped, caught it by the carapace. It stung her palm, a jolt like touching a live outlet. She gritted her teeth and twisted. The carapace popped free with a sound like a cheap clasp. She flung it into the fire-river. It hissed once and turned into a glassy bubble that burst without residue.

Rally stared at her, then down at the red welt streaking her palm. "Thanks," he said, voice smaller than he liked. "I could've…"

"No," Dani said. "You couldn't. Not yet."

They moved on, ash sucking at their boots as if practicing ownership. After a while the plain rose into a shallow swell. On its far side, a forest of poles appeared, tall, thin, irregular. From each hung a mask, hundreds of masks, some carved wood, some hammered tin, some a gray material like dried skin. The masks turned as if following them without moving, every eye slit a judgment. A sign over the path into the masks read: APPEARANCE.

"Do we have to go through?" Rally asked.

Jake scanned left and right. The poles stretched as far as the fire-rivers would allow. "We do."

They entered. The masks rotated slowly, and each time a mask rotated, a new face appeared. Dani's own face, younger, laughing in a bar with her academy class. Her face the morning after her first shooting, eyes red, hair slicked back in a bathroom mirror, toothpaste burning her tongue because she couldn't taste anything else. Jake's face in dress blues. Jake's face down in a cot, light pared to a knife edge, the ceiling a blank he could not forgive. Rally's face at twelve, front teeth chipped, trying to look hard. Rally's face at sixteen, tears he refused to let fall standing in his lower lids like full glasses.

The masks began to whisper. Not words this time. Breaths. In. Out. In. Out. As if teaching them how to keep moving.

They kept moving.

At the far end of APPEARANCE, the poles dwindled to nothing. The plain resumed, featureless, a hardpan of old sin.

A thin shape rose ahead, black on black, another arch, half-buried, no light beyond it.

Jake slowed. "Another door."

Dani's mouth went dry. "Or a mouth."

They approached in a shallow wedge, each trusting the other to see what they missed. As they neared, letters burned faintly into the arch's lintel, rising from the stone like bruises: ADMISSION.

Rally swallowed. "Like ticket?"

"Like *truth*," Dani said.

The arch offered no handle. Only shadow.

Jake looked at the ground. At their feet, their footprints lay in ash like a paragraph that had not decided its tense. He crouched, touched the center of one of Dani's prints. The ash collapsed and revealed stone beneath, etched with a single word: WITNESS.

He moved to his own. DEFENDANT burned there, faint but legible.

Rally stared at his. It showed two words, flickering back and forth, unwilling to choose. BOY. MAN. BOY. MAN.

He took a breath and said, steady, "Man." The ash settled. MAN remained.

The arch's shadow brightened by a tone only bone hears. The space within it felt less like a mouth and more like a throat.

Dani stepped to the threshold. Heat rolled out, not from fire, from thought. She put her hand into the dark and did not lose it. She looked back once, checked the eyes that had kept her alive this long, and nodded.

"Ready," she said.

The Deceiver's laughter had followed them this far, a thinning thread. It tugged once, twice, as if reminding them he could pull whenever he pleased. Then it went quiet, which was worse.

They went through.

The ash plain remained behind like a signature they had finally decided not to forge again.

The arch swallowed them whole.

No stone, no ash, no fire, just black. The kind of black that wasn't absence but pressure. Their footsteps vanished, no sound, no echo, no confirmation that the ground beneath them existed. The only proof of forward motion was the insistence of breath, harsh and ragged, carrying them deeper.

Then the dark relented, giving way to a chamber vast and hollow. Light dripped from the ceiling like liquid glass, pooling in thin rivulets across the floor. Each pool reflected not their faces but their deeds.

Dani stopped short. In the nearest pool she saw herself in the uniform, her nightstick slick with blood, her eyes wild. A civilian lay crumpled at her boots, faceless, nameless. The pool whispered: Necessary force.

Jake looked down. His reflection was the boy in Kabul, cradled in his lap, chest blown open, Jake whispering prayers he didn't believe in. The pool hissed: Mercy.

Rally's pool showed Jamal's face, younger than he remembered, teeth chipped, eyes bright. Jamal raised a toy gun, pointed it, laughed. The water whispered: Respect.

They tore their eyes away. The chamber stretched with dozens of pools, each one waiting to be looked at, each one ready to whisper a justification.

At the far end, a lectern rose from the stone. On it lay a single scroll. The scroll was bound with a red cord, thick as rope, knotted in a dozen places. A plaque at its base bore a single word: ADMISSION.

Dani's pulse climbed into her throat. "So that's the test."

Jake's jaw flexed. "You don't pass tests here. You survive them."

Rally licked dry lips. "What if we... don't?"

Neither answered.

They moved as a unit. Each step they took rippled the pools, voices hissing from water: Orders. Honor. Fear. Survival. The justifications grew louder, following them like a chant.

At the lectern, the scroll waited. The cord gleamed, waxy and red, as though fresh with blood.

Dani reached for it. Her hand hovered. "If I open it..."

Jake placed a hand over hers. "We open it together."

Rally's voice broke. "What if it writes itself?"

"It will," Dani said, and pulled.

The cord loosened like muscle unclenching. Knots dropped away, one after another. The scroll unfurled on its own, parchment sighing. Words appeared in black strokes as if a quill were moving, though no hand touched it.

It wrote their names.

Beneath each name, lines formed. Sentences. Not verdicts. Confessions.

- Dani Rivera, Shot without certainty. Claimed control. Carried badge heavier than truth.

- Jake Callan, Gave death the name of mercy. Accepted praise that was not his. Hid fear beneath orders.

- Rally Torres, Took a crown from a corpse. Chose respect over life. Called emptiness survival.

Rally stepped back, shaking his head. "No. No, I didn't say that. I didn't..."

"You did," the parchment answered in his own voice.

The pools all around them hissed approval. Yes. Yes. Yes.

Dani clenched her fists. The truth on the parchment burned worse than lies. Her throat hurt to read it. Yet some part of her, deep, buried, felt lighter for seeing it written.

Jake leaned over the scroll, reading his line twice. His hand twitched toward the parchment, then curled into a fist. "So what? It keeps our sins in a book and we get out?"

The parchment shifted. Fresh lines bled onto the page.

- Admitted. Not absolved.

- Admitted. Not forgiven.

- Admitted. Free to leave deeper.

The last knot of the cord dropped away. The scroll dissolved, ink scattering into the air, black motes drifting upward like ash caught in a draft.

The pools dimmed. Their whispers fell silent. The chamber shook once, like a gavel striking stone.

Then a door opened in the far wall. A thin slice of pale light.

Jake exhaled, the sound harsh. "That's it?"

"No," Dani said. Her voice was steadier than she felt. "That's the price."

They walked to the door. Rally dragged his feet until Dani caught his arm and pulled him along. At the threshold, all three looked back once. The pools lay still, mirrors gone blank. The scroll was gone. Only the plaque remained, carved with the word ADMISSION.

They stepped through.

The world changed.

They stood on a ledge above a pit the size of a stadium. The pit's floor churned with figures, thousands, maybe tens of thousands, arguing, shouting, clawing. The noise rose like a storm, every voice pleading its case. The air was thick with the stench of sweat and desperation.

"The Deceiver's Court," Jake muttered.

"No," Dani said softly. "Worse. The ones who never admitted."

Rally's face had gone white. The pit boiled with shades clinging to their excuses, their mouths open but their ears closed. Their words spiraled upward, tangling, suffocating. Above them, vultures of smoke wheeled, their wings stitched with laws that no one read.

The ledge beneath their boots shivered. From the far side of the pit, a new archway glimmered. Its lintel bore no word.

"Next step," Dani said.

Jake nodded once. Rally did not nod at all, but he moved when they did.

They began circling the pit, the roar of excuses rising around them like fire fed too much air.

Every footfall seemed to write a line in some unseen transcript; the more they moved, the more the record owned them.

The path was narrow, hacked crudely into the rock. No railing, no barrier, just a shelf the width of their shoulders. The pit yawned below, hot wind rising from the mass of bodies. The shades writhed and argued, pulling one another down, clawing for higher ground that never stayed theirs for long.

Rally hugged the wall, eyes wide. "They'll pull us in," he said, his voice trembling.

"They can't reach us," Jake muttered.

As if to prove him wrong, a shade launched upward, its body stretching on a spine of smoke, arms lengthening. Fingers clawed the edge of the path, nails clicking like knives. Dani kicked down with her boot, smashing the hand. The shade shrieked, more in indignation than pain, and fell back into the roiling mass.

"They can reach," she said flatly.

They pressed on. Every dozen yards another shade tried, leaping upward with accusations spilling from its mouth. *I was ordered! I was tricked! It wasn't me!* The words lashed like whips, stinging skin. Rally covered his ears, but the excuses found their way in regardless, digging deep, promising relief if only he'd believe them.

Halfway around, the path narrowed further, barely wide enough for one. Ahead stood a figure blocking the way. Unlike the others, this one was solid, flesh and cloth, not smoke. He wore a black robe trimmed with gold thread, his face hidden behind a mask of hammered brass. The mask had no mouth, only two slits for eyes.

"Admission accepted," the figure intoned. Its voice echoed without breath. "But not sufficient."

Jake's hand moved toward his belt, finding no weapon. "Then what?"

The figure raised a hand. In it was a set of scales, perfectly balanced though no weights sat on the plates. "Balance," it said. "The pit below, unbalanced. Your truth is only part. You must take weight from them."

The scales clinked once, impatient.

Dani stepped forward. "How?"

The figure gestured to the pit. Shades howled louder, sensing attention. "Pull one. Bear its weight. Balance, or fall with them."

Rally's stomach knotted. "You mean... we pick one of *them*? Carry it?"

The mask tilted. "Yes."

Dani's jaw tightened. She looked into the pit. A thousand eyes looked back, each promising innocence, each demanding belief. If she chose one, she'd carry its guilt. If she didn't, they'd never pass. She reached down, hand trembling.

Jake grabbed her wrist. "Not you. Me."

She glared. "Why?"

"Because I've carried ghosts before," he said simply.

He knelt, extended his arm over the edge. Shades surged upward, clawing, shrieking. He braced, grabbed one by the arm, and hauled. It came up screaming, its body thin as parchment, eyes wet and wild. The moment it hit the path, it collapsed into Jake's shadow, disappearing into him like smoke into a lung.

Jake gasped. His shoulders bowed under sudden invisible weight. His hands shook.

The masked figure lowered the scales. They tipped, wavered, then steadied at even. "Balanced," it said. The path beyond cleared. The arch glowed brighter.

They moved on, Jake limping under the unseen burden. Rally glanced at him, horrified. "What did it put in you?"

Jake's eyes were bloodshot. His jaw worked. "Excuses. All of his. They're screaming in my head."

"Can you..."

"I can carry it," Jake said, voice harsh. "Keep walking."

They reached the far arch. Its surface rippled like water waiting for a stone. The plaque above remained blank. They stepped through together.

They emerged in silence. Not ash, not fire, not voices. Silence. The kind that presses on the skull until the ears ring. The ground was smooth white stone, polished like marble. No cracks. No inscriptions. Empty.

A single chair sat in the center of the expanse. On it sat no one.

Then a voice filled the space. Calm. Cold. Familiar. It was the Deceiver, but stripped of charm, stripped of warmth. "You admit. You balance. And still you think you can leave."

The chair turned on its own. A figure appeared in it, but it was none of the forms they had seen before. It was Dani, Jake, and Rally, each in turn, faces shifting, their own voices echoing back at them.

"You," it said, "are your own judge."

The floor cracked beneath their feet. The white marble split, fragments drifting downward into endless dark. The chair rose higher, growing taller, until it loomed like a judge's bench over a courtroom.

"Last test," the voice intoned. "Convict yourselves, or remain here forever."

The choice arrived without ceremony, like a form pushed across a counter: a tiny box to check that changed everything.

The floor cracked wider beneath their feet. White marble split into shards, drifting downward into black void. The chair loomed above them like a judge's bench, immense, immovable, and on it their own faces flickered, Dani, Jake, Rally, cycling through every choice, every regret. The Deceiver's voice merged with theirs, until it was impossible to tell who accused and who defended.

"Convict yourselves," it commanded, calm as stone. "Or remain here forever."

Dani's heart thundered. She forced her boots apart, braced as though squaring for recoil. The face on the chair was hers now, but not steady. It shifted between her with a badge, her with a pistol, her bent over the boy she had shot. Her voice came from the figure, but not under her control. "You had power. You spent it on fear. You called it justice. Do you plead guilty?"

Her chest rose and fell. Her throat tasted of ash. To admit guilt meant she couldn't ever go back to who she'd been. To deny it meant she stayed here, drowned in mirrors. She swallowed and forced the words out.

"Guilty," she said.

The floor beneath her steadied. The fissures stopped spreading under her boots. Her reflection on the chair split apart, dissolved into smoke, leaving silence in her bones.

Jake's turn. The chair's face was his now, bearded, blood-smeared, eyes hollow. "You killed a boy and called it mercy. You bathed in honor that was never yours. Do you plead guilty?"

Jake's fists clenched. His breath came sharp. The weight of the shade he carried pressed harder in his chest, its excuses screaming to be heard. He forced himself to look up at his own face.

"Guilty," he said.

The shade in his chest thrashed, howling, but the word landed like an axe. The noise dulled. The floor under him solidified. The reflection's mouth closed, teeth bared, then disappeared into dust.

Rally staggered as the chair turned to him. His own face stared back: boy and man, child with chipped teeth, gangster with a pistol, king with a crown of ash. The voice was both young and old. "You took life to feel bigger. You traded

239

breath for respect. You feared nothing more than being nothing. Do you plead guilty?"

Rally shook, head snapping back and forth. His mouth opened, closed. "I…" He couldn't say it. His knees hit stone. His reflection leaned forward, mouth wide, demanding. "Guilty? Or silence?"

Dani crouched beside him. "Rally. Say it. It doesn't end you. It frees you."

His eyes brimmed, voice raw. "If I say it, then all I am is nothing."

Jake's voice was harsh. "No. If you don't say it, then that's all you'll ever be."

Rally's fists hit the ground. His voice broke. "Guilty!"

The floor steadied. The fissures sealed. His reflection screamed, a boy's scream and a man's at once, before shattering into fragments that vanished in the void.

The chamber went silent. The judge's chair dissolved into white dust, drifting upward until nothing remained but open sky.

A final arch opened before them. Its lintel bore one word only: RELEASE.

They approached together. Dani wiped sweat from her face with the back of her wrist, leaving a smear of ash. Jake staggered under the invisible weight but kept moving. Rally limped, his shoulders hunched, but his eyes clearer than before.

At the threshold, they paused. Behind them, the marble plain was whole again, untouched, as though the trial had never been. Ahead, the arch's light pulsed, cold and patient.

"Ready?" Dani asked.

Neither answered, but both nodded.

They stepped through.

The world shifted again. They stood in a narrow passage, walls of stone close on both sides. No pools, no pits, no courts. Only darkness, cool and steady, broken by a faint wind that carried forward. It smelled not of ash, not of fire, not of parchment. It smelled of earth. Real earth.

Rally let out a breath he didn't know he'd held. "Is it... over?"

Jake shook his head. "Not over. Just through."

Dani turned, looked back. The arch was gone. No door, no seam, only stone. Ahead the wind deepened, drawing them forward into something they couldn't yet name.

For the first time in what felt like forever, Dani's hand found both their shoulders. "We keep moving," she said. "Together."

They walked into the dark, and the passage swallowed them whole.

Chapter Ten: Witness in Motion

Night in the city was never dark; it was annotated.

Not lights, annotations. Notices tacked to iron railings, slips caught in the teeth of chain-link, paper birds roosting on crossbeams with clauses printed under their wings. Dani moved under the notes the way a diver moves under a ceiling of ice, aware of the thinness between breath and drowning. The Neutral District lay behind them, an abscess in the city's flank. Ahead, the lanes kinked and opened and kinked again, buildings leaning like litigants, the cobbles slick with a fine skin of ink no one had spilled yet.

They kept to the seams, gutter to alley, alley to narrow mews that smelled of damp brick and stone that had memorized arguments. The Archivist led, not because he was quickest (he wasn't) but because the city liked him. It stepped out of his way the way a court does when a clerk carries the book everyone agrees is necessary and no one wants to open.

"Left," he said softly, not looking back. "We'll take Marrow Lane."

Jake slipped in behind him, eyes doing the geometry they always did, counting sightlines, doors, ladders, the distance between cover and the nearest lie he could sell. Rally breathed too fast for a block, then throttled it down until his chest stopped advertising panic. The Defender came last, his suit shedding a slow, constant dandruff of paper lint. He looked like a man perpetually dusting off the world's shoulder.

"Marrow Lane?" Rally whispered.

"The city's old blood runs under it," the Archivist said. "It remembers where law came from before it learned handwriting."

They turned into a lane so narrow the windows leaned forward to listen. A wash-line strung overhead carried shirts of city gray, socks, a slip with a hem embroidered in tiny brass letters. The letters caught the light like notary seals and reminded Dani of the lock-shaped pin at that woman's throat. The book that was a mirror. The way their outlines had looked when the District decided to see them as less than people, more than entries.

Her left forearm prickled. She looked down. The cut she'd taken in the Precedent hall had scabbed into the word BREACH, neat as if someone had written it with a fountain pen under her skin. It didn't hurt when she flexed her wrist. It hurt when she ignored it.

The Archivist noticed without seeming to look. "It will call to its echoes," he murmured. "Gentler than a siren. More patient than hunger."

"How do we stop it?" Jake asked.

"Abeyance," the Archivist said. "A writ suspending enforcement for a set time."

"From the Temple," the Defender added helpfully, and then less helpfully: "They do a version with a ribbon if you ask."

Dani shifted her grip on the strap of her pack. "So we go to the Temple."

"Not in through the front," Jake said. He had a list of reasons and the city had more.

"Not front," the Archivist agreed. "There's a lower intake, a service passage for the Choir of Exceptions. The Temple pretends not to know it exists because the Temple cannot admit it needs exceptions at all. But the choir must rehearse somewhere."

The Defender brightened as if someone had told him today's filings were optional. "I adore rehearsal. It makes everyone honest for five minutes."

Marrow Lane opened into a little square with a statue that had been removed. The plinth remained, darker where something had stood protecting the stone from rain and judgment. A small brass plate still clung to the base, tarnished to green. The Defender bent and breathed on it, rubbing with his sleeve until letters surfaced.

"OBSOLETED MERCY," he read, pleased. "They're sentimental."

"Eyes up," Dani murmured. Blond paper birds perched on the pulley wires, heads cocked. They had quills for beaks and inked eyes. Nice work, if you forgot what they were for.

Jake followed her glance. "Notaries' pigeons."

"Ravens," the Defender corrected. "Pigeons carry bread crumbs. These carry crumbs of guilt."

They crossed the square with the absence of hurry that gets fewer questions than haste. The BREACH under Dani's skin ticked, a faint metronome in the muscle. Rally fell into step with her, not touching, aligning the way satellites align, distance maintained, gravity admitted. He kept his chin up. He'd learned posture in a room where posture was evidence; now he used it as a weapon.

A woman appeared at the far mouth of the square, pushing a cart whose wheels squealed for permission. The cart held teapots, dozens of them, each with a tag tied to its handle. She stopped as if Dani and Jake and Rally and the Defender and the Archivist had arrived for a fitting. Her hair was pinned up with pencils. A teapot's spout knocked gently as it settled.

"Restitution?" she asked in a voice pitched for counters and waiting rooms.

"We're moving," Dani said.

"Moving is a kind of restitution," the woman replied. She lifted a pot and poured into a paper cup. The liquid steamed and smelled like cloves and something medicinal. "This one is for breath. Six coins."

The Defender had a coin for every occasion and occasionally the wrong occasion. He fished out something too bright and slid it across the cart. The woman did not look at the coin. She looked at him. "Excommunicated," she said, weighing the word. "Delayed too often?"

"Just enough," he said cheerfully. "But we're paying. He paid."

The woman pushed the cup across the edge of her cart with one finger. The steam wrote the word PAUSE in the air and then didn't. Rally wrapped both hands around the heat the way a boy wraps his hands around a future he doesn't trust yet.

The Archivist bent very slightly, the way a man bows to the idea of gratitude. "We'll remember."

"You will," the woman said. "That one..." she pointed with her chin at Dani ", should forget when forgetting would help." She pushed her cart along, squeaky wheels complaining in a language that sounded like forms filled out in pencil.

"Temple," Dani said.

"Temple," Jake echoed.

They cut down Spindle Court where the doors had peepers shaped like ears and no one pretended they weren't. Beyond Spindle, the Temple District began to make its argument. It didn't announce itself with bells (yet) or spires (those came later), but with a neatness that emptied streets of litter and corners of anything that might look like refuge. The air had the smell it always had near places where people had agreed what things meant: limestone, chalk dust, the dry hush of papers cradled in drawers that opened without squeak.

"The Choir rehearses in the undercroft," the Archivist murmured. "We need the north intake door. It's painted to look like stone and has never succeeded."

"Guards?" Jake asked.

"Custodians," the Defender said with theatrical loathing. "They polish sanctity. Worse than guards. At least guards admit what they're guarding."

"Custodians," the Archivist corrected gently, "make sure the Temple forgets nothing it considers important. Which is almost everything."

They moved single file along a colonnade whose columns had been carved with vines and then sanded until the leaves looked like regrets. Paper birds watched from the cornice. One hopped to another's place and left a little fleck of ink the color of the city's sky.

Rally looked very hard at the line of light where the foundation met the paving stones, as if distance could lengthen under a stare. "We're just walking in?"

"We're witnesses," Dani said. The word still felt like a trick, a card turned that had seemed to belong to someone else until she realized she was the one holding it.

"Witnesses are admitted," the Archivist said. "What they're permitted to say once admitted is another matter."

They found the door by missing it twice. Painted to look like stone, it looked like stone in the way a mask looks like a face when you only have a second to glance. The Defender put his ear to it. He didn't look comical. He looked like a man in love with secrets and some of them in love with him back.

"Exceptions warm-ups," he breathed. "They're rehearsing 'Unless' in minor key. Efficient."

Jake drew a very small rectangle in the dust with his fingernail, then erased it. "How many?"

"Dozen," the Defender said. "And one conductor who thinks she deserves ironwork around her name in the program."

Dani pressed her palm to the door and felt nothing. No wire, no hairline tag, no precedent waiting to hum. That alone made her suspicious. "We knock?"

"Witnesses don't knock," the Archivist said. "They arrive."

He set his hand beside hers. The door considered them, then found the part of itself that wanted to present, and unlatched with a sigh that sounded like a chorus arranging their folders.

They went inside.

The undercroft was cool, and not only in temperature. Cool like polished stone that had never known skin; cool like a law before anyone tried to live under it. Arches held the ceiling up; light from grates overhead made squares on the floor where no one stepped. The Choir of Exceptions stood in a semicircle, holding folders the color of absences. Their mouths marked words silently as if the notes were what mattered and the words a courtesy.

The conductor lifted her hand. The air took a breath. "From the top," she said without turning to see them. "Unless. A-tempo. And smile with your teeth. Exceptions are a relief, not a burden."

The Choir began. Voices slid under each other and over, weaving a fabric meant to be worn by loopholes. Dani felt the music touch the BREACH under her skin and itched to scratch it. Jake stood slightly left of the center of the nearest pillar where a shadow fell and didn't think about shadows. Rally put his back against a column and tried to look like a boy who had always been where he was. The Defender shifted until his soles found the seam between two stones. He liked seams. They promised something.

The Archivist stepped forward. He did it the way a man steps into a courtroom when he isn't there to argue, only to make sure the record remains correct. The conductor's hand paused above the arc of the Choir's line. "We're closed," she said, still not turning. "Exceptions rehearse without witnesses. It keeps them honest."

"We're not here to watch," the Archivist said. "We're here to file."

She turned then. She was younger than Dani had expected, which made nothing better. The lock-shaped pin on her throat was small and very tight. Her hair had been taught to obey and did. "Who are you to file through me?"

"Archivist," he said simply. "Ledger."

Her mouth twitched around an argument too big to make with a stranger. She knew him, the way the city knew a particular bell. "You don't belong below," she said. "Archivists stay where the air smells of catalog."

"Today I carry a smell the Temple should care about," he replied. "BREACH."

Dani lifted her sleeve. The skin said it for her.

The conductor's eyes cooled further, then warmed by half a degree. "Who wrote it?"

"Precedent," Dani said. "When we walked through."

"Of course." The conductor flicked a speck of lint from the cuff of her robe with a motion that was either dismissal or prayer. "Everything here believes in consequences. Even the dust." She looked at the Archivist. "Abeyance?"

"Filed by a witness," he said.

"You?" Her gaze slid over Dani like a glove over a doorknob, polite, efficient, meant not to leave smudges. "You chose witness."

"It chose me," Dani said.

"That's not how it works." The conductor smiled without showing teeth. "But it's how it feels." She gestured with two fingers, and a boy in the second row, more shoulder than voice, with wrists still learning to be wrists, stepped forward with a folio.

"Form for Abeyance," the conductor said. "We can sing you the time if you like. One day. Two. Twelve hours if you like your hope concentrated."

"What does it cost?" Jake asked, because someone had to.

The conductor tilted her head. "Not coin." She glanced at the Defender. "Not delay. The Temple is bored with being late."

"The Temple is afraid of being late," the Defender corrected, very softly. "So it calls boredom by another name."

Her eyes might have flickered. Or the light might have hiccupped above a grate. "It costs an account," she said. "Witnesses don't pay with money. They pay by telling the truth where it hurts."

The word truth shifted the air in Dani's lungs. She looked down at her arm. BREACH looked back. "Where?"

"Here," the conductor said. "In the undercroft. Before the Choir. We will say 'Unless' at the right places and not save you where we shouldn't."

Rally shifted. Jake's voice didn't change. "What truth?"

The conductor's smile went out. "The kind that will hurt you next week if you don't say it today." She handed the folio to the Archivist. "Witness declaration. Then the petition lines. Then the hour. If you file now, we can write a day."

"A day," the Defender mused. "Enough to get very lost."

"Enough to get very done," Dani said.

The Choir stood with their folders open. The way they watched was not hungry. It was worse. It was professional.

The Archivist held the folio out. Dani didn't take it. Not yet. "If I declare," she said, "does it bind anyone else?"

"No," the conductor said. "It will hurt them for a bit." She flicked her eyes toward Jake and Rally and the Defender. "But it won't bind them. Witnesses bind themselves. That's the trick you bought with your card."

Dani took the folio. The paper had the tooth of something ready to bite. The petition lines waited with little boxes where boxes wanted a yes or no and little lines where lines wanted to be filled. Her throat went dry and then remembered how to be wet again.

"What if I tell it wrong?" she asked, hating the thinness in her voice.

"You can't," the conductor said. "That's the price."

Jake's hand moved, then didn't. Rally swallowed loud enough that one of the paper birds on the grate above cocked an inked ear. The Defender adjusted his cuff with the air of a man about to watch an opera he'd chosen despite knowing he would cry.

Dani signed her name where the line believed it deserved a name. She left off her surname. The Temple would have preferred it.

The Temple didn't need it. She wrote witness in the box that asked what she was, as if a box could hold it.

"Say it," the conductor murmured, and the Choir lowered their chins, breaths gathering. "Say the thing that is true and yours."

Dani closed her eyes and saw the book that had not opened. The lock-shaped pin. The boy's marble hand thrown forward in DISSENT. The blue strip Jake had set down on a bench. The way the District had wanted to write them into entries until they were only their worst verbs.

"I promised someone something I can't pay," she said. The words came out thinner than courage and truer. "I promised I would come back with him alive."

The Choir inhaled like a tide decides to change. "Unless," they sang, one word, a cup held out.

"Unless I can't," Dani said. "Unless keeping him alive kills the rest of us."

The word felt like treason in her mouth. It felt like relief too, which only made it worse. She expected the room to dislike her. The room didn't change. Rooms like this had filed worse.

The conductor nodded, almost kind. "Good," she said. "Now we can write your time."

She snapped her fingers; a clerk, no chain, only a ribbon around her wrist with the Temple's seal that left no mark, brought a pen.

"We need more than a day," Jake said.

"You need less than a lifetime," the conductor replied. "Everyone does. A day will do if you plan."

"Plan," the Defender said dreamily. "I have a very good one and a terrible one. The terrible one is fun."

"We'll take the good one," Dani said.

"For now," he agreed.

The Archivist watched the pen set the line that would hold the day as if watching rain write in dust. "Once it's written," he said, "we go to the Scriptorium of Binding."

"You'll need to," the conductor said. "Abeyance is a towel over a bleeding wound. The Scriptorium gives stitches."

"And scars," the Defender added. "They do lovely scars. Very legible."

"We're witnesses," Dani said. "We go where we can go." She looked at the conductor. "What happens when the day ends and we haven't stitched?"

The conductor's face did not change. "You'll learn another meaning for 'summary judgment.'"

The Choir exhaled together, and the word unless settled back into the bones of the undercroft like a tool put away. The conductor closed the folio and pressed a small wafer of metal to it. The metal looked like a coin and bore no mark. Dani felt it click against her palm, coolness seeping outward the way water does on skin.

"Carry that," the conductor said. "It tells the Temple to wait. It will not speak to Enforcers; they don't listen to anything but boots. Don't show it unless you must."

"How will they know?" Rally asked.

"They always know," the Defender said. "They just pretend they don't until it makes for better theater."

The conductor's mouth might have been about to try on a smile and then remembered where she was. "Go," she said. "Take the long aisle, left of the old bookcases. Custodians like the short one. It makes them feel effective."

They went.

The Archivist lifted his head slightly. "The Temple's hymn," he murmured, as though announcing a verdict.

The Choir intoned the ancient refrain, their voices flat with discipline rather than devotion:

"Unless the scales are balanced,
Unless the fire is clean,
No soul may cross the threshold,

No wrong may go unseen."

Then, almost as if in afterthought, they sang it again, softer, like a blessing meant for people they would never know. The long aisle was indeed long. The floor had been worn by processions with good shoes. Dani's steps fell into a rhythm she did not like. She carried the wafer and felt time ride in her pocket like a very polite wolf. Jake walked so close their shoulders nearly brushed and didn't. Rally stayed on her right where he could see both her hands. The Defender hummed under his breath and stopped when the Archivist cleared his throat as if clearing a page.

They reached a stair that went up to a door that did not pretend to be anything but a door. Outside, the Temple's morning had woken ahead of the sky. Bells began a conversation, one answering another, some agreeing, some filing exceptions, some appealing. The sound mapped the city for people who could hear maps.

"Scriptorium," the Archivist said. "We shouldn't be late."

"We're abeyanced," the Defender said. "We're not late until late takes interest."

They moved along a terrace rimmed with stone that had not been made to lean against. Custodians passed with brushes, polishing air. One glanced at Dani's sleeve, the faint shine where BREACH hid under her skin. His gaze paused, filed it, and moved on. The wafer in her pocket was a weight against panic.

"Down through the scholars' garden," the Archivist said, "and under the arch with the names."

"What names?" Rally asked.

"All of them," the Defender said brightly. "But only the ones people admit to."

The scholars' garden grew plants that looked like herbs and smelled like memory. Labels on sticks had been written by hands that liked small neat letters. Some of the labels faced the wrong plants on purpose. Scriptorium novices had to learn the difference between true things and the things that wrote themselves as true when no one objected.

Under the arch, the names were indeed names, thousands carved into limestone, overlapping, crowded, some in flourished hands, some printed like threats. Dani found herself scanning for her own and was ashamed of it. She didn't find it. She did find the blue of something pressed into a crack where the stone had resisted weathering. A ribbon thread. She didn't touch it. Jake saw it and not touching it too took everything he had.

The Scriptorium of Binding lived partly underground and partly in a human discomfort with uncertainty. Doors here were heavier; hinges confessed they had work. A woman at a desk looked up when they approached and then looked down again because the Archivist's ledger balanced the scale for them.

"Witness filing," he said.

"Window three," she said, "if the window admits. If not, window two pretending to be window three."

"Of course it does," the Defender murmured.

Window three was open. The clerk behind it wore spectacles that made her eyes larger without making them kinder. She had a stamp in her hand that she rolled over her palm as if warming it. "Name?" she asked without looking.

"Witness," Dani said.

"Everyone is 'witness' when it hurts," the clerk replied, but her tone turned the sentence into procedure, not cruelty. "Form?"

The conductor's folio slid under the frame. The clerk read without moving her head, as if her neck had been trained by years of looking at lines and never at faces. She set the folio aside and held out her hand. "Token."

Dani gave her the wafer. The clerk did not look at it either. She set it on a scale that had no weights, only numbers that decided what things were when they were put on them. The needle rose to an eight that meant something here. The clerk nodded as if the eight had argued its case and won.

"You have twenty-four hours," she said. "During which enforcement will not collect on the BREACH. It will, however, remember. We don't do miracles."

"We do stitches," the Defender said. "Lovely stitches."

The clerk ignored him. "If you mean to unbind the underlying instruments, you'll need a key."

"Which instrument?" Jake asked.

The clerk looked at Dani's arm as if stones were transparent today. "Promise," she said. "Left lung. Bad place to carry one; they rub."

Dani felt the room tilt a degree and corrected. "Key?"

"Your own word," the clerk said. "Given without coercion and with context. Said when no one asked for it."

"How do I do that," Dani said, "in a place where everything is a form?"

The clerk's mouth might have softened. "You don't do it in a place," she said. "You do it in a moment. We have a door for that. It opens badly."

"Perfect," the Defender said, clapping once and then apologizing to the room for clapping.

The clerk slid a pass across the counter. It was heavy little nothing, engraved with a spiral so shallow it was more suggestion than design. "Down the west stairs," she said. "Through the room full of empty chairs. Not the first door. The second, which thinks itself the first."

"Custodians?" Jake asked.

"Busy," the clerk said. "It's second-day clean. They'll be polishing inscriptions."

"Commissioners?" the Archivist asked, and the floor under the word seemed to check itself for level.

"Not if you're quick," she said.

They went. Jake scanned the shelves of bindings on the way past, vellum and leather and something that might have been made from a refusal beaten flat. The Defender dragged his fingers through the edge of a curtain of chains without touching any and somehow touched all. Rally read the wall mottoes and decided none of them were for him. Dani kept her hand on her pocket, feeling the wafer press through cloth like a small cold moon.

The west stairs curved tight as a throat. At the bottom, a room full of empty chairs waited without dust on their seats. Each chair faced a blank wall where something once hung and had been removed. The room remembered faces watching the space where authority used to be, and was better for forgetting. They crossed it, the way you cross a memory someone else tells you was yours.

The first door waited predictably where first doors wait. The second door waited where a mistake would look most like intention. Dani chose the second because she had learned how intention and mistake wore the same coat in this city. The pass dragged in her pocket as if the spiral wanted to align with something in the hinge. The door shuddered and then relented like a person taught all their life to say no who finally understood the question.

Inside, the air tasted like wet paper. The room had no furniture. It had a single mark on the floor that looked like the punctuation left by a sentence that didn't need it and could not be argued into taking it away. The walls were painted with the very faint outlines of letters and not the letters themselves, as if sound had pressed into them and left only its shape.

"Say it," the Defender whispered, as if he were in a theater and the prompter had lost the page.

"Not yet," Jake said. "We're not alone."

He was right. A boy, no, a girl of fifteen with hair cut blunt at her jaw and eyes that had been told to see too much, stood in the far corner with her hands behind her back. She wore a cloth badge at her shoulder in the shape of a page turned down at the corner.

"Witness room," she said, and the words humanized the space an inch. "I'm the reader."

"You read what?" Dani asked.

"What you say," the girl answered. "So it's not only you who heard it. That's how binding becomes less dangerous. Or more fair." She narrowed her eyes as if deciding which today was. "You have the time token. You have a filing. You have a BREACH." She nodded toward Dani's sleeve. "You have friends who keep standing closer and farther like a wave line, and that's making the room seasick."

Jake froze mid-shift. Rally froze too. The Defender put one hand dramatically to his brow. The Archivist did not move at all and thereby admitted the accusation.

"What do we say?" Dani asked.

"The thing that unhooks the promise from the organ," the girl said. "It's always a sentence people don't like hearing themselves say. Sometimes it's just a word people hate arriving at. Sometimes it's a song. If it's a song, you're in the wrong room."

Dani took a breath and made it intentional. The mark on the floor waited like the patient in a chair that barely held them.

"I promised to bring someone back alive," she said, "and if I keep it the way I said it, it will kill us. I can't keep it the way I said it."

The word can't scratched her mouth on the way out. The walls absorbed it like blotting paper. The girl nodded once. "And what can you keep?" she asked.

Dani swallowed. The wafer in her pocket felt heavier. "That I will not throw him away so I can keep something else tidy."

The girl's chin tipped. The room tilted with it. "That will do," she said, humane and brisk. "Lean down," she added to the floor, and the floor decided leaning was a kind of duty today and sloped half a degree under Dani's boots.

Heat moved along her ribs like a hand that knew where to hold without squeezing. The BREACH under her skin brightened and then dimmed, a coal decide-not-to. The wafer cooled further, a mercy the size of a fingernail.

"Bound?" Jake asked quietly.

"Unbound enough," the girl said. "You'll still be tired later."

"Later," Dani echoed, and felt the luxury of the word.

The girl looked past them toward the hall as if listening to a shoe put down two rooms away. "You should go the way you didn't come," she said. "Custodians are polishing 'Obedience' and they like the echo it makes from this door."

"The way we didn't..." Rally began, and the Defender took his shoulder like a steering wheel.

"Backward," he said. "We're witnesses. The city at least lets us break that rule elegantly."

They left the room and became people again on the far side of a door that did not admire them. The empty chairs watched them cross like polite ghosts. On the stairs, Dani's breath went shallow and then found depth. The Archivist adjusted the ledger at his elbow. Jake stole a glance at her sleeve and then at her face and decided he could do something reckless later as a treat.

They reached the corridor and the clerk with the spectacles. She stamped something they hadn't given her. "You'll hear from us at the gate called Bray," she said.

"Bray," the Defender said, delighted. "Like a donkey."

"Like a bell that refuses to be a bell," the clerk said dryly. "Go."

They went. The Temple's morning had decided to be daylight now. The bells brought their arguments to a close for the hour. The city breathed the way people breathe when they don't notice they're doing it. The wafer rode Dani's pocket. The mark on her arm itched less. Rally's shoulders were still too high. Jake's were lower than they had any right to be. The Archivist walked as if a page had been turned and he was all for it.

They crossed the scholars' garden with the names on the arch casting little lines of shadow on their faces. At the gate, a pair of Custodians polished a railing that looked a lot like a boundary. One was humming. The other was listening for whether the humming had gotten out of hand.

"Don't look guilty," the Defender told Rally.

"I am guilty," Rally muttered.

"Then look like a person who has mastered their hobby," the Defender said.

They passed the Custodians with the kind of nod that cancels the need for conversation. One of the paper birds turned its head and made a sound like a pen being uncapped. A polite threat. Nothing came of it.

They were three streets from the Temple when the city remembered it needed them for something else.

A figure in an overcoat the color of reasonable doubt stood in the crosswalk and put out a hand as if stopping traffic. He wasn't tall until your attention measured him, and then he was. He wore no chain, no pin. He wore a face that had denied a thousand petitions without ever being unfair to anyone he could respect.

"Commissioner," the Archivist said, and the ledger in his arm acquired weight.

The Commissioner's eyes moved from Dani to Jake to Rally to the Defender to the Archivist and back like a pen doing a tidy list. He did not smile. "Witness," he said to Dani, as if he'd been informed by a clerk he trusted. "You are out of the District."

"For now," Dani said.

"For now," he echoed. "It is a frivolous phrase." His gaze flicked at her sleeve and came back with an entire reading in the space between blinks. "You've abeyanced."

"Yes," the Archivist said, taking the answer out of Dani's mouth as if to save it. "Filed correctly. Signed and counter-signed. Choir heard her."

"The Choir will sing for anyone who can keep a beat," the Commissioner said. "I require a different meter." He raised his hand a fraction. The city quieted itself around the movement like a courtroom does. "State your heading."

"Bray," the Defender said immediately. "We're admirers of odd bells."

"Bray," the Commissioner repeated, and in his mouth the word acquired a history. "Of course." He looked at Dani again. "You've unhooked one of your promises. Not all."

"Not all," she said.

"Good," he said. "The city likes its stories complicated." He took a step back, which for a man like him was more permissive than a bow. "Proceed. Witness. Be seen."

He didn't move aside because men like him didn't. Space rearranged itself so he wasn't in the way. They passed him and he did not watch them, which was how she knew he would remember everything.

"What," Rally whispered, "was that?"

"Commissioner of Process," the Archivist said. "He doesn't enforce. He validates enforcement. If you imagine the difference is comforting, you haven't slept here."

The Defender shivered theatrically. "He smelled like a lecture I once had to give to a room that didn't want to pass."

Jake's mouth tugged. "You passed anyway."

"I did," the Defender said. "I was magnificent."

They cut south toward Bray, following signs that hadn't been put up by anyone with permission. The wafer grew heavier once and then light again, like a small tide had passed through it. The BREACH on Dani's arm cooled the way metal cools when the fire finally isn't interested.

Bray turned out to be a gate in a wall that didn't admit it was a wall. On one side, the city looked like itself, a little shabby, a little stubborn. On the other, it looked like itself, only two degrees truer. The gate post had a bell clapper but no bell; a rope and nothing to strike. Someone had carved a donkey on the post and then thought better of it and carved a bell over the donkey and then thought better again and sanded both until they were only suggestion.

A small woman sat on a stool beside the gate with a ledger much smaller than the Archivist's. She wore a smile that made you think of spines, the plant kind and the book kind.

"You took your time," she said. "I like people who take their time. They're the only ones who know what they're spending."

"Clerk?" the Archivist asked, though the answer was obvious.

"Keeper," she corrected. "Bray doesn't need a clerk. It needs someone who can hear when a bell is there even when there's no bell." She looked at Dani. "You have a token."

Dani handed the wafer over. The Keeper did not put it on a scale. She held it in her palm and listened to it like a shell, then nodded and handed it back. "You have until the third fall of sun," she said. "That's how Bray keeps time. It refuses hours and uses light."

"How many falls are there?" Rally asked before he could stop himself.

"Several," the Keeper said, grave as a judge and twice as amused. "Go through. Try not to promise anything on the other side unless you mean it twice."

They went through Bray. On the other side, the air smelled like rain that had considered falling in this city and changed its mind at the last minute. The street names had not been painted; they had been whispered into the corners and stuck. The people moving here did not look different, but they carried their shoulders differently, as if they had decided that shame would only be part of their posture on special occasions.

"Safe?" Rally asked.

"No," Dani said, and found herself smiling. "But better."

"Where to now?" Jake asked the Archivist.

"North Quarter," the Archivist said. "We need a book that isn't in the Temple. The Temple writes what it thinks. The Quarter writes what happens."

"The Quarter," the Defender said, happier than earlier and for worse reasons. "I have friends there who owe me, and enemies who might forgive me if I save their children from unemployment."

"Enemies," Rally said faintly.

The Defender patted his shoulder. "You'll love them. They have taste."

They headed north. The city changed under their feet again, not dramatically, but the way a language changes when you cross a border and everyone still uses the same words but means them a little better or a little worse. Notices on poles were written in chalk, not ink. Lines at counters were shorter and more likely to be people talking than people queuing. A man stood on a box and read out loud in a voice that made the word 'however' sound like a bridge and not a wall.

They crossed a canal that didn't pretend to be an aqueduct and were briefly grateful for water that didn't need to pretend. The BREACH in Dani's arm was a shadow now, not a flare. The wafer in her pocket ticked like something that had learned manners. The third fall of sun felt longer than it was. She let the feeling be a kindness and not a trick.

The Quarter met them with a street that had been two streets and decided to be three. Stalls said WHAT WE REALLY MEANT and others said WE'RE SORRY and under both were things that looked like objects, not apologies. A girl with ink on her fingers ran past with a sheaf of papers shouting "Corrections!" and people bought them the way people buy bread.

"Home," the Defender said, breathing it.

"Your friends?" Jake asked.

"The Threaders," the Defender said, as if identifying a species. "They take what's been written and show where the threads don't line up. They sell correction and the idea that correction is not the same as harm."

"Will they sell us what we need?" Dani asked.

"They'll sell us the map to it," the Defender said. "And if we're lucky, they'll forget to charge the second half."

They found the Threaders in a shop whose sign read THAT'S NOT WHAT WE MEANT and in smaller letters beneath, OR

MAYBE IT WAS. A bell rang when the door opened, the sound a little flat because it had been rung too often.

Inside, a woman with hair the color of the inside of an almond looked up from a table covered in paper sorted into the archaeology of habit. She wore a thimble on her middle finger and the thimble had a nick in it that told a story with no witnesses. She saw the Defender and smiled like a litigant who had decided to settle because a fight would take years.

"Excommunicated," she said fondly. "You owe me three drafts and a coffee."

"I brought four friends and a problem," he said, delighted, "and a coffee token I stole from a judge who never learned to drink it hot."

She clicked her tongue. "Marla Quince," she told the others without getting up. "I thread what the Temple doesn't, I cut what the Temple ties double, I mend what the city rips for sport. You're witnesses or fools or both; sit."

They sat on stools that were sturdy without promising anything. The Archivist set his ledger down with a respect it would have demanded if it could. Marla tapped it with the thimble and the ledger did not take offense. "Abeyance," she said, sniffing lightly. "Old Choir song on your fingers. Temple dust in your cuffs. Commissioner attention on your backs. You've had a morning."

"We need a book that isn't in the Temple," the Archivist said. "Binding record for a promise lodged behind the lung. Not a title page. The receipts."

Marla's mouth did something that might have been a laugh if laughter had been appropriate. "Receipts," she said. "Quarter has them. Quarter writes the footnotes the Temple won't let you attach to steps." She opened a drawer, and then another drawer inside the drawer, and then a box inside that, and took out a map drawn on paper that used to have something important written on it and now had something more important. "You'll want the Stacks under

Hallow," she said. "The way in is through an apology no one believed."

"Of course it is," the Defender murmured. "We always go through sincerity's back door."

Marla slid the map across. "That gets you in the hall outside the record room," she said. "You'll need a key for the cage. They use ordinary keys because they think nobody would dare." She glanced at the Archivist. "You have the key."

He patted the ledger. "I have the key."

Marla's eyes flicked to Dani. "You have the scars for it," she said, not unkindly. "Don't show them if you don't have to."

Dani set both hands on the table because otherwise she would have put one over the mark on her arm and she refused to be that obvious. "What will it cost?" she asked.

"Everything," Marla said sweetly. She tapped the thimble. "Or five pages in trade. Clean pages. Not stolen. Not torn from a book. You write what happened after you take what you came for. Not what you wanted to have happened. What happened."

"Witness," the Defender said, and bowed from the stool, which nearly slid out from under him. "We can do witness."

Marla pinned him with a look that had saved several men from divorces they would have won and hated winning. "You can do a version," she said. She turned back to Dani. "You can do it better if you let the boy write two of the pages."

"Rally?" Dani asked.

Rally flinched in three places he didn't notice. "I don't write."

"You do after today," Marla said. "Else the Quarter won't believe you were here." She pushed the map over again until it touched Dani's wrist. "Go before the second fall. The Stacks smell you coming if you're late."

Dani took the map. The paper was warm from Marla's hands. "Thank you," she said, and meant it.

Marla waved it away. "You'll thank me if you get out. If you don't, you won't be around to make me uncomfortable with gratitude." She tipped her head at the Defender. "Leave me the coffee token. You won't use it."

The Defender sighed extravagantly and laid down a small brass disc that made the table more polite for a second and then normal again. "I never get to keep anything fun," he complained.

"You get to keep being alive," Marla said. "It's not nothing." She showed her teeth. "Go."

They went back into the street that had become three. The sun found them between buildings and made the wafer in Dani's pocket glow without heat. The city did not pause for them. It did not scold. It watched, as it always did, for the moment when a step would become a precedent.

"Stacks under Hallow," the Archivist said. "Down by the apology."

"What apology?" Rally asked.

"The one for the flood," Jake said, reading the map the way he read threats. "They built a wall that kept the water out and the people in. When they broke the wall, they said sorry. The apology didn't hold water either."

Rally huffed a laugh despite himself. Dani let the edges of her mouth lift enough for honesty. The Defender walked the way a man walks toward a library where he once wept.

They headed for Hallow.

Hallow began where the streets remembered river. You could tell by the way the cobbles changed, their edges softened, the grout dark with silt that had learned to hold its breath. The apology lived there too, as advertised: a bronze plaque set in a wall of old brick, verdigris like tears at its corners.

WE ARE SORRY, it read in letters a little too proud to be contrite.

FOR THE WALL WE BUILT.

FOR THE WATER WE LET IN.

FOR THE PEOPLE WE KEPT INSIDE.

FOR THE ACCOUNTING WE CALLED MERCY.

Under it, in a smaller hand: WE WILL DO BETTER, entered as if the city had signed but no one could prove who held the pen.

"That's the door," the Defender said, delighted. "They hung an apology and discovered it had hinges."

"Not a joke," the Archivist said mildly. "Language is a mechanism here."

Dani ran two fingers along the edge of the plaque. The bronze was colder than the brick. Her fingertip came away green. "How does it open?"

"You read it," the Archivist said. "Not like an oath. Like a correction."

The Defender bowed toward the metal. "We are sorry," he recited, his voice losing its flourish and flattening into something almost honest. "For the wall we built..."

"... for the water we let in," the Archivist continued, and Rally found himself adding the next line before he knew he would.

"For the people we kept inside," he said, and his throat tightened because he had once, and it had been him.

Jake's voice carried the last line without warmth. "For the accounting we called mercy."

The plaque clicked once. The apology's last sentence did not want to be said by him. He said it anyway, because want didn't matter. "We will do better."

The wall unlatched, not outward, not inward, but away, as if embarrassment had learned kinematics. The opening was barely more than a seam until it wasn't. Cold air came out that smelled of ink and clay and the damp patience of basements.

"Half the city never forgave this place," the Defender said, ducking into the seam. "The other half only pretended to."

The Stacks under Hallow did not stack at first. They descended, a helical walkway down into a well of shelves that grew as they went, a throat swallowing them politely. Lamps hung from cables, not electric, not flame; they held a thin, sincere light like the light of a copy-room nobody had budgeted for but used anyway.

At each landing, a plaque: ERRATA. CLARIFICATIONS. RECEIPTS.

"Receipts," the Archivist said. "Third tier."

"Receipts for what?" Rally asked.

"For what we owed and what we pretended was owed," the Archivist answered, his palm on the ledger like a man easing a horse down stairs. "For promises and their payments."

Voices moved in the Stacks, soft as paper, real as knives. People worked down here, men and women and others who wore aprons that had never seen a kitchen, fingerless gloves gone shiny at the pads. They sorted sheets and stitched signatures and weighed little packets of words on pocket scales. No one shushed. They corrected.

A clerk with a pencil tucked through her bun stepped into their spiral. She wore a pin shaped like a comma. She looked past Dani to the ledger and nodded as if the Archivist were an old debt paying itself without argument. "Receipts cage?" she asked.

"Receipts cage," the Archivist confirmed.

"Then you'll want Sim," she said, glancing over the railing. "He's the one who knows where the cage thinks it's moved itself to. It likes to change its mind."

She cupped her hands and called down: "Sim! Ledger!"

A head popped out from a run like a ferret from a wall. Sim was older than the air and younger than the stones. He had a scar at his lip like punctuation. "Ledger," he said, the way some men said 'sir.' "Come see what your key fits today."

He led them along a catwalk toward a section whose shelves wore chain like jewelry, decorative, on purpose, the way a sign promises its own security and then a little more to compensate. The cage behind the chains was copper mesh; the lock wasn't a lock so much as a question that wanted the right answer or the right tone.

Sim gestured. "Today she's in a contralto," he said. "Yesterday, tenor. Depends how the air sits."

The Archivist set his ledger against a small pedestal that had grown there since the last time a ledger had visited. He lifted a brass tab from the book's spine, a thing that wasn't a key until it met the lock. When it did, the mesh hummed the way a kettle hums just before it commits to boiling.

"Ask correctly," Sim advised. "The cage listens to nouns. Not verbs."

The Archivist did not ask for entry. He asked for receipts. The mesh relaxed at the corners. The question unbent its hook.

Inside, a room the size of a courtroom if the court had been too embarrassed to seat a jury. Shelves ran to a ceiling someone had measured three times. Each shelf wore cards at the edge, names, instruments, dates, little diagrams that were not pictures but ways to remind the hand what it had already done.

"We're here for a binding lodged to a witness," the Archivist said softly. "A promise of return, alive."

Sim's mouth soured. "Courier's bond or defendant's pledge?"

"Witness," Dani said, the word discovering itself on her tongue again. "But it was made the way a courier makes them. Fast and without permission."

Sim spat ceremonially into his fist and rubbed his palms. "Then it went where fast things go," he said. "It caught a shelf that likes to pretend it's in a hurry." He led them to a run marked INSTR.: PLEDGE (IMPLIED). The cards had tiny red dots where the indexers had fought about whether implied could be filed next to explicit without getting ideas.

Sim trailed his fingers across the spines until a quiver passed up his forearm and into his shoulder. He stopped at a ledger half the height of a man and twice as moral. He tapped it. The book decided it wanted attention and slid an inch, then two, until it could be lifted without breaking anyone's hand.

"Receipts for promises to return," Sim muttered, reading the edge as if it were printed in a dialect that only he and the book tolerated. "Witness-lodged. Temple-adjacent. Quarter-indexed. That's a fight right there."

He set the book on a table that had not been there and opened it to the middle the way you open a door you don't own but know well. The page smelled like paper and something else, breath. Dani leaned in.

Columns: DATE, ORIGIN, SUBJECT, INSTRUMENT, WITNESS, NOTES. Names ran down the page in neat lines. Some had been crossed out and given little funerals in the margin. Some had flourished with annotations that had been corrected by kinder hands, then corrected back by hands with better handwriting.

"There," the Archivist said, touching an entry as if not to bruise it.

DATE: Day of the Flood Apology (afternoon).

ORIGIN: Temple perimeter, south gate.

SUBJECT: [Redacted by Temple / Quarter holds variant].

INSTRUMENT: Phrase (Return Alive), spoken, unregistered.

WITNESS: Initials unknown (female), accompanied by Minor (male), plus two.

NOTES: Witness carried precedence burn; subsequent abeyance possible; jurisdiction disputed.

The word Minor stung. Rally's mouth went dry. He wasn't anyone's minor anymore; he never had been, except in the ways that mattered.

"Variant?" Jake asked Sim, eyes still moving. "Quarter holds variant?"

Sim tapped the margin, where a thread had been laid into the paper and run under the ink like a vein. "Temple redacted the name. Quarter didn't. They filed it sideways so the Temple's blind catalog wouldn't find it."

"And the variant is where?" Dani asked.

269

Sim tipped his head toward a cabinet with a lock that wore the shape of a shrug. "In a drawer that thinks it's a step everyone forgot to build." He fetched a ring from his pocket, keys that didn't look like keys: a pencil stub, a washer, a folded paper star, a nail bent and unbent. He chose the nail and the lock sighed open the way men sigh when they realize they've talked themselves into the same fight again.

Inside lay a strip of paper barely wider than a ribbon. It had been written on with a pen whose nib had not liked the ink and said so, thinly.

SUBJECT: Boy carried under witness's protection. Known in Quarter as Rally.

Rally flinched. The room accepted the flinch as payment. "It's not a crime to be known," Sim said gently, hearing the noise he hadn't made. "It's a crime to be owned."

Dani touched the edge of the strip. The ink warmed, not to her finger, but to the name. The Stacks did not need lies. They needed clarity. She felt the promise behind her lung stir like a dog hearing its leash.

"How do we unbind it?" she asked. "We have abeyance for a day. I need proof the city will accept."

"Quarter accepts receipts," Sim said. "But you'll have to annotate it here and then take the annotation where the bell that isn't a bell can hear it." He meant Bray.

The Archivist slid his ledger closer. He drew the brass tab again, rotated it a quarter, and the tab became a stylus. He wrote not over the entry, but beside it, in the narrow column the Stacks had left for courage.

WITNESS DECLARES: Promise reframed to duty of care; excludes guarantee of outcome; forbids waste.

He paused. "Say the words," he told Dani.

She said them. The page took her voice like ink. The letters blackened a hair darker. The promise under her ribs burned and then cooled as if deciding it wanted to live longer than definitions.

Sim whistled through his teeth. "That'll hold here," he said. "It'll hold in Bray if you file before third fall. It won't hold in the District unless the District decides to be in a mood."

"It has moods?" Rally asked.

"Palate," Sim said. "Moods are for people. The District has tastes."

Jake's head turned slightly. The movement meant something had changed in the air. He didn't look at Dani. He looked at the dark between two runs of shelves where the light didn't land and where, for a second, the dark looked like a suit with reasonable doubt for a color.

"We have company," he murmured.

Sim swore with affection. "Citationers," he said. "They're allowed everywhere because they promise not to touch anything and then touch you."

Three figures folded out of the aisle. Not Enforcers. Not Custodians. Their coats hung straight; their hands were empty; their eyes carried the courtesy of auditors. Each wore a sash with tiny metal tags that whispered as they walked, dates, places, cases, boiled down to tokens the size of thumbnails.

"Good morning," said the first, a woman with hair tucked away like an argument she'd won. "We heard the word reframe without a petition." Her gaze found the ledger the way light finds a mirror. "Archivist. Witness. Minor. Delay merchant." Her eyelids lowered a millimeter. "And Sim, who tells the cage where to sit."

"You can hear reframes?" the Defender asked. "How intrusive."

"We hear everything that changes a verb into a noun," the Citationer said. "People don't notice when they do it. The city does." She nodded toward the receipt. "You're annotating an implied return into a duty of care."

"We are," the Archivist said, old politeness in his tone like dust not bothering anyone. "It's within Quarter practice."

"It is," she agreed. "But the subject is Temple-adjacent and District-interested." She extended a hand, palm up, not asking, offering the form of asking. "Bring it with you. We'll file in a neutral room."

"Neutral," the Defender repeated, tasting the word. "We've had enough of those for a decade."

Jake set two fingers on the table. "We have abeyance," he said. "Filed and stamped."

The Citationer's smile didn't move her mouth. "Abeyance is a courtesy extended to witnesses," she said. "Citation is the courtesy the city extends to itself."

"Meaning?" Dani asked.

"Meaning this is where your day gets small," the woman said, almost kindly.

Sim rubbed his lip. "Or," he said, "we could make a mess."

The second Citationer, a man whose cuffs had been laundered to the point of insult, sighed. "Sim," he said. "Not the index rain."

Sim's eyes gleamed. "Index rain."

He slapped his palm on a lever under the table that had not been visible until a hand that loved it reached for it. Above them, the lamps changed their minds. They brightened to proofreaders' light and then shivered, and in the shiver, cards began to slide from the edges of shelves, not to the floor, but into the air. Hundreds of index cards lifted like startled pigeons and then fell, not down, but in diagonals and eddies, spiraling. Each card carried a word, BROKEN, AMENDED, STRUCK, printed in bold, and another in faint pencil under it where a clerk had argued later.

The Citationers lifted their hands automatically to keep cards from their faces. The cards had edges sharp enough to prefer respect. The room filled with a white flurry that wasn't snow and yet made the same noise in the blood.

"Go," Sim hissed, as if he'd opened a fire door and expected flames.

Dani grabbed the strip with Rally's name and the page with the annotation. The Archivist flattened his ledger to his chest. The Defender scooped three cards out of the air and threw them at the

Citationers' feet: DELAY, DELAY, DELAY. Jake didn't throw anything. He moved for the aisle to their left because the aisle to their right was the one a man would choose if he wanted to look brave.

They ran under a storm that didn't fall. Cards kissed their cheeks and drew bright, tidy lines. The Citationers didn't shout. They didn't need to. They picked their way forward, brushing words aside like leaves, but even auditors are slower when the world is annotating itself in their eyes.

"Back stairs," Sim panted, past them and then ahead, because Sim knew his Stacks the way beekeepers know bees. "Past the misprints. Don't read them."

"Why not?" Rally asked, already reading one: JUSTCE.

"Because your brain will fix them," Sim said, "and the Stacks will take it personally."

They hit a flight of iron steps that hated shoes. The misprints lined the wall in frames, each a word with one letter awry. FATHERS became FATHOMS. PEOPLE became PEEL. LAW became SAW. Rally's vision tried to right them and felt the shelves bristle.

"Eyes on the ground," Jake said.

"Eyes on me," Dani countered, because the ground had tricks too.

They passed under a lintel that had been patched with three kinds of stone. A plaque above it read APOLOGY ANNEX. The door beyond wore normalcy like a disguise. Sim shouldered it and the door accepted the argument and let them through.

They came out in a room that had once been municipal. It had windows painted shut and radiators that had been disconnected and left in place the way museums leave bones where they find them. A long counter ran the length of the far wall. Behind it, a woman sat on a stool, knitting with string so thin it made no sense.

She looked up and took them in the way people in public jobs take in disasters: patiently, cruelly, choosing which part to address. "You made it snow," she said to Sim, not disapproving, merely acknowledging the weather.

"Index rain," he said, proud. "They love it. It confuses the magnetic fields in their heads."

She clicked her tongue. "Everyone thinks auditors are machines," she said. "They're people. That's worse." Her eyes found the strip in Dani's hand. "You got your variant."

"We annotated," Dani said. "We need Bray."

"Then you need the alley behind this building that thinks it's a courtyard," the woman said. "It opens on Bray if you apologize to the wrong wall."

"We're good at that," the Defender said.

"You're too good at that," she replied, and went back to knitting a line that might one day tie two other lines together in a way that made a pattern feel like mercy.

They cut through a door with EXIT written on it in letters the wrong size. The alley beyond smelled like wet stone and old Loctite. A stray cat looked up at them the way cats look at people who haven't earned the right to be looked at warmly and left.

"Wrong wall?" Rally asked.

"Which one doesn't deserve it?" Jake asked, already choosing.

The Defender pointed to a section where bricks had been patched with lighter brick and then painted to look like all the other bricks and had failed at both. "That one."

The Archivist spoke first, not reading, not reciting, simply saying what happened. "We shouldn't have built the wall," he said. "We shouldn't have called the ledger in our favor a kindness. We shouldn't have needed a flood to learn how to open a door."

The wall unclenched. They slid through into Bray's weather, the light with edges, the smell of almost-rain. The Keeper on her stool looked up, then back down, then up again in the sequence of someone whose ear had heard a bell that wasn't there and then had decided to honor it anyway.

"You moved quick," she said. "I like people who move quick after they take their time. It means they know what they're borrowing."

274

Dani set the annotated receipt on the edge of the Keeper's table. The strip with Rally's name she kept in her hand, not hiding it, not offering it. The Keeper held the page and listened to it. Listening, here, was more than listening. It was a way to weigh.

"Duty of care," the Keeper murmured. "Forbids waste. Excludes guarantee." She looked up. "That will do. Bray can hear that and not choke."

"What about them?" Rally asked, looking back the way they'd come.

"They don't own the bell," the Keeper said. "They just walk around ringing themselves." She slid the paper back and set a small punch on it. The punch left no hole, only a ring in the fibers that showed when you tilted it toward the light. "Stamped," she said. "Quarter will accept. Temple will pout. District will sniff. You have until third fall to make it mean something."

"Meaning?" Jake asked.

"Meaning you'll have to present the witness reading," the Keeper said. "Public. Square of Corrections. You say the thing you wrote beside the receipt where people can hear it. That makes it less easy to unwind later when you are tired and want absolution instead of accuracy."

"Public witness," the Defender said, practically giddy. "I love an audience for things that don't want one."

The Archivist's mouth did an expression he rarely wore: genuine worry. "The Square," he said. "They'll bring the Counter-Witnesses."

The Keeper nodded, unsurprised. "Of course they will. Otherwise what is the point of a square?"

Rally looked between them, then down at his fingers, ink-streaked from a card that had kissed him. "I have to write two pages," he blurted.

Dani blinked. "Now?"

"Quarter wants payment," he said, cheeks hot. "Marla said. Five pages for the map, two of them mine. If I wait, I won't write them. And then it'll be like the promise was still a promise the bad way."

The Keeper's smile was all spine again. "Sit on the curb," she said, as if telling him to sit on a throne. "Write. The Square will take your words warmer than the Stacks do."

Rally sat. The curb was not clean. It felt like a better desk than any desk had felt. He held the receipt with his left hand, because holding it made the right hand honest. He wrote. He did not write well. He wrote what happened. He wrote how he'd been the kind of boy who would do the wrong thing if someone called him by the wrong name, and how he'd kept doing it when people called him by the right one. He wrote that he had thought being carried under a witness's protection meant he wasn't walking, and how today he had walked, and how his knees still shook, and how he would walk again because he didn't like what being carried did to his spine.

He wrote until the paper had sentences and then had more sentences than that. Marla would still want three more pages, and that was fine. He tore the two sheets from the pad he had not remembered picking up and put them on the Keeper's table.

The Keeper did not read all of it. She listened to it. "Good," she said. "You wrote it like a person. Corrections hates poetry."

Rally barked a laugh that surprised him. "Me too," he said.

"Square," the Archivist said. "Before the second fall."

They set off, the city rearranging its interest around them. The wafer in Dani's pocket pulsed once and then quieted. The BREACH under her skin had become a scratch she could live with. Jake walked as if the ground were a chessboard he'd stopped believing could surprise him and had learned again that it can.

They were two streets from the Square of Corrections when the weather changed.

Not the sky; the air's attention. The papers on walls had different verbs on them now, WITNESS REQUESTED and COUNTERFILE READY. People moved the way they move when a crowd is forming, which is to say faster without admitting it.

"What's our play?" Jake asked, not looking at Dani because that's how you let a leader lead.

"Simple," Dani said. "We say it out loud. We let them say their piece. We don't ask for mercy."

The Defender sighed in theatrical bliss. "Honesty," he said, "as strategy."

"It's always strategy," the Archivist said. "It's just rarely anyone's first choice."

They reached the Square like ships make harbor, a little battered, a little amazed. The steps rose in tiers. A dais in the center held a lectern that had been scarred and sanded and scarred again. People gathered on the steps, workers with ink on their fingers, students with long pockets, mothers with baskets. The Square had a rhythm already. You didn't have to teach it how to listen.

Across from the dais stood a cluster of men and women in clean coats with clean eyes. Counter-Witnesses. They held papers too. A banner behind them read PRESERVE ORIGINAL INTENT in letters that had never been out in the weather before today.

The Keeper of Bray took her place to one side with a small book and a pencil she had bitten without shame. Marla was there as well, as if the map had come with her attendance. She lifted two fingers at Dani. They meant: pay later, speak now.

Dani stepped up. The lectern felt like a judge's bench stripped of its power and left only with its usefulness. She set the annotated receipt on it. She didn't clear her throat. She didn't need ceremony to say something true.

"I am the witness," she said. The Square accepted the noun without applause. "I promised to bring someone back alive." She let the sentence hang and felt half the city wince on behalf of the other half.

"The promise is now a duty of care," she continued, voice steady. "I don't get to waste him, or any of us, to look like a hero of my own story. I do not guarantee an outcome. I guarantee that I will not throw him away to keep anything else tidy."

Silence. Real silence. The kind that doesn't glare but expects.

The Counter-Witnesses conferred with their papers the way birds confer with wind. A man with a lapel that had held expensive pins in its day stepped forward. "If not guarantee," he said, "then what is a promise?"

"A direction," Dani said. "An obligation in motion. You know that, or you wouldn't need squares like this."

He pursed his mouth the way men purse their mouths when their argument wants teeth and they have only lips. "You weaken intention," he said. "You license failure."

"I remove theater," she said. "I forbid waste."

The Square breathed. A woman in the crowd raised a hand as if in school. "What happens to him if you fail him?" she asked. She meant the boy. She didn't say his name because brave people forget names and careful people remember them.

"I don't hand him to the District to prove I tried," Dani said. "I don't use him as precedent. I don't write him into anyone else's ledger for convenience."

The Keeper of Bray spoke without looking up from her pencil. "Filed," she said. "Stamped. Heard."

The Counter-Witness tried one more line because that was his job. "And when someone needs saving and your duty of care says not to go because your story won't be tidy?"

"Then we go anyway," Dani said. "And if we die, we die without pretending the word 'promise' kept us alive when it didn't."

The Square made a sound like consent if consent had elbows. The Keeper tore a strip from her book and set it under the receipt. The sun shifted. First fall had happened while they were talking; second would come faster if they looked at it too much.

Marla slid through the crowd to Rally and flicked his ear like an aunt. "Pages," she said. "You owe me three more later. These two will do now." She took them without reading them because she trusted the Keeper's ears.

The Archivist closed his ledger the way a man closes a wound he has dressed. Jake leaned his palms on the edge of the dais and let himself feel, briefly, something like a plan working. The Defender bowed to the Counter-Witnesses as if he were a villain in a play who knew the audience would enjoy him anyway.

Then the city, which had been very generous, remembered it was also itself.

Bells began. Not Bray. Not the Temple. A third sound, flat, unlovely, procedural. The sound law makes when it learns someone has found a gap and decides gaps are dangerous.

"Mobile jurisdiction," the Archivist said, not surprised, not pleased. "They're bringing a circle."

"In the Quarter?" Marla demanded, scandalized.

"They can't hold it," the Defender said. "They can roll it through."

Down the far street, a ring of iron advanced, men under it carrying it on their shoulders like a canopy. Inside the ring, reality already looked a degree neater. The ring had words cut into it at intervals: AUTHORITY, PROCESS, COMITY, PEACE. A circle of competence, moving. It didn't capture spaces. It captured moments.

"Under that," Jake said, jaw set, "they can take us."

"They can try," Dani said.

The Keeper tucked her pencil behind her ear and shut her book. "You made your read," she said. "You made your stamp. If they want you, they'll have to argue with the Square."

"They'll argue anyway," the Archivist said. "That's what they're for."

"Then we leave while we still mean what we said," Dani replied. "Hallow gave us receipts. Bray gave us stamp. The Square heard us. Next is getting him…" she didn't look at Rally; she didn't have to ", through this city alive without lying about what alive means."

"Fun," the Defender said, and meant it.

They left the dais as the ring drew near. Counter-Witnesses broke neatly to let the circle roll. The crowd shifted the way crowds shift when they aren't impressed but also aren't suicidal. The ring slowed as it came even with the lectern. It didn't stop. Competence never stops. It just recalculates.

"Third fall," the Keeper called after them. "Don't be late to the part of your life that matters."

They moved. The ring drifted like a moon beside them, trying to be their sky. The city made room and didn't. The receipt rustled in Dani's hand, a living paper. The wafer in her pocket cooled and knew, in its small metal way, that it had done most of what it could.

"Where?" Jake asked.

"North again," the Archivist said. "We have to fetch supplies from a place that doesn't sell anything."

"The Office of Unsolicited Aid," the Defender said cheerfully. "They keep a cupboard of miracles. They're labeled 'misc.' It's very funny if you like pain."

Rally breathed and didn't notice he had. The word WITNESS lay under his ribs the way a new muscle does, sore, useful, unwilling to sleep. Dani checked the angle of the sun against the roofs. Second fall coming. Third not far behind.

"We move," she said.

They moved, and the circle paced them, and the city waited to see whether today would be the day it forgave itself or took better notes.

The circle followed, steady, like an idea that refused to leave the room. People stepped aside for it, but not with fear; with irritation, like giving way to a cart that collected trash on a market day. Its words, AUTHORITY, PROCESS, COMITY, PEACE, cast moving shadows that bent across the cobbles, climbing walls, crossing faces. Wherever the shadows touched, the city grew momentarily more polite. Too polite. Smiles stretched thin. Quarrels froze mid-gesture and filed themselves away for later.

Jake hated it. He could smell compliance the way other men smelled blood.

"The Office is four streets north," the Archivist said. "Through the Quarter's market of favors."

"The market that sells things you didn't ask for," the Defender added, eyes bright. "It's magnificent. You'll buy six before you realize none are yours."

"Stay close," Dani ordered. Rally tucked in on her right, shadowing her stride, one hand brushing the paper folded in his jacket pocket as if to make sure it hadn't evaporated.

The Quarter's northern lanes spilled them into a square so tangled it looked like a knot tied by ten different hands. Stalls clustered under awnings patched with old petitions. Every signboard read like an offer: FORGIVENESS (LIMITED). OPINION (FREE TRIAL). RELIEF (PRE-OWNED).

Vendors called with voices trained by haggling. One tried to sell Jake an alibi ("Unworn, guaranteed to fit"), another dangled a small glass vial marked POSTPONEMENT. Jake ignored them all, eyes scanning the alleys where the ring might roll.

The circle did not enter the square. It paced along its edge, shadows lengthening. The Square of Favors bristled at its presence, as if even commerce didn't want jurisdiction looking too long at its tricks.

"There," the Archivist said, pointing past a row of stalls where lanterns burned despite daylight. A facade of stone columns leaned against itself as though bored of standing. A brass plate read: OFFICE OF UNSOLICITED AID. Below, in smaller capitals: NOTHING GUARANTEED.

The door opened before Dani touched it. A clerk stood there, small as a question no one quite dared to answer. Her spectacles magnified eyes that were not kind and not cruel, only exact.

"Filed request?" she asked.

"No," Dani said. "Unsolicited."

The clerk stepped back, allowing them in. The lobby looked like a bank stripped of money, a hall stripped of faith. Cabinets lined the walls, each labeled with odd categories: RAIN INTERRUPTED. FRIENDS ARRIVING. MERCY LATE.

"We need supplies," the Archivist said. "For travel under the third fall."

The clerk nodded once. "You'll want the Cupboard. Aisle four, end. Pick one thing. No more. No less."

They followed signs through rows of cabinets that seemed to multiply with each turn. The Cupboard stood alone at the aisle's end: a tall iron cabinet painted the color of resignation. A tag dangled from the latch: MISC.

The Defender rubbed his hands together. "Ah, the cupboard of miracles."

Jake grunted. "One thing."

Dani opened the cabinet. Inside, shelves sprawled with objects so ordinary they felt dangerous: a matchbook with one match left. A rope coiled with one knot tied. A clock with no hands. A single page torn from a ledger, blank but warm.

Rally leaned in. "How do we choose?"

The Archivist's voice was soft. "You don't. It chooses you."

Dani reached. The objects shimmered faintly, each aligning toward one hand, then repelling. Her fingers closed on the matchbook. It settled against her palm, weightless and heavy all at once.

The clerk's voice came from behind them. "That one burns only once. Burn the right thing."

Dani slipped it into her pocket beside the wafer. "We will."

The building groaned faintly. Jake's hand went to his sidearm though he knew it would be useless here. "They're outside."

The Archivist didn't argue. "The circle has the Office in its register now. If we step out, they'll claim us."

Rally looked from one to the other. "So what do we do?"

"We leave by the door they don't know about," the Defender said. He walked to the rear wall and tapped his knuckles along the plaster until it sounded more like wood. He pushed, and a panel gave way. A dark corridor slanted down.

"Basement?" Jake asked.

"Basement is too honest a word," the Defender said. "It's where the Office files things it didn't mean to help with."

They slipped inside. The wall closed.

The corridor twisted, stone wet under their boots, air thick with mildew and ink. Lamps guttered without flame, as though burning obligation instead.

At one bend, a door leaned half open. Dani glanced through and froze. The room beyond was full of chairs, rows upon rows, each occupied by a figure made of dust. Men, women, children, seated in silence, as if waiting for a verdict that had never come. A plaque above the doorway read: THOSE WE FAILED TO HELP.

"Keep walking," the Archivist murmured.

The stair slanted further down until the smell of river thickened. They emerged into a culvert running parallel to the canal. A grate overhead showed daylight flickering. Voices drifted, Citationers. The ring was close.

"Third fall soon," the Archivist said. "We must reach the next Square. The city won't forgive silence after that."

"Which Square?" Dani asked.

"Square of Motions," he replied. "Where people argue what happens next."

"Perfect," the Defender said, grinning. "My kind of square."

They hurried along the culvert, boots splashing through shallow water that glowed faintly with ink. Behind them, the circle rolled above the street, its shadows falling like bars through the grate. Ahead, a faint light widened, and the city's noise grew sharper.

They were almost out when Rally tugged Dani's sleeve. "Look."

On the culvert wall, scratched deep into the stone, words had been carved by some desperate hand: WE PROMISED AND WE LIED.

The letters glistened with wetness that wasn't water. Dani reached out, then pulled her hand back. The BREACH under her skin itched.

She looked at Jake, then at the others. "We don't stop," she said.

They didn't.

The culvert spilled them out through a grating that was more invitation than barrier. They climbed into a narrow lane where walls leaned like old men arguing. Beyond, the lane widened into steps, and the steps climbed into a plaza already alive with voices.

The Square of Motions.

It wasn't grand. No statues, no banners. Just tiers of stone benches facing each other across an open floor scratched with lines, straight, curved, overlapping like diagrams drawn by hands that couldn't agree. Each line glowed faintly, as if the arguments they had hosted still smoldered.

People filled the benches, not summoned, not waiting, but already there. The Square of Motions never stood empty. It was where the city came to argue what came next, and the city always needed something next.

As Dani led them into the plaza, the crowd shifted. Heads turned, voices bent, new lines began to glow underfoot, charting fresh contention.

"The circle is close," Jake said, scanning the arcades ringing the square. The iron ring rolled toward one entrance, its cut words, AUTHORITY, PROCESS, COMITY, PEACE, flashing in sequence like a refrain.

"They'll want to pull us into their jurisdiction mid-motion," the Archivist murmured. "If they succeed, the Square's voice is silenced."

The Defender rubbed his palms, delighted. "Then we make enough noise the Square won't shut up."

Dani didn't hesitate. She stepped to the floor's center. The lines under her boots shivered, forming a new circle, incomplete, waiting for words.

She held up the receipt, annotated, stamped, still carrying Rally's name. "Motion," she declared. "That duty of care be recognized above guarantee, that life be carried without waste, that precedent not devour the living."

The Square responded. A line blazed outward from her circle to the benches opposite. A man in a scholar's robe rose, clutching a sheaf. "Counter-motion: that a promise unfulfilled is waste by definition. Guarantees bind. Without them, words dissolve."

The crowd rumbled approval, dissent, curiosity. More lines lit.

Jake stepped forward, voice iron-flat. "Guarantees kill. They make corpses tidy so the ledger looks clean. Duty of care keeps us fighting even when we fail."

The Square hissed with overlapping voices. The lines underfoot crossed, tangled, glowed brighter.

The Citationers entered then, sliding along the benches. Their coats hung like shadows that had chosen to be fabric. "Motion irrelevant," the lead intoned. "Circle claims. Jurisdiction mobile. All arguments subordinate."

The iron ring rolled through one arch, setting its shadows across the plaza. A hush fell. Wherever the shadow touched, benches stiffened, voices dulled.

The Square resisted. Lines flared hotter, rebelling against neatness.

Dani's hand slipped into her pocket. The matchbook. One match. The clerk's warning echoed: Burn the right thing.

She struck it. Flame leapt, small, hungry, impossibly bright in the gathering dusk. She held it low, near the lines carved in stone. The fire licked them, and the Square caught.

Every line ignited, white fire racing along arguments old and new, intersections blazing like stars. The plaza filled with light not meant for human eyes, yet seen by all.

The crowd roared. Voices surged. The Square of Motions burned with its own defiance.

The iron circle shuddered. Its shadows bent and broke against the blaze. The words carved into it, AUTHORITY, PROCESS, COMITY, PEACE, warped, their neat edges blistering. The circle faltered, slowed, retreated half a pace.

The Citationers shielded their eyes, their politeness unraveling into raw anger. "Improper use of aid," one spat.

"Motion carried," the Square answered, every stone speaking at once. "Duty above guarantee. Waste forbidden. Precedent denied."

The match guttered and died. The lines dimmed, smoke rising like the exhale of something vast. The plaza quieted, but its verdict remained.

The circle rolled back, unable to press further. Its words still glowed, but less certain, like declarations whispered instead of carved. The Citationers withdrew, stiff and silent.

The Square's crowd dispersed in murmurs. Some looked at Dani with approval, some with unease, but all with recognition. A new motion had been carved into the city's bones, whether they liked it or not.

Rally stood straighter. He felt the weight of his name on the receipt lessen, not gone, not erased, but shifted. Duty now, not debt.

Jake exhaled slowly, watching the circle vanish into the distance. "Bought us time."

"Not enough," Dani said. She tucked the dead matchbook back into her pocket, lighter now, empty but not useless. Proof of what they'd done.

The Archivist closed his ledger. "Third fall approaches. The next Square waits."

The Defender smiled, weary and exhilarated. "Onward then. Until the city runs out of tricks or we run out of breath."

They left the Square of Motions as the sun dipped, its last light casting their shadows long. The city shifted again, corridors rethreading themselves, new dangers already aligning. But for the moment, they had bent the law to their survival.

And in the echo of burning lines, the city itself seemed to remember, if only briefly, that words can choose not to kill.

Chapter Eleven: Trials in the Fire

The cavern opened like a furnace mouth, heat shoving against them as if the earth itself were exhaling rage. They had left the bridge of sacrifice behind, yet the air ahead was hotter, dry as a kiln, merciless as a judge. Flames licked from fissures underfoot, tongues of orange and blue that snapped back like predators startled but not gone. The walls sweated fire. Sulfur gnawed their throats with every breath, bitter as coins dissolved into spit. A sound lived inside the stone, low and predatory, the way a building hums when it's thinking about collapse.

Jake swiped his forearm across his brow. Sweat ran anyway, stinging his eyes, carving clean tracks through soot. His training liked to call this kind of place an environment. The body disagreed. This was an adversary. He measured distance in lungfuls instead of yards and forced his breath into the square counts that had kept him human in worse rooms. "Welcome to the hard way."

Rally trembled though the heat pressed on him like an anvil. His shirt clung, salt stinging the arrow-burn carved into his arm; the shiver was bone-deep, older than heat. "Feels like... hell." The word came small and stubborn, a kid refusing to cry and doing it anyway. He tried to hide the arm, but hiding just made the pain smarter.

Dani kept her pistol up, muzzle steady despite the shimmer. She tracked corners that were curves until the heat straightened them. "Stay sharp. Nothing here is what it looks like." Her voice went flint on the edges, the tone she used when the map was now.

They moved as a unit without talking about it: Jake on point for reading ground; Dani at rear for keeping ghosts honest; Rally protected by both, center of gravity and risk and something more difficult to say. The tunnel pulsed with thunder, the floor alive under their boots like a giant's heartbeat. Sound twisted as they descended, rumbles into murmurs, murmurs back into thunder, until the air seemed to chant in a language just past hearing. Heat blurred distance; edges softened, then returned too sharp. Every step rewrote the floor's rules.

The passage yawned without warning. They stumbled into a cavern vast as a stadium, roof lost in shadow and heat haze. A river of fire cut the floor wall to wall, a molten band flowing with the convincing patience of a real river. Geysers hissed from vents, flinging up sheets of light that threw their shadows long and multiple. The firelight painted faces into the stone, grim mouths, judge's profiles, that dissolved when Dani looked straight and reassembled when she glanced aside, like memory when you tried to stare it down.

On the far bank stood creatures wrought of stone and flame. Centaurs, massive and terrible, human torsos fused with bodies of lava and basalt. Seams of magma pulsed like veins. Embers burned where their eyes should have been, steady as coals fanned by a bellows. Each clutched a black bow carved from obsidian, strung with thread the color of white heat. Arrows smoldered in their fists, heads already bright. Their discipline felt administrative, as if they had a schedule for killing.

One stepped forward. Hooves struck the scorched ground and sparks skittered. When it spoke, the voice rumbled like a landslide. "Souls who mock judgment do not leave."

As one, the others drew. Fire stretched into arrow-shapes, hissed, held. The gesture was beautiful in the way storms are beautiful, pattern inside violence.

"Down!" Jake barked.

They split. A storm of fire ripped the air. Dani dove right, dragging Rally with her; a searing hiss scythed past, kissing his sleeve and the skin beneath. He screamed, short and raw. Smoke curled off cloth. The stink of scorched cotton and meat hit hard.

Jake rolled behind a boulder barely big enough to matter. A second volley fractured against stone, heat slamming him like an oven door kicked open. His teeth rattled. He peeked past cover. The centaurs advanced in a measured line, no hurry, no panic, things that had been law long enough to be bored by it.

Jake's mind shifted into survival calculus. Wind direction, footing, Rally's slowing pace, all variables. "Dani! Left flank distraction. I'll take bridge."

She understood instantly. Sliding low, she fired not at the centaurs, but at vents erupting along the cavern walls. Steam and sparks exploded, masking their silhouettes. Jake grabbed a shard of fused glass, sharp enough to cut his palm, and hurled it. The chunk struck a centaur's knee joint, cracking the lava seam. The creature bellowed, staggered, then righted, angrier.

"Move!" Jake roared, charging toward the narrow bridge that spanned the fire river. He vaulted onto it, ducking an arrow that hissed past his scalp. The chain hand-rails burned his skin, but he dragged them forward anyway. "Dani! Now!"

She hauled Rally across, firing in disciplined bursts. Arrows screamed past, one burying itself in the stone at Jake's feet and glowing red-hot. He kicked it into the fire river. The centaurs pressed forward, hooves hammering, sparks spraying with each step. Their formation was relentless, but the team reached the opposite archway in time.

The centaurs stopped at the riverbank, their ember eyes fixed. One raised its bow skyward and loosed an arrow. It vanished into the ceiling. A moment later, stone thundered loose and fell in sheets. Dust boiled, choking them as they fled into the next tunnel.

The tunnel narrowed, forcing single file. Heat clawed every breath. Dani propped Rally against the wall and tore back his sleeve. His arm blistered, fluid seeping. She wrapped it fast, but her hands trembled at the memory of Chicago, the boy she hadn't saved and the sound the world made afterward.

"Don't," Jake warned softly, seeing it in her eyes.

"I'm not," she lied.

They pressed on until the walls became glass, slick and fractured. Every pane whispered heat like a hidden forge. The passage spat them onto a plain of broken glass that stretched to a horizon blurred by fire haze.

The voices came almost immediately. Whispered, tailored, cruel. Dani heard accusations of murder, Jake of calculated betrayal, Rally of fratricide. The voices insinuated themselves into the rhythm of their steps. Rally stumbled. "Make them stop," he begged.

"Noise," Jake said flatly, but his jaw clenched.

They marched across an endless glass desert, each crack exhaling both flame and venomous memory. Dani lashed Rally forward, repeating, "Eyes on me, not them." The whispers shifted sweeter, promising forgiveness if they surrendered. Sweat poured. Their boots stuck in softened seams. Each step forward cost more than the last.

At a ridge where the glass bulged like a spine, heat doubled. Voices sharpened into knives. Rally collapsed to his knees, weeping that he could see Jamal's grin just ahead. Jake and Dani dragged him upright, steel in their voices, denying the lies. The horizon stayed dishonest.

They walked until the muscles in their arches shook and the canteens lied about their weight. Jake marked safe panes with his knife, X after X, because procedure is a kind of mercy when belief is thin. Dani's boot sole separated; she wired it tight, fingers moving by memory. Rally counted breaths because numbers were the only words the voices didn't try to borrow.

The whispers adjusted, praising their endurance as if endurance were the real sin. Yes, keep moving. Drag your shame with you. That's all you're good for.

Jake ignored them. Dani did too. Rally tried, and his lips moved as though he were chewing stones. Each breath pulled fire into his chest, each step demanded belief he didn't have.

They reached a broad plate of glass fogged by trapped bubbles, the panes buckled and crazed with lightning-shaped cracks. Heat shimmered in curtains. Through the ripples, figures seemed to walk beside them, mirage doubles, a step out of sync. One of Dani's shadows turned its head to look at her when she didn't. She refused the invitation; attention is a kind of permission here.

Rally slowed, drawn toward a darker swirl inside the pane, a memory pulled like a coin from a pocket. He saw Jamal as if through water, hair plastered to his forehead after a run, breath coming in delighted bursts. The image smiled and lifted its hand in apology, as if the past could be rewritten with a gesture. Dani caught Rally's elbow and steered him hard. "Not yours," she said. "Not now."

The plain rose by inches into a tilt that punished calves. The voices found new registers: not accusation, not praise, but administrative patience. They spoke like clerks explaining procedures. To Jake: You chose operators and outputs. Your friend was a rounding error. To Dani: You called it a clean shot. The ledger still shows a child. To Rally: You practiced being seen until you pushed someone else out of the picture.

Jake's answer was a pace that never faltered, though the ligaments in his knees complained with each thrust forward. Dani's was a single word breathed on repeat between clenched teeth: "No." Rally's answer was to name, under his breath, the streets he and Jamal had run, Garden, Price, Ironhook, Mint, like laying planks across a gap one by one.

A section of glass flexed and refused to rebound. Jake tested it with the flat of his hand and pulled back as a hairline raced out like frost in reverse.

"Hard right," he said.

They angled toward a seam where two plates kissed. Heat gouted up between them, bright enough to scorch hair from shins. They leaped it, one by one. The seam hissed like something disappointed to be denied its due.

They found an island, a heaved hexagon jutted half a foot above the surrounding panes, its surface pebbled and opaque. The air over it shimmered less. Dani eased Rally onto it and stood guard, watching the heat distortions for motion that wasn't theirs.

Jake squatted, palms on thighs, breathing through his nose, counting square. Four in, hold four, four out, hold four. The counts had saved him in rooms with windows too high to touch and in alleys that narrowed into fists. They would save him here.

Rally stared at his boots. "I hear him when it gets quiet," he said, voice thin. "Not the voices. Him."

"Then we don't give quiet to him," Dani answered. "We give it to ourselves." She nodded toward Jake's square breath. "Borrow his metronome."

Rally tried. The first four counts snarled. The second set found edges. By the third, his shoulders dropped half an inch.

"Good," Jake said without looking up.

A ripple moved through the glass, a slow pulse like the plain itself taking a breath. Far ahead, the horizon did a small dishonest trick, lurched nearer, then snapped back to where it had been pretending to be. The plain wanted them to spend themselves on impatience.

"Up," Jake said, and they left the island.

They angled toward a less fractured field where the panes had cooled thicker, the bubbles smaller and more evenly spaced. Dani ran fingers along the knife-scratched Xs Jake left behind, little tacks of insistence in a place that wanted to smooth everything out to forgetfulness.

When the next assault came, it wore kindness. The voices turned warm, conversational. They offered amnesty with signatures already forged. To Dani: You did what the job asked. Sign here and the ledger zeros. To Jake: You made the only call. Put your initials and we'll call it mercy. To Rally: You were only ever trying to belong. Agree and the city will call it an accident.

"Refuse the premise," Jake said, nearly soundless.

Dani smiled without humor. "I was planning to insult the clerk."

"Save it," Jake said. "Insults get filed."

They climbed another low spine. The heat gathered at its crest like breath held. When they stepped down, the temperature dropped a fractional degree and the relief felt like a drug. It scared Dani how much she wanted more of it. Want is a handle the place can use.

Rally slipped. His boot skidded along a pane gone slick with condensing vapor. He windmilled, found the chain of Dani's forearm, and steadied. "Sorry," he said.

"Don't be sorry," she said. "Be here."

He nodded. "Here," he echoed, like a word you practice until it fits your mouth.

Past the next seam, the plain changed grain. The glass lost its pebbled tooth and went polished, almost mirror. Their reflections walked beneath their feet in shattered strips, faces stretched by imperfection. Jake's mouth looked crueler down there, Dani's eyes more tired, Rally's shoulders narrower. The reflections began to speak a half-beat out of sync, mouthing versions of their words that bent toward self-contempt.

"Don't look," Dani said. "Let them fail alone."

They didn't look. They counted steps and cuts and safe panes and breaths. The reflections went on talking, deprived of audience, and grew hoarse.

A wall of heat hit, one of the vents exhaled deep. The blast tried to push them back. Jake leaned into it like into weather. "Two more minutes of this," he said. "Then it breaks." He was right. The vent sighed itself empty and the plain stilled to the old murderous calm.

Far off, a line appeared where the glass ended against darkness. They didn't trust it at first. Distance lies here. But with each dozen paces, the line steadied into a cliff edge. The voices grew intent, sensing a limit to their jurisdiction.

They gathered every tactic they had and spent them all: square breath; counting; anger domesticated into stubbornness; the soft discipline of not answering insults; the humor that doesn't show on a face but keeps feet moving. They spent, and the edge came.

The glass plain ended in a bite out of the world. Blackness opened, breathing up heat from some furnace below. Across it hung a bridge of chain, two massive cables strung between rock mouths, with scorched planks slatted between. The whole thing swayed, slow, as if caught in the breath of something sleeping.

Shapes crouched on the span, hunched and waiting. Wings tucked. Teeth bared. Eyes banked like coals.

"Only the guiltless cross whole," one rasped, delight already in it.

"None of us are that," Dani said.

"Then we run the lie," Jake answered, mouth a hard line.

Rally's throat bobbed. "I can't…"

"You can," Dani said, and put his hand on the chain where her hand already was. "Both hands. Eyes on me."

Jake stepped onto the first plank. It groaned. The cables thrummed, a low chord. He didn't look down. A wind rose from the pit, sulfur and old, and pushed the bridge sideways. He rode the sway and took the next plank.

Rally followed, breathing the square counts out loud now like a spell. Dani came last, pistol out, the iron cold in her hand a good anchor.

Halfway, the demons moved. Wings snapped open in black sheets. One dropped to the slats, talons sinking with a hiss. The whole span kicked, bouncing Jake's knees. "The guilty walk heavy," it purred. "You will break the bridge yourselves."

Another swept past Dani so close she felt the vacuum of its wing. She fired. Smoke tore, the shape tore, then re-knit, laughing without breath.

Claws raked sparks from chain. Jake ducked and drove an elbow into a demon's throat. It weighed nothing until it weighed everything and then nothing again. The bridge lurched. Rally screamed as his foot slid off a half-charred plank into open air. Jake caught him by the strap and yanked him back so hard his shoulder popped.

The nearest demon leaned close, heatless breath like rotten silk. "Weakest link," it whispered into Rally's ear. "Let go. End the noise."

"Shut up!" Rally shrieked, and for a heartbeat his voice was two voices.

His eyes went black.

He turned, hands finding Jake's throat and driving him into the side chain. The grip was iron. The voice that came out of his mouth was layered and wrong. "He begged me long ago. I only waited."

"Don't, shoot him!" Jake rasped, clawing at fingers that did not feel like Rally's.

Dani's gun sight climbed from chest to head, dropped, climbed. "Rally! Fight him!" she shouted. "You hear me? Fight!"

For one second, human eyes looked out. "Dani," he said, and then drowned.

She fired not at him but at the chain overhead. The shot slammed shock through the cables. The Deceiver's hold slipped by the width of a breath. Jake wrenched free, hammered a fist into Rally's shoulder, and shoved him forward. The bridge toppled into a new sway. Demons shrieked and dove. Claws ripped planks free; wood and shadow fell together into the red below.

They ran. Running was a choice you make with a whole body, even when that body is a ledger mostly of pain. Jake hauled, Dani drove, Rally stumbled between them, eyes clearing, then fogging, then clearing again as if each second were a verdict argued and barely won.

The chain wailed like an animal. Links groaned. Behind them, the span began to eat itself, planks tearing loose, cable strands popping like old stitches. One demon clung and laughed; Dani slammed her shoulder into it and her muzzle into its grin and fired until the grin exploded into cinders.

The far ledge came near enough to deserve the word. Jake threw himself, caught stone with both hands, dragged his weight up with a noise he would never make again if he could help it. Dani shoved Rally ahead and then flung her own body after them as the last third of the bridge ripped loose and twisted away into the furnace.

They lay panting on the rock, ears opening to a new sound: wind that hadn't learned policy yet. The laughter faded down the pit like a promise filed for later.

Rally curled around his hands. "He wanted me to kill you," he said to the stone. "He was inside my mouth. I could feel the words before I said them."

"He doesn't get the lease," Jake croaked, rolling to spit blood. "We evicted him."

"For now," Dani said, binding Rally's arm again with cloth that hissed when rain from somewhere above touched it. "We move while he reorganizes his lies."

They stood into a climb that had no kindness in it. Steps hewn without rhythm broke their stride on purpose. Niches held faces in ash under words that wanted to become definitions: ADMIT. DENY. DELAY. APPEAL. WASTE. Rally slowed at the last. "It's right," he said.

"It's bait," Jake said. "And even if it weren't, it doesn't get your knees."

They passed into a long cut of corridor where a column rose with BREATH carved into it. A draft slid down from a fracture above and moved around them like a clerk considering a petition.

The voice that came from the stone had the sigh of paper. "State what you carry. State what you release. Pass with your breath or turn with your feet."

Dani: "I carry duty. I release guarantee."

Jake: "I carry cost. I release the math that makes people numbers."

Rally: "I carry him. I release letting him steer."

The draft exhaled. The corridor brightened by a fraction. "Pass," the voice said, bored with its own mercy.

They went through, into air that smelled like rain choosing where to fall. The ceiling opened by degrees into a jagged mouth that showed a sliver of gray sky. Wind came in honest and cold, lifting hair, making steam run sideways. For a long half-minute, none of them spoke. They let the weather write its small blessings on their faces.

"We don't stop long," Jake said at last, still hoarse, not unkind. "He's behind us."

"Quieter," Rally said. "Like shouting from another room."

"Then we shut the door," Dani answered, and tightened the binding on his arm while the rain inked faint lines down her wrists like signatures of survival.

They stood. They moved. The stone angled toward the world.

The ceiling split jagged and showed a bruise-colored sky. Wind poured in, cold enough to sting, and the first threads of rain found their faces and stitched them back into the idea of breathing. The drops hissed where they hit hot stone. Steam rose in animal shapes and then unmade themselves.

For a few breaths they simply stood there and let the weather write on them. Jake tilted his bruised throat to the open sky, accepting the small sting the way a man accepts a long overdue apology. Dani kept her gun in her hand but lowered the muzzle, face slackening as if the muscles that held vigilance had finally been permitted to fail for a count of four. Rally made a small sound, shock, relief, grief, all of it, then clamped his jaw and swallowed because the sound didn't help them move.

They crossed the gallery where the rock flattened into a lip just under the world's skin. Below, the city sprawled in grays and smeared neon, trams hissing like snakes over wet rails. Rooftops looked hammered from tin, alleys ran like ink. The Quarter crouched, its narrow-boned buildings making a map of corners where truth went to change clothes.

"We could disappear in that," Dani said. She didn't mean it, and Jake heard that.

"Disappearing's still a shape," he said. "He knows ours."

Rally dragged his bandaged arm tight to his ribs. The cloth had gone dark and glossy with rain and blood. "I don't want to disappear," he said, quiet as a promise made only to test if it could survive air. "I want to be seen and not die from it."

"You will," Dani told him, eyes still on the city. "Both."

They moved when the rain thickened from threads to sheets. The cut in the ceiling widened by the width of a heartbeat and then refused to give any more. The ledge sloped to a staircase hacked into the rock by hands that did not admire human stride. The steps were slick, the rise too mean. They counted out loud because rhythm was the rope you hold when the cliff wants you.

The staircase spit them into a culvert that smelled of iron, mold, and every decision the city had been forced to make and then dumped. Water clattered through grates clogged with leaves, then laughed once when it found a way through. Dani led them along the culvert wall with her free hand riding the rough stone; Jake ranged a step ahead when the tunnel narrowed; Rally kept between them like a secret they had decided to keep anyway.

The culvert mouth opened into a service lane no map bothered to name. Puddles held neon as if hoarding it for better days. A tram rattled a block away and the vibration arrived under their boots like distant thunder retold by cheap stone. Jake lifted his chin toward the market. Dani nodded. They moved in wedge again, because formation was a way to say no to chaos.

A food stall still steamed despite the rain, its owner pretending not to see the marks on Jake's throat or the boy's bandage. Dani bought a cheap scarf the color of streetlight and wound it around Rally's head to break the geometry of his pain. Jake bought three bowls of noodles with coins that looked too clean for the lane. They ate standing, heads bowed, letting heat shock their mouths into remembering the alphabet for hunger. The owner didn't look up. That was a kindness that would never put its hand out to be paid.

When they moved again, they looked for the signal the Keeper had promised: a waxed clinic sign with one letter miswired. Two short pulses, one long. The wrongness winked through rain exactly where it was supposed to be, though the street around it had changed the way streets do when no one with power walks them. Dani's mouth tilted. "Left alley, second door."

Rally started counting birds under his breath, kite, crow, swallow, gull, wren, as if each name were a plank laid across the gap between here and whatever came next. When the list ran out he started again, adding the liars among birds, the ones that thrive near

302

people: starling, jay. His voice steadied. Dani touched his shoulder without looking.

At the alley's mouth a boy glanced up the way children who have been told to unsee still see long enough to hate themselves for it. He dropped his eyes the second their gazes met. Dani moved them past without slowing, the urge to hand the boy a different life a hot ache she couldn't afford.

The door they wanted was wood swollen by years of storms. Jake knocked in a rhythm older than this street, older than Rally. Bolts walked back into themselves. Someone on the other side inhaled as if the air contained the truth and they were preparing to weigh it.

"Late," a voice like paper said. The Keeper opened the door as far as he needed to and then no further.

"Long story," Dani replied.

"It always is," he said, turning without ceremony.

Inside, the air smelled of ink, damp stone, and oil. Shelves climbed walls and wobbled under ledgers bound in cracked hide. Scrolls slept in bundles tied with brown string that had been knotted by hands that knew rope's real work. A desk sagged under maps: black routes, red Xs where safety had lost arguments. A lantern guttered, throwing their shadows across everything as if the building wanted to check the fit of them before deciding to keep them.

The Keeper looked smaller than his reputation and larger than his bones. Pale eyes. Cheeks hollowed by years that had made a ledger out of his face. He took in the bruise strangling Jake's throat, the way Rally leaned against a shelf as if shelves were made for people, the gun at rest in Dani's hand. "Compromised," he said, almost tenderly. "But not broken."

"Not yet," Jake said. His voice came sanded farther down than before.

The Keeper's fingers drifted over the map and stopped at a quadrant near the river. "The breach is here," he said. "Growing. If it takes the quarter, the city becomes your glass plain. Every street will give you back your face with a mouth full of accusations. Every bridge will be the bridge you crossed. The Enforcers won't matter because the rules will have changed."

Rally said, "If we close it?" and didn't sound like he believed the word close meant anything permanent.

"Then the city has a chance to remain a city," the Keeper said. "And you have a chance to remain yourselves."

Dani felt the tiredness in her bones moving around to see what it could steal. She set the bowl of it aside by force. "What do you need?"

"First, for you to eat," he said. "Then for you to listen." He gestured and a runner slid in from a side corridor with bread that had hardened into a moral and a pot of stew that tried to soften it. The runner didn't look at their hands either. Someone had trained the whole house to that particular kindness.

They ate because the body likes to be asked to live. Rally's hands shook only at the start, then steadied as the heat argued with the rain inside him and won a temporary ceasefire. Dani found she was hungrier than she had admitted to herself. Jake chewed as if the act were a contract he meant to honor.

When the bowls were empty, the Keeper rolled a fresh sheet across the desk. Symbols clustered like starlings around a single word the ink made too heavy: BREACH. He circled it only once. "It widens when the city lies to itself," he said. "When it bargains for safety by throwing small truths out of windows. The Deceiver is not just a creature, he is a method. If you reach the breach with yourselves unfractured enough to refuse his method, you can force it smaller. If you do not, you will feed it."

Jake rested his fingers on the desk's edge as if he were testing whether it would hold the next weight. "What waits there?"

"The thing that borrowed him," the Keeper said, and finally looked straight at Rally because looking at wounds is part of mending them. "And everything it has learned since."

Rally lowered his eyes. "He wants me because I'm easy."

"He wants you because you're human," the Keeper said. "Easy and human are not the same thing."

Dani touched the back of Rally's hand with a knuckle. He didn't pull away. She spoke to the Keeper without looking up. "We'll go. Give us the path."

The Keeper's hand drifted from the map to a narrow drawer. He drew out a metal tag on a length of cord, stamped with a sigil that looked like an alphabet that had refused to become letters. "Wear this," he said, handing it to Rally. "It won't keep him out. It will make him late."

Rally's mouth twitched. "Late is something." He looped the cord over his head. The tag lay against his sternum, cold and honest the way some kinds of fear are.

"Second," the Keeper said, looking to Dani now, "there's a woman at the river called Gray Isla. If the breach spills, her boat becomes a door he can use. She will pretend not to know that. She will call it business."

Dani nodded. "We convince her otherwise."

"You convince her to tie off her boat with a knot she can't untie alone," he said. "If she asks the price, tell her it's the fact she'll still have a river when the rain stops."

"And third?" Jake asked, because there is always a third.

"Third," the Keeper said, and for the first time his voice softened around something like hope, "you remember what brought you out of the fire. Not the plan. Not my map. Each other." He met each of their eyes, leaving his longest on Rally. "The Deceiver is a soloist. You beat him as a choir."

Silence tried to lay itself over the room. The rain on the stone made a different case. Somewhere above, a tram's brake squealed like something refusing to let go. The Keeper watched the sound pass through them and measured who they were after it went.

"Rest ten minutes," he said. "No more. He is not sleeping."

They found a corner against the shelves where paper had softened to the idea of cloth. Dani leaned her head back and let her body feel all the weight at once so she could set it down deliberately. Jake stood because standing hurt less than trying to rise again. Rally closed his eyes and counted birds until the names became a field he could lie in.

He felt it before he saw it, pressure in his chest as if a hand were testing the door. He opened his eyes to the room looking longer and thinner. The edges of shelves seemed sharper; the Keeper's lantern flapped its shadow like a startled bird. He didn't say anything because the first deception is always that saying it makes it real. The second is that not saying it keeps it from being so.

Jake was already moving. "He's at the lock," he said. Dani's hand found her pistol without the rest of her moving. The Keeper's expression did not change; only his eyes sharpened until the whites were gone.

Rally breathed square. The tag on his chest felt like someone else's coin. He said aloud, to make the room a witness, "You do not get me cheap."

The pressure eased, then came back twice as clever. It found the memory of Jamal and pressed on it as if it were a bruise that would say yes to anything. The gallery wind returned in his head, a laugh stitched to it. Rally began to shake. Dani put her palm flat against his sternum over the metal. "Here," she said. The word had weight because she was where she said she was.

Jake looked to the Keeper. "We can't wait," he said. "Tell us the rest on the run."

The Keeper's mouth almost smiled. "Good," he said. "It's a long story and the city prefers its stories moving." He swept up the map and rolled it tight, tied it with the same brown string that held old truths. He slid it into Dani's pack himself, an old man's hand trusting a younger one not because he believed in youth but because he liked the odds better than the alternative.

They left the way they came, the door swallowing them into rain that had found a harder voice. The alley had filled to the ankles. The boy who had unlooked was gone, replaced by runoff carrying onion skins and paper promises toward drains that would lie about their capacity until they failed. The city had a way of demonstrating its metaphors without asking for applause.

They moved uphill first to buy a line of sight, then cut down toward the river along a ribbon of street that sold parts for machines no one had repaired officially in years. Through the dirty windows, men with clean hands traded money for functions. Dani kept them to the sides of trucks that had forgotten their own plates. Twice she stopped them with a touch that said patrol and twice she was right. Enforcers moved past like men pretending they'd fallen in love with a rule.

Rally's legs had turned to arguments; he countered with stubbornness. Jake's throat burned each time he had to look up to scan. Dani's hands had begun to tremble, and she let them, because stopping tremble is energy wasted unless you're shooting.

They reached the rim of the river quarter where stone met water in a line the map had turned into something polite. In life it was a teeth edge. Barges hunched under tarps. A chain dragged against a bollard in a rhythm that made thieves think of sleep. Rain hammered water until the water forgot the shape it usually wore.

Gray Isla's boat was easy to find because it behaved like a citizen. It was tied too neatly, its deck swept despite the weather. A woman stood under a canvas that had resigned itself to being a suggestion. She wore a coat that had been mended more often than it had been owned. Her face was spare and alert in the way of people who can pinch out a candle with wet fingers.

"You're early for the ferry that doesn't run," she said when they were still a dozen steps away.

"We're late for the thing that will use your boat if you let it," Dani said. "Tie her with a knot you can't untie alone."

Gray Isla looked them up and down and revised half her opinions before the second blink. "Price?" she asked.

"That there's still a river when this storm remembers what it is," Dani said. "And that your name still means the thing it used to."

Gray Isla made a face that suggested she had retired the idea of her name meaning anything a decade ago and kept it anyway out of habit. She nodded once, turned, and began looping line in a way that would require three hands from three different people to free in a hurry. Jake watched her knots with the quiet respect of a man who believes in skill more than he believes in declarations. Rally stared at the water and told himself that the churn was only weather and not some larger thing boiling.

"You brought the metal," Gray Isla said over her shoulder without looking. "I can hear it. Whoever gave it to you wants you to keep breathing."

Rally touched the tag. "He does."

"Then take your breathing somewhere else," she said, but there was no cruelty in it. Only a tired knowledge that air is a commodity too.

They moved on along the river's lip until the water's sound changed. It deepened, lost the chatter of rain on surface, picked up a bass note that belonged to stone. The Keeper's map slid in Dani's pack like it wanted to be consulted. She didn't take it out. The city had colored the path in more reliable ink: trash stopped against a grate in a pattern that meant undertow; a lamppost vibrating at a frequency you felt in your bones; the way the stray dogs had chosen not to sleep under a certain overhang despite it being the driest.

"There," Jake said. He pointed to a set of stairs that went down into a service tunnel. Water sluiced along the cut, but the center tread was still visible. The tunnel was mouth-black. The air from it carried a smell like pennies sucked by an old god.

Rally paled. "I know that smell," he said.

"Yes," Dani said. "And we walk into it anyway." She put her hand on his spine and pushed gently. He went because he wanted to be the kind of person who went when pushed gently by her.

The tunnel swallowed city noise. The rain became a rumor. Their bootfalls expanded, came back graceful and late. Pipes ran along the walls, sweating. Old notices peeled away in slow banners, warning about fines that no one remembered how to collect. The light came from their memories of light.

After twenty paces, the whisper started. Not the glass-plain chorus. A different voice, amplitude set precisely to the distance between heartbeat and doubt. It did not accuse. It offered economies.

To Jake: You can get them there faster if you cut what slows you. Two is lighter than three. Math as mercy.

To Dani: You can shoot earlier this time and call it prevention. Prevention is a kind of healing if the ledger is the only god you pray to.

To Rally: You can confess in advance. If you say you are the worst thing, the worst thing becomes old news. People forgive what they are bored by.

They walked. The tunnel sloped, that bass note of stone growing. The air cooled until their breath made smoke that hung and then forgot. The tag on Rally's chest throbbed once like a bell touched with a finger. The pressure in his skull eased half a notch. He didn't thank the metal. He thanked the hands that had given it.

The floor leveled and widened into a chamber. Not built. Eroded. The river's old hand had been here when the city pretended to be forest. The chamber's roof arched low enough that Jake ducked, and Dani only barely didn't. In the middle of the floor the stone had split in a crack a man could lie down in and not be found until the city built a museum to explain why they hadn't looked.

Heat sighed up from that crack. Not the furnace heat of below. A lesser brother. The whisper sharpened and then went silent as if it had reached the place it wanted and was listening for them to speak first.

Rally swallowed. "Is this it?"

"It's the skin of it," Dani said. "The breach itself is deeper."

Jake pointed along the wall where scratches had been carved recently. Not words. Marks. The way men unable to write still tell each other a story they need to remember. Down. Then a broken circle. Then a line through it. "People tried," he said.

"And either they failed or they're still down there trying," Dani said. Her voice didn't decide whether to be respect or warning.

A ladder of old iron rungs disappeared into the crack. Water slicked them. Heat fog made each rung look doubled for a breath and then singular again. Jake tested the first with all his weight. It held. "We go one at a time," he said. "If a rung goes, you do not follow. You find your own way down."

"I don't like that plan," Rally said.

"It's the only one that doesn't rely on hope," Jake said. "Hope can ride on top of it, but it doesn't get to drive."

Dani went first because going first is how she took fear away from the men she loved. Jake waited until she was three rungs down and then started. Rally followed, jaw clenched, naming birds into the metal. The tunnel's voice narrowed to breath and drip and the sound old iron makes when it remembers winter.

They descended into heat that felt like a mouth opened to speak a word you don't want to hear. The tag grew warm. The whisper returned in Rally's head but softer now, as if it had been forced to move two rooms away and was trying not to be rude about shouting. He smiled, small and private, and put both feet on the next rung.

Below them, the chamber opened into a light that wasn't light, a brightness like a moral argued until it grew teeth. The breath of it hit their faces and set the tiny hairs along their wrists standing up to listen. Dani didn't look back. Jake didn't either. Rally did, once, to make sure the way back still existed. It did. The way back is the kind of lie you can keep around for comfort as long as you don't inventory it too often.

They climbed until the rungs ended and stone took over. The floor was a shelf around a deeper cavity, a throat in the earth. At its bottom the breach gleamed the color of a wound healing wrong. Lines of force stitched and unstitched themselves. The air hummed the note of a bridge cable pulled too tight.

"Now," Jake said softly, and for once the word wasn't an order. It was a prayer that wore the clothes of a plan.

They circled the shelf until they stood over the narrowest part of the glow. Dani unrolled the Keeper's map only long enough to confirm what her bones already told her. She put it away like a holy book you don't take out in the rain.

Rally felt the pressure find him again, gentle as a hand after a fight saying maybe we were both wrong. He closed his eyes and pictured the glass plain's X marks, the bridge's scream, Dani's palm flat against the metal, Jake's breath marching the square. He opened his eyes and spoke to the breach the way you speak to an animal you don't want to startle. "We're not here to bargain," he said. "We're here to make you bored."

The air shivered. Somewhere above, thunder decided it belonged to this room too and rolled in, late and pleased with itself. Dani drew her pistol and didn't aim it anywhere you could see. Jake's hands curled and uncurled like he was about to pick up a weight he respected.

"Ready?" Dani asked.

Rally nodded. "Ready."

The Keeper's eyes would later glint in lantern light when they told this part back, calculating cost already owed.

Top of Form

Bottom of Form

lantern light when they told this part back calculating cost already owed.

The glow from the breach flexed like lungs, inhaling their presence and exhaling a pressure that went looking for seams, bone first, then thought. Jake felt it test the bruises around his throat with the tact of a locksmith; Dani felt it comb along the barrel of her pistol as if metal could be persuaded to confess; Rally felt it press against the thin tag on his chest until the sigil warmed and rang once, a sound too small for ears and too stubborn for silence.

They stood together on the carved shelf, three silhouettes against a light that wasn't light. Steam hung in the chamber's throat.

Somewhere above them, rain found cracks and stitched its rhythm down the stone in threads.

"Square," Jake said, voice raw. Inhale four, hold four, exhale four, hold four. Dani matched him. Rally stumbled the first cycle, then found the metronome the way a scared animal finds a herd and breathes inside its timing.

The breach brightened at their refusal, then modulated to a color no spectrum volunteered. The hum softened into whispers tuned for each of them.

To Jake it said: You can get them there faster if you cut what slows you. Two is lighter than three. Math as mercy.

To Dani it said: You can shoot earlier this time and call it prevention. Prevention is a kind of healing if the ledger is the only god you trust.

To Rally it said, gentle as a late apology: Confess in advance. If you name yourself the worst thing, the worst thing becomes old news and no one looks too closely when you fail.

"No," Dani said. She did not raise her voice. She set the word down like a stone that would not move.

Rally's shadow lengthened across the wall and smiled while he didn't. He pressed the tag harder to his breastbone. "You don't get me cheap." His voice wavered, then steadied. "Not again."

The breach convulsed. Threads of light snapped, then laced themselves tighter, angry sewing. Dust fell in a dry hush. Jake widened his stance and cut an X into the floor with his knife, a small tack of insistence, a mark that said We were here and refused.

Jamal laughed behind Rally's left ear. Dani heard her mother hum the lullaby Dani had taught herself to forget. Jake's old commander repeated a number that added up to a funeral. Lies wore their best voices; that is their way.

"Here," Dani told Rally, catching his chin and bringing his eyes to hers. "Say where you are."

"Here," he said. Breath caught. "Here."

The chamber breathed with them. The glow faltered, flared, then narrowed by a finger's width. It didn't like boredom. It wanted drama. They denied it the scene.

Minutes, or the longer cousin of minutes, unspooled. Their legs shook. Rally's burned arm screamed with honest pain that helped. Jake's square counts roughened at the edges and came back truer. Dani's fingers trembled and she let them, because killing tremble doesn't help unless you're pulling a trigger.

The breach screamed then, not with sound but with an absence of it, as if a mouth opened wide and ate the noise. The void punched through their ears. Rally dropped to one knee. Jake bit his tongue hard enough to taste iron. Dani's eyes watered and she tasted rain and stone and refusal.

When the dark sound passed, the glow pulled inward, folding itself into a seam the width of a blade. It held, sulking. The chamber's temperature dipped by a degree and that small mercy felt like permission to breathe honestly for three breaths.

"It's smaller," Dani said, ragged.

"Not gone," Jake answered.

"Smaller is something," Rally whispered, and in his mouth the words did not sound like consolation; they sounded like policy.

He was still on one knee when the pressure changed. It didn't come from the breach this time. It came from him. The air around his face twitched, the way heat does above a stove set just high enough to lie about its intention. He flinched without moving. "He's..."

"I know," Dani said, and put her palm flat to the metal at his chest. The heat leaked into her hand until it prickled. "Breathe with me."

"Rally," Jake said softly. "Permission is a door. Don't be polite."

Rally shut his eyes, found the square, and shoved. For a heartbeat, his pupils filmed over black, and the chamber leaned in to see which way he would fall. Then the black rinsed away and left brown, human and tired and furious.

He laughed once, a broken bright sound. "He hates being bored," Rally said.

"Then we are his punishment," Jake said.

They did not wait for thanks from the wound. Gratitude isn't a currency here. They climbed. The iron rungs sweated; the heat licked at their ankles in lazy tongues as if the world below wanted one more taste. Jake went first and bled steadiness into the ladder. Dani followed, keeping Rally between them because between is safer than behind. The chamber narrowed to the idea of climbing and the faith that rungs would hold because they needed to.

Above, rain returned with its old honest arguments. They surfaced into the service tunnel like divers, coughing air like wealth. The river's bass note shook the stones underfoot. The ceiling wept in sympathetic threads.

"Gray Isla's knots?" Jake asked, because thinking about a knot is a way to think about a promise that holds.

"They'll hold," Dani said. She wanted them to. Wanting is the risk and the weapon.

They moved back through the tunnel. The whisper tried once more, thinner now, offered them paperwork: sign here to certify closure. Jake snorted and did not take the pen. Dani didn't answer and made that her answer. Rally laughed again, not broken this time, and the sound startled all three of them into grins that hurt.

At the stairs a ripple of people forced them into shadows: three Enforcers in slick coats, faces blank with the discipline of men who need rules to know who they are. One saw the wet on the floor and did the math wrong. They passed, their boots loud and official, their shoulders pleased with weight. Dani waited until the sound dissolved before she moved them.

The quarter smelled of wet metal and hot oil. The rain had softened to a steady performance. Gray Isla's boat rode the river without leaving much behind. Her knots sat ugly and effective, a language of refusal. She glanced over once, as if to count them, then returned to coiling line; some people prefer proof to stories.

"Keeper first," Jake said. "Then we make the rounds."

"The rounds?" Rally asked, voice small, then stronger. "Thank-yous?"

"Debt-checks," Jake said. "Promises. Edges. The breach shrank, but its radiance touched things. We find the touch marks and quiet them."

Rally nodded as if he had always known this was what came after victory. Maybe he had. He pulled the scarf down from his head and let rain slick his hair flat. He didn't look like a boy. He didn't look like a man either. He looked like transition, the moment when a door closes and you feel the ghost of the room you left on your back while your hand reaches for the next knob.

The Keeper's door took their old pattern and opened just as far as needed. The house smelled the same, ink, oil, damp, a mathematics of paper, but the lantern flame burned steadier as if the wind had reassessed its priorities.

They told it in one line, then another. The story didn't expand because they refused the urge to gild it. The Keeper listened with the stillness of water in a tall glass. When Rally said, "I told him I was here," the old man blinked slow, as if that sentence had been the only thing he'd been waiting to verify.

"You have bought us a dawn," he said when they were done. "Spend it."

"How?" Dani asked.

"By keeping morning from becoming nostalgia," the Keeper said. He slid a drawer open and took out three strips of rough cloth. "Ties. Wear them under your sleeves. If anyone asks, they are for luck. Mostly they are for recognition, mine, and those who still answer to me."

Jake wrapped one above his wrist, a private insignia. Dani did the same and tugged her sleeve down. Rally threaded his through the chain of the tag and tied it off in a knot he could undo with one hand. The Keeper watched, approving the economy of it.

"You will find echoes," the Keeper said. "Small places where the method you refused has already started its work. A stall where prices hurt a little more than they should. A patrol that smiles too long while asking where you're going. A door that makes people pay with apologies before it opens. Close those. It is unglorious. It is what dawn requires."

Jake inclined his head. "We'll take the eastern run. Markets first."

"Isla?" Dani asked.

"Her knots are saying no for now," the Keeper said. "When the sun pushes the storm off its chair, go and thank her anyway. People who tie good knots live longer when gratitude checks on them."

They stepped back into the lane. The city had started its slow brighten: not light, not yet, but the idea of light rehearsing its lines. Traders lifted shutters. A woman dumped a bucket of rainwater into the gutter and watched it choose a path. Somewhere a child laughed at nothing and made it sound like something. Enforcers wrote notes to themselves to look important.

They made for the market under the tram viaduct where stalls sold cheap futures: parts that promised function tomorrow, herbs that promised sleep tonight. The first echo found them before they found it. A butcher held a boy's hand too long while taking coins, thumb pressing against a pulse with the intimacy of ownership. The boy smiled because he had learned the smile that gets you your hand back. Dani saw the smile and the pressure and the ledger it would become in twenty such transactions. She stepped to the counter and set her palm on the wood. The butcher did not look at her, he looked at Jake, because a certain kind of man believes he understands orders when they arrive in a voice like Jake's.

"Release the boy's hand," Jake said.

"It's a greeting," the butcher said cheerfully, pressure unchanging.

"It's a leverage," Dani said. "Release it."

The butcher did, surprised at himself for obeying. He tried to laugh and found his throat dry. The boy didn't run; he stepped back and looked at Rally, as if the geometry of danger had changed and Rally might have the theorem.

"Price?" the butcher asked, because everything is a price in markets.

"Your wrist," Jake said.

The man offered it, baffled. Jake tied the rough cloth there, quick and clean. "When you feel this, you remember not to measure people like meat."

"What is it?" the butcher asked, rubbing the knot like a charm that might work even if he didn't believe in it.

"A reminder," Dani said. "One that hurts a little when you forget." She tugged on the knot hard enough to burn his skin. His eyes widened. The lesson found a home.

They moved on. A patrolman stopped them near the spice alley. His smile was too long and too certain. "Good people," he said, as if that could be true in the abstract. "Where are we going this honest morning?"

"Left," Jake said, and kept walking, because sometimes refusal is velocity. The man put a hand on Rally's shoulder. Dani set two fingers on the man's wrist. She didn't squeeze. She didn't have to. Her eyes told him the story of the last person who had put a hand where it didn't belong. He withdrew, the smile collapsing into its proper size.

"Echo," Rally said when they were past. "Small. But not small."

They closed three more before noon. A lender's sign that required apology before it admitted you; they turned the letters wrong side out. A set of scales weighted with a thin line of solder invisible unless you knew where to look; Jake scraped it away with his knife and left an X in the wood. A water seller who insisted on hearing the worst thing a woman had done before he would fill her can; Dani filled it herself and tied the rough cloth around the spigot. He called after them, angry until he was afraid of the knot's meaning and pretended otherwise.

Around the third echo, Rally stumbled. He caught himself, then didn't. Dani eased him to a stoop and pressed her palm to the tag without thinking. He laughed breathlessly. "I'm okay," he said. "It's just, when people ask for apologies as rent to move through the day, it feels like him. Like the method."

"That's because it is," Jake said. "He isn't a single voice. He's a culture that thinks it's tidy."

The storm thinned to a gauze that made the sun look like a coin you could spend if you were quick. They took that light as permission to cross toward the river. Gray Isla stood as before, knots like sentences a judge might admire. She watched them come and didn't waste words pretending she hadn't.

"Still tied," she said.

"Good knots," Dani said. "We came to say thank you."

Gray Isla shrugged, which is how some people say you're welcome when they aren't sure the words will fit. She eyed Rally. "The metal still warm?"

He touched it. "Enough to remind me."

"Keep it," she said. "But don't fall in love with it. Tools don't deserve that."

He smiled. "I won't."

They walked the last hour of storm with their bodies starting to believe they could make it to the next table, the next argument. The city's edges softened and then sharpened back as the rain committed to being done. Enforcers found less important things to do. The market settled into its routine of small negotiations that didn't wound.

Back at the Keeper's, the old man had found a second lantern and a gentler chair. He listened to their report of echoes with the attention of a gardener told where the frost had bitten. When Jake finished, the Keeper let the silence set like varnish.

"Good," he said. "The method hates tedium."

Rally smiled. "We're very tedious."

"For him," the Keeper said. "For me, you are excellent company." He stood with the slow care of a man who has made too many sudden movements in old houses. "Come back at dusk," he said. "I have lines to set and I prefer to hand you the bait myself. Also," and here his mouth did something close to tenderness, "there is a woman with a ledger who will be looking for you by then. She will have questions about a boy with a scarf and a bruise and a way of saying here."

Rally flushed under the wet and the grime. "What does she want?"

"To forgive you nothing and still choose you," the Keeper said. "If that terrifies you, you are not lost."

They left with that sentence folded like a note you do not read until the tram is loud enough to cover the sound your heart makes when you open it. The sun pushed the last of the storm off the roofline. A child found a bright coin in a puddle and announced it to everyone. A butcher untied a knot and tied it again, harder, because some reminders you keep until the skin under them learns the new shape.

Near the glassworks, a pane leaned against a wall, catching the new light. For a heartbeat, the three of them saw the glass plain in its surface, saw themselves smaller and farther and braver than they felt. Dani lifted a finger as if to poke a hole in the reflection, then let her hand fall.

"No more trials today," Jake said.

"Only errands," Rally answered, which is another name for the work that keeps evil bored.

They walked. Not heroes. Not cured. But aligned. And because the city had been bought a dawn, it spent it with them: tram brakes that squealed less, gutters that chose not to flood a doorway, a patrol that forgot the question it had meant to ask.

By the time dusk began to practice on the east side of buildings, they had closed eight echoes and marked three more for tomorrow.

Their sleeves hid the rough cloth bands. The tag cooled against Rally's chest to a temperature that felt like belief without fever.

They turned back toward the Keeper's. Lantern light was already preening in windows. Somewhere a cello made the evening choose a key. Dani touched Rally's arm and felt muscle that had learned the difference between shaking and ready. Jake's throat still bore the necklace of bruises, but his voice had found more room in it. The path behind them did not look safe. It looked theirs.

At the door, the pattern knocked itself, as if the house had decided they were allowed. The Keeper opened. He did not look surprised. The second lantern made his eyes catch light like coins cast upward in a poor man's joke.

"You came," he said.

"We were tedious," Dani said.

"Excellent," he replied. "I have a worse job for you." He smiled then, small and true. "But first, there is bread."

They stepped in. The rain outside finally remembered to stop. Somewhere under the city, the breach sulked smaller, bored and waiting for better entertainment. Above it, in a room full of maps and ledgers and a new loaf cooling on a rack dented by years, three people refused to provide it.

Morning would come. It would ask for unglorious work. They would do it. And when the breach opened its mouth again, and it would, they would feed it nothing but their refusal and the stubborn choir of their shared breath until it learned, again, that boredom is a kind of defeat.

For now, they washed their hands, sat where the Keeper pointed, and allowed the day to end without apology. And when the lantern flame leaned toward them as if to hear what came next, they let it. They owed no secrets to the dark. They owed each other everything the method could not name. And so, quietly, without speeches, they moved as one into the next necessity.

Chapter Twelve: The Mirror's Truth

The air shifted as they climbed, every inch a war between their bodies and the stone. Smoke still clung to their hair and clothes, bitter ash grinding into their lungs, but a draft threaded through the cracks ahead, sharp with pine and rain. Dani leaned forward into it like a drowning woman toward air. Her shoulders burned; Rally's weight was a firebrand pressed against her, every stumble threatening to pull them both down. Jake kept close on the other side, his hand braced beneath Rally's arm, his jaw clenched, steadying the boy with brute insistence.

The tunnel narrowed, walls splitting with veins of cold light. Each fracture seemed to glow faintly, not from torches or lamps, but with a buried shimmer, as though the mountain itself had been fractured by something older than time. Dani forced herself not to look too long. She had seen enough light below the earth to last her a lifetime.

"Almost there," she whispered, though her throat was scraped raw from smoke. The words came out more rasp than voice. She wasn't sure whether she meant it for Rally, for Jake, or for herself. "One more step."

The passage breathed wider, then suddenly yawned open into a jagged mouth. A rush of silver light poured through, moonlight pale and steady, not the flicker of flame or phosphorescence. The sight of it cracked Dani's composure, stars, countless stars scattered sharp across a black sky, impossibly vast after so long beneath stone.

Her knees buckled when she reached it. They staggered forward, Rally between them, until their boots broke into damp needles and soil. The forest floor received them like an embrace. Dani went to her hands, fingers clawing into cool moss, lungs straining for clean air. Jake dropped to a crouch, chest heaving, shoulders shuddering. Rally collapsed sideways and rolled onto his back, staring at the stars as if he'd forgotten how to blink.

For a long while they did nothing but breathe. Breath was enough, ragged, uneven, but theirs. Alive.

Then the mountain groaned. It began low, like a belly rumbling, then climbed into a roar that vibrated the soil beneath them. With a thunderclap, the cave mouth behind them sheared inward. Boulders crashed like drums of war, dust plumed into the sky, the black opening choking itself with stone. The underworld sealed itself in silence, erasing any sign they had emerged from its throat.

Jake leaned against a fallen rock, his hands trembling as he pushed back his sweat-matted hair. His chest heaved with every word. "It's done."

But Dani didn't answer. Her eyes had fixed on Rally. His face, too young to be worn so deep, was etched with hollows, his haunted eyes clouded with a tremor that wouldn't let go of his hands. He was shaking even though the night was cool and still. Dani thought of Jamal then, of the faces they had left buried in that dark cathedral of judgment. The echoes would not stay buried; they clung to the boy, they clung to her.

Jake followed her gaze, his own breath slowing. He rubbed a hand over his mouth. "What do we tell them?" he asked softly. His voice cracked, not with weakness, but with the exhaustion of someone too long carrying impossible truths.

Dani's throat worked. She lifted her head and let the moonlight wash across her face. "The truth no one would believe," she said. "That it was just a landslide."

The lie felt jagged in her mouth. Yet what else could they say? That beneath the mountain lived a tribunal of shadows, a machinery of law older than parchment and gavel, a city of thresholds where people were measured and discarded? No court aboveground would hear it. No jury would understand.

The wind sifted through the branches like benediction, shaking free a drift of needles. Somewhere deeper in the forest, an owl called, patient, deliberate.

Jake drew his knees up and braced his forearms across them, staring at the collapsed mouth. His eyes glinted in the moonlight. "If it's sealed, maybe it dies with it. Maybe we're the only ones who ever carry it forward."

Dani said nothing. She didn't believe it. Things older than law didn't die under a few boulders. They pressed upward, waiting for cracks. And people, always people, would give them cracks.

Rally stirred beside her, his breath still shallow, his body twitching in small jolts like a man waking from too long a nightmare. Dani smoothed his hair back, feeling the heat beneath his skin. The boy opened his mouth as though to speak, then closed it, eyes darting skyward again.

"You're safe," she whispered, though she doubted either of them believed it.

Hours later, the forest still clung to her senses. Dani walked alone into her small house, the door shutting with a hollow click. The air inside felt wrong, too still, too quiet after the mountain's voice.

She left her jacket draped across a chair, her boots trailing needles across the floor, and went to the bathroom sink.

The mirror met her with blank, familiar reflection. Dani Francis: homicide detective, survivor of things no report would ever capture. Her cheeks were smudged with soot; her eyes ringed with sleepless hollows. She should have felt relief. The case was over. The underworld was sealed. Rally was alive. She was alive.

Instead, her chest ached with something nameless, a pressure that wouldn't release.

She leaned forward, palms braced on porcelain, and touched the glass.

It rippled.

Her breath hitched.

The reflection wavered like water disturbed by a stone. Her face blurred, her skin paling as if washed free of color. Then her eyes lit faintly, not with the brightness of life, but with the residue of something eternal. A shimmer bled outward from her pupils, cold and certain.

Dani stumbled back, but the reflection did not mimic her. It raised its hand first, palm out, not in echo but in warning.

She knew then what her heart had whispered in broken dreams all along. She hadn't survived that first fall. When the cavern floor shattered beneath her body, she had left something behind. Flesh had carried forward, yes, but her life as she had known it ended in the dark.

Everything since had been judgment.

But judgment wasn't damnation.

It was Assignment. The word reverberated through her chest like a second heartbeat. Dani clutched the edge of the sink, knuckles whitening, as the glass trembled beneath her touch. The reflection, no, the figure in the mirror, held its hand raised, a signal as old as warning fires. Not mimicry. Not illusion. A command.

Her pulse thundered. Behind her eyes, memories flooded unbidden: the tribunal's endless corridors, the echo of boots striking marble, the way Jamal's name had dissolved into silence when the verdict swallowed him whole. She remembered the Archivist's voice, steady and dispassionate, reciting outcomes as if they were already carved. And she remembered Rally's refusal to surrender, his stammering insistence on being more than numbers.

All of it knotted together now, tightening around her like a binding oath. She wanted to deny it. She wanted to tell herself she was simply exhausted, that trauma made the mirror swim. But the presence staring out from the silver refused her excuses.

"You should be dead," she whispered. Her voice sounded like it belonged to someone else.

The figure in the mirror tilted its head, and her blurred reflection seemed to pale further. For a moment, the glass filled with a deeper darkness, a suggestion of endless stone corridors and the hum of law without mercy. She staggered back, heart pounding.

"No," she said again, louder. "I crawled out. I'm still here."

The figure's hand lowered slowly, but its eyes, her eyes, burned steady with the faint light of judgment. And in that moment she understood: survival had not freed her. It had conscripted her.

She was sentinel. Guardian of thresholds.

The word "sentinel" formed itself in her mind, not chosen but delivered, heavy as a badge placed on her chest. The mountain had sealed, yes. But the city beneath, the cold machinery of verdicts, the impartial cruelty of balance sheets, was older than stone, older than the law she'd sworn to serve. It would find fissures again, pressing upward through men and women willing to trade mercy for order.

Her duty was to stand watch at those cracks.

The mirror steadied. Her reflection solidified again into her own soot-streaked face, trembling and too thin. For a breath she thought the vision gone, but the ache in her chest told her otherwise. The burden hadn't lifted. It had settled deeper.

She turned away, pressing her palms to her thighs to ground herself. The house remained silent. The refrigerator hummed faintly, a sound almost alien in its domesticity after weeks of underground silence. Dani walked back into the narrow living room. Her jacket lay where she'd dropped it, badge still clipped to the lapel.

She picked it up. The metal was cold against her fingers. A homicide detective's badge. Proof she belonged to the law of men, the law written in statutes and argued in courtrooms. But tonight it felt different. Heavier. Like a seal pressed against her, binding her to two worlds.

Outside, wind shifted through the trees. She thought she heard laughter in it, thin, faraway, like children echoing in an abandoned playground. The sound needled her spine. She moved to the window, drawing back the curtain. The forest pressed close, branches swaying, needles whispering against each other. No figures moved. No shadows detached from the trunks. Still, the laughter lingered in her ears until it faded into the rustle of wind.

She closed her eyes and let her breath out slowly.

The badge in her hand felt as heavy as stone. With deliberate movement, she clipped it back to her belt.

"I hear you," she said, voice steady now. Not to the mirror, not to herself, but to whatever force had drafted her from the cavern floor upward.

The glass in the bathroom stilled completely. Her reflection became only her reflection again.

But Dani knew better. Every mirror was a doorway. Every reflection a test. And she was no longer free to walk past them as if they were only glass.

The house did not feel like hers anymore. Dani paced the narrow hall, brushing her hand along the drywall, half-expecting it to ripple like the mirror. Each surface seemed to conceal another depth, a threshold disguised as ordinary. She had lived here for years, a detective's small refuge, but now every angle carried suspicion: the corners of picture frames, the dark panes of the television, the dull shine of a window at night. Reflections everywhere. Doorways everywhere.

She set water to boil, needing the small act of routine. The kettle's hiss grew sharp, too sharp, until she switched it off before it screamed. The silence that followed rang louder than any whistle.

She pressed her forehead against the cupboard door. The wood was steady beneath her skin. She needed steady. Her body still ached from the climb, shoulders knotted where Rally's weight had dragged against her. Her lungs caught on the memory of dust. Her throat was ached raw from smoke. The kitchen light buzzed overhead, flickering once, and for a moment her pulse spiked, until it steadied again.

Enough. She poured the water, made tea with shaking hands, and sat at the table. The badge dug into her belt like a reminder. She pulled it free and set it on the table's scarred wood. The metal winked back at her in the low light.

"Still me," she muttered. The words had no conviction.

The knock came sudden. A firm rap at the door. Dani froze, tea half-raised. Another knock, slower, deliberate.

She stood and went to the peephole.

Jake.

She pulled the door open. His face was pale under the porch light, shadows carved deep into his cheeks. He looked older than he had that morning, before the mountain swallowed them whole. His shirt was streaked with dirt, his eyes ringed like hers.

"You're up," he said. His voice was hoarse.

"Couldn't sleep."

He nodded once and stepped inside without waiting. His gaze drifted across her living room, pausing at the jacket, then catching on the badge still lying on the table. His eyes flicked back to her, unreadable.

"Rally?" she asked.

"Sleeping. Finally." Jake rubbed his hands together, then flexed them as if the memory of carrying the boy still ached. "Doctor said he's not broken. Just..." He exhaled hard. "Shaken."

Dani gestured toward the chair. Jake lowered himself into it, shoulders sagging. For a moment neither spoke. The refrigerator hummed. The clock ticked.

At last Jake said, "You saw it too, didn't you?"

Dani's stomach clenched. "What?"

"The mirror." His eyes were sharp now, cutting through her denial before she could form it. "Don't look at me like that. I saw your face when we left him. You weren't just looking at Rally. You were looking through him."

She sank into the opposite chair, fingers pressed to her temples. The weight in her chest deepened. "It's not possible."

Jake leaned forward, voice low. "We walked out of something impossible."

His words sat between them like a verdict.

For a time they spoke in half-starts, circling what neither wanted to say. About the tribunal. About the silence that swallowed Jamal. About how the mountain's collapse had felt less like escape and more like a door closing them into another kind of service. Dani listened to Jake's voice, measured and weary, and realized he had carried the same burden since their first descent: that justice had outgrown their hands, and yet demanded them anyway.

"Then what do we do?" Jake asked finally.

The question was a wound. Dani stared at the badge on the table, its gleam sharp in the lamplight.

"We wait," she said.

"For what?"

"For the cracks."

Jake's expression twisted, half disbelief, half recognition. He leaned back, folding his arms. "You think this is just the start."

"I know it is," Dani said.

The silence that followed was heavier than stone.

Jake's words hung in the air, heavy as the mountain itself. Dani let them settle, let them press against the silence until she could breathe through the weight. Her hands curled around her mug, the tea inside cooling untouched. She thought of the reflection's pale face, of its raised hand that hadn't been hers.

"Jake," she said finally, voice low. "When you looked in the mirror... what did you see?"

He hesitated, eyes narrowing as if to test her sincerity. Then he glanced away, his jaw tightening. "Not me. Not really. It was like, like I was standing trial again. Every decision I ever made, lined up behind me. And the worst of them... they leaned closer." He shook his head. "I thought it was just me cracking. Stress. Smoke. Whatever."

"It wasn't just you."

The admission tasted like iron. Her chest ached as if she'd given something away.

Jake leaned forward, elbows on knees. His eyes found hers across the table. "Then it's not over, Dani. You know that, right? Sealing that cave didn't end anything. It just moved it."

She wanted to argue, to cling to the illusion of finality. But the badge on the table gleamed back at her like a verdict.

They sat in silence until the clock on the wall ticked past midnight. Every sound of the house felt magnified: the hum of the refrigerator, the creak of settling beams, the sigh of wind outside. Finally, Jake pushed back his chair.

"I'll stay close," he said. "Rally's not ready to be alone. And neither are you."

She bristled at the implication, but didn't argue. He was right.

Jake moved to the door, then paused. "When the cracks open again... do we tell anyone? Or do we just keep carrying it ourselves?"

Dani opened her mouth, then closed it. The truth was too jagged to name. She looked down at her badge, then back at him.

"When the time comes," she said. "We'll know."

It wasn't an answer. It was a delay. Jake seemed to accept it anyway. He left without another word, the door clicking shut behind him.

Alone again, Dani drifted into the bedroom but couldn't bring herself to lie down. The bed looked foreign, an artifact from a simpler life she no longer believed in. She sat at the edge, boots still on, staring at the dresser mirror across from her. Its surface reflected the room dimly, catching the lamp's glow.

Her own eyes stared back, hollow but steady. For a long moment nothing shifted. She almost convinced herself it was only glass.

Then the faintest ripple disturbed the surface. Not much, no wave, no distortion, just a suggestion, like the tremor of breath on still water.

Her throat tightened. "I said I hear you," she whispered.

The mirror did not move again. But she felt it: the presence still waiting, patient, like a judge who had already written the sentence but allowed the condemned to read it slowly.

She tried to sleep. For hours she lay on top of the covers, staring at the ceiling, her badge still clipped to her belt. Sleep never came. Every time her eyes closed, she felt the mirror waiting.

At last, near dawn, she rose. She couldn't stay inside anymore. She pulled on her jacket and stepped into the cool morning. Mist threaded the trees outside, wrapping the forest in pale ribbons. The world looked clean, reborn. But beneath it she felt the same weight, the same tension humming under the earth.

She walked to the edge of her yard where the forest began. The ground was damp, pine needles slick underfoot. She touched the trunk of a tall fir, grounding herself in its rough bark.

For a moment she thought she heard Rally's voice, soft, fragile, echoing her plea from the cavern: I don't want to be nothing. The memory broke her. Tears stung her eyes, spilling hot down her cheeks. She pressed her forehead to the tree and let them fall.

The mountain was sealed. The city was buried. But the cracks were everywhere. And she was bound to them now, sentinel of thresholds.

The mist thinned as the sun crept higher, a pale disc blurred behind the trees. Birds began to stir, their songs tentative, as though testing the air before trusting the day. Dani stood rooted at the forest's edge, her hand flat against the fir trunk, listening to the chorus build. Each sound felt fragile, like it could be shattered by a single echo from below.

Her phone buzzed in her pocket, startling her. She fumbled it out and saw Jake's name glowing on the screen. She hesitated before answering.

"You awake?" his voice asked, rough with fatigue.

"Barely."

"Rally's asking for you."

The words pierced her. She could still see the boy's trembling hands, the way he stared at the stars as though they were both salvation and threat. "I'll come," she said.

She ended the call and walked back through her yard, her boots wet with dew. Inside the house, she caught her reflection in the sliding glass door. For a heartbeat, she thought it moved on its own, lips whispering words she could not hear. She yanked the curtain closed, shuddering.

Rally's room was quiet when she entered. He sat propped against pillows, pale but awake, his eyes shadowed with the weight of what he'd seen. He clutched a mug of broth, hands shaking slightly. Jake hovered nearby, arms folded, as if keeping watch.

When Rally saw her, his lips twitched into something like a smile. "You came."

"Of course I did," Dani said, moving to sit beside him.

For a moment he said nothing, staring down at the blanket bunched across his legs. Then, in a small voice, he whispered, "It followed us out, didn't it?"

Dani froze. Her eyes darted to Jake, who looked away. The boy's words were too precise, too knowing.

"What makes you say that?" she asked carefully.

Rally's gaze lifted to hers. "Because every time I close my eyes, I see the doors. All those doors in the dark. They weren't locked. They were waiting."

Dani's stomach turned. She reached for his hand, steadying it between both of hers. "Then you don't close your eyes alone," she said firmly. "Not anymore."

Rally swallowed hard, then leaned against her shoulder. The boy's weight was light, but it anchored her as nothing else had.

Jake's eyes met hers across the room. He didn't speak, but the unspoken truth filled the space: they were not finished. The underworld had not been left behind. It had only changed its shape.

That night, Dani stood again before her bathroom mirror. The glass was still. Her reflection waited, patient, ordinary. Yet when she leaned close, she thought she heard something deep within it, a whisper like wind through stone, promising that the cracks would come.

She touched the badge at her belt. Its weight steadied her.

"I'll be ready," she said.

The mirror gave no answer. It didn't need to.

Her breath caught sharp in her chest. She lurched toward the mirror, hand outstretched, but when her fingers brushed the glass it was smooth and cool, nothing more than her own reflection staring back. No Jamal. No echo of his wide, pleading eyes. Just Dani, smudged, exhausted, trembling.

She pressed her forehead against the surface. "I remember you," she whispered. "I won't let them forget."

The mirror gave no answer, but a chill threaded down her spine.

She pushed herself away and moved into the living room, collapsing onto the couch. Darkness pooled across the floor as night pressed against the windows. She didn't bother turning on the light. For a long time she sat in the silence, listening to the faint hum of the refrigerator, the occasional groan of the house settling.

But silence was no longer empty. It brimmed with judgment, with the presence she had carried out of the mountain. Every corner of the room seemed to breathe. Every shadow seemed a threshold.

Near midnight, her phone buzzed again. She snatched it up, grateful for distraction. It was Jake.

"They're asking questions," he said without preamble. His voice was low, tense.

"Who?"

"Press. Parents. City officials. They want to know why half a block of the mountain sealed itself."

Dani closed her eyes. "And what did you tell them?"

"The line we agreed on. Landslide. But they don't believe it. Not all of them."

A long silence stretched between them. She could almost hear him grinding his teeth on the other end.

"Dani," he said at last, "what if it comes back? What if the cracks open here, in the city, in the precinct, anywhere? What do we tell them then?"

Her throat tightened. She had no answer. Only the mirror's pale hand raised in warning.

"We stand watch," she said finally. "That's all we can do."

Jake didn't reply. Then the line clicked dead.

Sleep evaded her again. When dawn came, she walked the streets before the city fully woke. She moved past shuttered shops, their windows gleaming faint in the early light. Every reflection caught her: her face doubled in a bakery display, her silhouette stretched thin across a laundromat window, her eyes staring back from a puddle in the street.

She felt watched from both sides of the glass.

At the courthouse steps she stopped. The heavy wooden doors loomed above her, polished brass handles glinting. She had walked these steps countless times in her career. Today they felt like an echo of the marble halls beneath the mountain. Judgment above mirrored judgment below.

She climbed the steps and stood at the doors but did not enter. Her badge weighed on her hip, her reflection faint in the glass panels. She whispered into the morning air:

"Justice isn't finished. It waits."

Then she turned away.

That evening, Rally came to her house with Jake. The boy's face was pale, but his eyes clearer than the night before. He held a notebook in his hands, its pages scribbled with drawings, doors, arches, mirrors. He opened it and pushed it toward her.

"They're everywhere," he said simply.

Dani leafed through the pages, her stomach tightening. He had sketched with startling precision: the tribunal's black corridors, the brass plates that had labeled forbidden offices, the mirrored doors that never opened. He remembered everything.

Jake's voice was low. "He dreams it every night."

Dani set the notebook down gently. She met Rally's eyes. "Then you're not alone," she said.

The boy nodded once. And for the first time since they had crawled out of the earth, Dani saw resolve instead of fear in his gaze.

The lamp threw a soft circle across Dani's living room, enough light to make the drawings legible and leave the corners of the room in a respectful dark. Rally sat small on the couch with the notebook open across his knees, each page a gate: arches and doors and hallways rendered with a precision that didn't belong to a boy his age. The brass plates she remembered had returned on his paper, Office of Prohibitions, Registry of Outcomes, Department of Breach, drawn in a hand that trembled but didn't falter. He'd even caught the cold shine along the handles, the ones no one touched.

Jake stood a few feet back, his shoulder against the wall, arms folded like he was holding himself together. There was dirt still ground into the seams of his shirt. He hadn't shaved; a gray stubble roughened his jaw. He stared at the notebook as if it were a piece of evidence he had to explain in court and knew he couldn't.

"They weren't just doors," Rally said. His voice was thin but steady. "They were waiting. Like they could hear us coming."

Dani crouched so she was level with him. The pages smelled faintly of pencil and old paper, familiar scents that felt almost indecent next to what the drawings held. She touched one corner with her finger and then drew her hand back; it felt like touching a warning sign.

"They still feel like they're waiting," Rally added, eyes flicking from the paper to the window glass and back again. "Not down there. Here."

Jake exhaled. "He's a kid," he said, more to himself than to her. "He needs sleep and quiet, not, this." He gestured at the notebook, at the shadows, at the way Dani kept glancing toward the hall where the bathroom mirror lived.

"Trauma doesn't invent brass plates lettered exactly right," Dani said quietly. "It doesn't invent the echoes in my head."

Rally closed the notebook and held it against his chest, as if he feared the pages might blow away. "It's not over, is it?"

Dani shook her head. "No."

The boy swallowed, nodded like he was making a pact with himself, and said, "Then I'm not going to pretend it didn't happen. If I pretend, it wins."

Jake pushed off the wall and came to the back of the couch. "It's not your fight."

Rally looked up at him. "It took me under the mountain. It tried to make me nothing. Isn't that already a fight?"

No one spoke for a long breath. Outside, a car turned the corner two blocks away; its headlights slid across the room and were gone. When the light moved over the framed photograph on Dani's bookshelf, the glass flashed. She couldn't help watching it for a beat longer than she should have.

She pulled a blanket around Rally's shoulders. "You won't fight alone," she said. "Not while I'm here."

That got a small sound from Rally, a sigh that almost wanted to be relief.

Jake's voice softened. "We'll keep you steady. We'll keep each other steady." He looked at Dani when he said it, and she understood the question inside it. Who steadies the sentinel?

She didn't answer. She didn't know.

Rally's eyelids grew heavy. He tried to keep them open, but sleep had its own gravity. His head tipped and rested against Dani's arm. The notebook slid; she caught it before it hit the floor and placed it on the table next to the lamp.

Jake said, "You really believe it."

Dani didn't look up. "I feel it."

"What? The thing under the mountain following us?"

"No. The thing that waits for the cracks. It isn't a creature. It's a kind of pressure. A need to make outcomes clean by breaking people smaller." She smoothed Rally's hair without thinking. "Somebody has to stand where it pushes through."

"That somebody being you."

"I'm the one it tapped." She lifted her eyes. "I didn't ask."

Jake rubbed a hand over his face. "You sound like you're describing a sentence."

"Maybe it is. But I've carried worse for less reason."

He almost smiled at that, and then he didn't. "What does that make me?" he asked after a while. "If you're the sentinel."

"You're the line next to mine." Dani let the words come without decoration. "When it tries the door next to mine, you put your shoulder there too."

Jake nodded once, like a man accepting an unpleasant but necessary shift. "Then we need rules."

Rally stirred and mumbled, "Rules?" without opening his eyes.

"Yeah," Jake said, voice low. "Simple ones. So we don't drown."

Dani considered. "No one stares into mirrors alone. Not for a while."

Jake added, "If it's a choice between telling a clean story and telling the truth, we tell the truth to each other first."

"And if a door looks like it wants to open," Dani said, "we don't pretend it's a hallway. We name it."

Rally made a small sound of assent and sank deeper into sleep.

They let the rules sit in the room like new furniture, awkward but useful.

When Rally's breathing evened, Jake adjusted the blanket and stepped toward the window. He looked out at the street, hands on the sill, the tendons in his wrists sharp under the skin. "There's something else," he said without turning around. "Dispatch called before we came over. A disturbance out on Grace Street. Neighbors say shouting, glass breaking. Patrol is backed up."

Dani studied the back of his neck. "You didn't tell me because…"

"Because you weren't done with him." He nodded toward Rally. "And because I hoped the call would go away by itself." He looked at her now. "But it hasn't."

Grace Street was three blocks over, a row of old houses with thin walls and porches that collected arguments. Dani felt the badge at her hip as if it had gotten heavier in the last ten seconds. The bathroom mirror at the end of the hall might as well have breathed.

She glanced at the sleeping boy; his face was soft, unguarded. "You stay," she told Jake. "I'll go."

Jake shook his head. "Not alone."

She weighed the choices and didn't like any of them. "If we both go, we leave him here."

Rally's voice floated up from sleep, barely a whisper. "I'm not glass," he said. "Go."

Jake's jaw worked, then set. "Take my car," he said. "I'll lock up and sit right here till you get back. If he wakes, I'll tell him you're doing what you do."

Dani checked her phone, grabbed her jacket, and slid the notebook under the lamp to keep its pages from shifting in a draft that didn't exist. At the door she paused, a line of cold threading down her spine as her eyes caught her reflection in the dark pane. For a second she thought the figure in the glass leaned forward before she did. Then it was only her.

She went.

The night smelled like rain that had changed its mind. Streetlights made small islands on the pavement. Grace Street's houses hunched together, old porches with railings that had been painted too many times. Two doors down from the corner a woman stood on her porch steps with a phone pressed to her ear, voice sharp with fear, while a man in the yard shouted into the ground like it had insulted him. The front window of the house was broken from the inside; glass glittered on the grass.

Dani pulled to the curb, cut the engine, and left the headlights on. She didn't touch the siren. Neighbors didn't need more noise to tell them where they already were.

The woman turned at the car door slam. "Are you with them?" she asked, chin jerking toward the house.

"With who?" Dani said.

"The police. Or whatever you are." The woman's eyes snapped up and down Dani's figure and caught on the badge. "Good. Because he's going to break more than windows. He already threw the mirror off the wall. Said somebody in it told him things. He's not right."

The man in the yard had stopped shouting and started pacing, mouth moving, hands flexing open and closed at his sides. Every time he turned, he cut a line across the lawn like a saw in grass. Dani let her breath drop lower in her body, the way she did when she needed to make space inside herself for someone else's storm.

"What's his name?" she asked the woman.

"Marcus."

"And yours?"

"Annalise." The woman's mouth trembled. "He's not violent. Not like this. Something's, wrong."

Dani nodded, and something in the nod steadied Annalise enough that she put the phone down without hanging up. Dani stepped off the curb and onto the lawn.

"Marcus," she called softly, not yet close enough to startle him. "I'm Dani."

He didn't answer. His eyes flicked past her to the car's headlights and then to the window he'd broken. A curtain breathed in the hole where the glass had been. The house's front room was lit by a single lamp; the wall where a mirror had hung was a rectangle of paler paint, a shape like an absence.

Dani took one more step, hands open at her sides. "I'm going to come a little closer."

His voice came back hoarse and low. "Don't." He stopped pacing. The muscles in his jaw jumped. "It's still in there." He pointed not at the house but at the space in front of him, as if the air itself had become a doorway.

"In where?" Dani kept her own gaze steady. "In the mirror you threw?"

"It talked." He swallowed. "It knew things I never told Annalise. It asked me to remember what I promised I'd forget. And then it laughed."

Annalise let out a small wounded sound behind Dani. Dani didn't turn. She felt the pressure that had followed her out of the mountain gather along the edges of the yard, not wind, not cold, but a waiting. She remembered telling Jake it wasn't a creature. She remembered telling herself to name the doors.

"Sometimes," she said, "a mirror doesn't want to show you your face. It wants to show you a debt. That's not the same thing as a voice."

Marcus let out a short, ugly laugh. "What does that even mean?"

"It means you don't have to answer it," Dani said. "You can let it talk itself out." She took one more step and felt the air change, something in the night stuttering like a skipped heartbeat. "You can also decide what to do with whatever it dragged up. But you decide. Not the glass."

He stared at her, breathing hard. "You sound like you know."

"I do."

"What do you do when it doesn't stop?"

"You stand where it wants to break through and you keep standing."

He glanced at the window again. "It wasn't the mirror. It was me."

"Maybe both," Dani said. "Maybe the glass just noticed you were ready to hear yourself." She let the words land and didn't press. "What did you promise you'd forget?"

He closed his eyes. When he opened them again there was something softer there, something rawer. "My brother," he said. "I told him I'd be at the hearing. I told him I'd stand up when nobody else did. I didn't. I told myself it didn't matter because the judge didn't care. He went away alone." His voice thinned. "I broke the mirror because I didn't want to see his face on mine."

Annalise's breath hitched. Dani heard her step down onto the lawn, then stop.

"Okay," Dani said. "So we're not talking about glass anymore."

Marcus gave a small shake of his head. "No."

"Then here's what you're going to do," Dani said, gentle but definite. "You're going to come sit on your own steps. You're going to breathe like a man who gets a second chance to keep a promise. In the morning you're going to call your brother's public defender and

340

ask what you can do. And the mirror you broke is just a thing that broke. It doesn't get the last word."

For a long moment Marcus didn't move. Then his shoulders sagged like a shout leaving a body. He walked to the steps and sat. His hands were shaking. Dani stood in the grass in front of him until the shaking slowed.

Annalise came to sit beside him and took his hand. "We'll call," she said. "We'll both call."

Dani looked at the dark rectangle on the wall inside, the ghost where the mirror had hung. For a second the shape seemed deeper than it should be, like a square of night had been nailed there. She felt the pressure ebb, like water dropping after pressing against a dam.

"Do you need patrol?" she asked quietly. Annalise shook her head. Marcus stared at his hands.

"You need to sleep," Dani told them. "In the morning, do what you said." She tapped the rail lightly with her knuckles, an ordinary sound to anchor what had just happened, and walked back to the car.

She drove the long way home. Windows reflected the car back at her, each pane a small story: a silhouette at a sink, a cat in a window, nothing but her own headlights. The town had the nerve to be ordinary. She let that steadiness soak into her until her hands loosened on the wheel.

When she eased the key into her own door, Jake stood from the chair with a start and then sat back, embarrassed. "Everything?" he asked.

"Held."

Rally was still asleep, the notebook half open across his chest. Dani eased it free without waking him and set it on the table. Jake watched her, eyes searching her face for cracks.

"What did you see?" he asked.

"Not what. Who." She told him enough: a broken mirror, a man remembering a promise, the way doors open when a person thinks they've run out of ways to be decent. She didn't say the pressure had risen in her throat like a tide. She didn't say she had wanted to run.

Jake rubbed at a spot on the table with his thumb. "And you kept it from spilling."

"For tonight." She felt the room respond to the words, some small, invisible slackening. "Tomorrow is tomorrow."

Jake's gaze went to the hall. "You going to look again?"

"In the mirror?" She thought of the dark pane, of the hand that had once lifted before hers. "No. Not to ask it anything. It answers to no one I want to meet."

He nodded, oddly relieved. "Then we sleep in shifts."

"I'll take first," she said. "You lie down on the couch next to him."

Jake made a face. "I snore."

"Good. Let whatever listens know we're loud."

He smiled at that, small and unwilling, and did as she told him. He stretched out, one arm draped across his eyes, the other resting on the cushion near Rally's shoulder. Within minutes his breath evened. The boy didn't stir.

Dani sat in the chair and let time pass without asking it for anything. The lamp hummed faintly. Somewhere inside the walls, the heater clicked on and the vents whispered. The house had its own heart sounds, and tonight she chose to hear them.

When the dark outside the window thinned toward morning, she stood and walked quietly down the hall. She stopped in the bathroom doorway and looked at the mirror. It was just glass. It was never just glass.

She stepped close enough to see the grain in her irises, the thread of a scar along her hairline she never noticed in ordinary light. She lifted a hand, then put it down again.

"I know what I am," she said, and her voice didn't waver. "Not a judge. Not a priest. Not the machine under the mountain. I'm a person with a badge and a spine. I will stand in front of the doors. You can press. I'll be there."

Nothing moved in the mirror. That was its answer.

She went back to the living room. Dawn spread thin gray across the floorboards. Jake snored softly. Rally dreamed without flinching. Dani clipped the badge more firmly to her belt and stood at the window until the sky lifted into color.

Justice wasn't finished. It had never been. It waited for the next defense to be weighed, the next promise to be kept, the next small act that kept the world from slipping through an easy crack.

When the day arrived and asked for her, she would be where she needed to be, between what insisted on being simple and what was, in truth, human.

The sentinel of thresholds.

Epilogue

The ridge lay quiet beneath the stars. In the weeks that followed, the collapse was called an earthquake, a tremor no one could explain. Official reports listed missing children, found alive but shaken, their stories too fractured to hold together. Parents wept, deputies shook their heads, and the news moved on.

But those who had gone below carried the silence of the City with them. Dani Francis returned to her post, but the mirror of her own choices followed her like a shadow. Jake Tinsley went back to his small house by the river, his neighbors noting how his gaze lingered longer at dawn. Rally Gillum walked softer, his scarred arm a reminder of how close judgment had come. And Nia Alvarez pressed pine needles into a scrapbook, as though they held a secret language only she could read.

No one returned to the ridge. The trails grew over, the entrances collapsed. Yet on still nights, when the wind cut through the trees, some swore they could hear a faint murmur rising from beneath—a susurrus of voices rehearsing lines they'd forget were fiction.

The City was gone. But its verdicts lived on in the living.

Thank you for reading In Defense of the Righteous. If you enjoyed this book, you'll find more thought-provoking works by Charles Patton—ranging from history and politics to leadership and fiction, at: ⊕ charlespattonbooks.com

Explore the full collection, stay updated on new releases, and continue the conversation.